Murder at the

CHRISTMAS EMPORIUM

Before writing her first novel, Andreina Cordani was a senior editor and writer for women's magazines including *Good Housekeeping* and *Cosmopolitan*. Her assignments included interviewing gun-toting moms on the school run, ordering illegal DIY Botox online and learning to do the splits in eight weeks.

She lives on the Dorset coast with her family where she reads voraciously, occasionally makes TikTok videos and swims in the sea.

Also by Andreina Cordani
The Twelve Days of Murder

Murder at the CHRISTMAS EMPORIUM

Andreina Cordani

ZAFFRE

First published in the UK in 2024 by
ZAFFRE
An imprint of Zaffre Publishing Group
A Bonnier Books UK company
4th Floor, Victoria House, Bloomsbury Square, London, WC1B 4DA
Owned by Bonnier Books
Sveavägen 56, Stockholm, Sweden

This is a work of fiction. Names, places, events and
incidents are either the products of the author's
imagination or used fictitiously. Any resemblance to
actual persons, living or dead, or actual
events is purely coincidental.

A CIP catalogue record for this book is
available from the British Library.

ISBN: 978-1-80418-746-3

Also available as an ebook and an audiobook

1 3 5 7 9 10 8 6 4 2

Typeset by IDSUK (Data Connection) Ltd
Printed and bound in Great Britain by Clays Ltd, Elcograf S.p.A.

Zaffre is an imprint of Zaffre Publishing Group
A Bonnier Books UK company
www.bonnierbooks.co.uk

To Lucia
Youdunnit

1

CHRISTMAS PAST

How can you tell that Christmas is coming? It's in the chill air, the redness of your cheeks when you come inside to warm yourself by the fire, the scent of cinnamon and ginger, your first bite of a mince pie. But for almost a hundred years, if you were a child living in the great metropolis of London, the Christmas season never truly began until your first visit to the Verity's Emporium Grand Festive Display.

Such a sight it was, in the days before wonders became cheap and arrived through the post in grey plastic packaging. Adults would flock there for the exotic scents, the delicious food and the fine craftsmanship. Children would come from miles around and press their faces against the windows to see the marvellous mechanical elves hard at work inside. They would beg their parents for a tub of Mr Verity's Unpoppable Bubble Mixture; or a toy cat with gossamer-soft paws which mewed when you hugged it; or the world's fastest miniature steam trains, which raced along smooth silver tracks.

They said the Verity family had a touch of wizardry about them, that they could weave magic into any toy and turn it from an ordinary trinket into something living, but if you asked Old Man Verity he would laugh and say that children's imaginations contained all the magic needed to make a toy come to life.

By the late 1970s, when Peggy's father took her on her first visit, things had already begun to shift. The world was changing, wanting things faster and cheaper, not caring how well they were made. But the Emporium resisted still, remaining a perfect bubble of Christmas joy.

Peggy was not particularly beautiful to look at – small and skinny with thin hair the colour of a muddy puddle. She had awkward, bony arms and legs, a naturally surly expression and a tendency to cry at loud noises or strong smells. Adults at the time called her 'sensitive', as if that was a bad thing. As if seeing and feeling the world at a state of heightened intensity was not a superpower. Father understood, though. That's why he had brought her here.

She had never been to London before, and the Tube station Father took her to was gloomy, with looming scaffolding, litter and grime piled in its corners. The Tube train pulled away, and she felt a waft of stale poison-filled air blow into her face. Down on the track, tiny blackened mice flitted to and fro, their clawed feet covered in soot. She slipped her mittened hand into Father's as he led her onto a fast-moving escalator.

'Careful,' he warned. 'Jump over the bit at the end. I don't want your feet getting stuck in the mechanism.'

Trembling, she gripped his hand harder and jumped over the hungry metal teeth, then emerged into a noisy, smelly road lit by the yellow glow of street lights. Everywhere she looked there was filth and disorder. Half the road was being dug up; cars and motorbikes jostled along, spouting fumes; a man in a suit rushed by, almost knocking her over onto a traffic cone. A half-demolished building loomed like a skeleton to her left, and as she passed, one worker fired up his pneumatic drill and she leaped in terror, throwing her arms around her father's legs.

'I can't walk like this, silly,' he said, prising her off. 'This is just what London is like. Everything is always being dug up and rebuilt. But the Emporium doesn't change. I went there when I was a boy, and it'll still be exactly the same.'

Father shook her off. He did not slow his pace as he wove through the crowds of smelly, busy people who rushed in and out of the shops, laden down with polythene bags and long rolls of Christmas paper. But although the shop windows were all lined with tinsel they sold boring things like office supplies, cigarettes and toiletries. Although . . . For a moment, she hesitated, her gaze snagged on a bright watercolour set in a stationery shop window and when she looked up again, Father was gone.

Her stomach dropped. She walked forward a few steps, became aware of the beer-sodden, smoky entrance to a pub. Surely he hadn't gone in there . . .

She took a step towards the open doorway. Inside, they were playing that Christmas song about war being over. People were singing along, roaring with animal laughter.

A man appeared, huge and red-faced, leaning against the door frame.

3

'You all right, love?' He was holding a pint of thick, dark liquid and there was tinsel garlanded around his bald bright-pink head. As he lurched towards her, a strand of it stuck to the bead of sweat on his forehead. *A monster.* She shrank back, looked away and as she did she noticed a dark alley next to the pub. It was only a few feet wide – the kind of place Mother always told her to avoid, although never saying exactly why.

The pub monster was advancing towards her, a foamy dollop of his drink flopped to the pavement. She shivered – the navy wool double-breasted coat Mother had buttoned her into that day was nowhere near warm enough.

And then, a wave of relief. There was Father in the mouth of the alley, rolling his eyes in that way he did when she didn't keep up.

'Come on, slowcoach, this way.' Father took her hand again and led her past a sign reading Quockerwodger Court, and into the darkness.

It was like stepping into another century.

The alleyway was narrow and cobbled, a single old-fashioned street lamp stuck out from a nearby wall. The lantern was flickering, its pale gold light different from the acid glow of the street lights nearby.

'It's gaslight,' Father said. 'That's how the streets were lit in the olden days. There are still a few left in London and this is one of them.'

The light lengthened Father's shadow as he led the way towards what looked like a dead end, but which was actually a sharp bend. And when they rounded the corner, there it was.

An impossible building – narrow and wooden-beamed with floors piled on top of each other like a crooked stack of books.

She'd studied the Great Fire of London at school and recognised the style, this building was old. Over the door a sign swung and creaked in the breeze: VERITY'S EMPORIUM. Every floor was bedecked with lights and a warm, inviting glow spread from the windows. Through the leaded glass she could see things – colourful, thrilling, sparkling things.

She stepped forward but then a thought made her hesitate. The Emporium reminded her of something, a tale she had read long ago about a shop which sold magical wares. At first these items looked like they would solve all your problems but then they spiralled out of control like a curse. When the customers returned to the shop they found it had vanished, as if it was never there. That's what this place looked like. Anything this alluring and beautiful had to be some kind of magic, some kind of trap.

She felt something brush her cheek, cold and gentle. A snowflake. And another one. Flakes whirling through the air. Forgetting her unease, she grinned.

'It's snowing!'

'Don't get too excited,' Father said, pressing his lips together. 'Snow doesn't settle in central London.'

But the impossibility of it was just what excited her. The store *was* magic, and this snow proved it.

Father opened the door for her and as she went inside she noticed an engraved wooden sign above the door.

> The pure of heart find joy within
> But hold here, ye who are steeped in sin

'What does it mean?' she asked Father.

'This store first opened in Victorian times; they liked to turn everything into a moral lesson.' Catching sight of her confused look, he smiled. 'It means naughty children don't get Christmas presents.'

A flush of fear passed through her. She'd taken that biscuit from the jar without permission last week, and just now, she had thought that man outside the pub was a monster which was probably rude and unkind.

'Am I steeped in sin?'

'Of course not.' Father laughed gently and chose to gild his reassurance with a lie. 'You're a good girl, which means only good things will happen to you.'

He ushered her through the door where the scent of pine needles, cinnamon and warmth drew her inside. Thoughts of being steeped in sin melted away as she caught sight of a spectacular doll's house display and rushed towards it.

Back then, Old Man Verity was still alive – pottering around in grey twill trousers, white shirt and braces, his back hunched from hours bent over in the workshop, his face wizened by a thousand wrinkles. He greeted Father like an old friend and hunkered down next to Peggy. She drew back, overcome by the built-in apprehension the very young sometimes have for the very old. Her eyes focused on the large mole above his left eyebrow. *Did he know he had hairs growing out of it? Did he care?*

'Give me your hand,' he said. He spoke with the kind of accent men used in Mother's favourite black-and-white films. Clipped and proper, as if he were just about to take off in his Spitfire.

She must have hesitated because Father stepped in and urged her not to be rude. Then he added: 'Mr Verity has a talent for finding the perfect toy for each child.'

Her hand shot out at lightning speed. 'I'm Peggy.'

Old Verity laughed, and his brow crinkled even more than it had already, creating creases between creases. The mole waggled as if it were alive.

'Peggy, you say? What a splendid name. We have another Peggy who lives here too, you really must come and meet her before you do anything else.'

She would have liked to linger, to touch and stroke and play with every toy on the floor, but her parents had drilled politeness into her. So she followed the wrinkly old man through a maze of wonders – here a clockwork Santa dishing out presents to a happy child. There a plush puppy so realistic she expected him to move. She reached out her hand to stroke a diorama of dancing mice, only to shrink back in surprise – their fur was warm!

'This way.' Verity led them into the wood-panelled lift, where a teenage boy stood in a smart, gold-braided uniform. He was a tall lad, lanky and all elbows and knees; his face was peppered with acne. Peggy smiled, but instead of smiling back, he looked away.

She blushed, embarrassed by the rejection.

'Ignore my son,' Verity said to her in a theatrical whisper. 'He is learning the trade, but has yet to understand that children are the most important people in my Emporium.'

The boy's face turned red as he attended to the lift buttons and as it rose jerkily upwards, Peggy looked between his face and his father's, wondering how someone who looked so ancient could have a son not much older than her. She was fairly sure Father wouldn't approve if she asked, so she held the question inside.

The lift pinged.

The top floor was even more spectacular – everywhere she looked there were toys, games, puzzles.

These weren't the sort of toys she saw on TV adverts. Nothing was plastic, and she already knew she wouldn't find the mono-grammed Sindy wardrobe and dressing table she had been coveting, but instead it was filled with things she hadn't previously known she wanted. A spinning top ballerina who performed an elaborate whirling dance, functioning model aeroplanes, a perfect Wendy house with gingham checked curtains and a sporty pedal car parked neatly outside.

'Watch out, the Toytown Express is about to hit your foot,' Verity warned and she realised she was standing on a train track. She stepped back and a tiny engine powered past, bright and shiny and puffing smoke, pulling trucks laden down with sweets. Peggy reached out and grabbed one, laughing. She had never seen a store like this before, where the toys weren't locked away in their packaging, where you could play with anything which took your fancy.

It was then that she noticed the piano music. Soft and tinkling, it picked out the song she had been singing at school this term, the 'Coventry Carol', but more slow, more delicate than her choir's rendition: *luly lullay, thou little tiny child . . .*

Verity noticed her listening.

'That,' he said, 'is Miss Peggy Goodchild, otherwise known as Clockwork Peg.'

'Oh,' Peggy breathed. 'Like me!' She didn't know any other Peggys.

To one side of the room, next to a shelf of neatly turned-out dolls, sat a woman in a pale blue Victorian dress, playing the piano. Her dark brown curls were twisted into a bun and tucked neatly into a ribboned cap revealing light brown skin on the nape of her neck.

It was only as she got closer that Peggy realised Clockwork Peg's movements were jerky and strange. Her arms moved, her head tilted in time with the music but her shoulders didn't shift.

'She's not real!'

Verity laughed. 'She's very much real, she just isn't alive. She is an automaton built by my grandfather. She has been playing this piano for almost a hundred years and if we keep her wound-up she will play it for a hundred more.'

Now they were closer, Peggy could see the automaton's jointed elbows, the fingers that flickered down onto each piano key. And, unnervingly, she could hear the click and whir of the clockwork which caused her to move.

Click *bye*. Click *bye*. Click *lul-* click *-la*.

The face, though, looked real. Deep brown eyes seemed to gaze at the sheet music, her lips shone, her nose was dusted with tiny freckles and her skin was several shades darker than the pallid flesh-and-blood Peggy standing next to her. This wasn't a pink-cheeked doll like the ones she had at home.

'Who is she?'

Verity laughed. 'That is exactly the right question,' he said. 'Although it would be more correct to say who *was* she. Peggy Goodchild was an orphan rescued from poverty in Jamaica by my family many years ago and brought to London. She had a genius for toymaking and worked here in the Emporium on some of our most magical creations. After she died, my grandfather made this clockwork automaton in her memory.'

He cast a glance at Father. 'Does she mind scary stories?'

She could see her father opening his mouth to say 'yes', and interrupted.

'No. Tell me.'

Verity bent down again, put his mouth close to her ear. His bristly moustache tickled her. 'They say her ghost still walks these halls at night.'

Peggy felt a delicious shiver. She should be afraid but she wasn't; she would very much like to meet her namesake in ghost form. She was sure they'd be friends. She reached out her hand to the automaton.

'Can I touch her?' She reached out, desperate to make contact, to hold the artificial girl's hand. She felt sure that when she squeezed, the jointed fingers would squeeze back. She was a lonely child, and longed for a friend like this, who would always be there for her provided you kept her wound.

'You can play with absolutely any toy in this Emporium, but Clockwork Peg is too old and delicate to be touched. Now, let me see, which is the right toy for you?'

The girl drew her hand back, fighting to hide her disappointment and the old man gazed into her eyes thoughtfully.

'I expect people buy you dolls, don't they?' he continued. 'But it's not dolls for you. You like to make things move, I think. A toy you can control. Wait here.'

In a flash, the old man was gone – the girl couldn't even see where he'd got to – but moments later he reappeared with a pleasingly large box in his hands.'

'A Peggy of your very own.' This Peg was a perfect replica of the automaton, right down to the pale blue dress and freckles, but strung to a wooden frame with near-invisible threads.

'A puppet?' The girl was a little disappointed, but too polite to say.

'Not just any puppet, a marionette.' Verity held the frame gently, tweaking the strings, and miniature Peg tossed her head angrily, then put her hands on her hips and walked away in a huff, every bit as if she were alive.

Now the girl was intrigued.

'You can show me how to do that?'

'I think you were born to do it.'

The rest of the visit passed in a blur – a lesson in puppetry, a trip to the Hall of Delicacies, where she drank a creamy cup of hot chocolate and devoured a gingerbread man still warm from the oven. Meeting Father Christmas who, with his bristly white beard and genuine jelly-belly, was definitely the real thing this time.

On the way home she held her Peg-puppet tightly against her and thought about the real Peggy Goodchild who had lived at the Emporium so long ago, in a time of sweeping ball gowns, fluttering fans, horses and carriages. At eight years old, life still seemed magical to her; she could think of nothing finer than being a poor orphan whisked away by a rich, eccentric family, given beautiful clothes and taken to live in an Emporium full of toys. It would be much more adventurous than living in a boring house with sensible parents.

It was only six months later, when she became an orphan herself, that she began to think differently. She had no extended family, nobody to take her in, and as she moved through the care system the only familiar face in her life was the puppet. She clung to it, using it to act out a better future, all her plans and dreams poured into one stringed figure until she was surprised it didn't crack open under the pressure.

At night she would lie, her puppet in her arms, staring up at the ceiling and fantasising about the Emporium, its beautiful halls, and twinkling lights, the staff who seemed to appear like magic whenever you wanted them, the toys you could play with endlessly. Sometimes she thought that trip to the Emporium was the last good, beautiful thing to have happened to her.

Nothing bad could ever happen there.

2

MERRY

MERRY'S WEATHER APP TELLS HER THAT IT'S THE COLDEST LONDON has been in years, saying that tonight will dip well below zero. The newspapers have gone into overdrive, predicting the first white Christmas in years but Sadie from the office – who reliably predicts the weather based on the twinges in her back – had told her confidently that it will be too cold to snow.

So logic dictates Merry should be freezing right now, but it is a peculiar characteristic of London that no matter how cold it gets, after five minutes fighting your way out of a crowded Tube station, you are ready to melt. As Merry weaves her way past the wine shops and overpriced sandwich bars, she feels hot and clumsy in her coat, layered over her hideous, scratchy Christmas jumper.

She has never been one for festive knitwear. In fact, she feels dubious about the whole Christmas thing full stop and she has never worn so much as a comedy Santa hat, until today. This is not what you would call a starter jumper, either – there's no tasteful Scandi snowflake pattern or subtle touches of silver thread. No, this is full-on multicoloured acrylic nightmare, featuring an image of Rudolph with fairy lights tangled around his antlers. It was only after buying it at lunchtime that day that Merry noticed the LED bulbs embedded in the yarn, which light up when you press a button on the sleeve, making it even more tortuously embarrassing to wear.

But there are no half measures. Not when it comes to the Plan.

The Plan, however, hadn't included wearing it tonight. Her boss Doug had forced this situation on her when he spilled latte over her at the end-of-year round-up meeting. Her skin still smells faintly of coffee and the aroma intensifies, tinged with sweat, as she darts through the Christmas Eve crowds.

'Ha, I suppose you could call this revenge.' Doug had laughed as she patted herself down with paper towels, and she had had to force a smile. It's true, she has spilled coffee on Doug, or over his desk on numerous occasions. There was the time she needed to divert his attention away from Sadie's late return from a 'dental appointment' (actually a job interview which Merry had lined up for her). Then there was the time Taranjit from art accidentally put one of her 'Doug doodles' on his desk and it was the only way to stop him seeing it. And of course the time he said something sexist and just deserved it.

Because although Doug was technically the boss at J.D. Stimpson Greetings Cards, it was Merry who ran the place. She pulled all the strings and knew where all the bodies were buried – most of them she had buried herself.

'What the hell are you still doing there?' her best friend Ross had asked recently. 'You're smart, you're efficient, you run that place with your eyes shut, you could do so much better. Why not just leave?'

The question had blindsided her, but Ross had a point. They had met at Stimpson's after university, bonding over the shared drudgery, but since then Ross and their fellow interns had all moved on to better jobs. Only Merry remained, sitting outside Doug's office writing terrible Christmas card poetry and messing with her colleagues' lives.

'I guess I like the people,' she said, shrugging. But it was a barefaced lie.

The truth is that she doesn't care enough about her career to do anything about it. These days she struggles to care about anything in her life that isn't Ross.

Merry isn't a romantic, she believes in very little – the detachment is probably what makes her such a good greetings card writer. Christmas spirit, to her, is a commercial wheeze and a fun opportunity to mess with people's psyches. But somehow that cynicism has never extended to Ross. She doesn't believe in soul mates, but they are soul mates nonetheless.

She just has to get him to see it too.

This year, for the first time ever, they are planning to spend Christmas together. She'd sold it to him as a pragmatic solution: they're both single, both have weird family situations, and nobody wants to be alone that day.

'You're going to have to enjoy it, though,' Ross had insisted. 'No groaning when I put carols on in the morning and absolutely no disrespect for *It's a Wonderful Life*. That film is sacred.'

'I can be Christmassy,' Merry had protested. She understood then that her dislike of Christmas was one of the things holding

Ross back from her. She had to be less sharp, less cynical, more tinselly. And that's when the Plan was born.

She would become so damn tinselly that Ross would be unable to resist.

She stops at the entrance to Quockerwodger Court, stands under a flickering street lamp and takes a couple of deep breaths. The key to gatecrashing exclusive invitation-only shopping events, as with all forms of con-artistry and manipulation, is confidence . . . and not showing up sweaty and breathless in a flashing reindeer jumper.

She smooths her dark hair down and touches up her lipstick, practising her assertive of-course-I-didn't-steal-this-invitation-how-dare-you expression in the tiny make-up mirror. She's not an habitual thief and she does feel a little guilty, but she squashes it down. Doug's not interested in this sort of thing anyway, and it's for a very good cause. And hey, she didn't even spill coffee over him to get it, just waited until he went out for an extended pub lunch. He should be grateful! She pulls the precious rectangle of card out of her shoulder bag.

Montagu Verity Esq. invites you to a special, exclusive event
Christmas Eve at Verity's Emporium

A chance for a select few VIP shoppers to sample the delights of London's unique department store on 24 December from 7.30 p.m.

Admission strictly by invitation only. No plus ones.

Ordinarily, Merry's reaction to this sort of thing would be one of disdain. Who needs an invitation to go to a shop? But the Emporium is no mere shop. A relic of the Victorian era, it had closed back in the Eighties when customers began to flock to out-of-town shopping centres. But earlier this year, the owner, Montagu 'Monty' Verity, reopened it to a fanfare of publicity and hype.

In an era of big brands, online shops and mass imports from faraway factories, the Emporium was different. Everything there, from the toys to the perfumes, was hand-made either by skilled artisans with many years of trade behind them, or by Montagu himself and his team of craftspeople – affectionately known as the Elves. And it was affordable, too.

At first it had been overrun, its ancient floors creaking under the weight of so many pounding feet. The authorities became involved and it was threatened with closure unless Monty agreed to control access and reluctantly he had instigated a ticketing and queuing system which made a visit to the Emporium well-nigh impossible for anyone who didn't have time to spend hours in line. Newspapers had written mournful columns about it, how Verity's bold attempt to bring old-fashioned shopping back into the world had failed because of twenty-first-century social media hysteria.

So this was Merry's only opportunity to get into the Emporium and buy the one present she knows will show Ross that she listens, that she cares. She can imagine it now, his eyes filling with tears as he opens her thoughtful gift.

Quockerwodger Court is a curious place. Merry had googled the antiquated word earlier and found it means a wooden toy that jerks its limbs when a string is pulled. It's a suitably old-fashioned name for a narrow, cobbled alleyway. Merry picks her way over the uneven surface, guided by a glow coming from around a sharp corner, and then the alleyway opens into a wider courtyard, lit by chains of fairy lights which sway slightly in the winter breeze. A burgundy-painted sandwich board bears an old-fashioned image of a finger, pointing customers towards a maze of barriers, the same sort of queuing system they use at theme parks or gigs.

But there is no orderly queue today, only a small trestle table outside serving hot chocolate and a trickle of guests making their way through the door. Tonight, the store is only open to the privileged few. As someone who is usually on the wrong side of the velvet rope, Merry feels a flare of resentment.

'It's quite something, isn't it?' A voice jerks her out of her train of thought – it's coming from a small man sitting on a camping chair next to the queuing sign. He is so wrapped up in scarf, hat, boxing-glove-sized mittens and a grubby padded jacket that must be at least two sizes too big for him that she can barely see the person underneath. He has brown skin with crinkles around his eyes that must have come from years of smiling. Merry immediately wonders what his deal is. Ross would say it was none of her business, but she can't help it.

'Um, yeah, impressive,' Merry says, looking at the mock-Tudor façade in front of her. Its quirky crookedness reminds her of Diagon Alley. 'Are you coming to the event thing?'

The man laughs, a high, nervous laugh. 'Oh no, not me! I'm not very popular in there. No! I'm just . . . I suppose you'd call me an unofficial historian of Verity's. I'm Gary Shrike, you might have heard of me – I'm @no1veritysgeek online.'

'So you know a lot about the place, then?'

'Probably too much for my own safety!' he says, winking so Merry knows it's a joke. 'Did you know that although Verity's didn't open its doors until 1885 the Verity family has owned this site for more than three hundred years?'

Merry nods politely.

'They're a fascinating family – merchants originally, who brought back the Seven Wonders of the World and then opened the store to share them with the people of London . . . But they have a dark past.'

Merry's scandal-sense is tingling, that need-to-know urge she can't seem to switch off. She stays silent, knowing that Gary will be compelled to fill the dead air between them.

'I'd say they were probably cursed from the start by the spirit of poor Peggy Goodchild. They still have their secrets too, like that Monty Verity, popping up out of the blue, reopening the Emporium. Where did he come from, may I ask?'

'I think I read somewhere he was a backpacker for years, travelling the world and learning all his artisan crafts.'

The man shakes his head sadly, as if Merry has told him she believes in Santa Claus.

'Yes, that's what he'd like us all to think, but there's far more to it than that. He's a smarmy git and his face doesn't fit.' Gary's smile is full of relish; it's clear he loves knowing more than the person he's talking to. Merry can relate to that. 'And then there's the building work they had done on those historic windows recently . . . Very odd.'

Merry is torn. She doesn't like talking to random strangers, but there's something interesting going on here, so she resists her urge to brush him off and hurry inside. Gary's eyes light up; he can tell he's got her. He rises out of his camping chair and grabs her arm, his voice low as he speaks.

'Listen, I can't get in there, they won't let me in, but if you see anything there at all, any historic papers about ownership of the building . . .'

'I'm just here for the Christmas shopping.'

Gary opens his mouth to reply, but then a voice calls out from the store-front. A young man in Victorian get-up is running towards them. Gary jumps, startled, and thrusts a leaflet of pink-coloured paper into her hand. 'Check out my channel for more information – and watch out. It's not all comfort and joy in there, let me tell you.'

Before Merry has a chance to respond, he dashes off into the alley. She crumples the leaflet up and shoves it in her shoulder bag just as the Verity's employee reaches her.

'Oh God, what was he saying?' the young man says, panting. 'He's always here creeping people out. I was supposed to be keeping an eye out for him, but one of the other guests just barged in with an uninvited plus one and it took ages to sort out . . .'

Merry surveys him, reading the situation. He's the one on the door, probably responsible for admissions. He's stressed, anxious to do his job right, and she needs him on side.

'Don't worry, I won't tell anyone about this,' Merry says, handing her invitation over as she does so.

Panic flares in the assistant's eyes at the very thought and he only glances at the invitation.

'Please, let me start again,' he says, adjusting his cravat nervously, his tone more formal. 'On behalf of Monty Verity and his team of Elves, I wish you the very merriest of Christmases. Please accept a complimentary hot chocolate to warm yourself up on this cold winter's day.'

Merry follows him over to a wooden table by the store's front door with several copper kettles on it. A brazier burns warm and bright, and there's a hum of excitement from other customers, sipping from earthenware mugs that look hand-made.

'You've got a VIP invitation, which means you get the VIP hot chocolate.' The assistant lays down the invitation and picks up the smaller of the two kettles, filling a mug with steaming hot dark brown liquid. 'It's extra nice, apparently.'

'It really is delicious,' the man standing next to Merry says, sipping from his own mug. He turns his gaze on her and unleashes a smile. Merry is sure she has seen this tanned, confident face before. He looks to be in his early forties and is incredibly well presented – gym-slim and wiry with close-cropped hair and the kind of beard that's trimmed so straight you'd think the barber used a ruler. Merry finds herself smiling back, even more flushed than she was before, and definitely regretting the jumper. It's ridiculous, he's not her type at all but his charisma seems to bypass all rational thought.

She keeps the entitled-VIP expression on her face as she sips the chocolate. It's scalding but meltingly good, and subtly spiced with Christmassy flavours.

'Lovely to meet you.' The man's tone is relaxed and friendly, his accent firmly Essex. 'I'm Dean Hallibutt, the Business Fixer.'

Merry keeps smiling but inside she's awash with guilt. Dean Hallibutt is Doug's favourite business guru. She remembers where she's seen his face now, in the memes Doug likes to share, peppered with inspirational sayings which read even more badly than the worst of her Christmas poems: *Know when to act, and act fast, Leaders gotta lead* and *Live the Legend you Make for Yourself.* Doug even made everyone watch Dean's TEDx talk on streamlining your business for the modern world last year. He would have been thrilled to meet him.

'I need to tick off your name, miss,' the assistant interrupts, pointing to a clipboard on the table.

Merry plays for time by putting down her hot chocolate, glancing at the list to see whose identity she can steal.

Evangeline Fall (and plus one). There's a tick next to this name, and the plus one has been added in pen, so they must already be inside.

Dean Hallibutt. Obviously not an option as he is still standing right next to her.

Benjamin Makepeace. She definitely doesn't look like a Benjamin.

Fran Silver. Ugh, that annoying overly perky chef from daytime TV, the one with the insincere, over-the-top laugh. She's too old and too famous to impersonate. Merry keeps reading.

She is just about to lay claim to be *Josie Clough* when her eyes snag on a name that makes her heart lurch.

Rita Gliss.

Oh. Crap.

Her system floods with fight-or-flight panic. Her first instinct is to run, to follow nerdy Gary's example and leg it down the alleyway. But then she sees there's no tick next to her name yet. Rita is not here. And anyway, she thinks with a flare of anger, why should Merry be the one to scuttle away? Why should Rita spoil her perfect Christmas plan? She thinks back to the advice she gave Ross when he was wavering about spending Christmas with her: *Stand up for what you believe in.*

And then a truly wicked idea enters her mind. It's risky, but the sheer naughtiness of it is too good to resist.

'Rita Gliss,' she tells the assistant.

'Welcome, Rita,' he says, making a flourishing tick. It takes Merry some effort to hold down the bubble of laughter inside her. What if Rita turns up later and doesn't get in? That would be priceless.

Then, of course, comes the fear: what if she turns up later and *does* get in? Merry will have to keep her eyes peeled and be ready to hide.

The assistant coughs politely. He is holding out a small basket.

'If you could just pop your phones in here.'

'Um, no?' Merry recoils, instinctively hugging her phone to her chest.

'I'm sorry,' the assistant says, 'it's Mr Verity's policy.'

'That doesn't apply to me, mate,' Dean says, directing his charm at the assistant. 'I'm not just here for the event, I'm here to meet Mr Verity and his associate.'

The assistant wavers under Dean's gaze and Merry watches in admiration. He's not being rude or demanding, he's just calmly stating: *This is how it will be.* Merry wishes the world worked like that for her.

The assistant has stopped reaching for Dean's phone now and he goes to tuck it away in his pocket, when a powerful voice interjects.

'I'm afraid the rule applies to all this evening, Mr Hallibutt.'

Merry looks up to see a tall, angular gentleman leaning against the store's open oak door. He is wearing a blue top hat and

23

Victorian-style frock coat, silken waistcoat and cravat. But this is no stuffy Victorian chap. His coat is a patchwork of different patterned fabrics. There's an African wax print, Chinese silk, Paisley, patches of delicate Japanese flowers. It's like he's taken a little swatch out of everywhere in the world and stitched them together. *No culture left unappropriated*, thinks Merry but she's also impressed by how well made the coat is.

He is using a red-and-white-spotted handkerchief to polish the top of his silver walking cane, and carries the self-satisfied air of a man who is Making an Entrance and knows it. Merry fights not to goggle at him. She feels strongly that people who dress eccentrically are desperate for you to stare, and that the worst thing you can do is give them what they want.

The man tucks his handkerchief away and smiles. 'Montagu Verity at your service.' He bows.

'Good to see you again, Monty,' Dean says, shaking Monty's hand, his phone still in his trouser pocket.

'Indeed, and how is your delicious hot chocolate?' Monty sniffs theatrically at the mug Dean is holding. 'Hmm . . . it's lacking something. One moment . . .'

The man rummages through his pockets, finally coming up with a twist of paper, which he opens carefully. 'I am given to understand that you like your food spicy, Mr Hallibutt – and this blend of spices should add an extra, pleasurable kick to your beverage.'

He sprinkles a pinch of the stuff on the top of Dean's mug, but somehow the paper slips from his grasp, scattering powdered spice all over the front of Dean's shirt. Dean's friendly smile slips slightly – he clearly cares a lot about his clothing – but

Monty dusts him down with his spotted handkerchief, apologising profusely.

'I am sorry, dear boy,' he says again. 'But how is your hot chocolate now?'

Dean sips. 'Oh,' he says. 'Wow!'

'You see, it was worth being lightly dusted, wasn't it? Now, do go inside and enjoy yourself. After all, it's Christmas!' Monty leans in, his lips close enough to tickle Dean's ear as he murmurs something, too quietly for Merry to hear.

Dean laughs – a rich, warm sound. 'OK, you got me.' Merry swears that Dean does a little joyful skip as he crosses the Emporium threshold.

Monty spins on the ball of his foot, a balletic move, and pulls Dean's mobile phone out of his sleeve, presenting it to the assistant.

'How did you do that?' Merry asks.

'A simple bit of misdirection,' Monty shrugs. 'Mr Hallibutt is an excellent man of business, but all mobile telephones are banned from Verity's, without exception. My beautiful emporium was filling up with influencers looking for . . .' he shudders, '*content*. They would spend hours in the store filming and taking photographs, not buying anything and, worst of all, not truly appreciating what they saw. They were taking up space that could be used by parents seeking the perfect toy for their children.'

Monty turns to face her and Merry tenses, suddenly sure he's going to kiss her hand. He looks like the type. But luckily this showman can read the room, and doffs his hat instead.

'And who do I have the pleasure of addressing?'

'Rita,' she says breezily, holding out her hand, keeping that confident smile in place.

'I think we both know that's not true.' Monty smiles. 'Rita has a highly distinctive look, which does not include such festive apparel.'

Merry folds her coat back over her reindeer-emblazoned chest, feeling the blood rush to her cheeks and chiding herself for her stupidity. Of *course* Monty would know what Rita looked like. But he doesn't look angry.

'You can tell me your real name, I won't throw you out. It is Christmas Eve, after all.'

'Merry Clarke,' she admits. She is often reluctant to say her name for the first time, especially now, on Christmas Eve and to someone so clearly obsessed with the festive season.

'Merry.' Verity beams. 'How wonderful. And are you?'

'Not particularly.' Merry gets this line every Christmas, and shoots it down without hesitation.

'Let's see what we can do about that.' He offers her the crook of his arm. 'Come, then, and see my Hall of Wonders!'

It's then she realises that her phone has been gently taken away from her and relocated into the basket. It's too late to protest, so she gives in, linking her hand through his arm. He leans in closer, his head cocked thoughtfully to one side, his gaze intensifying. He is too close now, his breath smells of cinnamon and fine cigars.

'Oh yes, you're definitely my favourite,' he says thoughtfully. 'Remember that, when things get hard. I'm rooting for you. I can't wait to see what you're capable of.'

3

Fran

Fran Silver is bewitched. The exterior of the department store is warm and welcoming, decked in strings of lights that don't look a bit like modern LEDs, and somehow have the soft yellowish flicker of candle flames. At the edge of her hearing is a faint tinkling sound. It's not the piped music you hear outside modern stores, it's less rhythmic than that, almost as if elves with bells on their hats are scurrying around just out of sight. It's just as beautiful as she remembers.

The Emporium was probably at the root of Fran's love for Christmas. Her mother had brought her here in its previous incarnation, when she was just four years old. She could still remember flashes of detail, a blur of colours and lights, a Victorian lady playing the piano, a huge clock with little wooden dolls dancing beneath, and the feel of a small carved toy in her hand on the way home.

'There are so many ghosts there,' Fran's mother had said. She hadn't meant it in a bad, spooky way. Talking to the dead had been Agnes's particular talent and ghosts had been part of the everyday fabric of her life. Fran had thought it embarrassing as a teenager but now her mother was gone she longed to have the gift herself. She got occasional flickers sometimes, enough to give her hope, but she didn't walk among the spirits the way that Agnes had. For all she knew, her mother could be here right now, in Quockerwodger Court in front of the newly reopened Emporium, and she would have no idea.

Her phone beeps, and Fran groans. It's the latest in a long stream of increasingly anxious WhatsApps from her friend and agent, Zelda. She has been ignoring them all the way here, swiping each one away unread.

What were you thinking?

Are you out of your tree?

I know you don't like shouting about your charity work but you turned down an effing OBE, Fran. It would have got you back on TV again, and earning proper money, not just reality shows. Don't you want that?

I want that.

My electricity bill wants that.

Stop ignoring these texts.

Don't make me call you, lady. You know I hate voice calls.

This last message, though, is different from the others – less angry, more worried.

You're not sick again, are you?

Fran can't ignore that one.

No not sick, she types. *Will explain later about gong. Merry Christmas, love xxxx.*

She is not sure how she's going to explain to Zelda why she had to turn the OBE down. Over the past few years, since her very public cancer battle and treatment, Fran has raised hundreds of thousands of pounds for charities. She has walked, run, cycled and on one occasion sack-raced countless miles, drenched herself in gallons of tough mud. Even now, her feet are still aching from the Get Stuffed Cancer Half Marathon Santa Dash two days before, and she has another event lined up on Boxing Day. She isn't doing all this for fame and recognition, far from it, but somehow it has transformed her from daytime TV has-been into up-and-coming national treasure.

Reality shows are clamouring for her. More so because being one of the few non-white faces from Nineties television makes her attractive to reality TV producers looking for some diversity in their retro celebrities. And she has accepted every single one, provided the profits go to charity. She knows how the industry works; knows an OBE would make her even more in-demand but still, she had no choice but to turn it down, and Zelda will never understand why.

So when the skinny white boy at the Emporium door asks for her phone she practically rams it into his hands. Zelda will keep messaging. She is not a person who lets things go – it's what makes her such a good talent agent, and why Fran doesn't deserve her as a friend.

Aaaannd there it is. After a brief holiday, Mr Guilt takes up residence in the pit of her stomach once again, dragging her round and down into a spiral of self-hatred.

To make matters worse, as she walks through the heavy oak doors of the Emporium she glances up and sees the moralising message above.

The pure of heart find joy within
But hold here, ye who are steeped in sin

She shouldn't be here, not really. She should have ignored the VIP invitation when it turned up two weeks ago. She should throw away this delicious hot chocolate which tastes like molten heaven. She should head home right now and donate to charity or something and . . . Oh my.

She is standing in a wood-panelled room full of sound and light – much bigger than she imagined from looking at the store's lopsided exterior.

The room has a high ceiling with a kind of gallery around the edges – a mezzanine floor. Dripping down from the centre of the ceiling is a myriad of crystal droplets, glistening like strings of tears as they move gently in the warm Emporium air. Tiny, winged figures flitter among them, weaving through the strands. They look like fairies, and Fran can't make out where they're hanging from and what's making them move. The room itself is bedecked in red, gold and green. Dozens of shoppers are browsing through the tables – just enough people to give the room a pleasant buzz without reaching frenzied pre-Christmas hysteria levels. Assistants in Victorian garb move among them, and in the corner a choir performs 'Hark! The Herald Angels Sing'. It's all quite, quite lovely.

Stop enjoying yourself, the guilty voice nags at her, but Fran steps forward anyway, taking a sip of her chocolate. Christmas is her kryptonite, it has always been too hard to resist.

'Ah, Ms Silver,' a voice booms, and she catches sight of Monty Verity standing amid the sparkles and lights in all his excessive Victorian glory. Her cheeks go hot. To be honest, she has a bit of a crush. She's always liked flamboyant men with a bit of showmanship about them and she's read that he's terribly good with his hands.

He's standing surrounded by a group of people, just next to the door, and beckons for her to join them.

'VIP ladies, gentlemen and gentlefolk, gather round!' he says. A small group of people drifts towards him and forms a kind of circle between the display tables, while the other shoppers continue to browse, trying not to glance enviously over their shoulders.

Fran had half expected the usual line-up of faces, celebrity freeloaders who go to the opening of an envelope, but this is an oddly mixed selection. The woman next to Fran looks like a normal, everyday person – if such a thing exists. She's shuffling out of a sensible beige coat to reveal a jumper featuring a giant Christmas pudding. Her grey hair is pulled into a severe topknot. She has granite eyes, and her sallow white face is the kind that Fran's mother would have described as 'lived-in'. There's a smear of hot chocolate at the corner of her mouth.

'Do I know you?' the woman asks in an old-school cockney accent. At first she thinks she's being told off for staring, but then realises the question is genuine – it's a telly thing. 'Yes, I do know you, you're that chef off *Morning All!*.'

'Not anymore,' Fran can't stop herself saying.

'They should never have fired you.' The woman's voice is threaded through with outrage. 'Fucking unforgivable, pardon my French, dropping you because you had cancer, then replacing you with that blonde idiot.'

That isn't entirely the truth, and shame niggles at Fran again but she lets it slide, especially as there is a tall, ivory-skinned woman bearing down on her, arms outstretched. She is elegantly dressed in shades of cream and white, her raven hair twisted into a loose knot at the nape of her pale, elegant neck.

'Why, Fran Silver, how incredible to see you after all these years!'

Fran blanks for a moment, the woman's face is vaguely familiar but . . . Then the unwelcome penny drops. It's Evangeline something from university. Wow, keen, keen Evangeline – voted person most likely to marry royalty by the college newspaper. She hasn't thought about her in years.

'Oh, Fran, how simply gorgeous to see you! What a fetching Christmas jumper, you look *amazing*. Look at your skin! What is it they say? Oh yes, "black don't crack", isn't it?'

After a lifetime in telly, Fran has gritted her teeth through more racially loaded comments than she could ever count. Her warm expression doesn't even flicker. Monty saves her from having to respond by clapping his hands.

'I see some of you already know each other, and others are famous faces known to us all!' He beams at Fran, and then over towards a tall, slender man in business attire who flashes a smile back. Fran doesn't recognise him, but he looks confident and put-together so he might be some kind of influencer. 'Allow me to introduce you all with a simple game. When I point at you with my cane, you will say your name, and tell me your Christmas wish – the thing you would like most in the whole world. Ms Silver, maybe you would like to go first?'

Monty's cane points right at her, and feeling the audience's attention on her, she switches instantly into live-TV mode.

'Well, my name's Fran Silver and yes, I'm on telly a bit. I suppose my Christmas wish is a cure for cancer.'

Verity sighs. His eyes close, his smile becomes cherubic and he leans closer. 'What a very noble and lofty goal, but I was asking about *your* true desire – the selfish one you nurture in the darkness, the one you are too polite and too civilised to mention in public.'

His eyes bore into her – too serious, too intense – Fran's warm, fuzzy feeling drains away replaced by a hot, prickly sensation. The ugly truth is building up inside her, and she clamps her mouth shut, afraid that if she lets down her guard for even a moment it will spill out.

Monty laughs. 'Oh dear, Ms Silver. I really was only teasing, there is no need to go digging for skeletons in your cupboard. I shall leave you to ponder and move on.'

His cane points at the grey-haired woman now, who looks up and gives him a friendly, crooked smile.

'All right, mister?' she says, sounding extremely cockney. She waits for Monty to answer, and when he doesn't, she continues. 'Anyway, yeah. I'm Josie, Josie Clough. I won a competition to be here tonight – luxury shopping trip plus a night in Claridge's, don't you know! I think I'm with Fran on the Christmas wish; cancer can do one.'

A bored expression settles upon Monty's face. 'Very well, let us all just choose a cure for cancer. Unless . . . what about you, good sir?'

This time the cane points at a small, finicky man in a dapper suit complete with waistcoat, bow tie and pocket watch – he reminds Fran of Hercule Poirot but without the moustache.

'My name is Benjamin Makepeace, of Makepeace and Sherwin.' When everyone looks blank he adds, 'We are antique dealers. My Christmas wish, as Mr Verity knows, is the preservation and restoration of the Goodchild automaton.'

Monty lets out a weary sigh. 'And I am sure Clockwork Peg will be ecstatic to see her greatest admirer here tonight.'

Benjamin Makepeace opens his mouth to speak again but Monty swings his cane to point at Evangeline.

'I'm Evangeline Fall,' she says. Oh yes, that was the surname. Fran is surprised to hear that it hasn't changed. At university she had been a compulsive man-chaser, hence the 'keen, keen' nickname. She'd never had much interest in talking to other women, which had enraged Fran, who had been going through her punk feminist phase.

'I am a girlboss,' Evangeline announces. 'I'm the founder of Yuletide Creations. We specialise in high-end festive decorations, which is why I am thrilled to be here in this most festive of places. And, oh yes, my deep, dark Christmas wish . . . well, a girl has to have secrets.'

Her eyes flicker over at the businessman Dean Hallibutt. Fran has never seen anyone genuinely bat their lashes before, she thought it was something only Betty Boop did, but Evangeline tries it all the same. Dean, however, is busy checking his pockets for a phone that isn't there. For a moment he doesn't see the cane pointing him.

'Ah, my turn! Well, I'm a thought leader and business consultant. I deep dive into companies, putting out fires and drilling down into their core competencies. I help them futureproof and disrupt their sector with innovative ideas.' He looks at the blank faces around him and gives an infectious, white-toothed grin. 'Sorry, got carried away with the jargon there. Basically, I fix businesses. The Business Fixer, that's my brand. Two point one million followers and counting!'

Dean comes across as suave but likeable. A self-made man, Fran decides. Someone who's been successful and wants his face, body and clothes to show it – hence the intense grooming – but is proud enough of his roots to keep his Essex accent.

'And your dearest wish?' Monty prompts.

'You know very well what I want for Christmas, Montagu Verity!'

'Indeed I do. Let's see what Father Christmas can do for you tonight. I have high hopes.'

His cane swings around to the young woman who, Fran notices, is wearing the exact same flashing Rudolph jumper as her. The girl gives Monty a calculating look, as if assessing what the right answer should be.

'I'm Merry Clarke. I don't have a business or a brand. I write greetings cards. I'm just here for the Christmas shopping.'

Monty smiles, reaches forward and ruffles her hair – Fran can see her fighting to keep her expression friendly.

'Why, Miss Merry, I think there is a little more to your visit here than—'

Just then a crashing sound interrupts him. It sounds like someone has taken every percussion instrument in an orchestra and dropped them from a great height. A small brass cymbal rolls down the floor towards Monty, spinning noisily until it falls flat.

A flustered-looking woman stands guiltily near a display of children's musical instruments, her hand over her mouth. She is at once a stranger and totally familiar to Fran. Back on *Morning All!* the marketing team had loved pigeonholing their viewers and this woman would be categorised as a WOFAA – Woman Over Fifty Accepting her Age. This joyous acronym was arrogant marketing speak for women who aren't interested in advertisers flogging them anti-ageing cream, but who will spend money on kitchen gadgets, gardening and classic fashion. The woman has dull grey eyes and an unsightly bump in her nose. Her pale face is bare of make-up, her hair is *au naturel* frizz, and she's wearing a mac with a pattern of sad grey rain clouds. As a nod to the season, she is sporting a fun pair of Christmas tree earrings. And her cheeks are flaming with embarrassment.

'Oh gosh,' she says. 'I'm so sorry. I tried to drag my case past this drum and . . .'

Fran notices she's lugging a large blue suitcase behind her.

'Oh, Barbara,' Evangeline sighs affectedly. 'I do apologise for my assistant.'

The WOFAA, whose name is evidently Barbara, is scuttling around trying to scoop up the scattered instruments and Fran moves to help her with her case. *Another good deed, even a tiny one, can't hurt.* Monty indicates a small nook by the door so that they can leave their coats and their bulkier bags.

'I'm sorry,' Barbara tells Fran. 'I'm going straight to the airport after this – I'm going to see my grown-up son in Queensland, I can't wait!'

'Monty, I thought you said it was no plus ones,' Dean Hallibutt says. 'I could have done with bringing my assistant too.'

'Ah, yes,' Monty says. 'The rules are strict but one of our VIPs cancelled at the last minute creating a space, and besides, Miss Fall can be terribly persuasive.' The words are flirtatious, but Monty's tone is less than flattering, and the look he throws at Evangeline is steely.

Evangeline blows him a kiss, and turns her gaze back to Dean.

'So the person who isn't coming, is that . . .?' begins Merry Clarke.

'The woman whose name you appropriated, yes,' Monty says dryly. 'A lucky choice on your part. But anyway, back to business. You have all been gathered here today to experience the world's most astounding department store,' Monty continues, his voice booming theatrically as he holds his arms out wide. 'My Emporium of delights! Follow me, for an exclusive tour of the building!'

He whirls around, the skirts of his coat flying out behind him, and points his cane onwards, weaving through the tables, bowing to a customer here, doffing his cap there, leaving the small party of VIPs to follow in his wake. Fran hangs back, pausing for a moment to make a mental list of the other guests' names. It's a habit she has picked up through years of public appearances and charity events when it's rude not to remember who people are.

Just as she is about to join the others, a strange feeling overcomes her. Suddenly, despite the warmth and the hot chocolate and the cosy Christmas jumper, she is cold. There's an odd sensation, like a slender, chill hand gripping at the back of her neck and she feels a sense of wrongness, telling her to go home now.

Was this one of the ghosts her mother had seen all those years ago? Or was she simply just imagining things?

On the far side of the room, Monty beckons urgently to her. It would be rude to walk away on a whim, a feeling. Fran is a decent, polite person – she has to be to make up for what she did. And so she stays.

4

CHRISTMAS PAST – 1981

KNIVES

AT THE CHILDREN'S HOME THEY CALLED HER KNIVES. THAT WAS the way of things there. There was a rapid turnover of children, catapulted out of bad situations into the Home then fostered out as quickly as possible so as to experience the more 'natural' environment of being part of a family. In places like this, there often wasn't time to remember names – at least so Knives said – so most of the kids were nicknamed after what had landed them there. Knives had been welcomed into the Home by Junkie Jill, who slept across the hall, and she shared her own room with a girl known only as Klepto. These were simpler, less sensitive times and the adults in charge, whom they were encouraged to call Aunties and Uncles, didn't even think to clamp down on the practice. They felt they had much bigger problems than a bit of light name calling.

Knives didn't have an issue with her nickname either. It kept the other kids in a useful state of fear, giving her the power to rule the place as she wished and to work on building her organised crime empire.

One Christmas, long ago, she had seen the musical *Oliver!* on television, and watching Fagin operate had opened up a whole new career option for her. Now, as the longest-standing resident of the Home (she made it difficult for them to place her in long-term foster care), she had her own light-fingered army at her beck and call. Some of the children who went on to foster homes or adoptive families, became fences, distributing her stolen wares far and wide. Ordinarily, Knives and her gang stuck to local high-street shops, lifting razor blades, batteries and other high-value items. But it was Christmas, and as a treat she had decided to expand into the City.

Most of London's department stores weren't worth the risk. They'd invested in security cameras, were policed by platoons of uniformed guards – Hamleys was a fortress these days. But then one of the other residents, Fire Kid, had mentioned the Emporium. Like a place from another time, she'd said. Eccentric, old-fashioned owner, she'd said.

It sounded perfect.

If her gang skipped school and dodged their way onto the Tube both ways, they could be there and back in the space of a day, with no money spent and the Aunties and Uncles none the wiser. She brought the best of the best, her elite squad: Klepto, Crash and Saddo. At the last minute she drafted in Fire Kid, on the grounds that she knew the layout of the place.

Knives was beginning to regret that. Fire Kid was weird and whiny, complaining about the funny smells on the Tube, fretting endlessly that they were going to get caught and refusing to wear the baggy jacket that Knives considered to be essential shoplifting equipment. Instead she had crammed herself into a navy blue wool coat that she had obviously outgrown. The sleeves only came down to mid-wrist, it was tight across her shoulders and the smart red buttons were straining to hold her in. It was also the ugliest, most old-fashioned coat she'd ever seen. It didn't even have a hood.

'You look like that wimpy Victorian girl from the film, the annoying one who fell out of a tree.'

'Pollyanna,' Fire Kid suggested. 'It used to be one of my favourite old films.'

Knives shrugged, not wanting to admit Fire Kid knew anything she didn't.

Fire Kid had only been there six months, turning up with a sad sports bag of clothes, smelling of smoke and with a sob story about losing both her parents in a house fire. She spoke with a plummy accent, pronouncing all her *ts*, and kept herself to herself, staying in her room playing with some old-fashioned puppet. Knives always felt she looked down on the rest of them.

'I don't need a big coat, I'm not stealing anything,' the kid went on. 'I'll tell you where things are, I'll act as a lookout, but nothing more.'

Knives made a disgusted noise in her throat. 'You'll do whatever I tell you to do, or you'll pay. You know that, right?'

Fire Kid didn't answer. Her gaze dipped to the pavement in front of her. She knew.

They probably never would have found the Emporium without Fire Kid; it was so tucked away in those back streets. But when Knives walked through the heavy wooden door into a sparkling, festive wonderland she knew they had made the right choice.

'Wow,' she murmured.

'I know!' Fire Kid smiled, and for a moment her eyes sparked with a happiness that Knives had never seen in her before. 'It's amazing, isn't it?'

'It really is – narrow aisles, big crowds and they don't even have anyone on the door! Candy from a baby.'

Knives lost no time in assigning duties. Crash and Saddo would work the ground floor, the Hall of Wonders as Fire Kid called it. The shelves and tables there were crowded with small merchandise which fit nicely into sleeves.

Knives herself would head upstairs to the toy department with Klepto, and Fire Kid would show them where the best stuff was.

Knives had long since trained herself to stop being a child, and remained unmoved by the stuff around her – dolls and puppets, teddy bears and soldiers. They weren't for her, and never had been. Still, as she passed a gilt-edged wardrobe of dressing-up clothes, she couldn't help running her fingers over the silk of the dresses. Before she knew it, she had a tiara in her hands, was lowering it gently onto her head.

She surveyed herself in the mirror, her eyes haughty. Oh yes, she could get used to this.

'Nice one,' Klepto smirked, taking the crown and slipping it into her coat.

Just then, Fire Kid whimpered.

'What?' snapped Knives.

'Nothing it's just . . . that man there. The one in the braces and the shirt. That's the owner, Old Man Verity.'

A white-haired man was standing over by the till, hunkered down talking to a child who was wearing a Pollyanna coat just like Fire Kid's. It must be some kind of posh kid uniform, Knives decided.

The man was really old – *prehistoric* old. She didn't think she'd seen anyone that wrinkly in her whole life. His back was bent practically double, his hairy arms dotted with liver spots, his hands weak and bony. He was simpering at the kid in that jolly way that some adults did. He looked weak and infirm, not much of a threat at all.

'Just keep working,' she told Klepto.

They moved efficiently round the hall, slipping things into their coats and sleeves as they kept half an eye on Old Man Verity and the other staff members. Fire Kid was worse than useless, hovering near a display of puppets similar to her own childish toy, talking to them and stroking their clothes when she should have been on lookout. After around half an hour, Knives' coat was full.

'OK, let's go . . .'

But Fire Kid was rooted to the spot, her eyes staring forward and – *oh, for Christ's sake* – her eyes were filled with tears.

'Peg,' she murmured. 'I need to see Peg before we go.'

She was staring at a piano on a raised platform on one side of the room. There was a girl in Victorian gear sitting at the piano, playing a Christmas carol. No, not a girl – some kind of cross between a doll and a robot. Weird.

Knives grabbed the kid by her arm, tried to pull her away but she was surprisingly strong, yanking herself free and running across the shiny wood floor to the piano. Knives groaned, then took off after her, trying to act casual and keep the contraband inside her coat.

To her disgust, the kid was hugging the giant puppet around the shoulder, murmuring into its ear. 'Did you miss your parents too?'

Knives shivered at the wrongness, the creepiness of it.

'Let's go, kid,' she ordered.

'One more minute.'

Knives felt a flash of temper, grabbed the kid's wrist, digging her nails in hard so they bit into the skin.

'Listen to me, or I'll make your life hell.' She yanked Fire Kid away, and felt a burst of satisfaction as Fire Kid lurched backwards into her. But then she realised Clockwork Peg was coming too, falling back, knocking the kid off balance. Knives tried to wrench her body around and away, but the kid fell on her. Then there was a crash, a clang as the robot thing tumbled down onto both of them. A wig and cap landed full in Knives' face, filling her mouth with hair and dust.

Then there were more clattering sounds, as all Knives' pickings flew out from the pockets inside her coat and rolled off across the floor.

'What have we here?' a voice boomed. Old Man Verity loomed over them, jocular no more. Fire Kid burst into tears. Knives pushed Peg's stiff body off herself, scrambled to her feet and tried to run, but Verity grabbed her by the ear – the way her granny used to when she was in trouble. His gnarly fingers pinched at her, grip surprisingly strong. He had a hold on her now and, looking into his eyes, she realised he was nowhere near as old as he looked, and that underneath that grandpa act he was a pure, hard-as-nails bastard.

'You little thief,' he snarled. 'I'll make you pay for this.'

Later, as she and Fire Kid sat on the Tube home, Knives was seething.

It was all Fire Kid's fault, and Verity hadn't even punished her – hadn't even suspected that she and Knives knew each other. No girl in a Pollyanna coat would ever hang around with the likes of her. He'd accepted the kid's sobbing, heartfelt apology and assured her Clockwork Peg would be fine. He'd ruffled her hair and called her by her real name, asked her how her own little puppet was doing. All the while gripping Knives tight by the earlobe, so she couldn't get away.

The worst of it, though, was when some sales assistants gently pulled the horrible doll thing back into place. The head had come loose and turned around facing backwards – glassy eyes staring straight into Knives' soul.

Old Man Verity hadn't called the police.

'I like to do things the old-fashioned way,' he'd told her. The punishment he decided on was far worse, far more degrading than a mere caution from the pigs.

Now, grinding her teeth with rage, she stared across the Tube carriage at Fire Kid. 'You'll pay for this,' she said.

Fire Kid sighed, slumped back in her seat, her face blank and unafraid. 'Whatever you say. I don't care anymore.'

Over the next few days, her fury only grew. She'd sworn Klepto and the others to secrecy but who knew how long that would last, and if word got out what Fire Kid had done, her grip on the other children at the Home would loosen. The punishment of Fire Kid would have to be savage, unmistakeable and a message to every snivelling boy and girl under that roof. And she had the perfect idea.

45

There was always much excitement surrounding Christmas dinner at the Home. The Aunties and Uncles pushed all the tables in the dining room together to make a horseshoe shape. Each child had a cracker, a party hat and a plate of what passed for Christmas dinner. It was utter chaos. Kids were pulling crackers, trading hats, jostling for extra roast potatoes. One boy emptied the entire tin jug of gravy onto his plate, causing outrage from those around him. It was easy to sneak away, do the thing, then creep back.

Nobody smelled the smoke at first – their faces were too full of food, but then wisps of it began to curl down the corridor into the dining room. The festive grins slid off the Aunties' faces.

By the time they got there with the fire extinguisher, Fire Kid's bed was a wreck, the yellow polyester bedspread melted and black, the paint on the wall next to it bubbled and stained. And in the centre of the bed you could still see a tangle of charcoal limbs and tattered lace that had once been a cherished stringed puppet.

The most delicious thing about it all was that the adults suspected that Fire Kid had done it herself. None of the other kids would ever tell, not when Knives had proved herself capable of such terrible revenge. And wasn't that how the kid had ended up here in the first place? The house fire which had killed the kid's parents was officially an accident, but two fire-related incidents happening to one child? The coincidence planted a seed of doubt. By the time spring had come, Fire Kid was gone – moved to somewhere more secure, more *therapeutic*.

Within a year of the fire, the Emporium itself had closed and a few months after that Old Man Verity was in his grave. And although she had nothing to do with either of those things, it still showed, for all the world to see, that nothing good comes to people who mess with Knives.

5

MERRY

MERRY IS MILDLY IRRITATED. THE PLAN HAD BEEN TO BLAG HER way into the Emporium, buy the snow globe for Ross then dash back on a late Tube to meet him and their fellow former interns for pre-Christmas drinks. Merry always feels a little excluded from their group – Jen and Farah coupled up pretty much as soon as they started at Stimpson's and she has always felt they like Ross more than they like her. She worries that not showing up will make them think even less of her. She also worries that Ross will somehow change his mind about spending Christmas with her. The last thing she wants is to be trapped here with this odd, mismatched group, following Monty Verity through his Hall of Wonders.

She could sneak off, of course, Merry is excellent at sneaking. But something is stopping her, that deep, urgent curiosity which Ross always teases her about. Some weird stuff is going on and she needs to know what.

She just wishes she hadn't left her hot chocolate on the table outside – the others are still drinking theirs happily and it's making her mouth water.

There are beautiful things everywhere she looks. On one side is a mirrored table piled high with glass baubles so rainbow-hued and delicate that they look like bubbles blown by a child. She keeps her eyes peeled, looking for snow globes – no, not just any snow globe but *the* snow globe. There's no sign, they must be somewhere else. Her eyes rest on a model of a brightly clad elf, posed as if he's polishing a crystal droplet. Then, to her shock, the elf moves, his little duster working back and forth, his other hand turning the droplet so he can polish both sides.

She jumps back, knocking a full-size reindeer covered in sleigh bells with her elbow which causes an embarrassing amount of jingling.

Monty chuckles.

'That's just one of my little automata – what do you think?'

Merry stares at the elf's rosy-cheeked face. She can hear a complex series of ticks coming from inside the elf's chest now and sees that his movements are simple and repetitive, but still oddly real.

'These aren't electrical, you don't plug them in, oh no. They are all perfect clockwork, made over one hundred years ago by my dear great-grandfather and his assistant Miss Goodchild. All I have done is revive them, given them a little oil and a lick of paint. Their old faces were – quite frankly – terrifying to the modern eye. In fact, my dear ancestor was quite the genius when it came to clockwork.' He points upwards. 'Behold!'

On the wall at the back of the store is a vast, complex mechanism of cogs, leading upwards to a large, carved wooden clock face. The cogs are moving, the pendulum swings back and forth, and from the depths of the mechanism comes a deep, solid tick far louder than the one made by the automaton elf.

'This is the Great Clock, one of the jewels of Verity's, as is the miniature store below.'

Beneath the cogs and pendulum there is a table, on which sits a perfectly rendered miniature cross-section of the Emporium, like a doll's house. She can see the beautifully crafted mini-store has three levels: a Hall of Wonders like the one she's standing in, above it the balcony floor, laden down with tiny miniature cakes and sweets. Finally there's the upper floor, which houses the toy department and teems with intricately carved Victorian dolls, trains and red-coated soldiers.

'I have endeavoured to keep the layout of the revived Emporium true to this model,' Monty explains. 'Hall of Wonders, perfumes and floristry on the ground floor. Then you will find the Hall of Delicacies and Discoveries on the mezzanine, and my Hall of Toys at the top.'

On the marble surface in front of the model Emporium stand five brightly painted wooden models. Each one is about the length of her forefinger and constructed like one of those jointed, wooden artist's models. She looks at the one closest to her. It's a woman, a little thicker in the waist and heavier in the bosom than the average doll. Her painted-on hair is styled into cornrow-type braids.

'That looks like me,' Fran Silver says, peering closely. The doll is wearing a colourful dress, which was very much Fran's style on

Morning All!, and on her chest is a little coloured ribbon, the kind charities use for fundraising. 'It *is* me!'

'This one might be me,' Benjamin says, peering at a figure in a pinstripe suit and bow tie.

'Well, my one isn't right,' the stylish dark-haired woman, Evangeline, says, running her hands over her flat stomach. 'It's far too *round*.'

'Hah, that one's got my hairstyle.' Josie touches the bun on the top of her head. 'It's so well made, look at the detail on my face! Blows me away how someone can do this with just some wood, paint and a few tools.'

She reaches out to touch the model, but Monty holds up his cane, stopping her.

'These figurines are indeed facsimiles of your good selves, hand-made by my finest craftsman. You will be able to take them home at the end of the evening,' he says. 'But the paint on them is still not fully dry. I would be grateful if you refrain from touching them until then.'

Merry is a little disappointed there isn't one of her, but then as a gatecrasher she can hardly expect full VIP privileges. Perhaps, tucked in a drawer somewhere, there's a Doug model that will never see the light of day.

'How many hours did that take to make?' Dean Hallibutt asks, peering at his own figurine, which is taller than the rest, and is posed dynamically, hands on hips. 'I mean, they're amazing but I can't imagine how this hand-crafted stuff makes sense, productivity wise.'

Monty sighs. 'My Elves insist it is worthwhile to put time and love into something, regardless of cost.'

'Yeah, but not if you ever want to make any money,' Dean replies wryly.

Monty goes to answer but then glances up at the Great Clock above him. 'It is time! Keep your eyes on the miniature store!'

The clock chimes eight – bonging like a smaller-scale Big Ben – and as it does, the toys in the mini-store come to life, whirling and dancing. On the ground floor a group of wooden Victorian shoppers appears, moving jerkily around inspecting the wares.

Merry is a Millennial. She has been relentlessly marketed to for the whole of her life so she is used to everything that surrounds Christmas being pitched as 'magical'. TV specials, heart-warming festive ads, a Lapland Experience, a sugar-free diet drink. This is the first time she's seen something that's truly worthy of that word.

'Have I finally impressed Miss Merry Clarke?' Monty asks.

'Yeah,' she admits. 'It's not bad.'

'Oh poor un-merry Merry,' Monty says, throwing an arm around her shoulders, 'who can't express a strong emotion for fear of getting hurt. Let the wonder of Christmas in, dear girl. You won't regret it.'

The wood-panelled Verity's lift is definitely not designed to hold this many people. Monty has taken the stairs but the rest of them are crammed in like Christmas crackers in a box. She is so close to Dean's chest she can feel the heat coming off him, catch the undertow of musk beneath the scent of his aftershave. Just as it's becoming too much, Evangeline somehow squirms between them asking if there is room for a little one, so Merry becomes crushed by a soft wall of cashmere.

'What a coincidence to find you here,' Evangeline gushes to him. 'How have you been? A little bird tells me there may be a television deal in the works. You must talk to lovely Fran over there about that! She's a national treasure, you know, what with all that charity work. But the things I could tell you about her . . .'

'Hey,' Fran protests. 'College was a long time ago. We all did a lot of silly things then.'

'I wasn't talking about college,' Evangeline says. 'But Fran we simply *must* catch up about your more recent activities. Give Barbara your number and we can do coffee in the New Year.'

Evangeline leans back towards Dean, invading his personal space to murmur something in his ear which, annoyingly, Merry can't hear. Instead she studies Fran's face. The usually perky TV star looks deeply uneasy.

And then the lift lurches abruptly and stops. They are stuck between floors.

Fran, whose breathing is already nervous and shallow, jabs the button for the Hall of Delicacies again, extra hard because everyone knows that the harder you press a button the sooner the mechanism will respond.

Dean pushes past Evangeline, bulling his way across the lift to the buttons. 'Let me look . . . oh shit, the alarm button just came off in my hand.' Dean jabs violently at the empty button hole. 'I don't know if it's even working now. Fucking piece of shit machine!'

'Steady on,' Benjamin says mildly from the opposite corner. 'Language! Ladies!'

'OK, come on then, Mr Antiques Expert, let's see what you can do,' Dean snaps back. He stares at Benjamin over the women's heads, shoulders set, eyes narrowed as if he's fronting up to someone in a drunken pub brawl. Where did this sudden aggression come from?

'Whoa there, cowboy,' Josie says wearily, pushing through the crowd to the buttons. 'Stand aside for a sec.'

She rummages through her roomy tote bag, pulling out a bunch of keys with a cry of satisfaction. Attached to the keyring is a miniature screwdriver.

'My sister-in-law got these posh crackers last Christmas. Totally worth it – this thing's well handy.'

She sets to work, unscrewing the control panel, and by the time Benjamin has said 'Do you think you should be doing that?' the panel is off. Josie reaches in and does something to the controls. The lift judders and starts to move.

'This model's an antique, it's temperamental,' she says. Then, noticing everyone staring, she adds, 'My ex-husband was a lift engineer. It's amazing the information you pick up when a man's moaning about work.'

Fran laughs – that raucous crack of laughter that made her famous, and Evangeline joins in with a high-pitched giggle. Josie gives one of those wheezy laughs that singles her out as a heavy smoker. Benjamin titters and even Dean's shoulders are shaking. The laughter builds, becomes uncontrollable and by the time the lift doors open, everyone is in hysterics except Merry.

'Well, I see you are all nicely warmed up,' Monty observes as they spill out of the lift, some of them wiping tears from their eyes.

'The lifts are shit,' Josie says.

'Ah yes, old machines can be very temperamental, can't they, Benjamin?'

The antique dealer's face becomes harsher, more judgemental. 'Indeed, especially if they are not properly maintained.'

The mezzanine floor smells even more of mulled wine and fresh baking, of mince pies and Christmas puddings. The others fall hungrily on the piles of glorious festive food. Merry sees Fran turn down a glass mulled wine, then grab it and down it like her throat is on fire. She sees Barbara having a giggling food fight with Josie, Benjamin eating a gingerbread man in one bite, Evangeline feeding Dean morsels of Turkish delight. He seems to have calmed down now, opening his mouth obediently for each little powdered cube. It's all a bit . . . much. It has a feel of last days of the Roman Empire about it.

'Dear Merry,' Monty says at her side, 'are you not having as much fun as the others?'

Merry searches for the answer she thinks Monty wants to hear. She's not sure why, it's just out of deeply ingrained habit. She comes up blank. All she can think of to say is, 'Things are getting a little weird.'

'Oh, that's just the Emporium Effect – we frequently notice that sensible grown adults revert to second childhood when they come here at Christmas time.'

An image of Rita flickers through Merry's mind. If she'd come tonight would they have ended up making up, giggling as they played dress-up or hosted a doll's tea party?

'But what about you?' Monty asks. 'Don't you feel it? The need to forget about your daily cares for a few moments and have a snowball fight? Or eat an entire Christmas cake?'

'A bit, I suppose. Not enough to actually do it.'

Monty's face falls in a moue of sadness, but then he snaps quickly back to his old self and shrugs. 'Well, give it time.'

He clicks his fingers and an eager-faced assistant in a long, corseted dress is standing at his side.

'It appears that my young friend has left her hot chocolate outside – please be so good as to fetch her a fresh one. Make sure it's the very best, from the VIP kettle, no second-rate stuff!'

Merry puts a little distance between herself and the others, moving over to the edge of the balcony. She can see the beautiful filaments hanging down from the ceiling more closely, the clever lighting which allows them to twinkle in an otherworldly way. She is not a fan of heights, but she allows herself a glance down to the Hall of Wonders below. There are fewer shoppers there now, people are beginning to drift home to spend Christmas with their families. She should be going soon, too.

'Please, Miss Merry, do not lean on this part of the balustrade,' Monty says. 'See the sign? Oh dear, Ruffles the elf appears to have dropped it.'

Nearby there is an elf automaton waving at her with a sinister series of clicks, a fallen sign at his feet. Monty puts the banner back into its hands and she reads: PLEASE KEEP CLEAR OF THE HANDRAIL. WOODWORM TREATMENT IN PROGRESS.

She shrinks back from the weakened balustrade immediately, feeling a surge of fear.

It takes Monty some time to herd them up the stairs to the third floor – Fran refuses point blank to get back into the lift and Merry can't really blame her. But when they do, they arrive in Narnia

– or at least they are in a forest of over-sized Christmas trees that tower up to the ceiling, covered in fake snow and minimally decorated, giving them a look of natural wildness. Here and there, between the boughs, Merry sees toys. Puppets and planes, dolls and puzzles. She can imagine how children would love to play hunt-the-toy through this miniature forest.

Fran is clearly heavily invested. She stops to wonder at everything, ooh-ing and aah-ing as if she is five years old. She has draped herself with a garland of golden ivy, and now she snatches a dress-up tiara from one of the boughs and tries to place it on Merry's head.

'Here you are, princess!'

Merry shies away instinctively, spilling some of her hot chocolate down the front of her jumper, but Fran isn't reading the signals and pushes the tiara forward again.

'Come on, lighten up a bit, crack a smile!' Fran makes the lights flash on her own matching knitwear and does a kind of jazz-hands gesture. 'It's Christmas!'

Ugh. Is this what Merry will have to transform into to convince Ross she doesn't hate Christmas? She really hopes not.

Just then, they arrive at a log cabin tucked away to one side, a sign on the door says SANTA'S GROTTO.

The area in front of the grotto is populated with automaton elves going about their business. One is hammering diligently at a toy soldier. Another is posed as if he is about to scale a long rope ladder with rungs made of candy canes, which hangs from the cabin roof.

'Let's go inside,' Josie says, but the wooden front door of the grotto is firmly bolted. Monty leans across the doorway with a smile.

'Alas, Father Christmas has departed. Christmas Eve is a very busy night for him.'

Merry is relieved the grotto is closed – she wouldn't have put it past Monty to force them all to sit on Santa's knee. But it's strange too. Surely Santa's grotto should be the highlight of the tour? Merry crouches down to inspect the fake snow around the front of the hut. It's not the standard nylon-fibre stuff the other department stores seem to use – it feels like it's made of individual crystals – and when Merry touches it, it leaves a handprint behind.

'Please don't do that.' Benjamin is at her side, disapproving. 'Imagine if we all did that, the effect would be ruined.'

Merry realises she can hear piano music, a Christmas carol being played. As they move on from the grotto, the toy department opens out before them, full of shelves and tables stocked with bright, hand-crafted toys. There is a car park of toy cars, scooters and balance bikes and nearby, a giant slope, made of dry-slope ski matting, sledges stacked beside it.

She can see where the music is coming from now – a plinth where an adult-sized Victorian doll sits, playing the piano with jerky movements. As she gets closer she realises the doll has seen better days. Her dark hair is ragged, her bonnet is lopsided. The fingers, which move jerkily over the keyboard, were once painted a warm brown but most of the paint has flaked away exposing worn wood beneath. There's something about it that makes her shiver – the way its eyes move, the creaking and clicking of its gestures. It's grotesque, like something out of *Doctor Who*. She half expects the jointed hand to reach out and grab her wrist.

'So this is the famous Clockwork Peg,' Dean says.

'The *priceless* Clockwork Peg,' Benjamin corrects him, pushing through to gaze at the automaton. 'Peg is a piece of our history, a stunning example of engineering left to rack and ruin . . .'

'Yes, we know.' Monty's tone is weary. 'I have received your many letters on the subject. For those of you not intimate with our history, the Goodchild Automaton is a reproduction of the Emporium's first toymaker, Miss Peggy Goodchild. She was a genius, almost as gifted as my great-grandfather, and he made this in memory of her.'

'I know *all about her.*' Evangeline speaks slowly, turning away from Dean for a moment to fix Monty with a strange kind of glare.

He avoids meeting her eye.

'Indeed, and I am happy we can finally welcome you back here to see her again in person, Miss Fall.'

'She is in a right state, though,' Josie says with genuine sorrow in her voice. 'Peggy, I mean, not Evangeline. It's so sad.'

'It is regrettable,' Monty sighs theatrically. 'The Emporium was closed for many years while I travelled the globe seeking new toymaking techniques and honing my craft. During that time there were squatters, and there were rats. I do, however, have plans to restore her to her former glory.'

'The same way you did with those automata over there?' Benjamin says. 'Coat her in modern paint and dress her in garish clothes? As Britain's foremost dealer in antique clockwork and automata, I . . . I can't allow it.'

He moves closer to Peggy, turning so he can gaze directly into her eyes, using the side of his finger to caress Peggy's cheek.

'She is too precious.' Frowning, he brushes at Peggy's cap, tutting as a cloud of dust flies off. Then suddenly, he winces.

'Ouch. Look here, Verity, I cut myself on a loose wire. And look how dusty she is! It's just unacceptable.' Benjamin draws his finger back, sucking it angrily.

'You are correct there,' Monty concedes. 'I am afraid our cleaners are a little reluctant to go near her. They are superstitious and rumour has it that the spirit of Peggy Goodchild haunts this precious piece of work.'

Fran is gazing into the automaton's eyes.

'Yes. There is something, something sorrowful.' Fran sways, her body unstable. 'Can I give her a hug?'

'I am afraid not – please, nobody else must touch Peggy this evening. It is strictly forbidden. As Mr Makepeace says, she is delicate.'

'Can I give *you* a hug?' Fran asks. Her words are slurring as if she is drunk, although she only had the one mulled wine earlier. Benjamin too is looking woozy, and Josie is running, whooping, towards the sledging slope, calling the others after her. Evangeline seems to have attached herself to Dean's arm and Barbara is sitting on the floor nearby next to a doll's house, a miniature piece of furniture in each hand. The Emporium Effect seems to be taking hold of all of them.

'This has been great, Monty, really,' Dean says. His voice is slurring too; he seems less masterful than he did downstairs. He taps his expensive watch heavy-handedly. 'But time's ticking!'

'Indeed, Mr Hallibutt.' He smiles. 'We are about to conclude our tour with one final display. Ladies and gentlemen, I ask you to fix your eyes on the ceiling over there, and in a few moments, you will see our very own version of the Northern Lights.'

The others turn around, but Merry senses another of Monty's misdirections. Sure enough, while the others turn their backs to watch a pretty light show, Monty reaches for a brass light fitting attached to a nearby panelled wall. It's screwed in rather low, at Merry's head height, and looks very old. Deftly, he twists the lamp to one side and with a click, a gap opens in the wood-panelled wall and he goes through. He is gone in moments, the door clicked shut behind him.

Merry gapes after him. An actual secret passage. Curiosity roars up inside her, hungry and impossible to ignore. She absolutely *has* to know what's behind that door. Making sure that none of the others are looking – she really doesn't want a raucous Fran trailing after her – she twists the lamp herself, and goes after him.

6

FRAN

BACK IN THE DAYS WHEN FRAN WENT OUT PARTYING THERE WERE some nights – some special nights – when wonderful things would happen. She would get talking to someone new, make connections and – *bam* – magic. Those were the nights when you'd find yourself dancing with a Russian count in a Mayfair apartment, talking about the afterlife with a drug dealer in an illegal drinking den, or trying to steal a monkey from London Zoo. This was fast becoming one of those times.

Fran never had a sledge as a kid – there wasn't much call for them in Camberwell. On rare snow days she and her friends had usually taken a Tesco bag to the gentle slopes of Ruskin Park, envying the posher kids with their elegant wooden sleds that could fit three or four friends. So as she speeds down the slope, Josie pushing her and laughing, she feels like she's fulfilling a lifelong ambition.

Gurgling with laughter, she scrambles to her feet and a feels a rush of dizziness. Her limbs are behaving oddly, and the edges of the world have become blurred and sepia-tinted, like she's living in an Instagram filter. But her cheeks are aching from smiling and it feels amazing. She climbs the slope again, throws herself on the sledge and rockets down, sliding beyond the edge of the matting and onto the toy department floor.

For this short time, she does not feel the loss of her mother, the weight of guilt she has carried for all these years – or even the strange, disorientating sensation she experienced when she saw Clockwork Peg earlier.

Look at me. The pull is still there, tugging at her attention, desperate to be noticed. None of the others seem to see it. Even Benjamin, who breaks off from sledging occasionally to gaze longingly in Peg's direction.

Maybe it's to do with the tune she is playing. Although it sounds like a lullaby, the 'Coventry Carol' is the darkest of Christmas songs, mourning the children massacred by King Herod as he tried to eliminate the young Messiah.

'Come on, Fran,' Josie calls. 'Let's go again. Race you to the top!'

Fran tears her gaze away from Peg and runs after her new friend, breathless with laughter. They race their sledges, they swap and race again, then she, Josie and Benjamin pile onto one sledge to see if they can make it go even faster.

At some point they wander downstairs to where the food is, grab as many festive treats as possible, and return back upstairs to picnic on the slope, drinking from tiny china doll's cups, and laughing.

From the top of the slope, Fran can see Dean hanging around outside next to Santa's grotto, and Evangeline, fluttering next to him, trying to hold his attention. He turns away but she pursues him, catching his arm with one pale, manicured hand. He shakes her hand off, rounds on her. It's too far away to hear what he's saying, but he's shouting. Then he reaches out, shoves her shoulder.

'Oi!' Fran struggles to her feet. 'Hands off her!'

Dean stalks away, off through the Christmas trees, leaving Evangeline alone in a fairy glen. She looks as though she might be crying.

The right thing to do would be to go and help her, but after Evangeline's words in the lift, Fran is afraid to get too close. What was it she'd said? *The things I could tell you about her.*

Fran feels sick. There is only one thing she can mean.

Luckily Barbara is already at Evangeline's side, helping her up, soothing her gently. But the sight has killed the carefree, festive vibe now and she feels her usual guilty rush of shame, despair and sadness.

She thinks of the people she's met through all her years of fundraising. Men running marathons to prove to cancer that they were strong, women reluctant to shave their heads because they don't want to frighten their children. And the kids – the kids were the worst of all. After the Santa Dash, they had lined her up for a photo opportunity with the needy children the charity was helping.

One little girl climbed onto Fran's lap and threw her arms around her.

Fran, who loves children but never really knows what to say to them, froze and randomly clicked into Santa Claus mode.

'So, erm, what do you want for Christmas this year, little girl?'

The girl's weight was sparrow-like, and she felt too bony as she fidgeted on Fran's lap. Her hair was just about growing back, her face tired from chemotherapy as she turned and gazed up at Fran.

'I just don't want to be in hospital for Christmas this year,' she'd said and Fran felt a twist of sadness in her guts. Then the girl's face lit up with a grin. 'Oh, and a doll as big as me that walks and talks. And an iPhone. And a Roblox smartwatch.'

Moments like that made her feel helpless. However much fundraising she did, she could never save that child's life. And even if she could, it would take more than that to make up for what she had done.

Fran is not sure what the time is, but her energy has begun to dip. Josie is yawning too, has sunk down into a discarded pile of dressing-up clothes. Benjamin's feet are sticking out of a Wendy house and she can hear him snoring. There is no sign of Barbara, Evangeline or Dean. They have probably gone home and Fran knows she should, too, but is suddenly struck by the fact that nobody is waiting for her except for her cat, the esteemed Mr Duncan Biscuits. He has a twenty-four-hour automatic cat feeder, though, so he won't miss her until tomorrow afternoon.

Maybe she could take a quick nap before she leaves.

She has selected a huge doll for the Santa Dash girl, hoping the charity will send it on to her. Now she picks it up and staggers over to Santa's grotto, wondering if the main man has a comfy bed.

The door doesn't open when she pulls it. She peers inside, through a window encrusted with fake snow. There's someone in there, someone wearing dark clothes, pacing back and forth.

Although she can't see their features through the frosting, the body language is angry, the shoulders bunched-up.

'Someone's not getting what they want for Christmas,' she tells the doll. The doll does not answer.

There's a large sleigh parked next to the grotto, piled high with furry blankets and throws – it's as good a bed as she's going to find. Within a few moments she has made herself a comfy nest.

She slips her hand into her bag, half-conscious – looking for a phone that isn't there – and as she does, her finger brushes against a piece of paper. Confused, she pulls out an envelope, tears it open to find a folded page, torn from a high-quality notebook. It's white, unlined, with silver edging around three sides and a rip along the fourth. It takes a few moments to unfold the creases enough to read – and then her blood goes cold.

Five words savagely scrawled in black fountain pen ink.

I
KNOW
WHAT
YOU
DID

7

MERRY

MERRY STUMBLES INTO THE PASSAGEWAY, AND BY THE LIGHT OF a bare bulb she sees Monty's back disappearing around a corner at the top of a steep flight of stairs. She follows him quietly, treading on each step as softly as she can. This building is old – the stairs are bound to creak – she can only hope that Monty is otherwise distracted.

At the top she emerges into a long, low-ceilinged room tucked under the eaves of the Emporium roof. It's a wide-open space and is filled with rows and rows of workbenches. Each bench is fitted with an Anglepoise lamp and magnifying glass, but is set up for something slightly different. On one, a row of toy soldiers shining in the half-light. On another, a delicately sculpted doll's foot lies on a pile of lace and vintage rags. A semi-carved eagle emerges from a rubble of wood shavings. Merry can't resist, she reaches out and touches its beak – the wood is sanded smooth as silk.

At the far end of the room is a blazing log burner, and over it hangs a portrait of an austere-looking Victorian gentleman. Monty stands next to the fire, talking to a man in a white shirt and red trousers, who is hunched over one of the desks. His voice is a low, angry murmur, his arms gesticulating wildly. Scenting secrets, Merry hunkers down behind the benches and treads softly, creeping closer, her ears straining to hear.

'Why won't you listen? This could be the answer . . . Well, at least this is bringing in money . . .' And finally, almost in a roar: 'I am Montagu Verity, dammit! I *am* the Emporium!'

Merry strains closer, and the top of her head brushes a metal ruler sticking out from the nearest desk. It clatters to the floor, ruinously loud. Monty stops talking immediately, and, hot with shame at being caught, Merry rises slowly to her full height. To add to the indignity, her Christmas jumper starts flashing even though she hasn't pressed the button. Spilled hot chocolate is probably not good for the wiring.

'Ah, Miss Merry Clarke, I am happy to say you are behaving exactly as I thought you would,' Monty says. His voice is back to normal now, the smiling entertainer. 'Well, there is no need to lurk there in the background, please come, come! Now you are here, you must let me show you around!

'This is where the magic happens. We do, of course, buy beautifully crafted wonders from all over the world but we also pride ourselves on our hand-made artisan pieces, and these are created here, in this very workshop by my own army of Elves.'

The man next to Monty makes a gruff, indecipherable sound.

'Is he one of your Elves?' she asks.

'Ah now, Rudi is something more,' Monty says. 'Every single person who works for me is a genius but this man here is the greatest genius of all. Rudi, this is our esteemed guest, Merry Clarke.'

Merry giggles awkwardly, which is odd as she's not usually one of life's gigglers.

Rudi still does not look up, but continues working intently on a small wooden figure in his hand. He's a big man, with broad shoulders, his rolled-up sleeves show hairy arms and sausage-like fingers with grubby nails. But between his fingertips he holds a paintbrush the size of a toothpick, and he is delicately touching up the face of the small wooden toy he's making.

'You must have such a steady hand to do that,' she says. People reveal more when they think you admire them and she hopes this will get him to open up. At first Rudi doesn't respond, but eventually his gaze flickers away from his work. It takes a moment for him to refocus his clear blue eyes on her. He is much older than she had first thought. His features are wrinkled, his white brows knit together as he looks at her, an expression of pain on his face.

'Rudi doesn't talk much,' Monty explains. 'But he makes magic with his hands.'

The old man returns to his work and she can see it's another jointed wooden model, like the ones she'd seen of the VIPs downstairs.

She thinks about the amount of time and effort that goes into making all this – especially compared to the minimal effort she expends on her greetings card poems – and wonders that anyone can afford anything in the Emporium. Dean was right – the store can't be making any money.

This figure looks like another of those jointed models but this one has a red-painted jumper with a tiny reindeer on it. A curl of hair flops down over one of its eyes just like . . . Merry's hand flies up to her own curl.

'Is that . . . *me?*'

Rudi doesn't answer, just stares at her, his eyes intense and sad. Instinctively, she backs away but then his wrinkled, paint-splattered hand shoots out, grabs her wrist. His mouth is open, struggling to form a word.

'D . . .' he says. 'D . . . D . . .'

'Oh dear, poor Rudi,' Monty says. Gently, he prises Rudi's hands away. He sweeps an arm around Merry's shoulders and leads her away. 'Don't you worry, old man. I'll take good care of her. She is, after all, still my favourite.'

Rudi continues to struggle to speak as Monty leads her away. He clearly doesn't want Merry to hear what the man is trying to say, which makes her even more desperate to hear it, and just as they reach the doorway, Rudi finally finds the words, his scream drifting after them across the work room.

'D . . . D–don't t–trust him!' Rudi yells. 'He l–lies!'

By the time they're back down on the shop floor Merry's curiosity is aflame and her mind is whirling with questions. She ignores the other VIPs who seem to be in hysterics over on the sledges, and follows Monty as he strides down the stairs to the Hall of Delicacies. The effort of trying to keep up and decide what question to ask first is making her more than a little flustered. Her head is starting to feel fuzzy, like it's wrapped in cotton wool.

Finally, Monty stops so suddenly Merry nearly crashes into him. He grabs a freshly baked mince pie from the counter, urges her to try it and more or less shoves it into her mouth. Merry tries not to choke on the (admittedly delicious) crumbly pastry.

'I can see you're confused,' Monty says. 'I'm sorry Rudi upset you. He is the best toymaker on the planet – and that includes every last one of Father Christmas's genuine elves, but he's not a people person. He is quite cross with me tonight, but it has nothing to do with you.'

Merry coughs and a cloud of icing sugar comes out of her mouth.

'Secret passages?' Merry says through the pastry.

'Oh, those,' Monty says, waving his hand. 'The original Mr Verity – my great-great grandfather – did not want the customer experience to be polluted by the comings and goings of staff. Sales assistants were meant to appear and disappear as if by magic, and so he built a number of hidden doors and passages to allow the staff to move seamlessly and noiselessly from department to department. You may have noticed that we still have fitted gas lamps – indeed, they still work after a fashion although we rarely have cause to use them. Some of these lamps are in fact levers, used to operate the tunnel entrances.'

Merry's mind is struggling to keep up. Who builds a place like this? It wasn't just a business put together by a man of commerce, it was a wonderland, a folly. She decides that every Verity from first to last must have been quite mad. *Now, there's a troubling thought.* She shoves that uncomfortable possibility aside as another burning question rises to the surface and although Monty seems to want to move away from her, she follows.

'But how do you survive?' Merry asks. 'As a business, I mean. Everything's so cheap and if you hand-make it all . . .'

A cloud of irritation crosses Monty's face, and then he smiles. 'A magician never reveals his secrets, Miss Merry. Let us just say that once again, it comes down to misdirection.'

Just then a loud *bing bong* echoes through the store as a tannoy crackles to life.

'Ladies and gentlemen, it is five to eleven and the store will be closing shortly. Please make your final choices and make your way towards the till. Thank you for coming to our late night shopping event, and merry Christmas!'

'Ignore her.' Monty smiles, showing a row of too-even, too-white teeth. 'That's just for ordinary guests – you're one of the special ones.'

How long has she been here? Time seems to move differently in the Emporium – the same way a child can spend all morning opening Christmas presents but it would only feel like five minutes to them. It's getting late, she has to get away from Monty right now, get Ross's gift, pay for it and join Ross and the others. But her head is still swimming, her eyes drawn to the sparkling crystal decorations which hang down from the ceiling in front of her, the fairy-like figures flitting between them. *So pretty.*

No. She has to focus.

'I've got to go,' she tells Monty. 'I've got something I really need to buy.'

Monty cocks his head to one side, and removes his hat solemnly.

'Of course you must,' he says. 'God speed, my child.'

It's not until she is back in the Hall of Wonders that she realises she should have asked him where the snow globes are.

The Hall is almost empty now, just a few stragglers paying for their wares and hardly any members of staff. She passes Evangeline, who is staring into a Snow White-style mirror, combing her hair and singing to herself like a Disney princess. Merry wouldn't put it past the Emporium to have created a magic mirror that shows you your Instagram-filtered face.

The Great Clock chimes – she tries to count the bongs but loses focus halfway, instead watching the clockwork dancers whirl around in the replica store. The line-up of personalised figures still gleams on the marble in front of it, but on the top floor of the model there's a new figure – a wooden toy Santa that looks like it's become caught in the mechanism, splintered and broken.

'Poor Santa got smashed,' she says to precisely nobody. Now, time to buy the . . . what was it she wanted to buy again? Snowy thing. Globe. Yes.

She stumbles through a tunnel of twinkling lights and as she does she sees Rita, lunging towards her out of the darkness. A scream rips out of her, but then she realises it's just another shopper, her brow creased with concern.

'Are you OK, love?'

'Yeah. Sorry, looking for the snow globes.'

'You want upstairs,' she says with a smile. 'Mezzanine floor, past the food, turn left at the stuffed animals.'

Merry wants to thank her, but her tongue won't really do what she asks any more. She waves a rubbery-feeling hand at her and wanders on.

The snow globes have a room to themselves. A round, dark -walled cavern lit by a revolving crystal chandelier which throws different colours onto the walls and lights up the tiny details in each glass bubble. Some are traditional festive snow globes but just more beautifully wrought. A polar bear makes a pilgrimage to Santa's North Pole; a teddy bear stands, looking lost, outside a cottage with warmth glowing from the windows. Others are darker – a cloaked figure hunched in a snow storm, pressing a baby to her chest. A little match girl shivering in a Victorian doorway. For a moment she is afraid she won't find the right one.

But then her eye snags on something – this is it.

Ross had showed her a photograph of it once: the Emporium snow globe his father had put out on the mantel at home every Christmas. It was a crowded winter fairground scene, with hot-chestnut vendors, a moving Ferris wheel, a carousel laden with happy children. It had been part of Ross's Christmases for his whole life and he had been devastated when it broke.

There are two fairground designs to choose from – one is identical to the one Merry remembers from Ross's photo, right down to the red-painted wooden base and the little boy dragging a sledge in the foreground. The other one is slightly different. Its base is a deep midnight blue, and instead of the kid with the sledge there is a couple in the foreground – a girl in a bright red coat, and a tall angular boy in a striped scarf, looking down at her. It looks as though they're about to kiss.

It's us, Merry thinks. *A sign that we really are meant to be.*

She hesitates – the sledge one is a perfect reproduction of the snow globe Ross lost; it's the one he would probably choose if he were standing here. But the blue one is pretty close, and it might send a message to Ross, showing them they had a future together . . . She chooses blue.

Time to pay up and leave. It feels like she's been in the Emporium for days now, but now Christmas is waiting. It's probably too late to meet Ross and the others now but she still needs to wrap the snow globe, get the turkey ready to go into the oven and arrange the presents under the tree before she finally goes to sleep.

The lights outside the Snow Globe Room have dimmed, which makes it harder to wend her way through the different departments. Everything blurs together in a whirl of glitter and sparkle, just like being in a snow globe herself.

Her eyes are heavy. It's as if her mind is like the store, slowly dimming, closing down. Rational thought cashing up for the day and going home. But in a tiny corner of her brain a thought sparks: *The others were behaving oddly too, but I'm only feeling it now . . .*

The feeling had started up in the toy department shortly after she finished her hot chocolate. She tries to focus – to work out what's happening to her – but the facts keep slipping away. Could Monty have put something in her drink?

His face shimmers in her mind, warped and grotesque, laughing. *You're my favourite . . .*

Ugh. Her skin crawls.

Instinctively, she reaches into her pocket for her phone but of course it's gone, taken from her by Monty.

Panic surges – dammit, where is she again? Some kind of narrow aisle that feels like a tunnel. Looking frantically around she sees a wall filled with ribbons, another wall bedecked with tiny silver things hanging from pins, then a display of taxidermy animals, wearing human clothes but still displaying beady eyes and sharp claws.

She backs away, spots a doorway behind her. Through the fuzziness of her brain a paranoid instinct kicks in telling her: *Be ready to run.* She slips the snow globe into her shoulder bag for safekeeping. And then she hears it, the Great Clock striking the hour again.

That way.

The bell tolls one, two, three times – she follows the sound, and only the sound as it counts down to midnight. How is she still here? How is it Christmas morning already?

And then, after the last chime strikes, the Emporium is plunged into darkness.

8

CHRISTMAS PAST – 1987

EVANGELINE

FOR YEARS AFTERWARDS THE SMELL OF SMOKE, STALE BEER AND sweat would remind Evangeline of her wedding. The bride was dressed in a burgundy gown with full satin skirt which was very much the worse for wear after an evening's abuse at the college's official Oxmas Bop. There was a wine stain on the left side of the bodice, a smear of cream on the waistband and a cigarette end clung to the hemline of her tulle underskirt. Instead of a veil she wore a net curtain laced with dust, purloined from someone's flat-share and fixed into place with a jewelled banana clip. In place of a bouquet, she carried a beer glass filled with mulled wine.

The groom had been dressed in black tie at some point but was now stripped to the waist and someone had prematurely scrawled JUST MARRIED on his chest in permanent marker. He could barely stand, but his best man was doing a sterling job of holding him upright. The assembled crowd parted to form a makeshift aisle leading up to the bar and sang 'Here Comes the Bride' with the style and tunefulness of the Muppets. All eyes were on Evangeline and her new college husband, and she loved every moment of it. She beamed, wondering what her mother would think if she could see her now. She couldn't decide if this marriage was the culmination of her mother's wishes for her, or a mockery of everything she held dear.

When Evangeline thought of her mother, the divine Lydia Fall, she pictured her at her dressing table, carefully putting on her face, and passing on her wisdom about the inner workings of love and men.

'Red lips to catch them, pink lips to keep them,' she would say, touching up her own in the triple mirror. 'Draw them in like a siren, then show them what a natural, home-making beauty you are.'

Then she would turn to her perfume, caressing her collection of scents with one manicured finger as she selected the right one: 'Once you know which scent pleases him, keep it the same. Wear it the first time you kiss, the first time you . . . go further. Train him to respond to it.' That was how Evangeline learned about Pavlov's dog and how the principle applied to bewitching a man.

Lydia was not unaware of feminism, or 'women's lib' as she called it, but she found the concept baffling. Why would you want to work and wear trousers and drink in pubs when it was so much easier, so much more fun, to be beautiful and to be kept? She had had four husbands, and in between marriages, she was never without an escort for more than a month. As a result Evangeline had grown up in boarding schools, moved house often and was accustomed to remaining in the background when at home as Lydia's relationships came first. She passed many a long summer in her room, losing herself in the historical romances Lydia had stockpiled, where the heroines were witty and spirited and love solved everything in the end.

Evangeline wouldn't have been able to go to university at all if it hadn't been for husband number four. Lydia held that it was a waste of money sending girls into higher education but her new husband had a holiday home on Mustique and planned to spend every winter there. The last thing he wanted was to hang around in London while Lydia desperately tried to marry off her daughter, so he was the one who convinced her that Oxford would be the perfect place to catch a man. In the autumn of 1987 Evangeline set off, her vanity case full of lipstick, scent and battered paperbacks, her head full of Lydia's maxims.

Her digs were small and poky – two single beds and two small desks in a wood-chipped wallpaper room with a sad little basin in the corner. Her room-mate was a weak and watery type of girl, a nobody with no family who never socialised. Her name was Peggy – a curious name for a girl these days, but it fitted her, odd little thing that she was.

After boarding school, Evangeline was used to sleeping less than six feet away from virtual strangers, but with Peggy there were awkward conversations. Window open or closed? Could we leave just one light on? The undercurrent beneath all this was, can we live together? Can we be friends? Evangeline felt a twinge of panic at the idea of spending three years shackled to wishy-washy Peggy, dragged down the social pecking order by association. She kept her answers brisk and impersonal.

When they finally settled in on their first night together, Peggy in her plaits and Evangeline's face liberally coated in night cream, they lay there in the dark, before Peggy spoke.

'I'm reinventing myself,' she said. 'University's a good place to make a new start, right?'

At those words, Evangeline's imagination flared, filling with images of her paperback heroines. She pictured herself as Angélique, the courageous beauty of Louis XIV's court, irresistible to all who laid eyes on her; or bold, green-eyed Marianne, skilled at swordplay and at catching the attention of Napoleon. She would not be a dutiful, domestic wife; she would be a siren, an adventurer. She would follow the path of love.

And love came in the form of Peter Winchall.

Peter and his best friend Kit Verity were an inseparable pair, although most people paid more attention to Kit. Not because he was good looking – the man was barely nineteen years old but already looked forty. His hair receded, his face already creased with laughter lines when he smiled. And he smiled a lot, which was what drew people to him.

'Premature ageing is a family curse,' he told her. 'But it's also a reminder that life's too short to be boring.'

If you were throwing a fancy dress party, Kit would be the one who turned up dressed as a caveman in a genuine bearskin, most likely with a willing cave-girl slung over his shoulder. He knew the location of every drinking den, every off-beat underground club, every adventure to be had. But it wasn't Kit who attracted her, it was Peter – who reminded her of stepfather number two. He was sweet, self-effacing, an untidy boy with hair which constantly stuck up at all angles and left-leaning politics. You would never know that he was a bona fide honourable, the eldest son of a baron and heir to an enormous country pile somewhere in Dorset.

Unfortunately, he was also completely devoted to a deathly dull-sounding girl who was reading English lit at Edinburgh.

'It doesn't matter, what she doesn't know won't hurt her,' she told her drippy room-mate airily, as she sat at her makeshift dressing table (which was meant to be a desk) applying a deep red shine to her lips. She surveyed her rows of make-up, the carefully chosen scents, her own luscious body. She was Angélique, she was Marianne, she was irresistible.

Peggy was sitting on her own bed, chemistry textbook open across her knees, staring at her. She did that a lot, like Evangeline was a science experiment to be studied.

Despite her bold words, Evangeline wasn't as confident as she sounded. Not until that night in early November. It was cold, the first of the Christmas events were being advertised, and they had been drinking since lunchtime. That irritating punky girl Fran Silver was there, being all boyish and loud, drinking pints, and trying to get everyone to dance. She was fresh, a novelty and Evangeline didn't like the way Peter and Kit looked at her. So as closing time drew near, she suggested the three of them go back to hers to keep drinking.

They were four in the end – Peter, Kit, and some other girl whose name she couldn't remember. Evangeline rushed around the room throwing scarves over the bedside lamps and kicking stray bras under the bed, hissing at Peggy to stay quiet and just read under the covers with a torch if she had to. Kit produced a bottle of tequila from somewhere and rummaged around looking for mugs while Peter stretched his glorious self out on her single bed. Drink had loosened him a little, and he was gazing at her, fixing her with a look that gave her vertigo. Hope flowered in her chest.

She smiled at him, then remembered Lydia's words – *Don't be too keen, you'll scare him off* – and looked away.

'Let's play spin the bottle,' the other girl said.

Kit laughed. 'I'm sorry, are we at a slumber party with Rizzo and Frenchy?'

The girl looked suitably stung, but Kit softened the blow by saying he was up for some kind of game, just not a silly teenage-girl one. Various card games were mooted but they were all too drunk to pay attention to the rules.

'What about truth or dare?' a voice said. To Evangeline's surprise, it was Peggy, who was perched on the end of her bed gazing at Kit, seeming not to care that she was wearing a floor-length Flannelette nightie.

'Yeah, I'm game.' Kit smiled wolfishly at her.

Evangeline felt a twinge of irritation, that Peggy could grab Kit's attention so quickly with no make-up, her hair in plaits and dressed as a granny. But it now seemed Peggy was part of the game, for better or for worse.

Peter and Kit had zero imagination when it came to asking questions of girls. *Are you a virgin? . . . What's your 'magic number'? . . . Have you ever, like, done it in public?* But at least they kept the subject firmly in the zone of intimacy, which suited her agenda.

In between rounds, Peggy manoeuvred to sit closer to Kit, gazing intently at him, studying his features. Evangeline groaned inwardly at her room-mate being so embarrassingly obvious. But then Peggy began asking the oddest questions.

'Does your family still own the Emporium on Quockerwodger Court?'

Kit looked irritated. 'Not *my* half of the family.'

Peggy had always struck Evangeline as the tactful type but she clearly had no understanding of how much the British aristocracy disliked talking about trade. The fact that he had to admit his family owned something as vulgar as a shop was clearly making Kit uncomfortable. But Peggy did not back off. 'But your uncle owns it, right?'

'My cousin now. It's not a shop anymore, just a valuable piece of property in the City, which he won't sell. That whole half of the family is weird.'

'I suppose the Emporium is a pretty eccentric place.'

Kit gave a bark of laughter. 'Eccentric is an understatement. My uncle was away with the fairies and since he died my cousin is turning his whole life into one extended gap year. Last thing I heard he was living with some tribe. No wonder the store closed.'

'But *why* did it close?'

Kit took another slug of tequila from his mug. His expression was guarded now, even though he tried to make his words sound casual. 'Oh God, I don't know, some kind of family thing.'

'That's not it, though, is it?' Peter said, suddenly leaning forward, his voice assertive. Evangeline hadn't seen him like this before, usually he wouldn't say boo to a goose. It must be the tequila.

Or maybe it was because Kit had been flirting with her earlier. She hoped it was that.

'Fuck off, Winchall,' Kit said.

The tension in the room rose, winding tightly between the two boys. Something had happened, something to do with this store, that Kit didn't want to share. And for some reason it had offended Peter's sensibilities. He wasn't backing down.

'OK,' he said. 'Truth or dare, Verity. What's the biggest thing your family ever stole?'

Peter's eyes locked onto his friend's, as Kit's expression went flat, his jaw clenched with fury. The annoying girl protested that that's not how you played the game, that Kit had to pick truth or dare first, but everyone ignored her.

'Mate, you've gone too far. Don't bring your politics into this.'

'Did I mention politics?' Peter asked. 'Go on, truth? Or dare?' His gaze flickered over to Evangeline, like they were doing this together and she felt a spark of connection.

'What's the dare?'

'Run naked across the quad.' Peggy cut in with that a little too quickly, and then her eagerness dissolved into blushes. Maybe Evangeline's first assessment had been right; she was developing a crush on Kit and her weird questions were just a way of getting his attention.

'Dare, then,' Kit conceded, peeling off his Superman costume.

Later, as Peggy and the other girl watched Kit whooping and screeching his way across the quad, Evangeline and Peter sat back on her bed together. They were close, the warmth of his arm brushing hers. The contact felt prolonged, deliberate. Electricity coursed through her, her heart pounded.

'What did Kit's family steal that was so bad?'

'A person,' he said. 'It was a long time ago, but his family is still hushing it up now.' He leaned over then and told her a secret, something Kit had told him in confidence, while drunk. Something that nobody else was meant to know. Evangeline's eyes widened in shock but she had heard worse things about these wealthy, powerful families. It didn't matter what it was, not really – only that they had a secret now, that she was more important to Peter than his best friend. His hand stroked her cheek, before moving to cradle the back of her neck. His lips were warm and soft moving against hers. It felt like she was falling. She was Angélique, she was Marianne, she was desired.

Two weeks later, they walked down the bar aisle together. Peggy was there, hovering at the sidelines, and Kit was officiating. He had somehow got hold of a genuine gold-trimmed bishop's mitre and swore that he was an ordained vicar and that the marriage was therefore legally binding.

'Wilt thou, Evangeline, take this tosspot, Peter, to be your awful wedded husband?'

'I do.'

'Are you sure? You could do a lot better, you know.' Kit winked and Evangeline found herself grinning back at him, basking in his attention.

'Ahem,' Peter coughed. Evangeline turned her smile on him, snuggling into his chest as Kit pronounced them Oxford man and wife. It wasn't a real marriage, just a silly, fun college tradition linking them together. Next year, as second years, they'd get to adopt a couple of freshers as 'kids' and show them around. But what Evangeline wanted was the photo. The picture of her, pressed against him, her hand nestled possessively in his sparse chest hair, the pink imprint of her lips on his cheek.

She sent one copy to her mother by airmail to Mustique with the words: *This is as close to marriage as I'm ever going to get, and by the way he's an honourable.* She sent another to Peter's girlfriend in Edinburgh, anonymously, in a plain envelope.

'I've told her,' Peter said in the New Year, as if he'd had any say in the matter. 'We can be together now. We're free.'

'Congratulations, old thing,' Kit had said airily and kissed her on the cheek. As he had done so, she felt that spark of attraction again, a pull towards this charismatic, wrinkled figure. Evangeline felt a stab of panic that she had picked the wrong man.

'There's something about Kit, isn't there?' she told Peggy later on. 'He's not *attractive*, not really, but I like the way he makes people laugh, I love the crazy things he does. And Peter can be so worthy, always going on about atoning for our ancestors' sins, blah, blah, blah. He even wants to remove the Rhodes statue at Oriel because colonialism was a bad thing. How absurd is that? No, Kit is far better suited to me.'

She leaned forward, close to the mirror, eyebrow tweezers in hand. But as she did, she caught a glimpse of Peggy's reflection – sitting at her own desk, a shocked expression on her face.

'Oh, please don't be prudish about it,' Evangeline said. 'Peter and I aren't *really* married, you know. These college relationships come and go, that's what uni is for. He won't be remotely upset.'

'But you really think Kit could like you back?'

There was a tremor in Peggy's voice. Of course, Evangeline remembered, she had some kind of a thing for Kit, didn't she?

But surely she didn't expect to get anywhere with that – he was too flamboyant, too aristocratic to be interested in a middle-class mouse.

Evangeline looked back into the mirror and smiled, the kind of smile she had seen on her mother's face many times, although she would never admit it.

'We'll see,' she said, airily. 'I like a challenge.'

9

FRAN

FRAN WAKES TO PITCH BLACK. SHE IS COLD, TOO, DESPITE THE fleecy blankets on the brightly painted sleigh. The lights in Santa's grotto have gone out, the model planes no longer buzz overhead, the music boxes have stilled. And Peg, over in her shadowy corner, is no longer playing her endless *luly lullay*. Fran's head feels thick, her mouth dry – she's been here many times before.

Fran has been sober for nearly five years now but before then, before Dr Raynsford took charge of her, she hadn't even been aware she had a problem. London life, especially in the entertainment industry, made it easy to slide into drinking. TV producers, PRs and the like would be eager to get you relaxed and happy, pouring Champagne, lining up shots and, later in the evening, lining up lines. Eventually, it became a badge of pride. When one of the tabloid gossip pages featured her in its Caner of the Week slot she'd been strangely proud. But by the time she wound up in Raynsford's office, a messy trail of catastrophically bad decisions behind her, she was shaking, weak and ashamed. And he hadn't pulled his punches.

'The deal is, you take care of yourself from now on,' he'd said. 'It's the least you can do.'

Drying out had seemed impossible then, but swamped with remorse as she was, she felt she didn't have a right to argue. Raynsford was getting her out of this whole cancer mess, it was up to her to make it count.

And so, she had stopped drinking. Those six words completely gloss over how painful, how difficult that journey had been. How many times she found herself at the corner shop with her hand closing around the neck of a bottle of red. How often she thought one drink wouldn't hurt, before finding out, yet again, that it really did. What had kept her going, kept her trying, was the knowledge that drinking, or at least that fun beginning part, made her feel happy, and she didn't deserve that.

So it has been a long time since she had woken up like this, in a strange place, trying to piece together the memory of what she had done.

This time, the memories are even more surreal than usual. She groans, as snatches of the previous few hours return to her: sledging down a fake snowy slope, putting on a puppet show, dancing a can-can with a supermarket cashier called Josie. She's quite glad nobody has their phones; at least it hasn't all been recorded for posterity.

How had it gone that far? The festive cheer of the Emporium would have given her a natural high, but not *that* much of a high. There is a tang of spices on her tongue, and she vaguely recalls drinking a glass of mulled wine at some point; could her tolerance to alcohol be so low now? *Drunk on one glass of mulled wine? Fran Silver, you're such a lightweight.*

God, she hates that word.

A rustle of paper in her hand reminds her of the note, the one she found just before she passed out.

I know what you did.

A stupid, drunken mistake that had got out of hand. She had accepted the guilt and shame long ago, along with the fact that she would be paying the price for the rest of her life. But she had taken a small comfort in the fact that it was still a secret. If someone else knows – if they told the world – there would be no coming back from that.

Who had slipped her the note? Lord knows she was so far out of it, it could have happened at any time. When she was sledging, during the doll's tea party, mid can-can – her bag had been lying right there on the toy department floor the whole time.

Whoever had done it, they're probably long gone. The store is clearly closed now and Fran is alone.

She groans, embarrassed. Trapped inside a department store on Christmas morning. Zelda's never going to let her live this one down.

'Hello?' A man's voice in the darkness, thick with sleep. Fran feels a rush of relief she's not by herself after all. For a couple of moments she struggles to attach a name to the voice.

'Benny, is that you?'

'Benjamin,' the voice comes back, correcting her. He sounds as embarrassed as she feels.

'Is Josie over there with you?'

'Josie? Oh, yes I remember. I don't know, I can't see a thing.'

'I'm here,' Josie's voice comes. 'What the hell was I drinking? I did have a mulled wine with that Christmas pud but bloody hell . . . I need a cigarette.'

'I don't think you can smoke in here,' Benjamin says.

Josie grumbles, and a few moments later Fran sees a dot of blue light, evidently Josie sucking on a vape.

Benjamin begins to protest again, and Josie scoffs.

Fran rummages for her phone torch for a moment before remembering the no-phones thing again. Then an idea occurs to her and she presses the button on her jumper. Rudolph illuminates.

Suddenly, the situation seems less sinister and more absurd. The three of them burst out laughing.

By the light of Rudolph and a couple of the Emporium's Magical Glowing Fairy Jars, they search for light switches, but none of them seem to work. It seems sensible for them to go downstairs to seek out any remaining staff, so Fran gathers up the giant doll in her arms and they set off, working their way down the oak-panelled stairs to the ground floor.

'There really should be illuminated fire exit signs,' Benjamin complains.

'They really should check their bloody shop floor before locking up,' Josie adds. 'I mean, I can't say we ever let this happen in Lidl.'

It's definitely weird, Fran thinks. OK, so she fell asleep under the blankets in the sleigh and it's entirely possible the others also crawled into little hidey holes where they could be missed by staff, eager to get home for the Christmas break. But if she were Monty, she wouldn't be impressed.

It's a little easier to see when they arrive in the Hall of Wonders. The lamplight from Quockerwodger Court seeps through the front windows and some of the fairy lights down here are battery powered.

And they are not the only ones trapped. Dean Hallibutt is hammering at the heavy oak door. Next to him stand Evangeline Fall and her assistant Barbara.

Fran feels a strange pang of relief that Dean is in here with them. Drunk numpties like Fran get into silly situations like this all the time, but Dean is a man of influence, someone who gets things done. He'll find a way out of this.

His appearance has unravelled since the beginning of the night, though. His suit jacket is gone, his tie is loosened and, for reasons Fran can't fathom, he is barefoot. Still, he is keeping it together, which is more than she can say for Evangeline and Barbara.

Barbara is methodically jiggling at the lock, shoving the door a bit then jiggling, then shoving again, her face stressed and tearful.

Leaning on the door frame next to them both, Evangeline holds a bottle of Champagne and is not helping at all.

'It's no good, Dean,' she says. 'The door isn't moving, and it's deserted outside – everyone's gone home for Christmas.'

'I'll smash the windows, then.'

A high-pitched yelp of horror fills the air – it takes a moment for Fran to realise the sound is coming from Benjamin.

'Please don't, just don't.' Benjamin's hands are joined together, pleading. 'This is a grade two listed building with original leaded lights dating back to the nineteenth century.'

'It's an emergency,' Dean says, grabbing a large glass paper-weight from a display and tossing it from hand to hand, testing its weight. 'We can't spend Christmas locked up in here! I'd pay for the damage and Verity would understand . . .'

He stops mid-flow, his brow wrinkling with thought. He places the paperweight down. 'This is weird,' he says.

'So you guys fell asleep too?' Fran asks.

'Yes, and so did Barbara,' Evangeline complains. 'Despite the fact that she was meant to be working.' Evangeline mimes drinking and Fran's cheeks go hot.

'That mulled wine must have been strong,' she says, feeling the need to come to Barbara's defence. 'It happened to all of us.'

'Oh, fuck,' Dean says, shoulders sagging. Benjamin makes a disapproving noise.

Evangeline links into Dean's arm, stroking it consolingly. 'Come on, there's no need to panic,' she says. 'I'm sure Monty or one of his staff will realise what's happened and come back soon with the key. In the meantime we might as well enjoy ourselves. We're locked in here with some of the finest foods and wines in the world, and I'm sure Monty wouldn't begrudge us helping ourselves to some of them.'

She waggles the Champagne bottle at Dean and an expression of deep discomfort crosses his face. Fran's not surprised. Hadn't those two been arguing earlier? She remembers seeing him shove Evangeline and shivers at the sight of her now shimmying closer to him.

'But what about my flight?' Barbara has stopped jiggling the lock now. Her voice is quiet and laden down with stress as she checks her watch. 'I have to be at Heathrow soon!'

'I'm sure there's a landline around here, tucked away in an office somewhere.' Evangeline waves her hand dismissively. 'Why don't you go and look for it?'

'I'll help,' Dean volunteers, but Evangeline holds onto his elbow.

'No, you stay here,' she says. 'Let's make a cosy nest and get comfortable.'

Evangeline walks past the Great Clock and the miniature Emporium beneath, the shadowy carved figures still standing guard outside it, and over to a nearby fireplace, which has been set up to resemble a Victorian Christmas hearth with two comfy chairs, blankets, an array of traditional toys, and stockings hanging from the mantel. There's also a small table bearing a tray with seven Champagne flutes. A strange number, that. Evangeline cracks the Champagne and pours out two glasses, then looks up to count the new arrivals.

'Goodness me, all of the VIPs! Monty evidently kept the strong stuff for us.'

Evangeline hasn't noticed the absence of Merry, but then noticing other women has never been her strong point.

Dean necks his Champagne and stares distractedly into the glass, as if hoping for more to appear.

Josie, who has settled into one of the chairs, snorts with laughter and grabs the neck of the Champagne bottle, helping herself since Evangeline has only poured one for herself and Dean.

'Well, I'm with you. We might as well enjoy Monty's hospitality while we can.' She pours one messily for Benjamin, who uses his white cotton handkerchief to clean off the silver tray beneath it. Fran notices spots of blood on it from where he cut his finger.

'I shall settle the bill with Mr Verity in the morning,' he says pointedly, handing Fran a glass and holding his own up in a toast. 'Merry Christmas!'

They all clink their glasses, an odd little Christmas morning gathering. Fran pretends to sip and licks the residue of the bubbles from her lips. It tastes like happy memories. She puts the glass down quickly.

'Well,' says Evangeline, claiming one of the chairs for herself. 'This is all rather pleasant, isn't it? I mean, it could be a lot worse.'

'Speak for yourself,' Josie huffs. 'I'm supposed to be in sodding Claridge's right now wearing a big fluffy robe, watching *Elf* and ordering a fuck-ton of room service.'

Benjamin winces, but has clearly given up on ticking people off for swearing. He sits in the opposite chair to Evangeline, sinking his head into his hands. 'I should be . . . well, I had no specific plans for the night,' he says. 'But I was rather hoping to take some detailed photographs of the Goodchild automaton and I wasn't even allowed to do that.'

'I should be celebrating the deal of a lifetime.' Dean's voice is mournful.

'You've got me.' Evangeline smiles. 'We can celebrate now.'

94

Dean gives her a mystified look. 'I told you I . . . wait, don't you remember?'

Evangeline looks away, biting her lip coyly. A curtain of black hair falls across her brow. 'I just thought you might have given it some thought – now we're stuck here together we've got a chance to talk.'

'You really are a piece of work,' Dean says. His tone is half admiring, half scared.

Fran stays silent, unwilling to reveal that there is nobody human waiting at home for her. With her mother gone, her last connections to her old neighbourhood withered away, and Zelda is her last remaining friend from her showbiz life. She says it's for the best, that friends would only drag her back to her old, partying ways but in truth she doesn't feel she deserves friends.

'Right.' Dean claps his hands together. 'Enough moping about. Time for action. I have no idea what game Verity's playing but this is obviously some kind of tactic aimed at me. I'm very sorry you have all been caught up in it but if we work together, I'm sure we'll find a way out. Let's recap the situation. Doors are locked. The light switches don't work and nobody has their phone. Evangeline's assistant is already off looking for either our confiscated phones or a landline. We should do the same.'

Fran has seen it before on-set, the way that some people automatically look for a leader to take charge of a situation, and others automatically assume it's going to be them. Still, it's good to see Dean back on decisive form.

'We'll split up,' he says. 'And bonus points if anybody can get the electricity working again. Josie, isn't it? You're with me.'

Evangeline makes a sound of protest, and Josie pokes out her tongue at her as she heads off in Dean's wake.

After fifteen minutes of searching, Fran is mystified. There are no side doors marked STAFF ONLY, no delivery area, not even a lavatory. It's weird, it's not realistic. It's as if they're trapped in the doll's house Emporium which lives under the clock rather than a real, functional building.

Neither member of her team is proving very useful. Benjamin keeps getting distracted by random automata, some of which are still moving and ticking in the darkness. And Evangeline seems to think this is a good moment for a catch-up.

'Really, I'm so proud of what you've done. Who could imagine it? Bovver-boots Fran from college becoming a TV star! I guess you had to unleash your ruthless side to get there, eh?'

Fran freezes in the act of rummaging around under a cash desk. 'What do you mean by that?'

'Oh, nothing,' Evangeline says airily. 'It's a cut-throat business, though, isn't it? I bet everyone on screen has lied and cheated and trampled their way to the top.'

Fran feels a flare of anger. She's heard this time and again, the idea that people 'like her' – in other words, a Black, working-class, first-generation Brit – only make it by cheating somehow. She's about to spit out a retort but there's something else in Evangeline's tone, a note of cunning. The realisation takes Fran's breath away.

Evangeline put that note into her bag.

She knows.

'Oh, there you are, Barbara.' Evangeline turns away from Fran and swans off to where her assistant is waiting.

Fran leans back against the panelled wall, trying not to hyperventilate, her mind whirring through questions. How did she find out? Why is she toying with her? What does she want? Her downwards spiral is halted by the sound of a sob. Barbara is crying.

'I'm going to miss my flight,' she cries. 'I knew I shouldn't have come here, I knew it. I haven't seen him in years, it took me months to save up the fare . . .'

Evangeline is doing a worse than terrible job of sympathising, so Fran steps in, putting an arm around Barbara, giving her a tissue.

'We'll get you out of here,' Benjamin says, with the air of a bold knight protecting fair ladies.

'Yes, we will,' Dean says. 'Keep calm, love, all we have to do is focus. The darkness is confusing us, we need light. Once we can see, we can get out.'

'The perfumery,' Barbara says.

'I think Dean smells sweet enough already,' Evangeline says.

'N-no.' Barbara is looking downward, twisting her sleeve nervously in her hand. 'I mean, in the perfumery there's lots of scented candles? That might give us some more light?'

'Candles!' Dean says loudly.

'Oh, great idea, Dean,' Evangeline coos.

The perfumery is laid out like an apothecary's shop with wooden shelves full of glass bottles, and cabinets with delicious-smelling drawers. There are no big brand or celebrity fragrances here, only round bottles with crystal stoppers, bearing names like Morning in the Library or After the Storm. In the darkness, though, it looks more like Frankenstein's lab. The eerie fairy-jar glow glints off the distended glass of countless bottles, illuminating the different-coloured liquids within. Dean leads the way to the candle display, distributing wicker shopping baskets.

'I've got a plan,' he says, and Fran feels a wave of relief that someone is doing something.

Barbara hangs back, lifting a perfume bottle labelled Sunday Suburbia and sniffing at the stopper. Fran sniffs, too, and it smells of cut grass and – irrationally – sunshine.

'I don't know how he makes perfumes this lovely,' Barbara says to Fran quietly.

'You don't have to take crap from Evangeline, you know,' she says.

Barbara smiles. 'It's kind of you to say, but I don't mind really. I'm a mother, I'm used to tantrums and unreasonable demands – although at least my son grew out of them!'

Fran smiles, glad that Barbara has teeth after all, and the fact she isn't loyal to Evangeline is good news. It means she can ask.

'Did Evangeline know who else would be coming tonight?'

Barbara looks at her quizzically and shrugs. 'Yes, she asked me to source a guest list – she likes to know if she's going to be meeting possible clients or attractive men – so I asked the Emporium and they forwarded it all to me.'

Fran shivers. Evangeline knew she was going to be here, but she'd faked surprise on seeing her.

'Did she mention me at all?' Fran keeps her voice casual.

'Not outright, but she did say something about meeting an old frenemy who had something to hide.'

Wow. A frenemy? Back at uni she and Evangeline hadn't even qualified for the 'fr' half of the word, let alone the latter part. Had she done something to hurt Evangeline in the past? Was that why she was tormenting her now? Fran tries to think, but comes up blank.

She's about to ask Barbara for more details, when a tremendous crash fills the room. Fran whirls around to see Merry, lurching from table to table, grabbing at a display of ball-shaped perfume bottles to keep her balance. They tumble and roll across the floor, smashing and releasing a bouquet of heady, clashing smells that hit Fran's nostrils in a wave. Barbara groans and coughs. Benjamin rushes forward, trying to help Merry to her feet, but her legs are buckling, she's sinking to the ground.

'I've gotta get out of here . . .' Merry slurs. 'I've been drugged.'

With those words, she loses consciousness.

10

MERRY

ROSS IS SMILING AT HER ON THE DANCE FLOOR OF SOME CLUB, back in the early days of their friendship, when they were trying out new things, when they told each other everything, thinking that they could eventually fix each other. He's sweating, his pupils dilated from whatever it was he took earlier, and on his face is an expression of pure bliss, of connectedness with the music. Merry took the same thing at the same time and feels nothing but a vague sense of unease.

'You need to learn to let go,' he yells in her ear. Her nerve endings tingle at the heat of his breath, so she has to struggle to focus on what he's actually saying. 'You can't go tripping if you're trying to stay in control, you'll just end up having a bad time. It's about losing your senses, embracing the chaos.'

Merry laughs, trying to sound free and happy but really her feet are hurting and she wants to go home and lie in bed while this stuff wears off.

'I don't think drugs are my thing,' she says.

'What?'

'I SAID, I DON'T THINK DRUGS ARE MY THING!'

'I think you're probably right. They're not my thing either, at least not anymore,' another voice cuts in, clear and pure without the sound of the club in the background. Immediately the dance floor recedes, Ross disappears, and Merry jerks awake.

The air smells strange; a heady mix of jasmine, lavender, cinnamon and sandalwood. She is lying on her side, looking straight at an elf, his head nodding gently, his rosy-cheeked grin flickering with candlelit shadows. *Still in the dream*, Merry thinks and then realises.

The Emporium, she's still in the Emporium. Merry jerks, knocking the elf flying, breaking into pieces. Clockwork cogs roll away from her. She's lying on the floor and someone has tucked a festive blanket around her and placed a plush puppy under her head as a cushion.

'Take it slow, don't get up too quickly.' It's the friendly, saccharine voice of telly favourite Fran Silver.

Oh God, she's been lying here, probably dribbling and definitely talking in her sleep, in front of Fran bloody Silver.

Merry gets up, very quickly, giving her an instant head rush. Her legs wobble under her as if they're made of rubber. She sinks back onto the floor. Fran gives her a gentle I-told-you-so look.

'Take your time,' she says. 'You've got plenty of it. I'm afraid we're all trapped in here. The staff have locked the doors and gone home for Christmas, and of course none of us have our phones. Just stay down there for a few minutes, until you feel better.'

Merry tries to get up once more but her legs are weak. As she sinks back into her chair, her jumper starts spontaneously flashing again. The woman sitting next to her grins, and then her own jumper starts flashing.

'Twinsies!' Fran smiles.

Ugh.

Merry blanks Fran and puts all her effort into dragging herself upright. She manages to totter towards the nearby fireplace, before sinking down onto a cushioned easy chair. The inside of her mouth is furry and dry. She needs water, she needs to get her bearings and then she needs to figure out what the hell is going on.

She seems to be trapped with all the VIPs from earlier on, and they are now engaged in a pointless-looking task. Benjamin the automaton guy is carefully and methodically removing items from the store window, stacking them up on the floor beside him.

'Hurry up, posh boy,' says Josie who is holding a lit scented candle in each hand. Behind her, that Evangeline woman is unpacking and lighting high-end candles by the dozen. Now her charge is awake, Fran has joined in too. Business guru Dean Hallibutt is overseeing the operation.

'OK, people, off we go, pick up the pace! Benjamin, you really don't need to be so careful.'

'These things were all hand-made, and they're not ours to damage.'

'What are they doing?' Merry murmurs to herself.

'It's the plan,' says a weary voice next to her. By the candle-light she can see Evangeline's assistant Barbara standing close by. 'We tried bashing the door and yelling, but central London is a ghost town at Christmas, especially in a back alley like this.

We can't find where our phones are hidden, can't even find the office, and Benjamin won't let us break the windows. So the idea, apparently, is to write a big sign saying HELP and put it in the window surrounded by candles to make it more eye-catching if anyone passes by.'

'Wow.' Merry is stunned. 'That is a really useless plan.'

The woman sighs and sinks into the chair opposite. 'I know. None of them seem particularly bothered about getting out of here – they all seem to think they're going to get rescued any minute – but I've got a bad feeling about this.'

'Me too,' Merry concedes. She's glad the woman said it first, but speaking it aloud creates a knot of fear in her stomach. She's been roofied – or at least drugged in some way – by cuddly Mr Christmas Monty Verity and then just left in the store while he and his staff went home, and her fellow inmates seem think the answer is some kind of cultish ritual.

'I'm Barbara,' the woman says, possibly assuming Merry has forgotten. She holds out a half-bottle of Evian. 'You must be thirsty. We all were when we woke up.'

Merry wipes the neck of the bottle with her sleeve, setting off the flashing lights again as she does so, then drinks gratefully, taking Barbara's words in.

'You mean, you were *all* unconscious?'

Barbara fills her in on what has happened. The general belief among the others seems to be that they all had too much mulled wine, dropped off and that the staff simply forgot them. How can they all be so naive? But then look at them. A businessman who is probably used to having everything organised by an assistant, an antiques dealer who lives in a weird posh bubble where people care about clockwork elves, a perky upbeat TV star . . . Nothing bad has ever happened to them, and she's sure they have loving families who will raise the alarm as soon as they realise they're missing. Merry's parents are on a mini-break in Prague, she'd be lucky to get a text, and for all she knows Ross will just think she's got a hangover and go back home when she doesn't answer her doorbell.

'. . . so my flight leaves in a few hours – my suitcase is over there by the door – but if I don't get out of here soon, I'm going to miss it,' Barbara concludes. 'I've got to do *something*. Something that doesn't involve candles.'

'Where are all the landlines?' Merry asks.

'There's a phone jack next to the tannoy over there, but there's no phone to hook up to it.' Barbara says. 'It looks like it's been ripped out.'

Merry feels another tug of unease in her belly. Shops need landlines, even ultra-modern shops, and the Emporium is far from that. Something is going on, something weird and horrible and not even slightly festive.

'Has anyone looked elsewhere – the other floors, or the work-shop maybe?'

'What workshop?'

They go quietly, leaving the others bickering on how best to complete Operation Candle in the Window. Merry would have preferred to go by herself, but Barbara's desperation to get out of here is even more acute than hers.

'I'm not even meant to be here,' Barbara says as the two of them make their way up the stairs by the light of their scented candles. 'The invitation said no plus ones, but Evangeline wanted me to help so she insisted. She stood outside the shop loudly demanding to speak with the owner. It was so . . .' She shudders with embarrassment and Merry feels a flare of kinship for the quiet woman. That sort of situation would mortify her.

'I'm not really supposed to be here, either,' she says. 'I just really wanted to buy a present for my friend.'

Barbara's head tilts sympathetically to one side. 'You poor thing,' she says. 'This is so unfair.'

Merry finds the right gas lamp and twists it, and with a quiet click, the hidden door pops open. The impressed reaction from Barbara is highly satisfying. But inside, the workshop is dark, the fire in the grate is dead and Rudi's bench is empty, cleared and wiped, the brushes cleaned and placed back in their glass jam jar.

There is not a landline in sight. Merry searches all the work-benches, plus the large, high bench at the front that she assumes belongs to Monty. She finds a screw sticking out of a wall, next to a phone jack that at least looks like it was fitted in the twenty-first century. So it's not that they never had phones here, they just don't now. The sickening feeling in Merry's stomach grows: someone has taken the phones. They have been lured to the Emporium, drugged, trapped here on purpose and prevented from calling for help. Why would anyone do something like that?

'What's wrong?' Barbara asks. 'You look scared.'

Merry plasters on a confident smile; she doesn't want a panicking Barbara on her hands. 'Nothing, just wondering how to get out of here.'

She casts about for a way to change the subject, to keep Barbara calm, and lands on the portrait over the log burner.

'I know it's silly,' she says, 'but in films portraits like this often have a safe behind them, and our phones could be in there.'

The painting is a full-length image of an elderly man in Victorian garb, not dissimilar in cut to Monty's favoured costume but sensible and brown. He is old, with whiskers and a cloud of white hair jutting out from under his hat brim. Unusually for a Victorian portrait, he is standing in a marketplace framed by palm trees. A woman with brown skin and a striped head wrap holds out a basket of bananas for sale and a child in a grubby apron hovers in the background, her hands behind her back, unruly dark curls flopping over her eyes. At the bottom of the gold frame is a plaque: EVERARD VERITY, FOUNDER OF VERITY'S EMPORIUM.

Monty had talked about him, she remembers. He'd been an inspiration to him as he too had travelled the world finding wonders and learning different crafts. He had also been the one who built Clockwork Peg.

Merry runs her fingers along the edge of the gilt frame, but it seems firmly screwed to the wall. Feeling foolish, she presses at the plaque and the different knots and bumps in the gilding but nothing happens.

Barbara suppresses a laugh, and Merry blushes hot, sweating in her acrylic jumper. She has always feared the mockery of others. The older woman's face softens.

'It was worth a try,' she says. 'What about looking through that door in the corner?'

The door is unlocked, and opens onto a tightly wound spiral staircase which eventually leads to a narrow roof terrace.

There's a flurry of wings as frightened pigeons flee their roost. A nest of discarded cigarette ends in one corner shows that the Emporium Elves have a strong nicotine habit. At the opposite end stands the twisted, rusty remains of something which might once have been a fire escape but now leads nowhere. Merry looks up, and sees rooftops stretching out in the darkness. Flat glass office façades nestle side by side with old-fashioned crooked chimney pots.

It's quiet. There's no traffic noise from the street, not even the sound of a passing aircraft. In the distance a car alarm shrills, but by London standards, it's a silent night. The stars are blotted out by a heavy, dark bank of clouds.

'There'll be snow tonight,' Barbara says.

'Nah, snow never settles in London. And Sadie from my office says it's too cold.'

'We'll see.'

They try calling for help, yelling, screaming and screeching into the night, but it's as if the clouds swallow their words. Merry is overcome by a sensation that they are all alone, the last humans in central London, while the rest of the world curls up by the fire with a warming drink or lies in bed listening for Santa Claus.

She peers over the rusted metal railings and looks down into a cramped loading area at the back of the store, then pulls back, shivering.

'Scared of heights?' Barbara asks.

Merry nods. There it is — that weird, prickly feeling in her feet that she gets whenever she looks down from somewhere high. She realises her fingers are gripping the frozen railings so hard it hurts.

'I had no fear when I was a kid,' Barbara says. 'I used to climb to the top of all the trees, higher than the boys. My boy was the same, but I couldn't watch when he did it. I'm not scared of falling myself, but the thought of him falling terrified me. Being a parent changes you, it makes you do desperate things.'

Although Merry would never say so, Barbara does not look like a tree climber now. She is small in stature, comfortable in belly size and moves like someone whose joints are a little stiff. She leans further over the railings, causing Merry's insides to lurch, and stares down at the rusted remains of the fire escape.

'I wonder if I could do it, if I could climb down. There's a drainpipe there, a few hand-holds, too. I'd do anything to get to my boy this Christmas, I really would.'

Merry had had Barbara pegged as the picture of common sense, but she looks at her now with new eyes. The fire escape is rusted through at the top; the middle section of the staircase is completely missing. Only the bottom part remains, about one storey high, and still reddish brown with rust, each step rotted to nothing in the centre. If the fall didn't kill you, the tetanus would.

'Please don't. You'll never get down there! What are you going to do, strap your suitcase to your back?'

'Oh, I'd ditch the case, just take my handbag with my passport and paperwork,' she says. 'Maybe I'll stuff a swimsuit in my pocket.'

'You can't be serious! Couldn't you just get another flight?'

'We scraped together for months to afford this one and Christmas morning flights were slightly cheaper! He's having his engagement party on the twenty-seventh and I . . . I just can't miss it. I've missed too much already.'

Merry wonders why she is so desperate – maybe they fell out and she's travelling out there to apologise. Maybe he ran away from home. She makes a mental note to find out later. For now, she watches as Barbara gazes longingly down for a few moments, and then draws back with a sigh.

'No, you're right, it's too risky. You're very sensible, you know.'

They are just passing the silent figure of Clockwork Peg on the toy floor when they hear the others, an approaching hubbub of chatter. Why are they all treating it like some kind of *Home Alone*-style festive sleepover? Merry hears Fran Silver's famous laugh, the smooth tones of Evangline. As they approach, Barbara seems to shrink into herself, taking a step behind Merry.

'Oh, there you are,' Evangeline says. 'Barbara, you really mustn't wander off, what if I need you?'

'What are you going to need her for in here?' Josie asks.

'I do think we should stick together, though.' Benjamin straightens his bow tie. 'It would be so easy to trip over something in the dark and have a nasty accident.'

'That almost sounds like a threat,' Dean says.

Benjamin splutters in protest, while Fran steps forward.

'We were worried, though,' Fran says, holding her candle aloft and peering into Merry's face as if looking for signs of injury. 'You hadn't been awake long and you were pretty dizzy.'

'I'm fine,' Merry cuts her off. Why does Fran keep trying to mother her?

She surveys them all; the part of her brain which she uses to mess with people's heads kicks into gear. Everyone here is like Clockwork Peg. They all have a specific set of functions and movements, they have something inside them making them tick. And if she wants to get out of here she needs to figure out what it is, and make it work for her. If she can convince one of them that something weird is going on, then maybe they can mobilise all of them into some kind of action.

Dean is the obvious candidate. His candle is larger than the others', with multiple wicks; it smells of manly musk and sandal-wood and she is sure his choice is deliberate. He walks ahead, clearly leading them all which suits Merry fine. She has no interest in challenging him for that position, putting herself at the centre of the group. So, in order to get what she wants, she'll have to talk to him.

She hangs back, knowing that he will notice and double back to round her up. He approaches, his brow furrowed with concern, and she feels a little fizz inside her at being the focus of his attention. How annoying. He's not even her type, Ross is. She squashes it down.

'Thanks for taking charge like that,' Merry says, knowing flat-tery will help open him up. 'It's good to know you've got this under control. But . . . do you really think we all fell asleep natu-rally? It just seems . . . unlikely.'

A shadow crosses his face. 'It is strange,' he says. 'I don't want to panic the others but something odd is going on here. I did drink some of that mulled wine earlier but that doesn't explain the way I fell asleep on the floor with a model train in my hand. Or the holes in my memory.'

'What holes?' Merry can't hide her surprise. Her memories of Christmas Eve are blurred in a crazy-night-out kind of way but they are all there, even ones she'd rather forget, like Monty's creepiness.

Dean looks uncomfortable. Expressing weakness is not easy for him. 'I remember going to my meeting with Verity. I remember playing with a train set. And then there are flashes of . . . well, anyway the rest of the evening is a bit of a blur. I can't even remember where I left my shoes.' He shakes his head. 'I don't *do* that sort of thing anymore. Last time I had a night like that was BizCon 2018 and that time there were Jägerbombs involved.'

'What do the others think? Do they have memory gaps too?'

'I haven't told them. We've got enough shit going on as it is, I don't want them thinking I'm off my game. I don't even know why I'm telling you now, but keep it under the radar, will you?'

'I won't say a thing,' Merry promises. And then a thought occurs to her. 'Your meeting – was it in some kind of office or meeting room? Were there phones there?'

'I . . . no, I don't think so. I can't bloody remember.' He bashes at the side of his head, as if trying to jog a memory loose. 'All I know is that the deal I wanted blew up in my face and I have no *fucking* idea why.'

Merry can see it again now, the traces of primal anger that Dean tries so hard to hide behind his thought-leader persona. She doesn't push it any further, and soon they've caught up with the others, who are standing outside the fake log cabin that is Santa's grotto.

'It's the only place we've not been to,' Fran is saying. 'You never know, Santa could have left his mobile on charge for the night.'

'Worth a try.' Josie shrugs.

When Monty led them past the grotto earlier in the evening it had been bright and cheery, but now in the candlelight, it looks less cosy and more like a horror movie cabin in the woods.

A sudden movement makes Merry jump, but then she hears the eerie tick-whir-tick and realises it's the automaton elves. They're winding down, the one at the bottom of the candy cane ladder is jerking strangely.

'Surely those things should have run out of juice by now?' Evangeline says, shuddering.

'Not if they're *hauuuuunted*,' Josie intones spookily, then cracks up laughing.

'Don't.' Fran's voice is suddenly serious. 'This really isn't the right time to start taking the piss out of the spirit world.'

Fran believes in ghosts? Interesting.

'It says "no entry",' Benjamin begins but Josie scoffs, pulls off the CLOSED sign and jiggles at the lock on Santa's door. It's not a proper door, so eventually it gives and swings open.

Just as Merry is about to go in, she notices Barbara hanging back, pulling tentatively at the candy cane ladder, as if testing its weight. Merry realises what she's thinking and feels a lurch of panic.

'Barbara, don't.'

The woman looks up, smiles sheepishly. 'It might be strong enough, the ropes are real . . .'

'Promise me,' Merry says. 'Your son wouldn't want you to get hurt. Better to miss your flight than that.'

Barbara steps back, until only the tips of her fingers rest on a wooden candy cane rung. She nods, and follows Merry into Santa's grotto.

Their candles flicker against the walls of the cabin. It's cosy. There are a few brightly painted chairs, stacks of faux presents on a small table and a sturdy throne-like seat for the big man himself. It's sweet and Christmassy and sparks memories of being taken to see Santa by her grandpa. Merry is preparing to question Barbara about her son when she hears a strange noise next to her, a tiny gasp, and sees Barbara put her hand up to her mouth: 'What's that?'

Over in the corner, a group of mechanical elves are crowded around a lump on the ground. Some are bent forward as if they're inspecting it. One holds a hammer out in front and is bashing at the shape. Another is digging at it with a little tin spade.

'It's probably Santa's sack,' Josie says.

'No it's not . . .' Fran peers closer. 'It's a reindeer costume.'

Now Fran has pointed it out, Merry can see the outline of a costume reindeer head at the top of the heap.

'Dean, try it on,' Evangeline says, with a high, girlish giggle.

Dean throws her an irritated look. 'Not my style, love.'

Evangeline gives a flirtatious trill of a laugh. 'Oh, go on. What was it you said to me that time: "I'll try anything once"?'

Hmm, Merry thinks. *So Dean and Evangeline definitely aren't strangers.*

Evangeline grabs one of the antlers and picks up the reindeer head. Dean opens his mouth to protest – and falls silent.

113

Merry's heart thuds hard in her chest. Because there is someone under that reindeer head – a man – and now his head is freed from the costume, it's lolling back. His tongue sticks grotesquely out of his mouth and around his neck is a thick, dark bruise, like a grey ribbon tangled and knotted around his throat.

It's Rudi.

11

CHRISTMAS PAST — 1995

BENJAMIN

BENJAMIN HAD TRAVELLED THROUGH SCHOOL AND UNIVERSITY without any major infraction of the rules. He had never sneaked out of school without official permission, not touched a drop of alcohol before the legal drinking age and was horrified when he found out that some of his closest schoolmates – even ones he had considered to be quite sensible – had tried drugs. As a child, his father had told him he had a weak heart, that he must avoid stress. Wrongdoing caused him great stress, so he never did anything wrong. Therefore, Benjamin Makepeace had never before in his life arranged to meet a shifty fellow in a dark alley and he wasn't very good at it.

Some twenty-five years of age, his style of dress had not yet hardened into the uniquely smart Benjamin of the future. He also had to bear in mind that he was about to commit trespass, and if one finds oneself compelled to perform a criminal act, one must dress accordingly. So he was dressed in his older brother's pea coat, a black beanie hat he had acquired for five pounds from a market stall in Berwick Street earlier that day, and a pair of trainers he had bought solely for this occasion. They glowed white against the grubby, litter-strewn concrete at his feet and they felt wrong, too spongy under his arches, more like slippers than outdoor shoes.

'Blimey, they're box fresh,' said a familiar voice next to him. 'You might want to mess them up a bit, or the crims in jail will have them off your feet in no time.'

Benjamin self-consciously tried to scuff the trainers against the grubby wall next to him, and Kit burst out laughing.

'It's a *joke*, Makepiss,' he said. 'You're just as serious as you were back at school.'

Benjamin winced at the sound of his old school nickname. He knew he'd had to talk to Kit about school at some point, but he wasn't looking forward to it. They had been in different years and run in very different packs – Kit's being popular, party-loving and outlandish, and Benjamin's being a pack of one very careful, studious individual. He really didn't want to get swept away in nostalgic chat about sneaking out after curfew and cigarettes behind the sanatorium when he had never done either of those things.

Kit's manner hadn't changed much in the years since they had seen each other – he was still overly pally and keen to appropriate cockney phrases like 'blimey' and 'mate' to seem less formal. But he had clearly inherited his family's premature ageing gene. Back at school he had been plagued with acne but now his adolescent face had given way to one of an old man, it was a mass of lines and his hair had receded drastically from both temples, leaving a quirky quiff at the front. Benjamin could understand how Kit had been forced to make up for his face by developing a big personality and it still packed quite a punch, sucking in all the air around him making it hard for Benjamin to breathe. He made jokes out of things Benjamin thought were serious, broke rules that Benjamin held as sacrosanct. At least he wasn't in fancy dress tonight – thank heavens for small mercies.

'Have you got the keys?' he asked.

Kit held up a bunch of old-fashioned-looking keys and the two of them went over to the front door of the Emporium.

'Hope you've brought a spare pair of underpants, Makepiss, because this place is almost definitely haunted. Are you sure you want to go in?'

Benjamin nodded. Trespass had been a last resort for him. He had written to the Emporium's owner, Mr Montagu Verity, almost a dozen times requesting access to study Clockwork Peg. He had cited his own background as an up-and-coming expert on antique automata, told him that his desire was merely to reassure himself that Peg was in a suitably preserved condition but adding that, should he ever wish to sell, Benjamin would be willing to make him a sizeable offer as he knew of several parties interested in acquiring her. If Montagu had responded with a no, Benjamin might have backed off but instead he didn't respond at all. No letter, not even a curt thanks-but-no-thanks compliment slip. Montagu had simply ignored him. Benjamin had asked around and discovered that Verity was travelling. Maybe he hadn't even received any of Benjamin's communications. Maybe he wouldn't even mind that Benjamin had paid his cousin Kit to 'borrow' the keys to the Emporium to allow him access.

'Oi, wait for me!' a woman's voice rang out.

Panicking, Benjamin leaped into the shadows, pressing himself against the wall. Kit laughed again.

'Calm down, Makepiss, she's with me.'

Kit reached out and the woman – who was wearing a short floral dress with black tights and heels too high to be suitable for trespassing – leaned in against Kit's side, snaking her arm around his waist. She was pretty, with brown curls and sparkling eyes and a broad thread of South London woven through her voice.

Benjamin stiffened. He knew Kit was married. He also knew that this wasn't Kit's wife.

'Ignore me,' the girl said. 'I'm a sucker for creepy stuff like this and when I heard Kit was coming here I couldn't resist it.'

Kit removed the wooden bar which marred the beautiful oak doors of the Emporium. But then when Kit went to undo the ancient brass lock, the door swung open.

'That's weird, it's not locked.'

'Rough sleepers maybe,' the girl said.

'Dad will go mad. He's not a big fan of this place, but it's *ours*. Well, it's our cousin's, at any rate. The idea of it being taken over by squatters might just send him over the edge.'

Benjamin felt worry gnaw at his chest. What if these squatters had damaged the automaton? But as they went inside, his mind wandered off into a pleasant fantasy involving him saving Peg from the abuses of a band of marauding squatters and being given charge of her as a reward. Images flew through his head: shaking Montagu Verity's hand; poring over Peg, somehow knowing how to repair her even though that definitely wasn't his skill set; unveiling her as the centrepiece of an exhibition of automata through the ages.

That pleasant dream warmed him as they walked through the darkened store, with only their torches to light their way.

'It's not as creepy as I'd imagined,' the girl said, disappointed. 'Too tidy.'

Benjamin was also surprised by its neatness. The ground floor, known historically as the Hall of Wonders, was bare and swept clean. It was cold, though, the kind of musty chill that comes from being left empty for over a decade. It was silent, too, just the sound of the stairs creaking under their feet as they made their way up to the top floor. Benjamin felt a draught coming from somewhere, his skin prickled with goose-pimples. Kit's girlfriend might not have been spooked, but Benjamin definitely was.

'BOO!' Kit jumped on the girl, grabbing her by the shoulders and Benjamin leaped into the air. He clutched his chest, thinking again about his weak heart.

She laughed, a pity laugh, and pushed Kit away. 'That's pathetic – you can do better than that.'

Benjamin was starting to like her, despite her questionable choice of company, and felt embarrassed that he hadn't asked her name. It was too late now. He shone his torch up to catch her expression, and the beam caught on a large gouge in the panelling. Someone had carved the word 'Knives', slashing deep, savage lines into the oak. The girl looked up at it and the smile melted from her face. This was clearly creepy enough for her now.

And then they heard the sound. A creak from overhead, a footstep on the boards.

'I knew it. Bloody squatters,' Kit said under his breath, but his voice was trembling and Benjamin saw him reach out his hand and link his fingers with the girl. She did not pull away and Benjamin wished he could hold someone's hand too. His darling wife Louisa was attending an auction house Christmas party tonight; he had been too ashamed to tell her why he wasn't able to escort her.

Kit swept his torch around, across the landing, and in the darkness they caught a glimpse, a small movement.

Rats, Benjamin told himself. That's all it is, just rats. But instinctively he knew it wasn't; the movement was more deliberate, less scurrying than a frightened creature's behaviour. Almost afraid to look, he directed his torch at it.

A hand, a tiny grey hand. He moved the beam up and found himself staring at a small face: glaring eyes, a twisted, sickening grin. And then it moved. Benjamin's heart hammered in his ribcage, he pictured it struggling to keep up. He listed the symptoms of a heart attack in his head: *chest pain, cold sweat, fatigue, nausea, shortness of breath . . .*

And then he heard it.

Tick-whir-tock . . . Tick-whir-tock . . .

Relief washed over him. He knew that sound.

'It's just an automaton.' He kept his voice light and airy, as if he had never been afraid.

He stared at the device – once it might have had rosy cheeks, peridot eyes and a cheeky grin but the paint on its wooden face was flaking now and part of its nose had chipped off.

'Bloody hell, I take it back, Kit,' the girl said. 'That is scary as fuck.'

Benjamin knelt down next to it, lifting its mouldy felt jacket to see the cage of metal underneath. It was beautiful, and clearly still in working order.

'It's not scary, it's a work of art. This piece is probably a hundred years old – can you imagine the wonder in children's faces when they first saw moving creatures like this in their toyshop? It's an elegant, simple design, a precursor to the larger model that I've come to see today. Nobody made automata like Verity's and it's shocking your cousin has left them in this state.'

The other two looked at him, uncomprehending, and Benjamin felt a flush of confidence. He may have been a lowly worm in the old school pecking order, but in the world of antique clockwork and automata he was a titan.

'It's natural to feel apprehensive,' he reassured the girl. 'It's called the Uncanny Valley. If something, particularly something animated, resembles us but is ever so slightly off we have a natural response of fear and unease. But when you look past that and focus on the incredible craftsmanship which goes into making each one, it's somewhat astounding.'

'I suppose that is quite cool,' she admitted. Benjamin smiled, warming to her even more.

'Wait until you see Peg.'

And there she was, isolated on her plinth. Benjamin had been here a few times as a child – it was where his love of automata had been born – and Peg had always felt like she was the centre of things, the heart of the Emporium. It was strange to see her sitting alone at her piano, next to a set of empty wooden shelves where toys had once been displayed. He reached out, caressed her cheek with the side of his forefinger. Her skin was rough, the paint flaking. Back when she was first displayed, the colour of Peg's skin, combined with the high quality of her clothing, had been a matter of some controversy. Back then, automata representing different cultures

121

and racial groups were common. There were dark-painted 'Turks' sitting on carpets or smoking hookahs, mysterious 'gentlemen of the orient' dispensing wisdom from fairground booths. The kind of stereotypes that, in the present day, Benjamin would refer to sadly as 'non-PC'.

But Peg was not a cultural cliché, she had been a real person. The flesh-and-blood Peggy Goodchild had been living in poverty and working in a watchmaker's shop in Kingston, Jamaica when Everard Verity had seen her talent and taken her in. He had educated her, brought her back to England, and when she helped design the first Emporium toys she had been feted by London society. She would have worn gowns like this on a regular basis so it was only right that her replica was beautifully dressed. Benjamin rarely thought of the real Miss Goodchild but at that moment he wondered if she had enjoyed, or even wanted, that kind of attention.

'Would you like a moment alone with your lady friend?' Kit snickered.

Benjamin ignored him and leaned in, examining the joint in her neck, her thin fingers, decayed with age but still able to move. Her hair smelled musty and old. It made him feel sad to the core.

Now, to business.

He lifted Peg's skirts – ignoring Kit's jeer of 'leave her alone, you pervert' – and examined her perfect feet, her sculpted calves. Above the knee she was all metal structure, her chest made of hollow bands of steel, housing the cam-shafts inside. And there in the piano stool was the lever which wound her. Gently, he began to turn it, and she started to play as smoothly as if someone had oiled her only last week. Benjamin smiled. She really was perfection. He moved on to unlace the back of her dress. There was something trapped inside, it looked like a bundle of papers.

'I'm not sure my cousin's going to appreciate this mauling,' Kit said.

'He shouldn't have left her to rot, then,' Benjamin snapped. 'Now, hold this torch so I can see.'

There was another noise, another creak that this time seemed to be coming from inside the walls. The three of them froze, instinct taking over.

'Kit . . .' the girl said uneasily. 'I get that the elf thing was just some kind of wind-up toy but . . . who did the winding up?'

Just then, the row of shelves next to them began to topple forward. Benjamin's heart lurched, he leaped away just as the shelves came crashing down, missing Clockwork Peg by inches. They were running, all three of them, the girl putting on an impressive turn of speed for someone in heels.

Benjamin ran, too, but as they reached the stairs he couldn't resist looking back for one final glimpse of his beloved. Instead, his beam of light found a face, a pale human face twisted with rage. He screamed.

Outside, the three of them leaned, breathless, against the Emporium's outer wall. Benjamin took a quick inventory. Chest pain: check. Cold sweat: check. Fatigue, nausea, shortness of breath: check. Benjamin braced himself for a squeezing pressure in his chest that, thankfully, did not come. Not a heart attack. Not yet.

'Fucking squatters!' Kit raged. 'I should go back in, turf them all out.'

The girl intervened – told him not to risk it, that they might be armed, that he had no idea how many of them there were. 'It's one for the lawyers, just come to the pub instead. They've got Christmas karaoke on at the one round the corner.'

On the threshold of the Marionette, the girl turned and said goodbye.

'The name's Jo, by the way, thanks for asking.'

Shamed, Benjamin cast his eyes down but made no move to follow her into the pub. The sound coming from inside – of someone torturing that song about scumbags and maggots – was enough to make him long for a nice bit of Debussy. He had no desire to join Kit and Jo but still, he'd like to have been invited.

'Well, lovely to catch up and all that,' Kit said blandly, then checking that Jo had gone inside he leaned forward. 'I'd appreciate it if you didn't tell people about my guest this evening. Don't want it getting back to my lady wife.'

Benjamin stayed silent, his lips pressed together in judgement. He'd been surrounded by men like this all his life. Men who called themselves gentlemen but who were arrogant, supremely self-confident, disrespectful towards women.

'Oh, sneer away,' Kit said. 'But you don't know what it's like. The nagging, the manipulation, the put-downs. The obsession with building her bloody business. She's a nightmare. I think she only married me because I'm a Verity.'

'I see,' Benjamin said although he didn't. 'Why do this, though? Why don't you leave?'

'We don't do divorce in my family,' he said. 'And besides, there's the ankle-biter. Once you've got kids, that's it. Life sentence, mate.'

Benjamin did not approve of what Kit was doing, and he didn't believe the man's excuses either, but he wasn't going to go about spreading gossip and breaking up families. He was just about to open his mouth and assure Kit he had no intention of telling, when a thought occurred to him. He had an advantage here, he should leverage it.

'I don't suppose you could get me into the Emporium again, after the squatters are cleared out? I really need to examine that mechanism. Of course I'd be happy to stay silent if you help me too.'

Kit laughed. 'Ah, bless, Makepiss is doing blackmail! I'll see what I can do, mate. Merry Christmas.'

From the tone of his voice, from the casual way he turned back into the pub and waved over his shoulder, Benjamin knew that Kit hadn't taken the threat seriously.

Bravo, Benjamin, he thought bitterly. Another avenue shut down because of his own inflexibility. A different antiques dealer would have taken Kit to the pub first, softened him with a few school stories and some off-colour jokes. A different dealer would have slid the blackmail in at the end elegantly, like a knife. But not Benjamin. Kit had been his only access to the Emporium and he'd blown it.

Later on, in a drinking establishment more suited to his own tastes, Benjamin ordered a decent whisky and tried to plan what to do next.

Montagu Verity would never sell Peg, he understood that now. Anyone who would sit on millions of pounds' worth of property in the City and let it rot would never be interested in making money. He should accept this. But the sight of her mouldering away in there, when she should have been on display in a museum somewhere, or be celebrated as the jewel of someone's collection . . . It was deeply troubling to him.

The thought of this stayed with him as he went home, as he went about his business, as he sped around the country in Betsy, his vintage van, seeking out new and exciting curios. All this while The Goodchild Automaton – a vital piece of his country's history – was being left to rot in an abandoned department store. His wife grew tired of him talking about it eventually and so there was no outlet for his feelings, nobody to tell.

There was nothing he could do, after all. Not without breaking even more rules, and he wasn't prepared to go that far. At least, not yet.

12

FRAN

FRAN HAS SEEN A DEAD BODY ONLY ONCE BEFORE. HER MOTHER passed away peacefully in her sleep, just two months before Fran was abruptly fired from *Morning All!* and her whole life spiralled out of control. She was often grateful that her mother never lived to see the debacle unfold, but then if her mother had been alive maybe Fran wouldn't have taken things so far, neglecting her body and her mental health. Grief messes you up, but grief plus public humiliation, plus too many mind-altering substances turns your life into an unholy bin fire.

Agnes Silver had deteriorated quickly – by the time the hospice called she had already passed away. Still Fran drove there in a cloud of shock.

'Are you sure you want to see her?' the carer asked, and Fran nodded. She knew it was what Agnes would have wanted. For all she knew, her mother was sticking around waiting to say goodbye.

Agnes had looked younger somehow, as if the cares of a hard-working lifetime had fallen away from her. This was the first time Fran had really tried to see the dead, desperate for one last conversation with her mother, but there had been nothing.

The body in front of her now is different. The man – stroppy Merry had called him Rudi – had clearly died violently. The lurid thumb prints on his neck, broken blood vessels in his staring eyes. His hands were resting loosely on his lap and she could see dark traces of something, probably blood, under his fingernails. He had fought to survive. If Fran's mother was right about the dead sticking around and he's still in the room with them, they're in trouble.

Fran shivers, pulling her arms around her.

Josie crouches down next to him. 'He's been strangled, poor bastard.'

Evangeline is clinging to Dean's shoulder and sobbing hysterically. Dean's expression is one of horror.

'Oh shit,' he says. 'Oh shit, no . . .'

Benjamin takes a throw from Santa's chair and lays it gently over Rudi's face.

Behind her there is a rustling noise, and Fran turns around to see Barbara backed up against the wall. Her eyes are wide, her doughy face pale. With a lurch of fear Fran realises what the assistant is thinking. They are trapped in here with a corpse – what if one of them is the killer?

The grotto falls silent, as all of them begin to realise the same thing.

'It must have happened before,' Dean says. 'When we were all asleep. The killer probably left when the store closed, thinking

128

nobody would find him until after Boxing Day. Yes. That's what happened.'

'Quite,' Benjamin says. 'I agree.'

Slowly, the others begin to make noises of assent too. They all agree that this is the best, most palatable version of the truth. That the killer was someone else who attacked this poor man and hid him in the reindeer costume so he wouldn't be discovered until after Christmas. But why surround him with clockwork elves?

Fran would rather not think about that.

Merry stoops to the ground and picks sonething up, a scrap of red and white cloth.

'It's Monty's, I saw him polishing the top of his cane with it earlier,' she says. 'I knew it. He has to be involved somehow.'

Fran shakes her head. She doesn't know why, but she's sure Merry is wrong. She racks her cloudy brain, it's something to do with what she saw last night . . .

'That doesn't make any sense,' Benjamin says. 'Why would Monty kill one of his staff? And if he did, he wouldn't leave the body in his own Emporium. That would just incriminate him.'

'Perhaps he's planning to come back and move the body over Christmas,' Merry says. 'Or perhaps he's here now, hiding somewhere in the walls. I told you, he drugged us and now he's locked us in. He's got some crazy plan for us all.'

Benjamin makes a scoffing sound; Dean shakes his head. Fran wonders if Merry really did take something with psychotics in it.

'Hiding in the walls?' Evangeline gives a trilling little laugh which almost makes Fran want to switch sides and back Merry. 'That doesn't make any sense. The person who did this must be long gone by now.'

'At least I bloody hope so,' Josie adds.

'It doesn't matter either way,' Dean says. 'But it's obvious we need to get out of here fast. I say we break our way out by force, we go home, we eat our turkey dinners and we don't tell anyone what we've seen. Let the police sort it out after Christmas.'

The grotto explodes into chaos as everyone begins to argue. Benjamin, predictably outraged at Dean's idea, promises to alert the authorities as soon as he is able. Barbara puts in that there is no way she's going to go to the police if it means missing her flight. And Merry, as if to herself, is chanting a litany of accusations against Monty.

'I *do* have evidence. This is definitely his hankie. And I saw him arguing with Rudi earlier, like Rudi was questioning his authority and – oh, for God's sake, I give up.'

'Well, if Dean wants me to keep a secret, of course I will!' Evangeline says, hanging on the crook of Dean's arm. 'I'm very good at keeping secrets when I want to, *aren't I, Fran?*'

Fran's insides churn. She hasn't forgotten the note – or her theory that Evangeline sent it – but recent events have pushed it into the background. Now the fear is back, roaring inside her head.

'Will you stop pawing me?' Dean snaps, pulling his arm away from Evangeline. 'When are you going to get the message?'

Evangeline stares at him, stung. 'What do you mean? I got *all* your messages. I don't understand why you're treating me like this.'

She begins to cry noisily and without real tears. Benjamin flutters sympathetically around her, shooting dagger looks at Dean. Barbara produces a plastic packet of tissues; Dean makes matters worse by calling her a fake and a liar, but the noise seems so far away; all Fran can hear is a whooshing sound of panic rising up inside her. All those years, all that careful concealment and now this . . .

Then suddenly a piercing whistle fills the air.

Everyone stops and looks at Josie, who has pulled off one of those two-finger whistles Fran could never master as a kid.

'In case you've forgotten, this poor bloke is dead. All this screaming and fighting in front of him, it's . . . well, it's disrespectful.'

Everyone, including Fran, hangs their head. Merry is glowering, though. Fran wonders why she finds her so irritating, then realises. *She thinks she's better than us.*

Still, Josie is right. If this Rudi person's spirit is still here, he wouldn't want to see this.

'Let's go,' she says.

'We should put the reindeer head back on,' Dean suggests. 'We don't want police knowing we interfered with a crime scene.'

'It's a bit late for that,' Fran says. 'Everything's covered in our fingerprints now. Whoever the killer is we just handed them a big advantage. And that reindeer head is *not* going back on.'

Sometimes there is power in being a WOFAA; in being older and not giving a shit, in being more confident that you know the right thing to do. Fran hasn't felt like this for years and she's missed it.

Dean has fallen silent but is staring at Josie and Fran like a sulky schoolboy, and Fran wonders if he has a problem with strong women. She knows that any minute now he will say something to reassert his authority.

'Right,' Dean declares, seizing a cricket bat from a nearby sackful of toys. He tosses it from hand to hand, testing its weight.

'Sorry about the grade-two-listed whatsits, Benny old chap, but I'm going downstairs, and I'm going to break some fucking windows.'

From then on, it's The Dean Show. He is the one who marshals them all downstairs, making sure everyone has a candle, getting Barbara, who keeps falling behind, to pick up the pace. He is the one who dispatches Fran to the Hall of Delicacies to fetch brandy to help with Evangeline's (quite imaginary but very irritating) shock and when she returns, bottle in hand and only a little sip sampled, she finds Dean in the window, shoving scented candles aside, the sound of breaking trinkets and Benjamin's protests filling the air.

He lines himself up, like a baseball player going into bat, and as he does, a memory flashes in Fran's brain. Something she saw earlier, before they fell asleep. Fran knows only too well that memory gaps caused by drinking never come back, they tear holes in your identity that stay there forever. She has no black holes in her memory of last night, but her recollections are still a bit fuzzy and confused. There's something on the edge of her consciousness, though . . .

Dean takes a swing, smashing the bat into the leaded window. Nothing breaks that time so he goes again, and again. Roaring with frustration, he rains blows on the glass over and over, but nothing appears, not even a crack.

'Oh dear,' says Evangeline, throwing back the rest of her brandy. 'Maybe you're not as strong as you thought?'

Wow, Fran thinks. *Evangeline Fall really is a piece of work.* Could she really be so petty that she's needling at Dean just because he rejected her?

'I'm sure you can do it, Dean,' Barbara says, and Evangeline glares at her in irritation.

'Shouldn't you be off doing something more useful?' she snaps.

Barbara hesitates for a moment, looking her employer up and down, and then, very slowly, folds her arms. 'I should be in duty free right now, killing time before I get on my plane to Australia.'

'Maybe you should stay in Australia,' Evangeline says. 'You're fired.'

Barbara gives a short, cynical laugh. 'I already quit hours ago, I just didn't tell you. Life's too short to run around after people like you.'

Fran cannot conceal her grin as Barbara turns on her heel and walks away. Not that she has anywhere to go beyond the fireplace nearby, but it's a splendid exit anyway.

'If we could just focus,' Dean growls. 'I need something heavier.'

He drops the bat on the floor with a clatter, stalks off across the shop floor, out of sight. There's a crashing sound and then he reappears with a six-foot carved nutcracker statue, straining under its weight.

'I'm not sure that's practical,' Evangeline says, and Benjamin makes an agonised squeak. Holding the nutcracker under his arm like a knight's lance, Dean takes a run-up and barges with full force into the glass pane. His body goes flying forward into a nearby display, and a clockwork elf topples down onto his shoulders. The glass is completely undamaged.

Benjamin gives a quiet little laugh.

Dean grabs the elf, smashing it on the floor.

'Have you got something to say, posh boy?' he yells at Benjamin. 'Think you can do any better? Do you? *Do you?*'

Dean struts up to Benjamin, banging one fist on his chest, just like Fran's seen gorillas do on Attenborough. She stares at him in disbelief. His shirt is ragged and untucked, his feet are bleeding from the broken bits of candle glass he trod on in the window. Dean doesn't even seem to notice.

'Oh, calm down, Captain Caveman,' Josie says. 'Look at the window. Look at it properly.'

Too shocked to do anything else, Fran goes closer to the leaded glass window and realises that it's protected by a layer of toughened glass. The old nineteenth-century windows are fully shielded from any impact.

'I need an axe, that's what I need. An axe would do it,' Dean says. 'No, a gun. Oh man, I tried an AK47 on a team-building exercise once and it was magnificent. That's what I need – a few bursts of an AK47 and these windows would be powder.'

'Would you believe it, I left my AK47 in my other handbag,' Josie says.

But Dean is not listening. He has returned to the front window and is throwing the statue against the glass, again and again, harder and harder, screaming.

'I've . . . got . . . to . . . get . . . out . . .'

It's several minutes before he drops the nutcracker to the floor and sinks back against the wall, rubbing his sore hands together.

Fran's not sure what it is – whether it's the way he rubs his hands, the defeated sag of his shoulders, but something about the movement ignites the memory in her brain, the one she's been struggling to recall. *Curled up in the sleigh, worrying about the note but unable to stay awake. Then – a sound, a movement. The door to Santa's grotto opened and a tall figure in a dark suit emerged, rubbing his hands on his trousers as he runs into the faux forest, towards the lift . . .*

Dean had been in the grotto last night.

13

MERRY

EVERY TIME MERRY THINKS SHE KNOWS ALL ABOUT HUMAN nature, something comes up to surprise her. The change in Dean is astonishing. The confident, charismatic Business Fixer is gone – he's a mass of insecurities now – his breath is ragged, his face shining with sweat in the candlelight.

'Windows, one, Dean, nil,' Josie deadpans and the businessman practically snarls at her.

Evangeline steps forward and peers closely at him, as if unable to believe she had ever been attracted to him. Merry feels the same. Not that she'd actually been attracted to him, of course. Nope. He's not her type.

Merry moves away from them, grateful to be swallowed up by darkness, and perches on a countertop next to the old-fashioned-looking till, kicking her legs against the panelled wood, letting her anger come out. They had ignored her in

Santa's grotto, laughed off her suspicions about Monty and now she was furious – but at herself rather than at them. She should have known better than to speak out. Nobody ever listens to her, nobody believes her. Nothing she says ever counts. It's no wonder she has to be sneaky to get what she wants.

She comforts herself by assessing all their strengths and weaknesses. Does she trust any of them as far as she could throw them? No. Could she make use of them somehow? Probably.

It's then that she notices the crack. Just behind the cash desk there is a slice of slightly darker darkness which wasn't there before. One of the secret passages has been clicked open. She looks down at her feet, thinking maybe she kicked a hidden button by accident. This passage could lead anywhere – to an office with a landline, an unlocked door . . . she feels a flutter of hope.

She picks up her candle – the label on it says CHRISTMAS MORNING and it smells of pine needles, wrapping paper and Champagne – and slips through the gap. She could call the others over, prove her point about the secret passages, but she doesn't even consider that option. She is better off by herself.

She slips inside. The passageway is only just wider than her shoulders and pitch-black. Merry's candle throws just enough light to show a few feet ahead, enough to see that there is brick on one side and the panels of the Hall of Wonders on the other. Pranks aren't Merry's style, but it occurs to her that she could freak out the others by tapping and knocking on the wood – or making ticking noises, pretending to be a haunted automaton coming to finish them off.

Evangeline would probably have hysterics, Benjamin would just get excited about the automaton. Fran would probably hold a séance. Dean would attack the walls with that cricket bat of his. Josie and Barbara wouldn't be fooled, though. They were both too solid and down to earth.

As a child, Merry had quite liked the dark. Hide and seek had been her favourite game. She had been a slight girl, able to slip between cracks that other people would not even see and once there she would curl into a ball and keep as still as she could, waiting patiently to be found. Often people would forget to find her. Friends would become distracted by snacks or television, her parents would pretend to play along but then occupy themselves with the crossword or a favourite TV show until she finally gave in and crawled out. Even her beloved grandfather would often wander outside for a smoke after a few minutes of looking. She told herself it was because she was good at hiding, but part of her was certain that she was forgettable. That if she disappeared from the earth overnight, nobody would notice she was gone.

Perhaps because of all the hide and seek, Merry's eyes adjust well to the dark and perhaps because of her natural sneakiness, she keeps her tread soft. Every little sound has her heart pounding.

The Emporium has rats. Of course it does, it's in the oldest part of London, the winding streets of the City, a stone's throw from the muddy Thames and the historic docks that were ground zero of the Great Plague. The drains under this building are probably older than the Emporium itself. At least, that's what Merry tells herself when she first hears the scampering, and a sound that's almost like footsteps.

Just then, her hand brushes against something – a metal door handle. She opens it softly and slides inside, lifting the candle to see what kind of room she has found – hoping for an office with phones, even a secret door out of here.

It's a toilet.

It's old-fashioned, with the cistern mounted high on the wall and a chain flush, but it's clean, and a nearby roll of quilted toilet paper and a folded-up Sudoku book show that it's still in use. It's not an entirely pointless place to discover after being trapped somewhere for five hours and Merry avails herself of the facilities.

Looking up, she can see a tangle of dusty copper piping mounted on the wall which doesn't look like part of the necessary plumbing. She folds the seat lid down and climbs up on it to look closer. There's a row of metal levers sticking out, each one with a yellowed label on it. HEATING. LIGHTING.

This must be the gas lamp system Monty had mentioned before he'd gone all *Black Christmas* on them. She uses her flashing jumper lights to see more clearly, then flips the lever. There's no hissing sound, no sign that anything is working. What now?

There's a small gas light fitting next to the cistern and as Merry leans closer to it, she catches the scent of gas.

She looks at the lamp, then her candle. This could be the stupidest thing she's done all night, but she removes the glass cover from the lamp, and holds the flame close.

There is no explosion. Her eyebrows are still in place, and the cubicle fills with a soft, warm glow – not as strong as electric light, but better than the candle. Merry's eyes, accustomed to the darkness, sting as they adjust, and she laughs softly at her little victory.

She has light. She's not beaten yet.

It's hard to force herself back into the darkness of the tunnel but she can't stay in the cubicle forever. She uses her small victory with the gas lamps as fuel to push her on, tells herself that the scuttling sounds aren't footsteps, but just large rodents looking for a meal. Not that this makes her feel any better.

To make things worse, she can't find the door she came through. It must have swung closed, and no matter how thoroughly she runs her hands along the wall, she can feel nothing but splinters. She finds herself at a fork, and realises she's gone too far.

That's when she hears a sound which is definitely, undoubtedly not rats. Looking up, she sees something looming in the right-hand passage. A human shape even darker than the blackness around it, which seems to be wearing a top hat. Panic floods her system and she turns around. The candle slips from her grasp and blows out as she flees into the left fork. She trips, pain blooms in her shins. She has run into a flight of stairs. Swallowing a scream, she scrambles up them, stumbling and flailing, all attempt at quiet gone.

The stairs are steep and narrow, with no hand rail, and when she reaches the top, she pauses, listens. There's no sign that the figure is following her, but there is absolutely no way she's going back down to retrace her steps, not when she can't even find the door she came through. Surely there's another door somewhere near here – then she can go back down the main staircase to find the others.

Reluctantly, she fires up her Christmas jumper. It might be helping light the way but it also turns her into a giant, flashing, moving target in case the shadowy figure – whom she assumes is

Monty – should decide to come up this way. What is his game? Why lock them in here with Rudi's body?

It would have made much more sense to keep the Emporium empty to cover up his crime more easily. But instead, he had trapped them all in here and Merry can't get her head round why. There had been some tension with Benjamin over Clockwork Peg, and some sort of meeting with Dean which may have gone wrong, but why target someone like Fran Silver, or poor Josie – or Doug, for that matter, who should be here instead of her?

She stops for a moment to peer back into the darkness as fear creeps through her bones. In the stillness she hears something, the off-beat out-of-tune sound of piano music.

luly lullay, thou little tiny child . . .

It's Peg. Merry must be near the toy department. She never thought she'd end up working her way *towards* the sound of the spooky clockwork girl, but it's good to know where she is going. She starts feeling the walls with her fingertips, aided by the flickering lights of Rudolph, until she finds a catch, and a door swings open.

She emerges onto the toy department, behind a large shelf stacked with Clockwork Peg dolls, right next to the piano. Peg herself is still playing, although more slowly now. She is winding down.

Someone must have wound her since the store closed. Was it one of the others – Benjamin, perhaps? Or is this further proof that Monty is lurking in the shadows?

The toy department is still in darkness, although there is some atmospheric light seeping through the leaded windows at the front of the building. Merry checks to see if they're reinforced like the ones downstairs, and it looks like they are.

Outside, the gas lamp flickers in Quockerwodger Court, casting light on Gary Shrike's abandoned camping chair. She wonders if he's at home with his family now, whether he'll be back in the morning to film more Emporium content. Perhaps he'll be the one to let them out. *Or to find our bodies*, Merry's brain adds unhelpfully.

Merry's bag is still slung over her shoulder – keeping the snow globe close to her is comforting somehow. Now she rummages through it and finds Gary's leaflet, which has worked its way to the bottom of her bag, under the snow globe. She flattens it out, peering at it in the jumper-light. It's called POOR PEGGY GOODCHILD AND THE HIDDEN HISTORY OF VERITY'S EMPORIUM.

The rags-to-riches fairy tale of Peggy Goodchild is part of the Emporium legend, Gary has written. *But the true story is one of exploitation, a child not 'rescued' but uprooted from her native country, used for her toy designing genius and who died a premature death within the Emporium walls itself.*

Under these words is a QR code, probably leading to one of Gary's videos about the subject. Merry looks over at the figure of Peg – whose playing has slowed to the point that she hits one key a minute – and feels a sudden rush of sympathy for the poor girl. She probably hadn't asked to be 'rescued' by Everard Verity, and had almost definitely not been up for being replicated as an automaton and used as a kind of nineteenth-century marketing curio.

'I bet nobody believed you when you asked for help,' Merry says – and then feels silly for talking to a bunch of cogs and wires. She walks back across the shop floor towards the staircase, studiously avoiding looking at Santa's grotto as she passes. But just as she's about to enter the forest of Christmas trees, Peg's piano sounds again, making her look up.

And then she sees it. The candy cane ladder which hung from the roof of the grotto is missing. Merry's stomach drops. Barbara has put her dangerous plan into action.

14

FRAN

FRAN SITS BY THE FIREPLACE, TRYING TO BLOCK OUT THE SOUND OF
Dean smashing things, of Evangeline taunting him, and Benjamin
flapping about trying to calm him down. She doesn't want to go
near him, or even look at him now she knows what kind of man
he is. Violent. Hateful. And maybe even a killer. Once again
she feels the loss of her mother. Agnes would have known –
maybe because the spirit of Rudi would talk to her, or maybe just
because she had the uncanny ability to see past people's façades to
the ugly truth beneath.

'We need to work together,' Benjamin is saying, sounding a
little like one of Dean's business memes. 'That's what's going to
get us out of here.'

That's us completely doomed then, Fran thinks. Merry's away somewhere on a secretive mission of her own. Barbara has stomped

off to lick her wounds after her row with Evangeline. Josie is watching from the sidelines, her face unreadable.

And as for Dean, it's as if that attempt to smash the window has opened a floodgate within him. The calm, managerial persona which had so reassured her at the start of this nightmare has evaporated, replaced by a snarling beast. A beast which Evangeline insists on poking.

'Come on, then, oh, glorious leader.' Evangeline is giving Dean a mocking bow. 'What now?'

Dean picks up a glass bauble and dashes it against the floor in response. 'What will it take to get you to leave me the fuck alone?'

Evangeline bursts into tears. 'I don't get it,' she says. 'You were so kind to me before, what have I done?'

'I don't know, let me think.' Dean counts things off on his fingers. 'Stalking me online? Saying I sent messages I never sent? Trying to stick your tongue down my throat in the toy department earlier?'

'You're cruel,' Evangeline says, turning away from him. But that's a rich accusation coming from the woman who was so nasty to her assistant, and who taunts Fran at every opportunity she gets with whatever it is she knows.

Fran shivers. What is she going to do?

The brandy bottle is on the table in front of her, and Fran catches a whiff of it on the air, feeling a twist of longing she hasn't felt in years. She has already failed this evening. First, with the mulled wine she evidently drank which made her fall asleep, then with the slug of brandy she had had while bringing it down for Evangeline. Another mouthful won't make much of a difference to that. These are exceptional circumstances.

Fran doesn't notice Merry appearing at her side, but suddenly she's there, like a magician without the puff of smoke. Her face is pale, distraught, and she looks like she's struggling to know who to speak to. Dean, previously the self-appointed leader, is currently shredding an undeserving fluffy toy. The others are all occupied by him and heaven forfend she speak to Fran herself. Merry seems to come to a decision and – to Fran's surprise – she grabs a candle and reaches up to a light fitting next to the fireplace. As soon as she touches the flame to it, the lamp ignites, spreading a glow across the shop floor.

It's not bright, but it's enough to grab everyone's attention.

'The historic gas lamps are still working!' Benjamin says. 'How incredible. All part of what makes it a listed building, of course.'

'It's not going to explode, is it?' Evangeline asks, looking at Benjamin rather than Merry, who got the thing working in the first place.

'I'm sure if it's still connected to the gas mains it will be certified as safe.' Benjamin's voice sounds confident.

'You mean, like all those regulation fire escapes that weren't there?'

Benjamin's face clouds. He seems to have such unwavering faith in health and safety, fairness and law. Fran wonders if he's ever had a bad thing happen to him that he hasn't been able to make go away.

'Please, I need you to listen,' Merry's voice cuts through everything. It's wavering slightly, pleading. 'Barbara's gone. She's found a way out.'

145

The air on the terrace is freezing, but its freshness is welcome after so long spent indoors. She hadn't realised how sickened she had been by the constant Christmassy aroma of cinnamon, ginger and pine needles. The terrace is barely big enough for the six of them to stand on. Fran notices that Merry stays pressed close to the door.

There is a light dusting of snow on the tiled floor, as though someone has sprinkled icing sugar on it.

Dean, who has been silent all the way up the stairs, not even reacting to the secret passages, speaks. He sounds calmer now, his voice faint and distant as his fingers brush against the few white flakes on the railings.

'I put a bet on for a white Christmas. I just won a grand.'

'*That's* what you care about?' Evangeline says. 'I think we have bigger things to worry about, like who killed Rudi and how we're going to escape this place.'

'I don't give a shit who killed Rudi,' Dean snaps. 'I just want to get out of here, and away from you.'

Next to the iron railings are letters traced in the sparse snow-fall, a parting message from Barbara.

SORRY MERRY.

'I made her promise she wouldn't risk it,' Merry says.

The candy cane rope ladder, stolen from Santa's grotto, has been hooked over the broken iron railings. It doesn't reach all the way to the ground but peters out some six feet above the bottom half of a broken metal stairway, which must have been a fire escape at one point but is now jagged and rusty. Barbara must have climbed down and then somehow dropped onto the decrepit metal. How she'd escaped being injured is a miracle.

146

She must have been absolutely desperate to get out. Fran looks at Evangeline with loathing.

'Bloody hell, go, Barbara,' Josie says. 'The girl's got hidden skills – you wouldn't catch me climbing down there.'

Fran looks at Evangeline, expecting her to be upset that her assistant has deserted her, bracing herself for a tirade about Barbara's unreliability, but Evangeline is peering down at the ladder, appraising.

'So who's going to try it next?' she says.

'I'm sorry – what?' Josie says.

'I think all we need do is wait for Barbara to send help,' Benjamin adds. His teeth are chattering and his arms are crossed and stuffed into his jacket to keep his hands warm.

'Oh, come on, she's not going to send help,' Evangeline scoffs. 'You heard what she said – she'll be halfway to Heathrow by now. She only cares about herself and her stupid son.'

'Surely she'll call the police before she gets on her flight?'

'And risk being held in London while they start a murder inquiry? I don't think so. She looks like a lovely mumsy lady but she's more cunning and selfish than people think. Appearances can be deceptive. Can't they, Fran?'

Fran feels a twist of panic, bites back a response. *Don't provoke her. Keep it nice.*

Evangeline steps away from the ladder, looks up at Dean. 'Come on, then, glorious leader, this is your chance to show everyone what a real man can do in a crisis.'

'You're having a laugh, aren't you? I'm not climbing down that thing.'

147

'So let me get this straight – curvy, dumpy Barbara can do it, but you can't? What happened to "fitness is my religion", what happened to "he who dares wins" and all the other stuff you said to me? Oh yes, and let's add one more lie to the list. The biggest whopper of them all: "I'll call you."'

'Oh, come on, woman.' Their tones of voice have shifted, as if they are retracing old steps – they knew each other before. That explains why Evangeline was so familiar with him when they were first trapped.

Evangeline advances towards him. Her creamy cheeks have gone bright red in the cold, genuine tears trickle down her face, streaking her mascara. She holds a hand to her chest.

'I thought we had something. I thought there was a connection and then you just vanished. Then – when you got back in touch and said sorry – I . . . I was a fool to think you'd changed your mind.'

'What? I have no fucking idea what you're talking about, you mad stalker,' Dean flashes back. 'Fine, I'll admit I ghosted you before and that was shit of me, but I didn't send you any messages after that. And fine, you want me to risk my life climbing down a rope to save your bony arse, I will.'

Dean climbs onto the railing and throws one leg over. His feet are still bare – grubby now with smudges of blood. He must be freezing but he's refusing to show it as he sits astride the metal barrier. Fran hears a sharp intake of breath from Merry beside her – the girl has gone positively grey.

'Fitness *is* my fucking religion,' Dean says, holding onto the railing and lining himself up next to the ladder. 'Who dares does win. But I did lie about wanting to call you.'

148

Gripping the green rope of the ladder, he tests the first candy cane with his toes. Everyone falls silent, even Evangeline.

'Feels all right to me,' Dean says. 'Stronger than I thought.'

When he puts his weight on it, the ladder lurches, the ropes creaking and straining. Fran remembers the assault course she did for the Branscombe's Disease Trust – she knows how rope ladders can swing around and how hard it is to keep your footing even when you're balancing on proper solid rungs rather than decorative wooden candy canes. She glances anxiously down – it looks like a long way, and a lot of rungs.

Dean lowers himself by one more rung, and as he does, Fran notices something – a series of scratches on the inside of his wrist. *As if someone has been gripping him hard, fighting for their life. Maybe even trying to stop him strangling them.* There had been blood under Rudi's nails, she remembers.

Dean takes another step down and Fran's heart lurches. Is she watching their saviour, or a killer? If he reaches the bottom, will he even get help or just skip the country and leave them trapped?

Dean takes another step, and his face disappears from the top of the balcony.

'He's doing it! He's doing it!' Evangeline crows. 'Oh, Dean, you're amazing! I take it all back!'

Fran leans over the edge of the balustrade and watches as Dean slowly makes his way down, rung by rung. The ladder is shaking furiously. From above, she can see his hair is thinning on top, blowing in the breeze. His knuckles are white. Her heart thunders in her chest as he takes another cautious step down.

And then – CRACK. A rung breaks.

Dean drops a few feet, his hands gripping the ropes until his knuckles go white, one leg flailing into thin air, fragments of ladder plummeting several storeys down to the hard concrete courtyard below. He looks up, face blank with panic. 'Shit!'

Evangeline screams. 'Oh, Dean, go faster! Quick – before it breaks!'

'No, come back up,' Fran calls.

Dean hangs there, frozen with indecision. *The secret to good business is knowing when to act, and to act fast.* Another of his favourite sayings. But now he can't move either way. He's too far down to be able to scramble quickly back up, but not near enough the bottom to fall without seriously injuring himself. Every new step, up or down, will put him in danger.

He pants – it comes out almost like a sob, and then decides. Better to try escaping than scramble back up. *Who dares wins. Leaders gotta lead. Live the legend you make for yourself.* He takes another step down. And another.

He has covered about six feet and is moving fast now, treading as lightly as he can on each rung, holding the ropes with his hands rather than trusting the rungs. *Let him make it.* Fran repeats the plea over and over in her head like a rosary prayer. *He's going to make it.*

CRACK. CRACK.

Two canes break at once under his feet. Shards of red and white wood tumble to the ground – his legs flail wildly out, his hands sliding down the rope. He roars in pain and terror and one hand slips. Evangeline screams. Josie shrieks in horror and Dean looks up at them, eyes pleading them to do something, anything to save him.

And then the rope snaps. Dean's mouth is open in a long, agonised cry and he is falling. His body bounces off the broken fire escape steps below with a sickening crack, and then falls down into the yard beneath.

'Shit,' Josie murmurs. 'That was like fucking *Die Hard*.'

Nobody replies. Evangeline is curled on the ground, whimpering. Merry is still pinned to the wall, her face a mask of horror. Fran and Benjamin gaze down at Dean. His leg is twisted at an odd angle, and behind his head a pool – no, a flood – of deep red spreads rapidly outwards. Fran has never seen so much blood come out of one person so quickly. Dean's eyes are open, staring at the dark, snow-laden skies.

15

MERRY

THEY STAY ON THE ROOF TERRACE FOR AS LONG AS THEY CAN BEAR the cold, calling down to Dean, hoping for a response. Merry calls, too, even though she knows that he is dead. She is almost relieved that he is, because otherwise he'd be trapped and in pain, and there is no way they can help him from up on the roof. His body lies in the gated delivery area at the back of the store and although several buildings back onto it, the windows are all dark. Nobody lives here in the City. Not anymore.

Curled against the wall, Evangeline weeps ugly tears.

'I . . . I killed him. He died because of me.'

Merry looks over at Fran. Ever since they were trapped here, Fran has been the caregiver, the comforter, the diffuser of difficult situations – sitting with her when she was unconscious, calming people down in the grotto. But she keeps her back turned away from Evangeline, her eyes staring out at the London skyline. Instead, Benjamin is the one who gently coaxes her to her feet.

'I don't get it,' Josie says. 'How could the ladder hold Barbara's weight but not Dean's?'

'Dean's taller and worked out,' Fran says quietly. 'Muscle is heavier than body fat . . . And maybe Barbara cracked some of the rungs on the way down, so that when Dean stepped on them they broke right away.'

The two of them lean forward to look down at Dean again, causing Merry's stomach to churn. Two deaths in one night. One clearly murder, one an obvious accident, but Monty has both their blood on his hands. He is the one who locked them in here.

Even though her teeth are chattering and the height makes her sick, Merry hangs back as the rest of them retreat inside. She doesn't want to be near them right now; she needs to think.

She remembers the VIP list at the beginning of the night. Everyone who is stuck in here now was on that list except for Rita, who never showed. Merry pictures Rita sitting at home by her perfectly trimmed Christmas tree, watching the news tomorrow morning and thinking about what a lucky escape she has had. But then Rita has far worse things to worry about.

At that, Merry feels a pang of guilt. Maybe she pushed things too far before. Maybe, when she gets home, she should fix this.

For now, she is trapped in a gilded festive cage and needs to figure out why. Fran and Evangeline clearly knew each other from sometime before, Evangeline and Dean have history too. But the others are perfect strangers.

There has to be something which connects them all. With an inward groan Merry realises exactly what she is going to have to do to find out. She's going to have to open up to them.

The Great Clock in the Hall of Wonders says it's twenty to three now, so it's no wonder the inmates' energies are flagging. Merry has lit most of the gas lamps, and their light is strangely comforting. Benjamin is trying to light a fire in the grate, holding a sheet of wrapping paper over the flue and mansplaining the technique to Evangeline. Firelighting, he says, is a dying art.

The mundane distraction seems to have helped Evangeline. She is huddled on the floor next to the fire, wrapped in a hand-woven cashmere blanket taken from a nearby display, an empty brandy glass in her hand. Her sobs have slowed to nothing now, her breathing calmed, but she is still wrung out and pale.

Fran sits opposite her, holding the brandy bottle loosely in her hand. She has already taken several slugs of it. For shock, she says, even though nobody has questioned her.

Josie has withdrawn a short distance away, scrabbling through her tote bag, a cotton number emblazoned with the words JINGLE ALL THE WAY. She produces a vape and pulls on it, letting out a sigh of relief.

Merry takes a deep breath and steels herself for what she is about to do. Her usual tactic for getting information is to probe people with gentle questions and reveal nothing of her own life. People always prefer talking about themselves, anyway. But her fellow Emporium inmates are all guarding their secrets closely.

And if you want people to show you their weaknesses you have to share something of your own.

'It's my birthday today,' she says.

Everyone turns to face her. Fran's expression is a mask of overacted sympathy. Benjamin is horrified. Evangeline is still a shocked blank.

'Yay, me, I'm thirty years, two hours and – she checks the clock again – forty-three minutes old.'

Thirty. It's hard to say it out loud. Where had twenty-one-year-old Merry expected to be by this time? Not working at the greetings card company, not still waiting for Ross, not trapped in a retro department store with a bunch of idiots and two corpses, that's for sure.

'Ha! That's why your parents stuck you with Merry,' Josie says.

'It was either Merry or Holly or Carol.' Merry shrugs. 'I've made my peace with it.'

She has often wondered how she ended up with that name. Her parents weren't especially the merry type, despite a fondness for decent red wine, and neither were they particularly Christ-massy. Had they hoped for a bright, cheerful uncomplicated child? They hadn't got one. Being christened Merry – the epitome of festive happiness and good cheer – had clashed with the sheer bloody-mindedness inside her and forced her to become, instead, secretive, dour and cynical. Maybe naming her Holly would have made her *less* prickly.

'Well, happy birthday, my dear,' Benjamin says, struggling to his feet to shake her by the hand. 'Many happy returns.'

'Are you OK?' she asks suddenly, noticing that the scratch on his finger is still red.

'Oh, that's just Peg's love bite.' Benjamin quickly puts his hand back in his pocket. 'Although I wish I had my phone – I'd be searching symptoms of tetanus right now. I really am shocked at the state she is being kept in.'

'Happy birthday, sweetheart,' Josie says. 'Thirty really isn't old, you know. You might feel like it is but wait until you're staring down the barrel of sixty.'

'Hear, hear,' Fran says with a shudder. She stands up and holds her arms out for a hug. Merry stiffens but lets Fran close her arms around her, trying to ignore the waft of brandy coming from her breath. This is for the greater good. After knowing Fran for only a few hours she understands that what motivates her is being a Good Person™ and so the best way to win her over is to let her. She feels Fran let go of her tension as she hugs.

'Come, come and sit down,' Fran says.

She draws closer to Benjamin's tiny, pitiful fire. She didn't realise how cold she had got outside, staring down at Dean.

'I was meant to be spending the day with my boyfriend,' she adds, stretching the truth a little, but Ross is not here to correct her. 'We were going to eat our body weight in Celebrations, watch our favourite Christmas films on a loop, play the stupid board games he loves . . . It was going to be perfect. I only gate-crashed this event so I could get a Christmas present for him.' She can't quite bring herself to show them the snow globe, to tell them all her hopes. It's too personal.

Fran covers Merry's hand with her own. Merry tolerates it.

'I came here because of Dean,' Evangeline confesses. Merry's gambit has paid off. 'I mean, it was partly for work. I love this place. The wreaths and garlands are excellent quality and I can mark them up quite considerably from Monty's absurdly low prices. But I came here last night because I knew Dean was invited. We've . . . I think you must realise now from what he said that we have history. We met last year on PeelYu and, well, things moved pretty quickly. There was a real . . . a connection between us, you know?'

'What the hell's PeelYu?' Josie asks.

'It's a high-end dating app . . . erm, I've heard . . .' says Fran. 'It stands for PLU – People Like Us – and you have to be pretty fancy to get onto it. Not that I tried and they turned me down. Not that I'm bitter.'

'There's a very strict vetting process,' Evangeline confirms, not noticing Fran bristle with outrage next to her. 'You have to be nominated by two existing users. I met Dean through the app and we just clicked. There was chemistry but we connected on a personal level too. I got what he was trying to achieve. He was working on some beauty company restructure and he was a bit clueless about such a feminine industry. I gave him advice, he even talked about getting me on board as a consultant. Then we slept together and after that . . .'

'He ghosted you,' Merry prompts.

'I do not get ghosted. *I* do the ghosting.' Evangeline's Botoxed brow tries to crease with irritation. 'But . . . yes, he stopped messaging. Then about a month ago he got in touch and apologised and we started messaging again. It was wonderful – that connection we'd had before was there again, even stronger than ever. And when I saw on his social media that he was coming here, I thought, why not engineer a meeting? What harm could it do?' For a moment she's her old self – coy and flirty. But then she remembers and her expression crumbles.

'I wish I'd stayed at home.' Evangeline's voice wobbles but does not break. She takes a deep breath – the kind that yoga teachers tell you to do – and then shakes her head, as if freeing herself of clinging guilt and sadness. 'What about you, Fran? What brings you here? One of your usual do-goody things, or something a little more personal?'

'What's your game?' Fran snaps. 'A nice bit of bonding by the fire so it hurts more when you stick the knife in later?'

Evangeline holds her hand up to her breast, which Merry now understands is what she does when she is about to express Big Feelings.

'Whatever do you mean? Why are you talking to me like this? I'd expect better from a national treasure. You don't want to ruin your reputation.'

Fran stands, glaring down at Evangeline. Her hand goes into her jeans pocket, as if she's checking that something is still there. She pauses for a moment, her mouth working as she forms words but chooses not to say them and instead she turns away.

Internally, Merry is breaking out the popcorn and settling in to be entertained. This is fascinating. Fran has been so kind and nicey-nicey – the exact reflection of her TV persona – since she has been here, but look what's underneath. A flawed, touchy person who has a big juicy slice of beef with Evangeline's name on it.

Merry lets the silence fall, hoping the argument will escalate but Benjamin, in a quintessentially British way, speaks to cover up the awkwardness.

'Well, I'm here for the most boring of reasons, Christmas shopping. I came to buy a gift for my wife,' he says. 'She's had, a, difficult time of late and I think she deserves something special. Something that isn't an antique piece of clockwork. She loves perfume, and this place is famous for its bespoke scents.' He takes a sparkling bottle from his pocket and holds it up.

'That sounds lovely,' says Merry.

'I reckon you were here for more than that, though,' Josie probes. 'You're into all that clockwork stuff – you were pretty interested in good old Clockwork Peg upstairs. Are you sure you haven't got an elf stuffed under your waistcoat?'

'Very funny,' Benjamin snaps. 'Those elves are a travesty. If they still had their original faces they would be worth a small fortune but, in modernising them, Monty Verity destroyed them. I cannot bear the thought that he might do the same to the Goodchild Automaton.'

Merry feels a tingle of excitement. She can see the connections and interplay between them all clearly now and knows how they'll react when prompted. She can rely on Josie to poke fun at authority and undermine pretension. She can trust Evangeline to always turn the topic of conversation back to herself. Benjamin is a rule-keeper. And Fran – clearly there's something between her and Evangeline, something which angers her far more than it does the interior designer. But she's still no closer to figuring out what they have all done to deserve being locked in here.

'So you won this trip in a competition, Josie?' Merry asks.

'Yup,' Josie confirms. 'Lucky me, eh? I've been desperate to see the old place since it reopened but I live up North now and trains cost a fortune. When I won this I thought it was a godsend.'

'And it was just a trip for one?'

That seems odd to Merry. She has not spent Christmas with her family for years now, but she knows she is in the minority. Why would anyone launch a competition when the prize involves spending Christmas Day alone? And why would Josie want to come?

Josie shrugs. 'I wanted to bring my eldest niece, the one who's sick, but they were really strict about the plus ones.'

'So nobody's going to know you're missing for a while,' Merry says. 'What about you, Benjamin?'

Benjamin looks down at his feet. 'My wife is . . . not waiting up,' he says.

'And I thought I'd be spending it with Dean,' Evangeline sighs. 'In fact, I was so certain; in his messages he even spoke about me meeting his mother.'

'Are these the messages he denied sending?' Fran cuts in. 'Face it, Evangeline, you were probably talking to some con artist overseas who hacked Dean's account. Did he tell you you were a beautiful lady? Ask you to send him money at all?'

'Shut up,' Evangeline snaps. 'Let's not start talking about liars, shall we, Fran?'

Just then, the Great Clock strikes three. Merry, who has pins and needles in her legs, pulls herself to her feet and stretches, walking over to where the little clockwork shoppers are dancing. There's the broken Santa figure on the third floor, but she notices something else.

The wooden model of Dean Hallibutt has been moved. Before, it had stood proud and tall on the marble shelf in front of the replica store. Now it lies just outside the Emporium door, and it's been smashed to pieces, as if it fell from a great height.

16

FRAN

As Zelda always used to say, when it comes to getting drunk fast, you can't beat booze that makes you cough. The expensive kind that people say they drink for pleasure, but you have to teach yourself to tolerate. Fran treats herself to another slug of brandy. It's good stuff and it burns fire down through her gullet. She coughs and splutters, then feels the bloom of warmth in her stomach and the sheer, melting relief of giving in.

The list of things Fran has forbidden herself has grown longer over the years. It started with straightforward things: holidays, parties, freebies, but then it expanded to anything and everything which gave what she saw as selfish happiness: friends, comfort, rest. Yes, she allowed herself a few small pleasures – the warmth of a cat curled into her lap, the satisfaction of a Christmas tree well decorated – but her day-to-day life is one of self-denial. She doesn't deserve any kind of comfort.

But now, with that one sip of brandy, the floodgates have opened.

She has moved away from the fireside chat and Evangeline's spite, curling up in the window space among the remains of the scented candles and splinters of nutcracker statue, staring at the alley outside. She prays for a passer-by but there really is no such thing. Nobody comes to this ancient part of the City at Christmas. It must be lonely for the ghosts.

From the other side of the room, she hears Evangeline's voice drift over to them, her inane trill of laughter. How can she find out what Evangeline knows? What does she want? And, most importantly, how can Fran silence her?

Another thought comes to her which scares her even more. When they are rescued, there will be police, there will be questions, there will be background checks. Secrets come tumbling out after crimes like this, so even if Evangeline doesn't say a word, the police could still find out what she'd done.

She can't just sit here watching an empty alleyway. She has to do something, anything to get out of this situation and keep suspicion as far away from her as possible. The best way to do this is to figure out what's going on herself, to present a nicely gift-wrapped story to the police and keep the focus away from her own past.

She notices Merry staring at the clock, then – after checking the others aren't looking – moving off towards the secret passage she had talked about earlier with a candle in her hand. Merry is definitely sneaking about more than she ought to be. She was the one throwing around accusations against Monty earlier. Perhaps to direct suspicion away from herself?

Fran does not take a candle when she follows, but instead decides to follow Merry's light. The passageway is dark and narrow, designed for people with slender Victorian-sized figures, Fran decides, snagging her hip on a splinter in the back of the wood panelling. She wonders if some of them are still here, listens out for whispers of their ancient conversations in the stale air.

When Merry reaches a fork, she takes the right one, treading quietly, stealthily, looking all around her. Fran moves as softly as she can, tries to stay at a distance, but she must have made some kind of sound because Merry rounds, holding her candle high in the air.

'Who's there? If that's you, Monty, I'm not scared. I'm not.'

Merry's voice is trembling, brave and frightened and vulnerable all at the same time. Fran feels a rush of guilt. 'It's just me! Harmless old me.'

'And that's supposed to make me less afraid? For all I know you could be working with him.'

'Do I look like a criminal mastermind?' Fran presses the button that lights up her jumper for emphasis. Merry makes a sound in the dark that's almost a laugh.

'If you are it's a good disguise.' Her voice is gentler now. 'Just don't creep about behind me. I'd rather you stayed close so we can both listen out for anyone else sneaking around. I didn't explore this passage before, what with Barbara leaving and . . . and Dean. I thought it might lead to that back door area we saw from the roof.'

The passageway comes out into some sort of warehouse area. There are rows of neatly stacked boxes, a large metal shuttered door which is locked and completely immovable, and an office.

Merry locates a gas lamp and lights it, illuminating a dingy cramped room with desks which look like they date back to the Seventies and chairs which are only marginally more modern. There's paper everywhere and a few chunky old-style computer screens – the kind that take up half the space on your desk. There are no actual computers, though, and on the messier desks there's a gap in the paperwork where a landline phone must have stood.

'Don't you think it's weird, that all the phones have been removed?' Merry says. 'There's nothing – not so much as a Wi-Fi router.'

'Not even a fax machine,' adds Fran.

'Surely even Monty isn't *that* retro.'

Fran feels the cold dead weight of certainty in her chest. Merry was right all along – the Emporium is a giant, festive, glitter-encrusted trap. The Emporium is not so old-fashioned that it doesn't take card payments, and for that she's sure they'd have to have an Internet connection. Which means all of it has been taken away to stop them from calling for help. It's a crazy idea, and one she wouldn't even entertain if she were sober. This sort of thing happens in Agatha Christie novels, but they're not snowed in in an isolated country house or marooned on a storm-blasted island. They're in one of the biggest, busiest cities in the world, and yet there is nobody, not one neighbour or passer-by, here to help them. They are trapped in the gaslit gloom with Rudi's body growing cold upstairs, Dean lying broken in the yard outside. No electricity. No phones. At the heart of civilisation and yet completely cut off from it.

And to Fran, a woman who has waited seven years for the axe to fall, it makes perfect sense. She deserves to be here. Maybe the others do, too. Her hands are shaking as she lifts the brandy to her lips again.

Merry, meanwhile, is pushing papers around, rummaging through in-trays.

'What are you looking for?' Fran asks.

'Stuff. Anything really.'

'That's helpful.'

Merry gives a sigh of exasperation. 'Look, I'm hoping we find a way out, I really am, but I think it'll help to understand what's going on. So I'm looking for paperwork about tonight – letters, email printouts, invoices – anything that tells me why you lot are all here.'

'You're here, too,' Fran points out.

'Yes, but I'm not supposed to be. I nicked my invitation from my boss, Doug. The rest of you were lured here, and someone's messing with you.'

She opens a desk drawer and starts looking through it. It's clear the conversation is over.

Fran takes another sip of the brandy, but it's not warm and comforting now. It's a familiar shift, that moment when the drink isn't doing its job anymore and carrying on will make her feel worse, not better. She doesn't stop, though. She never did.

And so, Fran begins searching too. The top drawer of the nearest filing cabinet is locked. In her experience the locked drawers always contain the best shit, so she forces it open using a metal ruler she finds on a nearby desk, feeling grateful Benjamin isn't here to disapprove.

It's a mess – as you can expect from a business which relies on paper as much as this one seems to. She pities the poor accountant who has to digitise all this at the end of the financial year. There are slips, one-page invoices for things like 'snow plus P&P' She sees one invoice for *Window Work*, the signature completely illegible. The window reinforcement work was recent, and had been paid for by a third party. Very weird. She also spots a slip scrawled by hand for payments to someone called Doug something – didn't Merry say that was her boss' name? She's about to call Merry over when her hands brush against something, a battered leather portfolio rammed at the back of the drawer.

She has been discarding anything that looks too old – this doesn't feel like it's about ancient history to her – but the portfolio is good quality, embossed with gold which indicates something important lies within. The sheets inside are newer than the portfolio, printed on a modern printer. She flicks through pages and pages of clauses and sub-clauses. In some ways it looks like a cross between an entertainment contract and an NDA – a non-disclosure agreement – between M.R. Verity and someone called Nigel Smallhouse. It talks about 'the role' and swears both parties to secrecy.

Maybe Nigel Smallhouse is the resident Santa? But this is a pretty heavy contract for a seasonal worker. One phrase in particular jumps out:

M.R. Verity is the sole shareholder and will remain sole owner of the Company. Provided Mr Smallhouse complies with the terms of the agreement, and in particular the non-disclosure terms, he will be entitled to 20% of profits.

Why is this Smallhouse guy getting a cut of profits from the Emporium? That's definitely not a standard Santa agreement.

Fran's brain is cloudy, confused. This paper doesn't mention anything about Evangeline or Dean or any of the others but it feels important. She puts it aside before picking up another file marked INVOICING 2024.

'I've found something,' Merry says. 'A letter from Evangeline.'

Fran jumps up with jackrabbit enthusiasm and rushes over to a desk, where Merry is leaning over a piece of paper. It's good quality paper, not dissimilar to the note burning a hole in Fran's pocket right now, and it's printed out, but signed with Evangeline's outlandish signature.

Darling Monty,

Regarding the ivy wreaths and silk garlands, it appears there has been a misunderstanding. I had no intention of passing them off as my own designs. I simply told my client that I was responsible for the placement of the wreaths, incorporating them into my overall vision for the Winter Wonderland ball at their property. Anything else must have been a misinterpretation on my client's part. I understand my assistant also placed them on my website at a highly marked-up price and for that I apologise. The wreaths have been removed from sale and my assistant has been dismissed.

I do resent the accusation of profiteering but I am not surprised by it. I am a lone businesswoman running a high-end enterprise and as such I am used to having to work twice as hard and be twice as good as my male counterparts. I hope we may continue to do business in the future, and that your ban on my entering the Emporium may be lifted.

I heard an interesting tale about the Emporium's history many years ago. It could be of great interest to the press, but such a thing would pain me greatly as I always felt we had a connection.

I'm sure we could sort this out amicably, over a drink or two.

Kind regards,
Evangeline Fall

'She was banned from the Emporium,' Fran cackles. 'She blames sexism, then tries to flirt with him while threatening him with press exposure. That's so Evangeline!'

Deep inside her brain, a tiny little voice is reminding her that she is no longer permitted to talk like this, that bitching and gossiping is not acceptable, not nice. But what Evangeline does is wrong, too, so isn't she just standing up for herself? Yes, that's it. She's standing up for herself.

'If she was banned, what's she doing here?' Merry asks, very sensibly. 'And Benjamin didn't seem very welcome either. Maybe this is all about them, somehow?'

'But that doesn't explain Dean,' Fran says. And then she decides to share her suspicions. 'I think Dean killed Rudi.'

For a moment, Merry pauses in her rummaging and narrows her eyes. It looks hostile, but Fran is coming to realise that this is her thinking face. Fran explains about her memory of the grotto, the scratches on the insides of Dean's arm.

'It's a theory,' Merry says. 'Dean had gaps in his memory which means he could have done it and then just, sort of forgotten – or blocked it out somehow. He was acting weirdly after we found

Rudi's body, and he has got a temper. But he came here for some kind of business meeting with Monty. The deal of his lifetime, he said. Why would he end up killing Monty's best craftsman?'

'And it doesn't explain Evangeline,' Fran adds. 'She's definitely part of it somehow.'

Those narrowed eyes again. 'You really don't like her, do you? And she does seem to have it in for you.' Merry's voice is far more gentle than usual as she says this, but Fran doesn't recognise the change in tone, just feels relieved that Merry has seen Evangeline for what she is.

'You're right, she does, and you don't know the half of it!' It feels good to say it out loud, to allow herself this tiny sliver of honesty.

'You knew her at university, right? Do you think it's a coincidence you were both invited?'

'No, she brought me here, I know she did. She wants to stick the knife in.'

Merry makes a sympathetic noise and a wave of positive reinforcement washes over Fran.

'I'm sorry, this is such a shitty situation,' Merry says. 'I just can't figure out why she'd have it in for you so badly. What did you ever do to deserve all that?'

Fran lets out a ragged breath like a sob. Merry isn't as spiky as she first seemed. She understands. Maybe she should just tell her, get it off her chest, swear her to secrecy. She imagines the sheer relief of saying the words out loud.

'I . . .'

It's on the tip of her tongue. It wants to come out, it's *desperate* to come out. Merry leans forward and for a flash – a fraction of a second – Fran sees eagerness on her face. It passes quickly, Merry reins it in and rearranges her features into an expression of sympathy, but it's too late. Merry's warmth is an act, a manipulation to satisfy her nosiness.

'I can't say.'

Fran pushes the secret down, cramming it back inside her like the stuffing in a teddy bear, and turns away.

'Anyway, you don't need to know about that. You can see from the evidence that Evangeline's involved.'

'You can tell me if you like,' Merry says gently. 'I won't say a word.'

Anger, aided by brandy, flushes through Fran's body. 'You'd like that, wouldn't you? Don't think I haven't noticed you snooping around.'

She's touched a nerve. Even in the gaslight, she can see Merry's face is flushed.

'Don't think I haven't noticed that you're not as nice as you seem on TV,' Merry flashes back.

With those words, the fight goes out of Fran. She turns and leaves the office, plunging back into the darkness of the passage.

No, I'm not nice. Not at all.

People want you to be nice when you've had cancer – she's seen this from the way people react to her, and heard it from people she's talked to through her fundraising. They want you to be brave and gracious and grateful. They don't want to see grumpy days or bitter days or why-me days. When Fran had shared her journey online she had kept it all positive, brimming with gratitude. And people had bought it. They hadn't seen the rage and grief swirling inside her, they had seen what they wanted to see.

In a way, she's grateful that Merry saw through the Nice Fran act but she's also disappointed. Because if she truly wants to make amends, the act has to become real. She has to be as nice and good and virtuous as she pretends to be. Alone in the darkness, she puts the brandy bottle down on the floor and walks away from it. She has to be better than this.

Just then, she catches a glimpse of light up ahead – a flickering candle. A stab of panic hits her – maybe Dean didn't kill Rudi, maybe the real killer is still lurking somewhere in the Emporium waiting to silence them all.

She presses herself into the wall, hoping to hide in the darkness. The figure is coming towards her in fluid, confident strides but then just before it reaches Fran, it takes a turn to the left. It's too dark to see the figure's face, but it's not tall enough to be a man, and the candlelight glances off a thin, pale feminine wrist. Evangeline. It has to be.

She heads up a steep staircase, and Fran follows, taking care to step on each tread at the same time as her quarry. It's steep and Evangeline moans slightly as she climbs, but Fran's calves are like steel after all the Santa dashing, she follows effortlessly. Nevertheless, she wishes she still had the brandy for comfort.

When Evangeline reaches the top of the stairs she stops at a seemingly blank bit of wall, placing her candle on the floor before confidently running her fingers along the panels until a catch clicks and a hidden door opens. Trapped halfway up the steps Fran stays frozen, watching.

Evangeline pushes the door open, then bends down to retrieve her candle. Just as she does, enough light is thrown on her face for Fran to see that it's not Evangeline after all.

It's Josie.

17

CHRISTMAS PAST – 2007

DEAN

THAT YEAR, DEAN'S CHRISTMAS DINNER SHOULD HAVE BEEN fish he had caught himself off a coral reef in the Maldives. Gifts should have been exchanged under a palm tree – Nicole would have bought him a new watch for his collection, he would have bought her that Ralph Lauren bag she had her eye on. He would have been tanned, relaxed, his body dusted with pale sand. She would have been wearing that white jewelled bikini that did things to Dean's insides whenever he looked at her.

But recent financial kinks, plus Nicole revealing herself to be a grade A bitch, had put the kibosh on that. No bikini tingles for poor Deany-boy.

Instead he was here, in a cramped dining room, sitting at an Ikea table and staring down at his mum's classic Christmas spread. It hadn't changed since he was a child: dried-out turkey, ready-made pigs in blankets from Morrisons, boiled sprouts because you had to have sprouts, plus peas and carrots because nobody ate the sprouts. Before tucking in, they pulled red and green crackers, exclaimed over the plastic dice or fortune-telling fish inside, put the paper crowns on their heads and laughed about it as if they were doing something outrageously silly.

And at the end of the meal, as ever, Dean's father laid his knife and fork together on his plate and said: 'Another cracking spread, Nance! Well done, love.'

The sameness of it made him seethe with fury, filled him with the urge to dash his plate against the wall and scream at Mum to go watch an episode of Nigella, for fuck's sake, and learn to cook a sprout. No matter how hard he tried, how many followers he gained on his newly minted YouTube channel, how many books he published or courses he taught, it felt like normality was always lunging out, trying to pull him back down into an ordinary existence of nine-to-five, pints down the George, weekends on the sofa.

He'd seen the lads from school in the pub last night.

'Oi oi, it's Train Boy!' Kyle had laughed.

Still that bloody name. Just because he'd liked model trains as a kid.

It should have been satisfying, seeing them all there in the same booth they'd drunk in since they were sixteen years old, talking about their dead-end jobs and struggles to get on the property ladder. But then, he was there in the pub, too, wasn't he?

They'd been duly impressed by the watch, the suit, the chat, but it hadn't changed anything.

'You still got train tracks running round the walls of your penthouse flat?' Callum asked.

'My girlfriend collects modern art, actually. She invested the money she got from modelling and it's worth a couple of mil now.'

It was all true, ignoring the fact that they'd split up and the penthouse was hers, but said out loud it sounded fake. *I've got a girlfriend who's a model. You wouldn't know her. She goes to another school.* The lads fell about laughing. Dean had laughed along with them, his hands clenching into fists under the table, holding in the rage.

At times like this, it wasn't Nicole's face that haunted him, it was the face of that woman. The one who had come to one of his first courses, the Wicked Witch of the third row.

'You're just an ordinary bloke. A walking logo with nothing underneath.' Nothing hurt like the truth.

He'd drained his pint, left the pub before he snapped and did something regrettable, like punching Kyle in his stupid, unshaven, gammony face.

Dean was fully aware that he had anger issues, even before Nicole had screamed it at him in one of their final bust-ups. Knowing about it made it an even bigger source of frustration. Rage was unproductive, wasted energy, it was off-brand. And yet it was still undeniably, immovably fucking there.

'Penny for your thoughts, love?' Nancy asked. Christmas dinner was over now, and she cleared his plate away. 'You're not thinking about that girl again, are you? There's plenty more fish in the sea. You remember Claire's daughter Izzy? She's single now, she's got a good job at the Nationwide and she was always very pretty. Maybe I should get Claire to pass on her number?'

Normality lunged at him again, his anger whip-cracked in response.

'God, Mum, just shut up!'

She drew back looking hurt and Dean pulled himself together again. 'I mean, it's not really about Nicole. I just had a bit of a business setback, that's all.'

'I knew it.' His dad shook his head. 'He's lost everything, Nance. It's all gone down the tubes.'

'There's always a place for you here if you're skint,' Nancy added.

'That. Will not. Be necessary.' Dean was fighting the rage so hard now, his knuckles were white. He took a couple of deep, diaphragmatic breaths, like the guy on the self-hypnosis CD suggested and continued. 'It's not that bad. Really. I just should be more ahead right now. I see other guys doing the same thing as me – the videos, the courses, the books – and they're getting more attention than me.'

'That doesn't matter,' Nancy said. 'As long as you put in the hard work . . .'

'That's exactly the problem, he doesn't work hard enough,' her husband added. 'He wants to go from zero to Alan Sugar in five minutes and the world don't work like that.'

'That's not it,' Dean repeated. 'Hard work gets you to a certain level but what sends you stratospheric is fame. It's brand. I want everyone to be talking about the Business Fixer.'

Nancy, who had an empty gravy boat in one hand and an empty serving dish in the other, still found a way to hug him – although she did spill a couple of drops on his trouser leg.

'You do your best, love, that's what counts,' she said.

Dean bit the inside of his cheek. He wanted to yell: *Doing your best is not good enough. Average is not good enough.* Nothing but one hundred and ten per cent of his efforts, years of fighting would get him to the top. Did Jeff Bezos spend Christmas Eve in the pub with his former school bullies because his more successful girlfriend had dumped him? No, he did not. Did Elon Musk have to say polite things about his mum's sprouts? Nope. They were human missiles, powering towards their next billion.

Dean did not help with the washing up; he went upstairs to his old room, threw himself on the single bed.

The room, like Nancy's Christmas dinner, had not changed. The wall was lined with shelves, a train track running around each one. He reached out and flicked a switch that had been lovingly built into his bedside decades ago and the trains began to move, slipping smoothly back and forth on their rails, over bridges, under tunnels, through perfectly rendered miniature stations. Even now, despite his resentment, the click–clack sound soothed him. His eyes sought out the pride of his collection, his dad's old OO-gauge Verity Flyer – hand-made, painted fiery red and perfect in every detail. Nothing could beat those old Emporium trains, his father always said, and they went for a fortune on eBay these days.

Train boy. He would always be Train Boy and would never be able to hide it. *An ordinary bloke . . .*

The Wicked Witch hadn't seemed particularly threatening when she first walked into his Fixing Your Business course six months ago. The course was going through a few teething troubles. The idea had seemed simple on paper – to build himself up as a brand, he had to produce self-help guides, tweet advice, post videos and – this was the real moneyspinner – run courses. Charge a fortune, hold a small collection of no-marks in the palm of your hand for six weeks, then send them off into the world as walking advertisements for Dean Hallibutt. It was visionary. All business would be done like that in the future.

However, teaching hadn't been quite as piss-easy as he had thought, and the Witch had noticed. Every week she'd been there in the third row with her questions, asking how he knew things, how he could prove his methods would work, what his experience was.

Ageist cow. She clearly didn't think someone as young as him could have achieved so much. She was exactly the sort of person who wound him up – a typical middle-class woman who had married a posh bloke with money, had a kid and wanted to set up a little sideline in perfume-making to 'fit work around the children'. She was such a cliché and no amount of statement lipstick and business plans could hide it.

Still, when she had asked for a five-minute coffee after the course ended, he had briefly been flattered. The five-minute coffee was part of his schtick: 'Say you'll grab five minutes, but drinking hot coffee always takes fifteen (if you don't let them order espresso). Use those fifteen minutes to sell hard and you can achieve anything.' The fact she remembered it showed that his messaging was getting through. And so he had gone.

When he'd slid into the booth opposite her, she smiled a slow, sharkish smile revealing a row of perfect white teeth

She drew a pale-yellow folder out of her laptop case and stroked it with her perfectly manicured fingers. Her nails were blood red, her skin pale and creamy by contrast. She had probably been hot when she was younger and although her face was still pretty fresh, he could see the age in her hands. That was always where it showed. She was far too old for Dean's tastes.

'I thought I should let you know, I've been doing some research on you and your so-called business interests,' she said.

And then she had laid it all out – the mountains of debt, the borrowing from Peter to pay Paul; she had paperwork Dean hadn't even known existed and God knows where she'd got it from.

'The fact is, Dean, you don't actually have a business at all. Of course, there's bits here and there – that SEO agency you set up, some trademark and domain-name ownership. You must have a small income from your YouTube ads but really, the rest is all hollow, there's no consultancy work that I've ever seen – you've never actually fixed a real business, have you? You're just an ordinary bloke. A walking logo with nothing underneath. And I learned more about personal branding from my room-mate at university who basically just told me to wear red lipstick.'

Dean's response came straight out of the Alpha Businessman playbook – bluster, denial, denigration of his accuser. The woman just sat there until he was all blown out.

'What do you want?' he said finally.

'My money back, plus an extra fifty per cent for my wasted time.'

The rage had surged inside Dean and before he knew it, he lunged forward, grabbed the woman by the throat, pinned her up against the wall of the booth. His heart pounded, a sense of rightness, of elation flooded through his mind. His anger sang with the joy of freedom.

And then he realised what he had done.

The woman was calm, a tightness in her lips the only sign that she might be afraid. *Shit, the witch was strong*. Her eyes met his and he knew that she had won.

'I . . . I'm sorry,' Dean stuttered. The words were useless, pointless. He'd attacked a woman. In his family there was no worse deed than that. He looked around: the barista was staring, shooting a worried glance at the Witch.

'I'm OK,' she told him calmly. Then she looked back at Dean. 'I think I'll be requiring a little bit more now. You know – to help my business take flight.'

In time, the shame Dean felt was absorbed into his anger. She had made him do it. She had provoked him with those words, those vicious words.

If she had said con artist, fake or hustler, he would have been fine. But she'd said *ordinary bloke*.

Now, as he lay on his bed, Dean felt a whisper of something brushing against his forehead. It was his tissue paper crown from dinner earlier. He ripped it off, scrunched it into a ball until the red dye came off onto his hands. The Verity Flyer sped past again through a forest of miniature trees, effortlessly smooth.

So he was ordinary. He would always be ordinary. And he was done hiding it. Instead, he would weaponise it.

An idea clicked into his brain.

He snatched up his BlackBerry. He started by searching the Verity Flyer – one had recently gone for £800 online which was nice to know but hardly going to make his fortune. But below that were other links about Verity's trains, about the Emporium itself. *A classic case of an old-fashioned business that refused to move with the times.*

He jumped up from his bed, snatching the Flyer from its tracks. Even now it felt different to the other trains in his collection, heavier and more real, as if the engines really were being driven by a tiny stoker shovelling minute pieces of coal. It was the best – but it was too good. People didn't want things like that now, they wanted quick, affordable, does-the-job products. No wonder the Emporium had closed.

Train Crash Businesses became his first viral hit. Filmed from his childhood bedroom, talking about his passion, the words had come easily. He found a rhythm, mixing business-speak with the Essex slang he'd grown up with and using the Emporium as a case study about how old establishment companies adapt or die. What he – the Business Fixer – would have done to fix it. Instead of being the loser banging the door to get into an exclusive club, he was the maverick outsider throwing stones at the windows. And it worked. From that video came more subscribers, more exposure and more opportunities. Trad publishers offered him a book deal, trad businesses asked him in as a consultant. And the women – oh boy, the women loved a success story. He'd never let another woman get close, though, not after Nicole. Instead, he blazed a trail through the dating sites, staying charming but also clear that commitment wasn't going to happen.

'Love 'em and leave 'em,' his dad said the following Christmas, a hint of admiration in his voice, even as Nancy winced.

From then on he spent every Christmas with them, basking in their quiet pride, posting online about how it's important to return to your roots.

Throughout it all, though, his anger remained. An ugly, unglamorous beast chained in his chest, fighting to get free. Sometimes he'd lose control. Twice he'd had to pay off a trauma-tised employee – thank God for non-disclosure contracts – and it wasn't uncommon for him to punch holes in the wall. He tried deep breathing, hypnosis, even yoga, but that high, heady flush of rage in his chest was addictive, and couldn't be contained by hippie stuff. And as the years passed he started to wonder if keeping it inside was the answer. What if the solution was the same as it had been before?

Don't hide it, weaponise it.

18

MERRY

MERRY WATCHES FRAN WALK AWAY, BACK THROUGH THE DOOR into the tunnel, sees her grab the brandy bottle but leave the candle.

So, the lovely, perfect Fran Silver from daytime TV turns out to be a drunk, selfish, vain woman with secrets to hide and a huge grudge against Evangeline. Merry is starting to like her now. Maybe that's why she's so stung by what Fran said about her snooping around – or maybe it's because her words were so close to something Ross said to her once. But she can't think about that now. Thinking about Ross and the doubts he has about getting together will only make her unravel, and she has to stay focused on the current, deadly trap she's sitting in. It all leads back to the Emporium. Evangeline herself had some kind of falling-out with Monty and the letter she has just found backs up the idea that Benjamin did too:

Sir,

I find the letter of the tenth to be forthright bordering on rude. I have no ill intentions towards Clockwork Peg at all. I merely wished to make you an offer. The Goodchild Automaton is a unique creation rivalled only by the work of Pierre Jaquet-Droz. She is a delicate, finely balanced piece of machinery and at her age she belongs in a museum, not on a public shop floor where she is at risk of damage from customers and their children. Please consider my offer or I will be forced to take drastic action.

Forgive me for the strong wording of my letter, but I care greatly for the preservation of our heritage.

Best,

Benjamin Makepeace

Makepeace and Sherwin

The threads are all coming together. Evangeline and Benjamin had some kind of dispute going on with the Emporium. Dean had some kind of business connection too. Fran had seemed like Monty's biggest fan when they first arrived, but is definitely hiding something. But when Merry tries to think of a connection Josie might have, she's stumped. Or her boss Doug, for that matter. There's still something missing.

And speaking of which . . . Merry suddenly realises that when Fran stormed off she was probably headed straight to the Hall of Wonders to confront Evangeline, and she's missing it. Damn. She hefts her bag onto her shoulder again and runs to catch up, the snow globe knocking against her hip as she runs.

Weirdly, Fran is not there when she arrives in the Hall of Wonders – maybe she got lost in the passages on her way back. Instead, only Evangeline and Benjamin sit on the floor around the fire. The scene is strangely intimate. Evangeline reaches forward, her hand covering Benjamin's. Instinctively, Merry softens her step as she draws closer.

'Thank you,' Evangeline is saying. 'You really are a wonderful listener. Your wife doesn't know what she's missing. You're a very open, gentle human being. I can't remember the last time I felt such a good connection with someone.'

'Well, like I say, it's nothing,' Benjamin says. He sounds flustered, but does not withdraw his hand from under Evangeline's. 'You've been through a lot, and sometimes it helps to talk.'

'And you swear you won't tell anyone?'

'Word of honour. I never break that.'

Evangeline chuckles, but there's a sadness behind her light, tinkling laugh. 'Thank you. It feels good to talk to you, but nobody can ever know. Especially Fran.'

'Of course, of course. I have to say I'm surprised, though – she seems like a nice sort.'

'Let's just say she's good at performing.'

Just then, Merry becomes aware of a movement at her side. Fran bursts out of the passage and strides forward.

'You shut right up, Evangeline Fall, before you slander yourself.'

Evangeline scrambles to her feet. She's clearly stiff from all that time on the floor, but she styles it out, places her hands on her hips. Merry senses another movement behind her. It's Josie, cramming something into her tote, which is looking much

185

plumper than it was before. There's no time to process this detail, though, not while Fran is completely losing it. Evangeline tilts her chin, holding onto her dignity.

'I have no idea what you're talking about. You've been acting like this ever since we got locked in here. Benjamin, have I done one single thing to deserve this kind of behaviour from Fran?'

'Well, I – I can't say I want to get involved . . .'

'Well, I haven't. It's you, picking away at me, making your sarcastic little comments.'

Fran's face is twisted with rage in the flickering firelight.

'So you're saying you didn't write that note?'

'Yet again, Fran, I have no idea what you're talking about.'

Fran gives an incoherent roar of rage and storms over to the door where most of the shoppers stowed their things. She grabs Evangeline's cream leather slouchy bag and returns to the fireplace, up-ending it over the rug. Luxury ephemera tips out – expensive lipsticks roll across the carpet, a jar of face cream follows, then a high-end purse, leather soft as butter. But with all this comes an avalanche of Emporium goodies – tiny, jewelled music boxes, carved figurines, bottles of fragrance.

'You've got a lot of stuff in there,' Josie says. 'Planning to pay for it all, were you, or just getting the five-fingered discount?'

But nobody responds – Fran has sunk to her knees and is raking through the debris, muttering to herself. Evangeline is there, too, grabbing her bag, trying to scrape things back in.

Fran seems to find what she's looking for – a brown leather-bound notebook, pages edged in silver. She flicks fervently through.

'Hah! There it is. I knew it! You wrote that note. I can see where you ripped the page out.'

Evangeline looks at her, stony-faced. 'I still have no idea what you're talking about.'

'Don't deny it,' Fran screams, throwing the notebook at Evangeline. She grabs a screwed-up paper out of her pocket and flings that at her, too. 'The evidence is right here!'

Benjamin gets to his feet and steps between the two women. He's probably planning to say something like 'Calm down, ladies.' Merry braces herself for how that's going to go down. But then he looks down at something lying on the floor between them and stops. It's a familiar, dark rectangle.

'You've got a phone,' he says. 'Evangeline, you had a phone all along?'

Everyone in the room stares at Evangeline. Merry goes still with shock. Fran must have been right, she is involved somehow.

'I *knew* it,' Fran repeats, her voice a low growl. 'What's your game?'

'That's . . . not my phone,' Evangeline says. 'Well, it is, it's a spare I use for personal apps, like PeelYu. I knew Monty was going to confiscate my phone before I came in – I know how much he hates them, so I smuggled an extra one in so I could take photos of stock for clients.'

'And you didn't think to tell us about it until now?' Josie asks, her tone heavy with scepticism. 'Even after we found a FUCKING DEAD BODY IN SANTA'S GROTTO.'

Merry stares at Evangeline, watches her take a breath, evidently trying to get her story straight. She's definitely lying about something, Merry can always tell when people are lying. But at the back of her mind, hope is rising. They have a phone. This could all be over.

187

Her imagination flashes forward – going home. Having Christmas. Ross unwrapping the snow globe, stunned at what Merry had to go through to get it. Freedom.

Benjamin snatches up the phone. It's a high-end model, of course, sleek and black and far too stylish to be hidden away by a phone case. He flips it over, and Merry can see that the screen is smashed. Benjamin holds his finger over the power button, but the phone doesn't respond.

'It's been like that all night, I swear,' Evangeline says. 'I think I dropped it when Barbara and I were stumbling around in the dark and it's been dead ever since.'

'Oh, you *think* you dropped it,' Fran mocks. 'You're lying about this like you lied about everything else.'

'Oh, that's rich coming from *you*,' Evangeline says. 'I think these people should know what sort of person you really are. Why don't you tell everyone here about how you—'

Fran lunges at Evangeline, who yelps as both women topple back into the display of crystal baubles. There's an explosion of shattering glass as Fran lies on top of Evangeline, struggling for purchase.

Evangeline speaks again.

'You see, she's a hypocritical bitch who—'

Fran shoves her hand hard over Evangeline's mouth.

'Ladies!' shouts Benjamin, but nobody pays any attention to him.

'Fran, she's not worth it,' Josie yells, grabbing at Fran's shoulders.

'I can't stop!' Fran's voice comes out as a choking sob now. 'Not until I know she's going to be quiet. Evangeline, please, you can't say. You can't.'

Evangeline thrashes and fights, her hands flail up, catching Fran in the eye. Fran's grip loosens for a moment, long enough for Evangeline to shout 'Stop!' but then Fran's hands are down again, covering both her nose and mouth. Evangeline's eyes widen with fear.

'You're suffocating her,' Merry says, her voice too quiet for Fran to hear. She is frozen, her body afraid to take direct action, to even move without thinking through every ramification first. Merry has spent her life stirring pots, gently pushing people to do what she wants them to do, but she has never directly stepped into a fight before. Fran is weeping now, her eyes streaming with tears, her grip on Evangeline's face pressing harder and harder.

'Stop!' Benjamin is the one who grabs Fran by the shoulders, pulls her back and away from her victim. She tumbles towards Josie, who lays a hand on her, holding her back, but Fran's fight is gone. She is sobbing hysterically.

First Dean and now Fran, both people with charming, confident exteriors who have seeds of desperation buried deep inside them that erupt into violence. *Not me, though*, thinks Merry. *I can't even take a step forward to save someone's life.*

She doesn't know what's worse.

Evangeline is half-coughing, half-sobbing. Her lipstick, which has remained mysteriously fresh all night, is smudged across her face. Her eyes are hollow with shock.

'I'm sorry,' Fran begins, her voice cracked.

'Just leave me alone, all of you.' The words come out in a furious sob. Then, in a storm of tears, Evangeline turns and runs.

19

FRAN

FRAN IS SHAKING ALL OVER, HER HEART POUNDING, HER BODY drenched in sweat.

'That was a bit much, Fran,' Josie says quietly. Benjamin just stares at her in silence. And Merry – creeping, conniving Merry – is watching her with her eyes narrowed. Her thinking expression.

A part of her is exhilarated. Yelling at Evangeline had given her a high as she tapped into the rich and venomous vein of anger that had been buried deep inside her. But then . . . She looks down at her hands, trembling, aching and still slick with Evangeline's spit. She had been out of control. She could have killed her; she *would* have killed her. The horror of this realisation overwhelms her.

The others are staring at her with a mixture of pity and fear. They are expecting an explanation – they want Fran to tell them why their cuddly cancer-campaigning national treasure would do such a thing – and she can't think of anything to tell them but the truth, and that's unthinkable, however much it seems to want to come out.

Fran turns on her heel and runs in the opposite direction to Evangeline, into the secret passage she came from just minutes ago.

Her heartbeat is slowing now, she can think straight, absorb her surroundings. She notices a lamp glowing around a corner which is strange – she hasn't seen any gas lamps in the passages before. Instinctively, she moves towards the light and it leads her out through a door which seems to be covered in a mosaic of mirrors, and onto the mezzanine floor.

She emerges near the counter in the Hall of Delicacies and sinks down behind it. The drunk feeling has leached out of her, but she doesn't think she will ever stop shaking, and when she closes her eyes, all she sees is Evangeline's terrified face, her hair sticking to her forehead, her eyes wide. *This is the real you, Fran.*

All those years of charity work, of denying herself all but the smallest of pleasures, of trying to be a good person, pretending to be someone who deserves to live a full and cancer-free life. They all meant nothing because deep down she is rotten to the core.

And there is no way that Evangeline will back off now; when she goes back to the group she'll tell them everything she knows.

Briefly, ever so quickly, the thought flitters through Fran's mind. *If only Evangeline were dead.*

Fran shakes her head. She's not a killer . . . but then, she so nearly was. And just then, Fran faces an awful, undeniable truth about herself. If she had a chance to make Evangeline disappear off the face of the earth without getting caught, she would do it. *Maybe we're all ruthless killers deep down inside, no matter how many fun runs we've been on.*

It's then that she hears movement on the other side of the counter.

Evangeline is standing there, leaning against the balustrade, looking down at the atrium below. And next to her is a figure in a top hat and frock coat. Merry was right, Monty was involved.

'I kept my half of the bargain,' Evangeline says. 'I never breathed a word to them, just as you asked.'

Fran feels a surge of rage at the vindication of her suspicions. Evangeline *was* involved – that two faced snake.

'I wasn't just doing it for the money, I thought we were friends.' Evangeline's voice cracks into a sob. 'But this was all part of your plan, wasn't it? It never was Dean talking to me on PeelYu, was it? It was you all along.'

It's then that she notices the way Evangeline is standing, holding her body stiffly, her fingers curled tightly around the balustrade. She is afraid, and Fran can see why. One of the glistening filaments which hang from the ceiling into the Hall of Wonders below is looped around Evangeline's neck, like a noose. Evangeline begins to weep.

Fran takes a step forward. 'Monty, stop!'

As she does so Monty draws back and kicks Evangeline hard in the back of her knees. Evangeline shrieks as her legs give way and he pushes her hard. The balustrade splinters and breaks and she falls forward and down, suspended from the filament by her neck. Her body writhes, legs thrashing as the filament swings back and forth over the Hall of Wonders below, her hands at her throat, trying to pull away the sparkling noose. The only sound that comes from her mouth is a dry, sickening choke.

Monty's silhouette whirls away, in that trademark flurry of coat skirts, and he is gone, leaving Evangeline twisting and struggling in the air.

Fran screams.

20

MERRY

MERRY IS BY THE DOOR, JUST ABOUT TO START SNOOPING THROUGH people's bags, when she hears the crashing, splintering sound. A section of balustrade smashes to the floor just feet away from her and then there is a single, deafening scream.

She jumps to her feet, horrified by the sight of Evangeline swinging from the ceiling.

Do something. She failed to act last time, now she forces her body to move, dropping her own bag with a clunk, racing to the centre of the room and climbing up on one of the tables, scattering tangled puppets as she goes. She reaches up but still Evangeline is too high up – her kicking feet over a metre above her.

'Here, quick!' Benjamin appears from the shadows, struggling to carry another display table, mashing baubles and trinkets as he swings it towards her. They hoist it up onto the table below

Evangeline, and Benjamin – who is a little taller than Merry – clambers up. Something falls and hits him on the head, bouncing off to one side. It's one of Evangeline's shoes.

But Evangeline's legs have stopped kicking now. Her arms, which had been clawing at her neck, hang limp at her sides, and she twists, like a Christmas fairy hanging from the ceiling.

They're too late. She's too late again. But still Benjamin reaches out, leaping upwards. For a moment he is airborne, arms flailing, flinging himself around Evangeline's legs. He finds purchase, clinging on in a way that could only have made things worse for Evangeline had she been alive, before the filament suspending her from the ceiling finally breaks. Merry throws herself out of the way as the two come crashing down.

For a moment there is silence. Benjamin moves, groans. His breath is ragged.

'Are you hurt?' Merry asks. His skin has a greyish tinge, there is a sheen of sweat on him, and he will not let go of Evangeline.

'No. A little chest pain, that's all. It's just a little heart thing. I've been dealing with it all my life. But it doesn't matter. Not when Evangeline . . .'

Merry does not have the energy to stand. Instead, she crawls across the soft carpet, through piles of puppet debris, splinters digging into her palms.

Evangeline's eyes are open, her face tortuously twisted. Merry never usually touches anyone unless she has to, but she clings to Benjamin's shoulder to stop herself from collapse.

'Oh my God.' A hollow voice behind her tells her that Josie is here too. And then she hears a sob from above.

Peering down from the gallery a pinched, frightened face. Hands gripping the broken balustrade.

'Fran, what the fuck did you do?' Josie roars.

'It wasn't me,' Fran sobs. 'I swear, it wasn't me.'

Benjamin and Josie are on their feet, looking up, shouting up at Fran. Accusations flying, denials, aggressive defences. Merry would usually be listening to it all, storing up little nuggets of information, but she can't stop looking at Evangeline. She looks so afraid, so much in pain. The sparkling filament has cut into her neck like wire. There's blood in some places where the hundreds of tiny crystals have bitten into Evangeline's skin. Surely those decorations shouldn't have been strong enough to hold the weight of a human being. She finds the broken end and takes it in her hands. It's much thicker than she thought it was, more of a nylon cord than a delicate strand. It's hard to tell, looking upwards in the gaslight, but it seems sturdier than the others above.

It's also knotted, as if the loop was waiting there all along, ready for someone to slip Evangeline's head into it and push her. A pre-prepared noose.

Someone has been planning this for a long time. Someone has had access to the Emporium to set this up. To reinforce the windows and remove the phones. To conceal a noose-strength Christmas decoration among the thinner filaments hanging from the ceiling. Fran hated Evangeline and she's definitely hiding something, but there is no way she'd murder someone she's just argued with in such an elaborate, attention-grabbing way.

She struggles to her feet, turns to where the others are still yelling up at Fran. And Fran is weeping, gibbering, 'It's Monty. I saw him. Merry was right, it's Monty.'

It's chaos. Nobody is thinking, everybody is shouting. Merry feels a wave of frustration coming over her, realising that if she doesn't speak up, take control of what's happening, then the whole situation will escalate again.

'Benjamin,' she says, choosing the least shouty of her companions. She keeps her voice low and reasonable, and it stops him in his tracks. When he falls silent, Josie stops shouting, too, and Merry continues.

'Think for a minute! There's no way Fran could have done this.'

'Oh, come on,' Josie says. 'It's obvious. Evangeline knew something and Fran was desperate for her not to tell. Now she conveniently turns up dead?'

'You have to admit it doesn't look good,' Benjamin adds. Fran gives an agonised cry from the floor above. Merry's first instinct is to roll her eyes and walk away but if they're going to get out, they need to keep it together.

'Listen, Evangeline was *hanged* from one of the Christmas decorations.' Merry's voice falters for a moment at the sheer horror of what happened. She feels a bubble of sadness pushing up inside her, for a woman she barely knew and never really liked.

She takes a breath. Continues.

'If Fran wanted to kill her she might have pushed her off the balcony or smashed something over her head, but this was already set up, ready to go, premeditated. Fran attacked Evangeline because she was out of control. No way did she sneak into the store before tonight and do all this.'

Josie nods reluctantly. 'Yeah, I see what you mean. And no way would she have been able to get Evangeline close enough to put the noose around her. Not after what had just happened. It had to be someone she trusted.'

'She was talking to him,' Fran adds from above. 'She was saying she'd done her part and asking to be let out and then he just . . . turned on her.'

Evangeline was working with Monty. It made a weird sort of sense. She had provoked Fran and Dean into acting rashly, and she and Monty had exchanged some pretty weird looks earlier. But where did her blackmailing letter fit in? Maybe that's why Monty turned on her. Merry shudders.

'Monty knows the secret passages,' Benjamin adds. 'He did something to the windows . . .'

It all comes back to Monty. He'd been cranking the gears since they got here. Asking them their secret Christmas wishes, making little digs, blinding them with cheap conjuring tricks and misdirection. Winding them up like good little automata and letting them loose on each other.

And he was still here, messing with their heads.

Well, two could play that game.

Merry is sure there is no way out. They're up against someone who knows the place inside out, everything will be locked down. And yes, Barbara had found a way around this, but she can't imagine Monty making the same mistake again.

Their best chance to take control of the situation is to get ahead of him and to do that they need to arm themselves with knowledge. They have to – *ugh* – work together.

She drags Barbara's suitcase and Dean's bag over to the fireplace, where Benjamin and Josie are sitting, staring into space, still processing the shock.

'Fran accused me of sneaking around earlier,' Merry says. 'So I think we should do this together. I'm going to go through Dean's, Evangeline's and Barbara's stuff to see if there's anything in here that can help us.'

She rolls the suitcase towards Josie. 'Can you use your screwdriver thingy to break the locks?'

Josie burrows into her bag for her keys, only opening it as wide as she needs, and holding the top together afterwards, as if she is guarding something precious. She sets to work, and the lock is off in seconds.

'I don't think we should be doing this,' Benjamin says. 'It's vulgar. No, it's downright *wrong* to snoop in people's private things. Especially now they are . . . no longer with us.'

Merry knew there would be some push-back from Benjamin, but for the first time she wonders if he is right. Sometimes she forgets that other people don't have her innate, built-in curiosity that seems to trump all sense of right and wrong. Benjamin's strict moral code fascinates her. It must be so difficult to live like that.

'Have you ever broken a law, Benjamin?'

'I wish I could say no but yes, I have, when I was younger and more foolish. I trespassed in here to look at Peg. But it was for the greater good – she was being shockingly neglected.' He gives a high, nervous laugh. Merry notices again that his skin is unnaturally waxy in colour. Perhaps he had a more serious reaction to Monty's sleeping potion than anyone else. He did say something about a 'heart thing' earlier.

'*You* sneaked in here to look at Clockwork Peg?' Josie asks, a strange smile on her face.

'It's a tragedy, it really is. She needs careful restoration, then to be displayed somewhere safe, not kept in the middle of a toy department full of children. Did you know there was an incident in the Eighties in which a child knocked her over and she fell to the floor? She was never quite the same after that.'

A thought pops into Merry's head. 'So if you had the chance, you might even steal her?'

She doesn't listen to his response – a spluttered denial – but watches his expression instead. His previously pallid face has gone livid red, his jaw is working up and down as if chewing invisible gum. A picture of discomfort. He really is a terrible liar.

'How would you go about stealing a full-sized wood-and-metal woman?' Josie asks. 'She's bloody heavy.'

'I never said I . . .' Benjamin stops and sighs, giving up. 'I prefer to think of it as a rescue. I know some people – one meets people like this in the trade sometimes – people who can help you liberate certain items. A private collector I know was willing to take her on, keep her a secret, and restore her to her former glory.'

He sighs, sitting back onto a broken display table. 'I was planning to slip away during the shopping trip last night. I had arranged to collect a set of keys a staff member had agreed to lend us. But then I accepted a mug of hot chocolate and before I knew it I was sledging in the toy department.'

'Oh right, "borrow!"' Josie laughs, digging through neat piles of dull, M&S clothing in Barbara's case. 'No judgement from me, mate. I like you better now I know you can be a bit naughty too. But I really fucking wish you had those keys.'

So Benjamin meant to steal Peg? Merry does not react, but files the information away, letting Josie and Benjamin chatter as she flicks through Evangeline's leather-bound notebook. It's not a personal diary but more a book of to-do lists that she shares – no, *shared* – with her assistant. Her spiky handwriting, as well as Barbara's more rounded scrawl, fills the notebook. Most of it is businesslike; client names, including a few minor celebrities, and shopping lists of outlandish Christmas decorations: *Taxidermy reindeer x 2. 100m silk swagging. Sleigh.*

Fancy.

But there are occasional doodles and scrawls in the margin – stars and whirls she must have drawn while she was on the phone. Hints of a hidden self which make Merry realise that she never got to know Evangeline, and that now she never will.

Near the back is a page documenting Dean's movements. *Tuesday: Speech at Westminster Uni. Xmas Eve: Emporium!!* Next to that date, she had even listed what she was planning to wear. *Barbara: get cream cashmere sweater from dry cleaner's.*

Evangeline had definitely been low-level stalking him and Dean had clearly not been interested. So why had he started messaging her on that posh-people's Tinder app? And why had he denied it?

Because it wasn't really him. The answer is obvious. Merry's not into posting on social media, but she does have an Instagram account which she uses for snooping on other people, and it's constantly besieged by fake men sidling into her DMs with lines about how lovely she is. Perhaps someone – read, Monty – had set up a fake PeelYu account in Dean's name to give Evangeline hope, to lure her here.

This is all a bit close to the bone, because wasn't hope what brought her here, too? The snow globe, with its model of the perfect couple at the fairground, weighs heavily in her bag. Her plan to nudge Ross out of the friend zone into soul mates territory is just a bad as Evangeline's stalking. Worse, even, because Ross has already knocked her back.

To be fair, it hadn't been a 'never', more of a 'not yet'. They had been out late that night. Merry had scored them tickets to an open-air screening of one of Ross's favourite Studio Ghibli animations. She'd brought a picnic like the ones Ross said he'd always loved – a 'proper' one with a tartan wool blanket and a real wicker basket. With crockery and sandwiches and a chilled bottle of white.

'You've made it perfect,' Ross had said. But his voice was uneasy, it hadn't sounded like a compliment.

Still, they had laid out together, gazing at the screen, the night sky, the people around them who were shifting and fidgeting on the stony park lawn. Merry could feel Ross's body close to her, as if there was a force field around him, drawing her in. She was afraid to make the first move, to break the spell and scare him off but she couldn't just wait here forever, setting up these perfect kiss-me scenarios that never came to anything.

She reached out and, with her little finger, brushed against his hand.

Ross made a whimpering sound. Merry wasn't sure if it was sheer pleasure or the pain of holding himself back. Emboldened, she slid her hand over his. He turned to face her and she smiled.

But then his body tensed. He moved his hand away, turned on his side to face her.

'Mez, I . . .'

'I know, I know,' Merry said hastily, her face hot with embarrassment and regret. 'Friends. Best mates. Got it. Won't do it again.'

'No, it's not that it's just . . .' Ross gave a sigh, and sat up. Merry didn't like being lower down than him so she sat up too.

'It's all this,' he went on sweeping his arm out to cover the picnic basket, the screen, the warm night air. 'My favourite film, my favourite smoked salmon sandwiches. The lovely basket. You keep doing this. Setting up scenarios, trying to make things happen. Love's not like that – or it shouldn't be. It's about knocking about together, having fun, feeling something in the moment and just acting on it. This process of arranging things just so, it reminds me . . .'

Oh God, don't say it, Merry prays. But he does.

'It reminds me of my mum.'

Merry feels a cold thud of disappointment. Of opportunities closing down. Of rejection. Reminding your beloved of their mother is never good, but when the mother in question is a conniving, cunning queen of passive aggression it's devastating.

'I wasn't trying to control you,' she said. 'I just wanted to do something nice. I know you love this film. I know you love picnics. I provided both, what's wrong with that? You're seeing things that aren't there.'

Ross had drawn his knees up in front of him, holding his arms around his legs protectively. He looked away, and Merry felt guilt roll over her. The words she had just spoken were bordering on gaslighting. She was fully aware she had a habit of tweaking situations to get the desired result. But sometimes she wondered what was wrong with that? How else could she reach him? And comparing her to his mother was a low blow.

'I'm not Rita. Not in any way. Aren't I the one who always said you had to break free from her? I hate the way she's treated you.'

'No, I know,' Ross said. 'But you have to understand I'm a bit sensitive to this stuff right now. And this – whatever it is – with us. I don't want to mess it up. I don't want to lose you as a friend.'

She let shame and mortification win, shifting her body away from him, helping herself to another bloody smoked salmon sandwich.

'Mez, I know you're not my mum. I'm sorry. But sometimes you just have to be patient and let people make their own decisions.'

Now, in the cold semi-darkness of the Emporium, Merry understands what it feels like to be under someone else's control.

She picks up the crumpled paper Fran threw to the floor during her argument with Evangeline, unscrews it and reads. *I know what you did.*

Yet another piece of manipulation designed to push nice, fundraising and possibly-an-alcoholic Fran into a meltdown. Oh, he was good.

She is desperate to know what Fran did, but it'll have to wait. She reaches for the slim man-bag that belonged to Dean and opens the catch. She will make do with these secrets for now.

There's not much in there. An expensive set of earbuds, a wallet containing several platinum cards and a membership card for an expensive gym, but no cash or twee photos of loved ones. A dog-eared bit of white pokes out from the back and Merry slides out a business card. Working at J.D. Stimpson means she's absorbed a decent enough knowledge of paper stock and print quality to know that this is a low-budget design – not the sort of business card she'd expect to find in Dean Hallibutt's wallet. It says:

Gary Shrike
@no1veritysgeek
#verityslondon #veritysthetruth

The card is scuffed and grubby at the edges. Dean didn't grab it from Gary outside last night, it's been in his wallet for some time. It's an unlikely combination. Dean was all about opportunity, about chasing the mighty dollar – Gary looked piss-poor and is fixated on a Victorian department store that nobody cares about when it isn't Christmas. There must have been something in it for Dean.

Next, she pulls out a red envelope, the same kind that Doug's Emporium invitation had come in. The invitation card is gone, of course, but inside is a handwritten note.

My associate is willing to do business after all. M.R.V.

There's also an A4 bound booklet. She pulls it out and sees the grey, angular Business Fixer logo on the front.

VERITY'S EMPORIUM PROPOSAL

The document is heavy on numbers, impenetrable pie charts and business terminology, but flicking through, a few things jump out. Dean spoke of his 'deep personal connection' with the Emporium and his 'profound respect for its values', which is usually what people say when they are about to tear down said values. She flicks to the last page, hoping for some kind of summing-up paragraph.

In short, I would waive my usual fee and exchange my business expertise for a share in the company and a seat on the Board. By solving your supply issues I would be able to increase your profit margins by over seventy-five per cent.

Merry had already known that Dean was here to do a deal, but getting a seat on the board? That didn't seem like Dean's style. As a consultant he usually went into companies, mansplained what they were doing wrong then moved on, but not before posting a bunch of videos about it online.

The answer comes when she flicks through the proposal again and notices another logo tucked away in the pages for a company called Leaping Lords Productions.

. . . as per the proposal I sent earlier, Leaping Lords feels that a documentary series about my work with the Emporium – transforming it into a business for the twenty-first century – would make great viewing and catapult both the Business Fixer brand, and Verity's Emporium to international fame. Past documentaries about other stores have had a significant impact on brand recognition and customer footfall.

Now, that makes sense to Merry. The 'deal of a lifetime' wasn't just about money, it was about super-charging Dean's brand, taking the Business Fixer to the next level. And somehow Rudi had done something to blow it apart. She adds that to her mental list of things she absolutely has to know.

'Nothing here,' Josie says, breaking her reverie. She's holding up hideously bland beige T-shirt which looks just Barbara's style. 'Just a few summer clothes for Australia and some Christmas presents for her kid. A scarf. A really boring-looking book. I hope she made her flight.'

Merry hopes so too. At the back of her mind she's been wondering if Barbara made it out at all, or if she came to some harm. Fran should have been back by now, too. It would be wise to stick together from now on.

Benjamin is tapping at his pocket watch, a predictably antique specimen. 'It's stopped, dash it.'

He gets up and walks over to the Great Clock to reset it. And then he stops.

'I think you need to see this,' he says, his voice flat.

He holds up his candle and the light flickers on the model Emporium. There's the mangled Santa on the third floor, the broken Dean model on the ground outside. And now there is a third figure suspended from the ceiling of the miniature atrium. It's the one with the festive wreath, the one Evangeline said looked nothing like her. It's still swinging slightly, as if the person who put it there has only just left.

21

FRAN

FRAN RUNS IN THE DARKNESS, THROUGH THE SECRET PASSAGES. She is not thinking, has no idea where she is going, can't even see beyond the flashing lights of her Christmas jumper. All she wants to do is get away from Evangeline's broken body, from the accusing faces she saw down in the Hall of Wonders.

Evangeline is gone. Fran's head is filled with horror. All traces of drunkenness have seeped away from her but now she's caught in a loop of sights, sounds and feelings. She can hear the wood crashing, the sickening, choking sound, the precise, jerking dance of Evangeline's legs, as they struggled to gain a foothold on thin air. And the helpless immobility in her limbs as it had happened. Fran knows now that she would never have been capable of anything as bad as this. She is not a killer. She's not sure the others will believe it, though, whatever Merry says.

Images flow through her head as she runs. She thinks about home, and comfort, and the precise tone of Mr Duncan Biscuits' purr when he knows she's holding a packet of Dreamies. She thinks about Dr Raynsford and how much her behaviour has let him down; about Zelda, still clinging on as her friend and agent after all these years. She had cut herself off from most of her friends, thinking she didn't deserve them, but she hadn't thought until now about the fact it hurt Zelda, too, that disconnecting from her friend was also an act of selfishness.

Her lungs are burning now, her elbows and knees bruised from running into hidden steps and walls. Out of breath, she drops to a walk. She has no idea where she is.

She should feel vindicated. She'd been right all along, Evangeline was in it up to her neck. But she doesn't feel like that at all. Not after what she just saw. Monty had clearly promised to pay the woman for her co-operation, but then he had turned on her. Fran knows now that nobody is going to walk out of here alive. *I give up. I might as well just curl up in the darkness and wait for him to finish me off.*

She leans back against the wall, the will to fight draining away.

And then she feels it. A soft tug somewhere in her belly; a sense that something is nearby, that it wants her to follow.

Her mother would definitely have followed and so Fran does too.

Her mind races. Who or what is guiding her? What do they want? But every time she questions it too much she loses the connection. Fran takes in a long breath, lets it out, tries not to overthink.

Up a flight of stairs, around a corner, and she finds herself drawn to a small wooden door – about half the size of a normal door. It sticks in the frame but after a couple of pushes it opens.

The room inside is only just big enough to stand up in. A tiny gas light burns on the wall and there is a narrow metal-framed bed rammed against the far side. Much as Fran would love to sleep, there is nothing inviting about the withered, sagging mattress.

'Who slept here?' she asks the darkness. But the presence doesn't answer.

She runs her hand over the metal headboard and sees that the white paint has been scratched away, made into an intricate pattern of swirls and flounces and fleurs-de-lys, the kind of pattern made by someone who can't help but create beauty even when they're locked in a tiny room like this. And at the heart of it, a set of initials. M.G.

It takes her a couple of moments to figure it out, and maybe without the presence there she would never have done so. Peg is short for Peggy. Peggy is short for Margaret. M.G., Margaret Goodchild, had slept in this tiny windowless room.

'I don't understand,' Fran says. 'You were part of London society, you were hailed as a genius – why did you end up living here?'

She stares more closely at the swirls in the headboard and then, like one of those old-fashioned Magic Eye images, the shapes resolve themselves into something quite different. Letters. Words, hidden in the pattern.

Daughter. Mother. Slave.

This couldn't be right. Enslavement had been made illegal decades before Peggy was brought here. 1807 – the date had burned itself into Fran's brain during a long-ago history class. But

209

then, Peggy had worked when Everard Verity told her to work, slept where he told her to sleep – how was that any different from slavery? Tucked under the bed is a medium-sized wooden box, and inside are the tattered remains of a pillow, a blanket. A makeshift baby's cot.

'You had a baby, and he locked you up here because of it?'

Of course there is no reply, but Fran's instinct fills in the gaps. This is where the real Peggy Goodchild had ended her days – illegally enslaved, holed up in a cell in the Emporium. And then after she died, Everard Verity had made a clockwork recreation of her, playing an endless song of loss on her piano. It's sickening.

Shoved further under the bed, behind the tiny cradle, she notices something else – fabric in a modern shade of green, the glint of a zip. It's some kind of holdall. She lowers herself down flat, trying to tug the bag free without touching the desperately sad cradle. It's stuck, caught in the under-springs of the mattress. She grabs the tag on the zip and tugs harder. The zip gives, undoing a pocket at the end of the holdall, and something rolls out.

It's a small vial, very much like the ones Fran used to photograph when posting about her cancer treatment. This one's not familiar to her, though. It's empty, but for a smear of powder at the base of the jar. The label bears a name which is vaguely familiar, but too long and too complicated for her to retain in her memory, and it's covered with biohazard signs. Fran drops it immediately. It's some kind of poison.

This bag, it must be Monty's. He must have been hiding out here, using this as a base in between sneaking out to watch them, to hurt them. He had lit the gas lamp in here. And he could be back at any moment.

Just then, she hears the unmistakeable sound of footsteps coming up the stairs outside. It's a light, soft tread. Someone is creeping up on her.

Panicking, Fran grabs the vial, dives out of the open door and runs out into the passage, away from the stairs, but she's too late. There, holding a candle in one hand, and peering through the darkness at her, is Josie.

'Thank fuck, we thought he'd killed you,' she says.

'And you came looking for me?' Fran is doubtful, she feels fear slithering through her belly. Josie knows her way around these tunnels all too well. Maybe she was looking for Fran, or maybe she's also colluding with Monty and was coming to pick up his supply of poison.

'Course. Like Merry says, we should all stick together.'

'*Merry* said that?'

Josie shrugs and turns back along the corridor. Fran follows uncertainly. She should tell Josie about what she saw in the little room, about the vial in her jeans pocket. But if she's working with Monty . . .

'Hurry up,' Josie says impatiently, and as she does, one of the handles on her bag snaps and it falls to the floor, gaping open. Fran moves forward to help but Josie pulls the bag towards herself, almost snarling to keep Fran away.

Josie moved quickly but there was still enough time for Fran to see it. The faint sheen of sharp metal in her bag. It looks like a knife.

22

MERRY

BENJAMIN IS SICK. HE REFUSES TO ADMIT IT, FORCES HIMSELF TO
stand upright like a soldier on parade but he is swaying, and his
eyes look bloodshot and strange.

'I'm fine,' he says. 'Just a little tired, is all. I'm usually in bed
by nine thirty with a cup of cocoa. And Louisa always says . . . I
mean, she did always say, before she moved out, that I was like an
eighty-year-old man trapped in a fifty-four-year-old's body . . .'

His shoulders sag.

'She moved out? I'm sorry.' Merry's not sure if she means it
or she's doing it to get information out of him. It's probably a bit
of both.

'I lied when I said I had only broken the law once,' he says.
'I broke it again, another time and she covered for me. I think she
lost all respect for me that day. And when she found out about
my plan for Clockwork Peg . . . I can't say she approves. She

moved out three days ago. She's staying with her mother; she won't even speak to me.'

He is weeping now, tears flowing silently down his cheeks.

'And although I searched this place as well as I could – although the whole Emporium is full of wonders – I can't find the right gift. I can't find the way to say I'm sorry.'

'I don't think there is a present for that. You have to say it. You have to use words.' Merry finds that her hand has crept into her bag, that she's gripping the snow globe. 'Sometimes if you want something, all you have to do is ask for it outright. Tell her you're sorry. Tell her how you feel, then leave it up to her.'

You just have to ask. The truth in those words stops Merry in her tracks. She has never asked Ross outright how he feels. Instead, she has laid a complex trail of signs and signals which confused and even irritated him, hoping to prompt him to make the first move. Maybe that's what she should do, when this is over. No engineered perfect Christmas, no mood-setting music and persuasive presents. Just tell him, and then trust him.

But first, she has to get out of here.

She and Benjamin are standing in the far corner of the Emporium, where a group of Victorian-style dolls is lined up in front of a large blackboard. They hold slates in their stiff little hands, set up to look like they're in a fake schoolroom that hasn't existed since the early twentieth century. *Seriously, who buys this stuff?*

She kicks the dolls aside and grabs a nearby piece of chalk, clearing the board with her sleeve, ignoring the subsequent flashing lights of her jumper, and writing 'Verity's Emporium' in the middle, and all of their names around the outside.

Next to Dean she writes: *Attempted takeover. Working with Gary Shrike to uncover scandal. TV show.*

She moves on to Evangeline's name, writing: *Passing off Emporium products as her own. Some kind of blackmail re Emporium's history. Colluding with Monty?*

'I think that last part is true,' Benjamin says. 'She told me, as we sat by the fire, that she was in debt and had accepted a large amount of money from someone to come here. She told me she had agreed to "play along" with the plans for last night.'

Merry has to fight to stop herself from grabbing Benjamin. 'What else did she say? Did she confirm it was Monty?'

'No, she just said it was supposed to be a prank, and if we all played along we'd be let out in the morning. I must admit at the time I found it reassuring but now . . . She was evidently lied to. Monty, or whoever has us here, does not intend us to survive Christmas.'

Benjamin's voice is strangely calm as he says this. He sinks down onto one of the dolls' desks, in an odd pose, holding one arm with the other.

Merry's jaw sets. No way is she going to let some pound-shop Willy Wonka get away with this.

'I am not going to let that happen,' she promises him. Merry is not in the habit of making promises, and she intends not to break this one. She turns back to the board.

Next to Benjamin's name, she puts: *Trespass. Plans to steal Peg. Other lawbreaking???*

She raises an eyebrow at Benjamin, who gives a little whimpering noise, like he is in pain, but does not elaborate.

Then she turns to Fran's name.

As if on cue, Fran and Josie appear from the shadowy doorway behind the cash desk.

'I found her! She's not dead!'

Fran peers at the chart Merry is making, and Merry flushes.

'I suppose this is what the inside of your brain looks like all the time,' Fran says. It doesn't sound like a compliment, but Merry still can't see what's wrong with thinking this way, of parsing through cause and effect on instinct. If she was a police officer or a politician or some kind of campaigner for social justice she'd have changed the world by now.

You could do so much better. Why not just leave?

As usual, Ross had been one hundred per cent right.

Here she was, thirty years old, and she had wasted a whole decade of her mental energies keeping Doug from blowing his top with the design department, manipulating the office refit so she didn't end up sitting next to Egg Sandwich Ed – and trying to get Ross to love her.

'I'm doing this for everyone,' Merry says, indicating the words on the board. 'Me included. So come on, Fran, spill.'

Fran fidgets with a ring on her finger.

'All I'll say is that the thing I'm hiding, it's nothing to do with the Emporium. I love Christmas, and I love this place, or at least I did when I first got here, but I've never had anything to do with it. Full disclosure, I was at university with Monty's cousin, but he was a bit of a wanker and I avoided him as much as possible.'

Merry keeps silent, holding Fran's gaze. The others are following her every lead now, just watching. But she can see that Fran is not going to break.

'You're just going to have to trust me, Merry. This is something you're never going to know.'

Fran cannot know how provocative that statement is, how the thought of not knowing will nag and nag at her like a hangnail catching on her Christmas jumper. Under ordinary circumstances, Merry would back off and find out later, but things have gone too far for that.

'Just tell me,' she says, taking a step forward, invading Fran's personal space. 'It could save our lives – it could be the key to everything. Is it about money? All that charity cash?'

A look of horror crosses Fran's face. Merry is onto something.

'That's it, isn't it?' Josie cuts in. 'You've been thieving, haven't you? What kind of scum nicks charity cash?'

A range of expressions flicker across Fran's face. She looks as if she is going to cry or protest, but then she shrugs.

'Yeah, that's it.' Her voice is colourless, as if she's surrendering. 'You're right, I stole a load of charity cash. I *am* scum. The worst kind of person and I belong in jail. Write it up on the board.'

Josie is cursing her, calling her any and every name she can think of, but to Merry something about Fran's story is unsatisfactory, ill-fitting, like a too-small winter coat.

Quietly, while the others are distracted she moves on to her own name, just as she promised Fran, and tries to be honest.

Gatecrasher. Shouldn't be here. No dealings with Monty or Emporium before tonight.

Her chalk hovers next to the board, her fingers gripping so tightly it shakes. Everything she has written is true, but it's a lie to say she has no connection with the Emporium at all. Taking a deep breath, she writes: *Ross.*

Moving on swiftly, not wanting to spill the details for the others, she turns her attention to Josie's name.

'It's time for you to share now, Josie,' Fran says. 'I saw you sneaking around the passages earlier. What were you doing? What are you hiding in your bag? If I'm guilty, then you're guilty too.'

Josie sighs and reaches slowly into the top of her tote. Fran tenses, positively shrinking away from her. But all Josie draws out of her bag is her vape.

'Sure. It's not a big secret or anything, it's just nobody bloody asked me. I used to live here.'

23

CHRISTMAS PAST — 1995

JOSIE

IT WAS A COLD WINTER THAT YEAR; THE LOCK ON THE DOOR was so encrusted with frost Josie had worried that her key wouldn't work, but she slid it gently in and felt a rush of relief when she heard it click. She didn't have much luggage; she'd never really had many possessions. Growing up in care and being an experienced thief herself made her cautious about acquiring too many things.

She had left the system with a few savings from her organised crime experiments which had seemed like a lot, but turned out to be nowhere near enough to get her started in the real world. And five years on, she had even less than that. A C&A bag of second-hand clothes, a dark, yellowing bruise around her neck from the man she had been living with and an old-fashioned set of keys that she had hung onto for no particular reason. There was no

support system there for her now, she had nowhere else to go –
except for the only place that had ever felt like home.

That first walk through the deserted shop floor had made Josie
want to cry. The Hall of Wonders, which had been so full of life
and colour, the bustle of people, the chimes of the Great Clock,
and the steady tick-tock of the automata – was now empty but
for a few tables, the odd carved wooden figure.

The Great Clock had a sheet hanging over it, and in the Hall
of Toys Clockwork Peg was similarly shrouded, like a ghost. Josie
reached out and pulled the sheet from her, gazing into those life-
less brown eyes. If she looked closely she could still see a slight
scratch on Peg's shoulder from where she'd crashed down on top
of Fire Kid all those years ago, on her first visit here.

Old Man Verity had told her then that he believed in old-
fashioned punishment. When he'd dragged her off, she'd braced
herself for the clip round the ear her stepfather had often dealt
out. Or worse, a beating.

She hadn't fought him, though – her body had muscle memory
and a deep down belief that she deserved this. She deserved what
was coming her way – wasn't that what her stepdad had always
said? And despite her mean mouth, her talent for cruelty and
the reputation she had built in the Home, the feeling that you
deserve nothing but punches doesn't go away.

Verity dragged her through a hidden door, up a terrifyingly
steep flight of stairs before letting go of her wrist. She found

herself in some kind of workshop, with rows and rows of people chipping and carving at wood, winding springs, polishing ceramic. One was replacing a cog on a broken elf. *At least he's not taken me somewhere alone*, she thought. She could scream – surely one of these people would help her.

On the downside, with Verity standing between her and the door, there was nowhere to run.

'You're an orphan?' he asked her.

'I don't know,' Josie answered, giving a shrug to show just how little she cared about this. 'Dunno where my real dad is.'

'Nobody knows you're here, do they?'

Josie's unease grew.

'Yeah, they do. I told my big brothers, they're hard bastards, been in loads of fights. You don't want to mess with them.' That last part was true, the first part, not so much. Both brothers were in prison up North and were not big on letter writing.

'Well, I know exactly how you're going to repay me.' Verity pulled off his jacket, rolled up his sleeves and she flinched back. *Here it comes.* 'You're going to work in my shop.'

An apprenticeship, he had called it. Learning through hard work.

Once she had realised there was no danger of physical violence, Josie's fear had turned to contempt. She had told him exactly where he could stick his idea, with eloquence and anatomical precision. A job? She didn't need a fucking job, she was building her own mafia.

She had marched out of there, caught up with Fire Kid who was moping in the alley outside, and went back to the Home, fully intending to wreak more havoc. She burned Fire Kid's stupid puppet, swore Saddo, Klepto and Crash to silence, and got on with business.

But she couldn't get that store out of her head. It wasn't the pretty lights, the grotto or the toys that stayed with her but the glimpse she'd had, behind the scenes, of the workshop. People making things with their hands, taking a bit of wood and finding smooth, beautiful shapes inside it.

And so she went back and threw herself on the mercy of the old man. For the first six weeks she worked on the shop floor, fetching and carrying, stacking shelves with train sets and teddy bears and rows of Peg-puppets very much like the one she'd burned.

Up in the workshop after hours, she would watch the old man teach his son the skills he needed, seeing the boy's hands confidently shave off just the right amount of wood to turn a rough sphere into a face with expression and life. Verity had noticed her interest and, eventually, held out a chisel from his own personal set.

'Stop watching and start doing.'

The boy — they all called him Mister because of his initials — had never said a word to her as they sat side by side; she assumed he didn't like sharing his dad's attention with a scuzzy little orphan. And slowly she made progress. She'd never be as good as the Veritys — it seemed to be in their blood — but she was good. And as she worked, her mind began to spread out beyond the confines of East London, the Home, the Aunties and Uncles. With a set of tools in her hands she was worth something, she could make things.

As she worked, she caught the odd snatches of gossip – a disagreement with the other 'posh' side of the Verity family who despised the store. Some kind of legal issue about the property. But the Emporium seemed so old, so immovable, she had never thought to be afraid.

And then one morning she had turned up to find the store closed. There was no sign of Verity or Mister, just a man in a suit standing in the Hall of Wonders handing out P45s.

The news reports she saw at the Home had put it down to the death of the department store, the rise of out-of-town malls, the fact that hand-made trinkets couldn't compete against cut-price imports. But rumour among the employees was that it was something bigger than that. The posh Veritys had been bankrolling the store for years and they'd found something out; something the old man had been hiding, so they cut him off.

Grief had killed the old man, and Josie had gone back to the Home, back to petty crime, but her heart hadn't been in it after that.

And now, the Emporium was her home. She hadn't even stolen the keys, the old man had given a set to her for safekeeping a week before the closure and she'd never seen him again to give them back.

Steeling herself against sadness and decay, she headed upstairs to her favourite place – the workshop. It was eerily quiet now without the constant sanding, sawing and chattering of the Emporium Elves. The pegboards which had been used to keep tools were empty, the Anglepoise lamps had all been stripped out and scrapped. But the low-ceilinged room was warmer than the rest of the store and the stove still worked, even if it smoked a little. She wondered whether the neighbours would see the smoke and report it to the posh Veritys, but there weren't really any neighbours to speak of, just city wankers scuttling between offices and wine bars.

At first, she amused herself by smashing mirrors, breaking furniture, carving her name into the walls. She fed most of the desks from the office into the fire but left the workshop tables untouched, as well as the oak chair and table the old man used to do his own work.

Sentimental, Josie chided herself, grabbing the table to prove she didn't really care. But as she was about to snap off one leg, she noticed a little drawer she hadn't seen before. It opened to reveal a small leather roll of tools, the ones he had used for his smallest, most intricate carvings.

Josie did smash the table, but instead of burning it, she broke a piece off the leg and began practising.

Growing up, Josie had always hated winter. The long nights, the way the darkness fell before the end of school. The way other children would be buzzing with anticipation – making lists, decorating trees, pretending that life wasn't shit. But this year, she loved it – the endless darkness, just her, the fire, the scrape-scrape of her tools as she recreated the toys Old Man Verity had taught her to make. No drunken, volatile man to tiptoe around, no dead-end, dead-eyed job to go to. No need to be the hardest person in the room when she was the only person in the room.

During daylight hours she would venture forth into the commuting crowds of city wankers, lifting wallets from their pockets as they pushed their way through the station or lined up waiting to go into the Tube. She ate well that year.

By night, the Emporium, which had once been Verity's kingdom, was now hers.

She took care of it as best she could. She tidied up the things she had smashed, stacking the remaining tables in the office. She also liberated the army of elves from a store cupboard on the workshop floor. Those little bastards were a total lifesaver, and lots of fun. Once, someone – probably another homeless person looking for shelter – had smashed one of the historic front windows, opened a latch and come inside. Josie had wound up a jolly elf and set him walking slowly across the room at the intruder – they had left pretty bloody quickly. Josie felt a bit guilty, but not bad enough to share her kingdom.

She explored every secret passage until she could walk them with her eyes closed, finding the dark and cramped room where some serving girl had slept. It was a sad, dank little place and although when the stove was lit it would be warm, Josie had no desire to spend any time there. Sometimes she would go down to the toy department floor, remove Peg's dust sheet and wind her up, just for a little bit of company.

'Sorry I knocked you over,' she said. 'It was a shitty thing to do to a fellow orphan. It was funny the way you fell on Fire Kid, though.'

Peg played a chord in a minor key, as if sounding disapproval.

'Yeah, well, I'm sure Fire Kid isn't living rough in a shop right now.'

Peg's head tilted with a click. She played another chord, and Josie felt a wave of loneliness come over her. She shifted awkwardly on the piano top, crossing her legs.

'You know why they called me Knives?'

Peg did not answer; Josie decided to tell her anyway.

'I was fucking scared ninety-nine per cent of the time when I was a kid. My mum dumped my stepdad and he smashed our place up and told Mum he was going to come back and slaughter the lot of us. "If I can't have you nobody can," that kind of bullshit. So I thought I'd be prepared. I took every knife in the kitchen and hid them all over my body. I stuffed them up my sleeves, down the waistband of my tights, in every pocket of my coat. There was no way that bastard was going to get me.'

Peg's fingers paused, hovering over her next chord. She was winding down, but Josie took her pause to be an interest in the story.

'The knives were what got me in the end. I didn't wrap them up properly and they cut me. My teacher called the police when she saw the blood seeping through my uniform. I was seven.'

In the silence of the Emporium Josie thought about Fire Kid, about herself, about kids everywhere that have crappy stuff happen to them.

That night, she began the Special Project. It took her months of whittling and carving, of scavenging the workshop for tiny metal pieces that had fallen between the cracks in the floorboards. She began making something beautiful.

As winter closed in, Josie prepared for her second Emporium Christmas. She brought in extra fuel gathered from London's parks, picked up some stray plastic garlands she'd found blowing in the street, hummed carols to herself as she warmed hot chocolate on the stove. Then she heard the unmistakeable sounds of people. Not fellow squatters or druggies looking for a place to use. They weren't sneaking. Their voices rang through the store. The unmistakeable tone of rich wankers.

For a whole year, nobody else had entered the store legitimately and Josie had almost forgotten that the Emporium wasn't truly hers – that the Verity family still existed, even though the old man was dead. She wondered briefly if it was Mister, come to reclaim his property and open the Emporium again, but ruled it out because the people downstairs were actually speaking out loud.

She crept to the stairwell, winding up the elves who stood guard there, and then fled to the secret passages, concealing herself within the walls but following the sound of the rich wankers as they progressed to Peg's floor.

It was a simple matter to push the shelf down on top of them, to scare them off. This time, she took care not to knock Peg over – they were friends now.

But Josie knew that this was the end.

In the early New Year, they came. Security guards to flush out any squatters; locksmiths to change the locks. She was working on the special project when she heard them and had just enough time to snatch it up, along with the Old Man's tools and hide them under the floorboards in the workshop. Then she fled into the secret passages, hoping they didn't know about them.

But they had brought a Verity with them who was guiding them through it all. Wide beams swept across one passage as she flung herself into another. Fear flared in her mind – not that she would be caught, that was inevitable, but that she would never see her tools or her special project again.

'There!' a posh voice said. 'Did you see that? Someone moved! COME QUIETLY! IT'LL BE MUCH EASIER FOR YOU.'

It was not easy for her. She fought, kicked and squirmed. Posh boy – who looked almost as wrinkled and knackered as the old man had so must be a relative – kept up a running commentary all along about what a firecracker she was, until one of the security guys slipped his fist under her arm and punched her in the gut so hard she stopped struggling. They took her sleeping bag, her grubby pile of clothes and cried out in triumph when they found her stash of rich wanker credit cards. They took the figures she'd carved, too; they assumed by the quality that she could never have made them and must have appropriated them from the store.

And that was how Josie 'Knives' Cavanagh – homeless person, care survivor and former aspiring crime lord – received her first ever criminal conviction and lost everything. The old man's tools, along with the almost-finished special project remained buried under the workshop floor of the Emporium where nobody would ever find them.

Later that year, Josie went back to retrieve them but by then the place was too well boarded up. The rich wankers had won again.

24

MERRY

IT'S EASIER TO SEARCH THE OFFICE WITH THE FOUR OF THEM. THEY rifle through papers together then pile the ones that look relevant up on a desk in the centre of the room.

'So that was you, who pushed the bookcase on me when I came to see Peg?' Benjamin says.

Josie shrugs. 'Must have been.'

'And that's why you were sneaking around the secret passages – you were looking for Old Mr Verity's tools?' Fran asks.

'Yeah, I was, not that it's any of your business.'

Fran clams up, her eyes downcast. Fran and Josie had had a strange little friendship vibe going on until recently, but Fran's revelation about stealing the charity money had trashed that. Merry understands – Josie had mentioned earlier that her niece was having cancer treatment – but there's still something iffy about Fran's story. It's the way she hasn't made any move to justify herself, to explain that the money was 'just resting in her account' or plead mental health issues. She just confessed and accepted Josie's scorn. People don't usually act like that.

Merry stares at her companions and inside her mind she can see the connections shimmering between these seeming strangers. Fran was at uni with Evangeline, Evangeline had flirted online with Dean, Josie had once attacked Benjamin. But she's not connected to any of them at all.

'Do any of you know Doug Stimpson?' she asks. 'He's my boss, the one I stole the invitation from. If we can figure out that connection, too, it might help.'

'There was a Doug something on an invoice,' Fran says, searching through a pile. 'Yes, here it is.'

The invoice turns out to be for the sale of five hundred high-end greetings cards. The most innocuous thing Merry has ever seen. And that's precisely the problem. Doug Stimpson is a no-mark. After a decade with the company, she knows practically everything about him. His shoe size, his opinions on this year's *Strictly* finalists and whether *Doctor Who* has gone Too Woke. The way he tells everyone he is six feet tall when he's actually five ten; the fact he never washes his hands after going to the toilet, believing that you need a healthy amount of germs on your hands. He is not a man with deep, dark secrets, and if there is a connection between him and the Emporium beyond a one-off sale of cards, surely Merry would have sniffed it out by now.

'Take a look at this,' Fran's voice interrupts. She is holding the clipboard the Victorian guy on the door had been using just hours before. 'It's the VIP guest list for last night,' she says thoughtfully.

Merry moves closer, looks over Fran's shoulder at the printed-out list, the Victorian gentleman's neat little ticks next to the names. There is a hot-chocolate ring on one corner of the paper from where Merry rested her mug. It feels like she's looking at a relic from the distant past.

'Here's Evangeline.' Fran's voice trembles at her name but she forces herself to continue. 'Barbara the plus one, Dean, Benjamin, me, Josie. And who's this, Rita Gliss? The perfume lady? I didn't see her.'

'She never showed.' Merry keeps her tone neutral.

'Yeah, or maybe she did and her body's stashed in a secret passage somewhere,' Josie says darkly. Merry shivers. She's not the biggest Rita fan in the world, but she doesn't want that.

'The thing is, Merry.' Fran's voice is quiet, cautious like a therapist nudging a client towards an uncomfortable feeling. 'There's no Doug on here either.'

'Well, no, there wouldn't be, I got in pretending to be Rita.'

'No but don't you see? Your boss's name should still have been on here, like Rita's, even if he didn't show up.'

Merry feels sick. She should have seen it a long time ago. She's supposed to be intelligent, she's supposed to be good at winkling out the truth, but she'd been wilfully blind to this. Fran is right. All the other names had been printed out on the list, with just Barbara's *plus one* added on after in pen. Doug should have been on it too.

'And come to think of it, my name was written on the invitation card,' Fran continues. 'Was Doug's on yours?'

Merry shakes her head; she remembers how she'd thought herself lucky that his name hadn't been on there, how it had

230

made the invitation all the more stealable. Her face has gone hot, her skin prickling as the others turn their gaze onto her again.

'Don't you think it's a bit weird that you're still in here too?' Fran's tone is still gentle, but firm. 'Barbara was trapped here by accident and Monty – or whoever is behind all this – let her get out. But you're still here, Merry. Whoever it was knew you'd steal that invitation. You *are* meant to be here.'

Merry's heart is hammering now, she's too weak, too shaken-up to protest. How could someone predict that she would steal an invitation? That would mean they knew about her and Ross, about the snow globe, about her own sneaky nature. It means that the killer knows her almost as well as she knows herself.

For a moment, Ross's name flits through her mind. He is the only person she's been honest with, the only one who would know her well enough to predict her movements. But she pushes the idea away. It's too ridiculous to imagine sweet, kind and open Ross doing something like this to her.

But then, Ross has some issues of his own . . .

She feels an overwhelming urge to run away, but separating herself from the group would be madness, especially now she knows for sure there's a target on her back too.

After this, Merry is much less useful in the searching of the office. She sits on a side-table, watching the others flit back and forth, piling papers onto the central desk, sifting through them; thinking about Ross, and home, and wondering why she is here. There is a box next to her, and she rifles through it half-heartedly but it's full of toys. Not Emporium toys but cheaper, more tinselly versions of them. There's a spray-painted jack-in-the-box made of plastic and metal, and a rough approximation of a Peg-puppet which doesn't move properly when you pull its strings. At the bottom of the box, a paper compliments slip with Dean's Business Fixer letterhead.

Here's a few samples to show you what can be achieved by outsourcing.

So Dean had wanted to replace the workshop's toys with cheaper imports, putting Rudi out of a job. She wonders if they'd got into some kind of fight about it but can't quite square that idea with the quiet mouse of a man she met in the workshop.

'Look, here it is,' Fran says, holding up a leather binder. The others are crowded round, flicking through a pile of papers.

'Interesting,' Benjamin says. 'This definitely isn't a Santa Claus contract. The agreement was signed last year and is ongoing, with very large monthly payments and shares of profits going to Mr Smallhouse. And then . . .' He flicks to the back of the papers, and freezes, an expression of pure shock on his face as he holds out a slip of yellowed paper.

It's a ragged newspaper cutting, a review torn from the *Yeovil Bugle* celebrating a sell-out performance of the local theatre's production of *Charlie and the Chocolate Factory*. There's a headshot of the lead actor in the corner of the cutting, with the caption: SMALLHOUSE: CHARISMATIC WONKA.

'Oh no, this has to be wrong.' Fran's voice is faint.

The photo is small, and not the best quality but it's clear enough.

'Nigel Smallhouse . . . is *Monty*?'

'Hah!' Josie shouted. 'I bloody knew there was something off about him. I used to know Mister Verity a little bit back in the day. He was just a kid but he was gangly and shy. I mean, I know we've all changed, and I hardly expected him to recognise me after all those years, but he could barely talk back then – and now we're expected to believe he's the Greatest Showman.'

'And then there was his face,' Benjamin adds – the excitement has given him renewed energy, showing flashes of his old, animated self. 'I knew Montagu's cousin Kit a little from school and met him again when he brought me here. The Verity men show their age dramatically early. It's a family trait. I never considered it before, but the gentleman we thought was Monty looked quite youthful for his supposed years.'

'Oh, shit, yeah,' Josie adds. 'The old man looked bloody *ancient*. He had wrinkles on his wrinkles.'

Merry remembers Gary Shrike's words when she first got here – *his face doesn't fit*. An uneasy realisation is creeping over her. *Premature ageing . . . chronic shyness . . . M.R. Verity . . .*

'Is there any mention of Monty's full name in the contract?' she asks quietly.

Benjamin picks up the document and flicks through again, studying each page with his practised eye for detail. 'Nothing that I can see, but . . . Oh, here it is under their signatures. Montagu Rudolph Verity.'

Rudolph. Merry's heart drops, and Fran's realisation is just seconds behind her.

'Rudi.'

'The master toymaker,' Josie adds, a peculiar sadness in her voice. 'He was so good.'

'Dean must have known the truth,' Benjamin says. 'This document says clearly that Rudi would remain in control of the business, so his meeting last night must have been with both of them. But why did he not say anything?'

But to Merry the answer is obvious. 'Well, before we all fell asleep, Dean would have been keeping the secret to protect his investment and after . . . Well, he had holes in his memory, but I think he knew on some level that he'd killed Rudi. He wouldn't have wanted to tell us they'd had a meeting.'

'Wait,' Josie says. '*Dean?*'

Fran nods agreement, telling them about seeing him come out of the grotto, the scratches on his arm, reminding them about Dean's flashes of temper.

'I only met Rudi for a couple of seconds,' Merry says, 'but I could see how committed he was to his hand-made gifts. And Dean . . . well, he changed after drinking that hot chocolate – lost control more easily. I think he might have just lost it with him.'

'I can believe that.' Benjamin shudders, remembering how Dean had lunged at him earlier. 'And so the true owner of the Emporium is gone. And now for some reason, Monty – or Nigel – has us all trapped here . . .'

As the four of them think about Nigel Smallhouse, something shifts from sadness to anger. Fran stands taller, crosses her arms. Josie's eyes acquire a hard, narrow look, her jaw set. Benjamin, although unsteady on his feet, curls his hands into fists. Merry, too, is boiling with rage.

It's one thing to be stalked through the shadows by Montagu Verity, mysterious puppet-master of the Emporium, but to be terrorised by Nigel Smallhouse, jobbing actor? It feels different somehow – intolerable.

'There are four of us, and one of him,' Benjamin says.

'Yeah, and I know this place much better than he does,' Josie adds, with dawning realisation.

'What are we doing waiting here to get picked off one by one?' Fran's face is etched with fury. 'I saw what he did to Evangeline. I'm not letting that happen to any of you.'

They look at each other, ready to go to war, but with no idea where to go. Where could he be hiding? What's the one place in the Emporium that they have been avoiding all night?

'Santa's grotto,' Merry says.

'Worth a try,' Josie agrees.

'Let's get him!' Benjamin shouts. His eyes are wild, his face twisted into an unaccustomed expression of savagery.

They pick up weapons along the way. Benjamin seizes the cricket bat Dean had threatened him with just hours before. Fran grabs an oversized wooden candy cane. Josie doesn't grab anything, just holds her bag close, slips her hand inside, ready to grab whatever she has in there. It looks like she is already armed. Merry feels a flutter of uncertainty – after what Dean and Evangeline did, what Fran almost did, can she really trust that everyone here is on the same side?

'We need a plan,' she says.

'We fucking kill him,' Josie snarls.

'No, I mean we need to sneak up – otherwise he's just going to disappear through a trapdoor. Then maybe Benjamin and Fran hold him down and you get him to talk, Josie. I bet you can do scary.'

'I can definitely do scary. I will try not to kill him, but no promises.'

235

This feels good, this energy, this anger, this sensation of working together – it helps her shove her suspicions to one side. They creep as best they can, but it's not easy. The Emporium is alive, ancient boards groaning under their every step.

When they arrive in the House of Toys it is completely still but for the sound of their progress. Merry thinks again of Dean, leading them through here the first time, fretting about the gaps in his memory. Dean and Monty – or Nigel as she has to start calling him – must have been conspiring to push Rudi out, bring in a flood of cheaper products and make the Emporium more like a normal, profit-making store. When Rudi resisted then Dean – high on whatever was in his hot chocolate – had lost control.

Benjamin must be thinking about Dean, too, as he rushes towards the grotto door and kicks it open. Unlike the rest of the store, it's a temporary structure made of cheap plywood and splinters off its hinges. Benjamin roars, some primal instinct coming out of him as he steps inside.

There is darkness. There is the hunched shadow of Rudi surrounded by elves. And there is a figure in the gloom, seated on Santa's throne-like chair.

'There he is,' Fran growls.

He seems smaller somehow without his coat and hat, but it's definitely Nigel Smallhouse. There's something off about the way he's sitting, though. Not like the evil lord of murder and mayhem, but slumped, his head lopsided, his eyes closed. And now she's closer she can see he has been bound to the chair with rolls and rolls of festive tape.

Oh no.

The righteous anger drains out of all of them. Benjamin drops the cricket bat. Fran suppresses a sob, her hand covers her mouth.

'Is he dead?'

Josie feels for a pulse. 'No, he's not. Just unconscious.'

The man's face is slack and without his staged bluster, his confident moves and distinctive costume, he seems small and sad. Merry pities him. But the fear which left her such a short time ago is seeping in again now. Back in the secret passages she'd seen a figure in a top hat and assumed it was Monty, but it could have been anyone.

It could have been one of them.

Fran is evidently thinking the same thing.

'I saw someone in a top hat push Evangeline,' Fran says. 'But what if it wasn't him?'

They look at each other. And then they all start talking at once. Accusing, counter-accusing. Josie is shouting at Fran now, saying she must have been the one who pushed Evangeline all along, that she is a liar and a thief.

Then Benjamin whirls on Merry.

'You're the one sneaking around all the time, going through people's things, pushing us to reveal our secrets. And you were the one who kept throwing the suspicion on Monty.' Something in Benjamin has changed, his face is desperate, sheened with sweat, he is clenching and unclenching his fists and his hands are shaking.

The others are looking at her now and she feels hot, exposed under their gaze.

'Yeah, you're right,' Josie says, switching sides so abruptly that Fran's jaw drops. 'Funny how you were the one who found the gas lamps and the secret passages. You've always been the odd one out. Who are you, really? What kind of name is Merry Clarke?'

Merry is blindsided by the shock, thrown off-balance by being the centre of everyone's attention. *This is what you get for sticking your neck out, for trusting people.*

She wants to defend herself. She wants to ask why Josie kept the Emporium's secrets to herself for so long, and what she has in her bag. But Merry just isn't used to standing her ground like this. She can't even speak – just lets the accusations wash over her.

Her gaze flickers towards Fran, but she is saying nothing. She's probably relieved that they're not attacking her anymore.

Those feelings she had before – of being part of a team, of working together to figure this out, they had been a lie. She has nothing in common with these people, she is better off by herself.

Leaving the others is dangerous, she knows it, but she can't stay here. On shaky legs, biting her lip hard to stop herself crying, she walks out through the grotto door without a word.

25

CHRISTMAS PRESENT

NIGEL

AT SIX FORTY-FIVE P.M. ON CHRISTMAS EVE, NIGEL SMALLHOUSE examined himself in the full-length mirror in his office. He straightened his top hat and twirled, watching with satisfaction as the skirts of his coat flew about. Monty Verity's signature move. A bubble of glee rose up inside him, the way it did before every big performance. Soon the special guests would be here and he was prepared to blow them away.

He did a few of the warm-up exercises they had taught him at drama school all those years ago, and waited for the feeling to come over him. It amazed him every time, the way he could slide out of Nigel Smallhouse's soul and into Monty's, inhabiting the character completely and escaping his own worthless life.

Although what was once an effortless process was becoming harder and harder.

Bzzz. Just as he felt the Montyness overtake him, the phone on his desk vibrated. His eyes instinctively flew towards it, jerking him back into his own Nigel self. What was it now? Probably another message from tonight's escape room client, with even more impossible demands. Another reinforced rope on the ceiling, perhaps? Some mild tinkering with the lighting system? Or more bespoke wooden models? Running escape rooms in the store – locking people in and setting them a series of fun puzzles – had been a lucrative sideline for him. Rudi tolerated his money-spinners, even helping out on occasion by making exclusive toys for influential guests. And Nigel was proud of how well they usually ran, but this particular client was driving him to the point of insanity, wearing him down with a barrage of constant demands.

He picked up his phone, glancing at the screen. Then he saw a name there that made him drop it back onto the desk with a clatter. It wasn't the escape room client, it was much, much worse.

The number was programmed into his contacts under the name Bob, but Nigel had no idea what his real name was. All he knew was that he was a big man with limited patience who knew how to twist an arm in just the right place to make it break.

Where's my fucking money nobhed.

Dread pounded in Nigel's chest, even as his inner Monty shuddered at the spelling.

Nigel urged himself not to panic. If tonight went well, he'd clear his debts with Bob, and maybe even some of the others, and have some to keep back for the New Year's Day races. He just had to keep his head and make sure everything tonight ran as smoothly as a creepy clockwork elf.

When he had first accepted M.R. Verity's offer of becoming his flamboyant alter-ego, Nigel had looked at his contract, complete with its cut of profits, with absolute glee. No more dodging Bob's calls. No more scraping by in regional theatre rep. But he had signed up to the project under the incorrect assumption that Rudi Verity was a sane, level-headed businessman, rather than an eccentric idealist.

Even though the store's reputation had gone viral – even though people were queuing to get in and Monty was fast becoming a celebrity in his own right – the business was making a loss.

The original money Rudi had brought in through investors had drained away quickly, and the last of Rudi's own fortune had disappeared into the money pit at the beginning of December. The more aristocratic wing of the family was refusing to help out – some kind of ancient quarrel about who really owned the property. And those viral videos would dry up completely once Christmas was over. Nobody wants a cosy magical store past January. In the New Year, the Emporium would have to close. All thanks to Rudi's damnable obsession with selling hand-crafted items at ridiculously low prices.

'Every ch-child should have something hand-made,' Rudi had said in one of his rare full sentences. And though his reluctance to talk made him seem weak, the old boy was stubborn.

It wasn't simply Nigel Smallhouse's greed that had led him to start talks with Dean Hallibutt. It was Monty Verity's passion for saving the emporium, too. It was surprising how often Nigel's and Monty's needs aligned.

Nigel was no expert, but Dean's business plan had made a lot of sense; he had investors lined up, a TV deal in the pipeline.

'All you need to do, old boy, is convince my silent partner,' Nigel had assured him, in Monty's gilded tones.

When he saw him on the guest list for tonight's escape room, he had thought it the perfect chance to engineer a meeting and make it look like an accident. Now all he needed to do was get into character and make it happen

He tried again to transform into Monty, tipping the brim of his hat and raising an eyebrow just like Gene Wilder did when he welcomed you into a world of pure imagination.

Bzzz. A series of aggressive emojis filled his screen. Loan sharks used emojis. Who knew?

Fuck. He couldn't do his Monty thing with this Neanderthal harassing him every fifteen seconds.

In an impulsive flash of panic, he shoved his phone into the old-fashioned safe under the desk, locking it firmly, its walls too thick for him to hear any further buzzes.

He just had to hold on for one more night. And who knew – maybe the deal with Dean would be secured, too, and then things would become easy. There would be wealthy investors, a TV role and – if and when he was finally unmasked – his acting skills would become the stuff of legend. He'd fooled the entire country, after all! He'd be inundated with roles.

So come on, Monty, he told his reflection. *Show yourself.*

And then there he was, the flamboyant owner of the Emporium. Eyes twinkling, a crooked smile upon his face. Slowly, the soul of Montagu Verity settled over Nigel's quivering shoulders. He drew himself up, and smiled a slow, wicked smile.

Now, on with the show.

Good lord, that Merry girl had been difficult to shake. Monty watched her stumble off in search of a snow globe and checked his pocket watch – it was after 10 p.m. The brief about her hadn't been wrong. *Obsessively curious, instinctively sneaky*, the notes said. *Hates being the centre of attention, will ask lots of awkward questions.*

Indeed.

It hadn't been helped by the fact Merry had left her first hot chocolate outside and spilled half of the second cup over her hideously vulgar jumper, but by the time he finally left her, she had seemed suitably disorientated – although regrettably not as loosened-up as the others. The client did say that the drug might affect each person differently.

Monty was aware that this Christmas Eve escape room had a slightly less playful feel. Usually escape room clients actually knew they were in an escape room, for example, and did not require drugging to keep them there. But when he had raised his misgivings with the good Mr Watton, who was arranging matters on behalf of the client, the gentleman had simply added a zero onto the offer and Monty had accepted.

And there was the added advantage that Dean Hallibutt would be considerably more malleable, thanks to the drug in the hot chocolate.

'Believe me,' Watton had said. 'This will keep him loose and agreeable, and if you add those extra sprinkles on top, he'll be putty in your hands.'

'How do you know all this?'

Watton's tone had been reassuring. 'My client is an experienced chemist,' he said. 'It'll work, trust me. Now, can we trust you to deliver the full package my client expects?'

'Absolutely.'

By the light of the bare bulbs in the tunnels, Monty checked his fob-watch. He was running late. He still had to go upstairs, collect Merry's wooden model and place it on the fireplace with the others, but that could wait. Rudi would already be in Santa's grotto by now; he had to find Dean and get him upstairs to make this deal happen.

Over the past few months, Nigel had found that the grotto was the best place to talk to Rudi. Hidden in his Santa suit, he could find the words that eluded him when he was just plain Rudi Verity. And in the grotto, surrounded by everything he stood to lose, surely he'd be more likely to see sense.

He arrived in the Hall of Toys to see that the partygoers had wound down, exactly as predicted. Josie and Benjamin were slumped over by that ridiculous sledging slope which took up far too much valuable retail space on one side of the Emporium. TV chef Fran Silver was curled in Santa's wooden sleigh, looking peaceful and cosy – but Monty couldn't be sure that she was fully asleep. As he took another cautious step forward, the door of the grotto burst open and Dean strode out. He was wild-eyed, had lost his jacket and – for some inexplicable reason – his shoes. His face was twisted with rage.

'Ah, Hallibutt, dear boy . . .' Monty began, instinctively retreating towards the lift.

In one fluid motion, Dean grasped him by the cravat, lifting him up and pressing him against the lift door.

'You fucking fraud,' he snarled, flecks of spit landing on Monty's face. 'You lied to me. This isn't even your fucking shop. And someone gave your so-called silent partner a dossier full of lies about my financial dealings. All in all I am Not. Fucking. Happy.' With each of those last words, he slammed Monty against the wood panelling, again and again.

Monty's arms grew weak from struggling, his head was blooming with pain. And then Dean shifted his grip, tightening his hands around Monty's neck. Squeezing, squeezing. *How can his hands be this strong?*

Monty – no, he was definitely Nigel now – fought to breathe, his limbs twitching, his head about to explode. He felt something warm trickle down the inside of his leg.

This is it, the end. I died for my art . . .

'Put the man down, Hallibutt,' a calm, clear voice cut in. Dean loosened his grip in surprise, turned around and backed off so quickly that Nigel knew he was being threatened with a weapon.

Over his shoulder Nigel could see a figure in a reindeer head mask. Rudi? No, not broad enough to be him. Whoever it was was holding a gun that looked horrifyingly real.

The figure pointed it at Dean. 'Now, go downstairs and play with your trains, you little twerp. Enjoy the time you have left.'

Astoundingly, Dean staggered away, confused, scratching his head.

Nigel whirled round to thank his saviour, but the reindeer just stood there, eyes glinting inside the mask. A cold shiver travelled down Nigel's body as realisation dawned.

'You?' he said. '*You're* the escape room client?'

'Dead right. And now you're going to come with me to hide out for a few hours and watch things unravel.' There was a short, dry laugh which had nothing to do with humour. 'It's going to be fun.'

26

FRAN

A PART OF FRAN FEELS STRANGELY BEREFT WATCHING MERRY walk away. Somehow over the last few hours her opinion of her has shifted, sensing that her stand-offishness comes not from a sense of being superior but a kind of crippling shyness, a fear of showing anyone who she really is.

She looks at her two remaining companions. Josie, who had seemed so warm and funny at the beginning of the night, is looking at her with loathing. And Benjamin . . . there's definitely something wrong with him. That burst of aggressive energy has left him shaking and weak. He leans back against the grotto's wooden walls, mumbling something about being so very tired. Fran rushes forward and helps him sink to the ground more gently.

'Thank you, I feel quite . . .' Benjamin's former wild-eyed anger has gone. He just looks exhausted now. She helps him prop himself up on a sack of soft toys by Santa's throne, fetches

247

a blanket from the sleigh outside and lays it over his lap, urging him to get some rest. He needs medical treatment, fresh water, but right now all she can offer is this.

'Listen, you guys,' she begins. 'I really don't think Merry has anything to do with this.'

'Maybe you're working together,' Josie says, but there's no true viciousness behind the statement. When Merry left the room, the angry energy had drained away.

'I could say the same of you,' Fran says. 'You've lied a lot. Why didn't you say you used to live here? Why didn't you just tell us about the secret passages? You could have got those gas lights working yourself.'

Josie shrugs. 'Old Man Verity never told me the gas lamps still worked. And I didn't want anyone to know I used to be homeless. It's a pride thing – surely you get that?'

'There,' says Benjamin. His voice is faint now, his hand is raised, trembling as he points his finger. 'On the chair. Envelope.'

Fran sees it now, a slip of paper which must have been placed flat on Nigel's knees, but slid off to one side at some point. She slips her fingers down the side of the chair, reluctant to touch Nigel's sleeping form, and pulls it out. It's a bright red envelope, the kind that Christmas cards often come in. It's addressed *To the survivors*.

'Don't touch it,' Benjamin says. 'Fingerprints!'

Fran is almost reassured by this flash of Benjamin's old personality returning, but she doesn't listen, rips open the seal. It's a standard old-school Christmas card, like the ones her mother used to buy as a multi-pack in Clinton Cards. On the front, a drawing of Santa in his workshop, surrounded by old-fashioned

248

toys. His cheery face is smiling as he balances a marionette puppet gently in his hands.

Inside, someone has stuck a piece of paper over the printed rhyme, replacing it with a new poem.

> *Welcome, this merry Christmas Eve*
> *To a magical store for those who believe*
> *The pure of heart find joy within*
> *But 'tis death to you all, steeped in sin*

> *'Twas in this season, warm with wine*
> *You all stole what once was mine*
> *So Happy Christmas one and all*
> *Each of you deserves to fall*

'That's awful.' Josie winces.

It is pretty terrible, but that's not the point. Merry had said they were being manipulated, that Monty was in the shadows pulling their strings and she was right – even if she was wrong about it being Monty. None of them had written this dross – even if Merry had the requisite skills. They were here because they were being punished.

'What the hell did we steal?' Fran says aloud.

'Ahem, *charity money*,' Josie flashes back. Fran has completely forgotten her false confession.

'I've never stolen anything in my life,' Benjamin says faintly. And then realises what he has said and adds: 'At least not yet. And surely whoever wrote the poem can't be talking about Peg? Clockwork Peg belongs to Rudi and Rudi is . . . not in a position to do anything about it.'

'Well, I've stolen so much stuff I can't even put a number on it,' Josie says. 'I haven't done anything like that for years, though. Got my brothers' kids to think about now.'

Fran keeps looking at the card, the phrase *steeped in sin*, an echo of the inscription over the Emporium door.

'It's not about stealing money or property,' she realises. 'It's about the sin. We've all . . . I don't know . . . sinned somehow.'

Benjamin whimpers, whether it's in pain or recognition Fran can't tell.

'If we're counting sins I don't know where to start,' Josie says. But a sad, guilty look crosses her face, as if she is thinking about the very worst thing she has ever done. Just then, Fran notices something discarded in the corner behind the chair. Two empty glasses.

She picks up one glass and sniffs. The now-repulsive smell of mulled wine hits her – cinnamon, orange and cloves. Each glass contains a smear of deep red, a few granules of spices. One drained by Monty/Nigel, the other probably sipped by the killer. They had been working together, up to a point, then the killer had wanted Nigel off the chessboard, without permanently hurting him, even though they clearly don't have a problem with murder.

Maybe Nigel – massive fraud that he is – didn't deserve death in the killer's eyes.

Just as she's about to put the glass down she notices it. A smudge of red lipstick. She stares at it. At last a genuine clue, one left by accident, not a breadcrumb set up to lead them astray.

'Whoever's after us, it's a woman.'

Josie lets out a cry, almost like a sob, hugging her bag close to her, her face stricken. She murmurs something to herself, it sounds like 'fire kid'.

At the same time, Benjamin gasps, 'Agatha Christie!'

Both women turn to look at him, and he beckons them closer. 'Please, I have to tell you something. I think it's my heart. It's always been weak and the stress of this evening . . . well.'

'What can we do?' Fran asks. She doesn't even know CPR. Why did she never learn CPR?

'Just listen,' Benjamin says. 'I have to tell you my sin. I need someone to know. Last Christmas, I nearly killed someone.'

27

CHRISTMAS PAST — 2023

BENJAMIN

ACCORDING TO THE PLAQUE BY THE DOOR, THE GEORGE WAS the most haunted pub in Sussex, boasting no fewer than three ghosts. Two human, one spectral stagecoach drawn by six horses. Benjamin was not sure whether to count the horses individually which would bring the total to eight. He mused on this for a little while to distract himself from what he was about to embark upon.

He was used to doing deals over drinks in dark corners of country pubs, but this one felt different. This was the kind of deal he had only heard about before, whispered rumours at auctions and fairs, usually attached to dealers of a question-able reputation and known thieves. He professed horror at such practices, as any decent gentleman would, but he also had some of these men's business cards tucked into the filing cabinet at his shop.

Not that he would ever use them, of course. His trespass into the Emporium had only reinforced the idea that every time he broke the rules, he would be caught, or punished in some way.

Probity had its advantages. It had become a central part of his reputation as an antiques dealer. A straight arrow, he would never inflate a price, never underestimate when valuing, then sell cheaply to a friend – although he was careful to point out that this did not make him a pushover. Anyone trying to take advantage of his honesty received short shrift. He was proud of the reputation he had built, which is exactly why he should have ignored the email that pinged into his inbox several weeks ago. But he couldn't, not when the subject line was *Clockwork Peg*.

The sight of her, rotting away in that cold, abandoned Emporium, had haunted him more than a pub ghost ever could. He saw her face when he closed his eyes, imagined the rust which must be forming on her joints, the effect of the damp on her hand-made gown. The Veritys had ignored his calls, his letters, his well-received article in the popular *Automata Today* magazine arguing passionately for her preservation. Benjamin did not naturally tend towards anger, but the arrogance of the family, sitting on a historic figure of such incredible importance like that, made his blood boil.

And then the email had arrived. It was cleverly written, so it would never stand up in court as evidence, but it made clear that a party was interested in acquiring Peg, and was willing to pay for his assistance in doing so.

He had committed this crime night after night in his own head, thinking about the skills and equipment required to move a heavy, delicate automaton while attracting no attention. But now he was sitting here in a nook next to the fireplace, nursing a flat lemonade and increasingly thinking that this was some kind of police set-up.

It was quiet in the pub, considering it was 8 p.m. and Christmas was only days away. Decorations were minimal; some shiny pull-out garlands on the ceiling which cheapened the haunted pub atmosphere, and a large Santa-shaped collection tin on the bar. Generalised guilt had made Benjamin shove a twenty-pound note in that before he sat down. The barman, a young man with a neatly trimmed beard, was polishing glasses. Did barmen even do that in real life, or just when they were undercover police officers trying to look busy? In the nook opposite sat a red-haired woman reading an ancient paperback, Agatha Christie's *The Adventure of the Christmas Pudding*. Was it his imagination or did her eyes just flicker his way? At the bar, a man in check shirt, cords and green wellies checked his watch and tutted. Was he glancing at the door, waiting for someone to arrive, or just watching Benjamin?

Benjamin's heart began to race. He had learned a lot more about heart health since his trespass into the Emporium, knew that he was feeling anxiety rather than a heart attack. But the breathing exercises which usually helped weren't scratching the surface.

'There you are.' A man slid into the seat opposite him. He was in his late sixties and his suit was well made, although it had clearly been made for someone else. His accent denoted safety, a member of the upper middle classes. He presumed this was the Mr Watton who had signed the email. 'Did you run here? You're sweating.'

'N-no. I hid my van in a side road and walked. It has the company logo on it and I thought I'd be discreet.'

254

The man laughed. 'I was told you'd be cautious. Are you sure you're up for this? You know the right people?'

The thought of someone else doing this – of another, less careful dealer laying hands on Peg – served to harden Benjamin's resolve.

'Mr Watton, I am the *only* man who can do this for you.'

Watton smiled. 'That's what I like to hear. Now, a drink.'

He ordered whiskies, sixteen-year-old Laphroaig – Benjamin's personal favourite. Watton had done his research.

'I really shouldn't,' Benjamin said. 'The van – I'm driving.'

Watton rolled his eyes. 'I can't work with someone who doesn't seal a deal with a drink.' The man stared at Benjamin, unblinking, intimidating. And so Benjamin drank.

They discussed prices and practicalities. The difficulty of accessing the Emporium. The front windows had been boarded up after an incursion by squatters some years before, and also there were the original nineteenth-century leaded lights to be considered. This was not a standard smash-and-grab.

'We could . . .' Benjamin clammed up as the Agatha Christie fan walked past their table and out of the front door. He leaned forward and continued in a low whisper, waxing lyrical about the degree of packing and protection that would be required to move her.

'Will we also be requiring the piano? It's a conventional pianoforte dating back to the early 1800s. It's not a part of Peg's mechanism but it has been hers for a very long time.'

Watton showed a flash of irritation. 'I'm not getting a bloody piano mover involved,' he snapped. He saw Benjamin bristle and added, 'My client has already acquired a suitable instrument, and a display case to ensure that the artefact is kept in perfect atmospheric conditions.'

'Is there nothing you can tell me about the client's identity?' Benjamin had heard of collectors from Saudi and the Emirates swooping in, snapping up valuable items in the way the British imperialists once did, locking them away in their palaces. He felt strongly that Peg would not like the heat.

'I'm under strict instructions to say nothing,' the man said. 'You'll just have to trust me that my client is every bit as committed to this automaton as you are. I can't see it myself but mine is not to reason why. Safe to say, you are both on the same side.'

'And the Veritys? They'll never know?'

'Why would they suspect anything? You have a spotless repu-tation, that's what makes you the man for the job.'

Benjamin felt a little sick. The taste of the whisky reared up in his mouth again and he swallowed in a ludicrous attempt to force it back down. He felt shifty and uncomfortable.

Just then, Watton's phone vibrated and Benjamin jumped, glancing around the room again. The man behind the bar was definitely staring at them, reaching for his phone, holding it up. *Christ, he's going to take a photo.*

Benjamin's heart beat out of control. This didn't feel like 'just' anxiety.

'Are you all right?' Watton's tone was curious rather than concerned.

'Weak . . . heart . . .' Benjamin said. 'I must go.'

He stood abruptly, spilling Watton's drink. He couldn't stay here a moment longer, couldn't even pretend to Watton that he was comfortable. He fled, the sound of his companion's laughter echoing in his ears as he ran. Outside the fresh air hit him, rain soaked his skin quickly, gusts of wind slamming the raindrops into his body. He had left his umbrella in the nook but there was no way he was going back for that now.

By the time he reached the van he was fighting for breath, and soaked through with rainwater and sweat. *Heart racing. Cold sweat. Fatigue.* Benjamin leaned back against the sides of Betsy, his lovingly restored vintage Morris Minor van, and breathed, waiting for the panic to go away, for the world to realign into the cosy, comfortable life he usually took for granted. He could get in the van and drive away, spend a quiet Christmas with Louisa, never contact Watton again.

He composed the denials in his head: 'I really had no idea what sort of man I was meeting. I left as soon as I realised. I was shocked and appalled . . .'

But then, what would happen to Peg? Nobody else cared about her, nobody in the world, except him and this mysterious client. He took a deep, ragged breath and although his heart was still hammering and his hands were still shaking, he turned the ignition key.

Just as he eased Betsy into first, the sound of sirens filled the air, getting closer. The police were coming for him! Benjamin reacted with a stab of sheer panic. He slammed his foot onto the accelerator, gunning Betsy around the corner, away from the siren sound, speeding away from this godforsaken village as fast as he could.

He didn't see the shadow ahead until it was too late. He heard a dull thud, saw a blur of hair and limbs slamming onto Betsy's bonnet – a woman thrown around like a helpless doll. Like Peg.

Benjamin stamped his foot hard on the brake pedal, but it was too late. The figure rolled off the bonnet, crumpled onto the road, and it was only then that he realised his headlights weren't even on. He flipped a switch and saw . . .

It was the woman from the pub, her red hair plastered against her face, the tattered book splayed out on the tarmac in front of her. She was pale, unmoving, her eyes closed.

Benjamin opened the door, started to climb out, but then hesitated.

He had sped around a corner, his headlights off. He had drunk two whiskies, forced down him by Watton. He shouldn't even be here.

And the woman looked dead.

Curtains twitched in a cottage window opposite, a flicker of Christmas lights shone out onto the street from within. In a moment there would be witnesses, police, questions, his reputation would crumble and Peg would rot forever in her abandoned store. Benjamin, already in fight or flight mode, panicked again, and got back into the van.

Only Louisa knew. He could never hide anything this big from her and the next day he walked her out to the garage, showed her the dent in Betsy's bumper and found, to his horror, a twist of rain-soaked red hair caught in the windscreen wiper.

'How fast were you going, Ben?'

'Too fast. I was seeing that awful man about Peg and I . . .'

'Clockwork Peg again. Benjamin, you've got to let this thing go. And you know you have to go to the police about this.'

He told her he would do it tomorrow, then he said after Christmas would be better, and each time he thought he meant it. The truth was, though, that Benjamin was never going to hand himself in. He had lived an unimpeachable life up until now, and what good would it do anyone if he went to prison? And without him, Peg would rot away in the abandoned Emporium.

'My work is too important,' he told Louisa finally.

'You're an antiques dealer.'

She did not shout or threaten to turn him in, that wasn't Louisa's way. She stood by in silent judgement as he washed the blood off Betsy, threw the hank of red hair on their sitting room log burner. She listened to his justifications with one delicately raised eyebrow answering only, 'Hmmm.'

But from that moment her respect for him evaporated, and their partnership began to fail; the solid, well-made joints clogging with rust, the fabric they'd woven between them polluted with mould.

28

FRAN

BENJAMIN FALLS SILENT, HIS SHOULDERS SAGGING FORWARD IN shame.

'What happened to her?' Fran asks.

'Well, I didn't hear from Watton for quite a few months after that. He cut off contact completely until the news broke about the Emporium reopening. So she just stayed here, getting more and more decayed.'

'Not Clockwork Peg.' Fran grits her teeth. 'The woman you knocked down in the street.'

'Ah, yes. Sorry. Not feeling quite well. She survived, thank goodness. There were reports on the local newspaper site the next day saying that a woman had survived a hit and run in the village. Another report appeared in the New Year asking for witnesses, saying that she had suffered life-changing injuries and had to undergo surgery several times.'

'But by then, you'd got away with it and decided to keep schtum,' Josie puts in.

'Yes. Yes, I did.'

'Charming.' Josie sneers, leaning back against a pile of teddy bears. 'What a fucking hypocrite. All that crap you talk about obeying the rules and honour and all that, and you just leave a woman lying in the street.'

Benjamin makes a noise which sounds like a small sob, but Josie presses on. 'And you still care more about Clockwork Peg than you do about her.'

'Josie, ease off,' Fran says. 'There's no point, not when he's this ill . . .'

'Oh, and you can talk. You're a hypocrite too – how much of that money did you steal? How much?'

Josie stands, and Fran notices her bag is still held close to her, hugged across her chest. She remembers the knife. Josie has done bad things, dark things in her past. Is she capable of hurting her now?

'You know, when I first met you last night I was so excited,' Josie continues. 'My niece has just finished chemo – there's this other treatment she wants to have in America and I thought, Fran will know about it. I even thought you might help me raise money to send her there. But you turn out to be every bit as bad as the other rich wankers here. That money you stole, that could have gone to help someone like my Ariana, that could save someone's life. What did you spend it on? A holiday? A new Christmas jumper?'

'I'm sorry,' Fran says wretchedly. She wants to tell Josie she's not a thief but the truth is far more shameful.

She pulls herself to her feet. Her body feels heavy and bone tired. It's nearly five in the morning and apart from her drugged sleep earlier she hasn't rested at all. They are all coming unravelled.

'I'm worried about Merry,' she says. 'I'm going to find her.'

'Suit yourself.'

'Look after Benjamin while I'm gone, will you?'

Josie's response is a curse and, even though it's not safe outside, Fran steps out of the grotto with relief.

She knows she has just done something foolish, that she is safer by far with the others, despite Josie's knife, but she also knows that Merry is in danger.

And that's why she's here, isn't it? She might have been lured in by some unseen killer to pay for her sins, but her purpose here is to ensure the others survive even if it means sacrificing her own life. This is how she will make amends.

She looks out across the Hall of Toys – at the sledging slope where they'd had such a brilliant time, and at Clockwork Peg in the shadows by the cash desk. She thinks of Benjamin touching the clockwork girl earlier, cutting his finger, and moves closer to inspect the far side of Peg's face.

Just like before, there's a feeling about the automaton, a low buzzing presence that's grown stronger now since her experiences in the corridor.

She is afraid to touch Peg herself, given what happened to Benjamin, but there is a jar of candy canes on a table nearby, and she uses one of those to brush Peg's dark curls aside.

And there it is, protruding from her cap, shiny and silver but so small you wouldn't notice it unless you were looking closely. The point of a needle.

It's the kind you would find in any sewing box. Looking closely she sees another one glistening in Peg's hair, and another just behind her ear. But why would someone do something like this?

She closes her eyes and remembers Benjamin brushing the dust off Peg's cap, cutting his finger, putting it into his mouth . . .

Fran draws back suddenly. The dust. There was poison in the dust. It must have come from that vial Fran found earlier. Benjamin had touched the dust, pricked his finger and then sucked at the wound the way most people instinctively do when they cut themselves.

Someone had put those needles there, knowing that Benjamin would be unable to resist touching his beloved Peg, knowing that he would cut himself, relying on him to suck the wound.

He had been poisoned by his true love.

Fran pulls the vial from the pocket where she stashed it, studies the label. This is a medical drug, similar to the chemotherapy ones which were so familiar to her, and suddenly she realises where she saw the ridiculously long name before. She'd read about this – it was an experimental drug used in the States to treat Branscombe's disease. She'd talked about it with Raynsford who had said it was showing good results but in many patients it placed undue pressure on the heart.

The drug had been in the dust. The dust had given Benjamin heart failure.

Fran is about to pull away, to run back to him, when she feels that sense, that tug again. *Look closer.*

Peg's elegant wooden shoulders stop just below the line of her bodice. Fran uses the candy cane to move the fabric away from her, and sees that beneath her clothes Peg is a simple metal cage. There is something just inside the cage, a fold of old-fashioned paper. Cautiously, using a tissue to protect herself, Fran reaches in and pinches the corner between her first two fingers. It takes a couple of tugs before the paper comes out.

It's an ancient letter, signed by Everard Verity. The writing is scrawled and difficult to read, but Fran can just about make out the message of it. He is acknowledging that Peggy Goodchild is his illegitimate daughter, expressing profound regret at her death, and instructing the recipient to seek out her son in the orphanage where he had been placed and pass ownership of the Emporium onto him.

Fran shakes her head, a wave of sadness overcoming her. Why does this not surprise her? Peggy was actually a member of the Verity family – hidden because of her illegitimacy and, Fran is sure, the colour of her skin. Everard Verity, visionary purveyor of wonders, was just a horny old coloniser after all, and the family must have been hushing it up ever since. Had Peggy even known the truth about her parentage, or had she died believing she was simply enslaved?

She gazes at the automaton, and for a moment she sees a shape behind it. Her skin prickles. This is the closest she has ever come to truly seeing someone in the afterlife, the imprint of a girl long since gone.

She folds the paper, stuffing it into her bra for safekeeping.

The shape wavers and Fran's belief wavers too – did she just see something real, or the product of her semi-exhausted state and her desperation to inherit her mother's gift? But she has known from the start that life isn't a case of black and white, real and imaginary. At Christmas your belief shapes your reality.

264

It's then she sees a shadow flicker behind the cash desk. Someone is watching her.

'Merry? Is that you?'

Silence.

She calls again, edging away from the piano.

Benjamin's words from earlier pop back into her head. Merry really is the odd one out of their little troupe; creeping around, avoiding sharing with the others unless it suits her. Could she be involved, the same way Dean and Evangeline had been? Fran had once been a trusting soul, but tonight has shaken that trust to the core. Fran's hands curl into fists. She wishes she had brought Dean's cricket bat out with her.

She is about to retreat to the grotto when a sound distracts her. One she hasn't heard in hours.

Ping.

And then the unmistakeable sound of a lift door opening. Warily, Fran turns away from the automaton, advancing through the forest of Christmas trees towards the sound. The light is on inside the lift, the doors are open and there, propped up against the panelled back wall, glowing like the ordinary everyday thing it is, is a phone.

It's not broken, like Evangeline's handset had been. The screen lock is off and she can see a generic picture of a sunset, plus all the basic apps you get when you first set your phone up. And, in the top right corner, five tantalising bars of reception.

It's a trap, of course it is, but it's a *phone*. Calling 999 is Benjamin's only chance right now. If she can think smartly enough to get this – if she can beat the odds – she can save the others, and surely that helps redress the balance of what she has done? The key, she knows instinctively, is not to step into that lift. Somehow, the lift is the trap.

It gives an impatient *ping* and tries to close its doors. She jabs her finger on the brass button to keep it there, looking around for things she can use.

She settles on a small Christmas tree, about waist-high, and jams it into the door to keep it open. Then spots her old friend, the elf with the sign: TOYS AND SANTA'S GROTTO THIS WAY.

The sign is about three feet high and slides easily out of the elf's grip. Her first idea is simply to kneel on the floor, reach into the lift and try and sweep the phone towards her with the sign. One jab hits the screen – it doesn't even wobble, and she realises with dismay that the phone has been stuck down somehow. It's not going to be that easy.

But still: five bars of reception.

She will not give up. Even though a tiny logical part of her brain is screaming that this will never work, she will not give up. She will save them all.

She tries a different tack, standing up and leaning forward, holding her hand on the edge of the lift door and pivoting her body forwards, without letting her toes cross the dividing line into the lift. It's not quite far enough, so she stands on one leg and pivots even further down, discarding the sign and reaching with her fingers. She can almost touch it . . .

Just then, someone shoves her hard into the lift. Fran tumbles forwards, her head hitting the floor. She is stunned for a few seconds, groans, just as she rolls over she can see a hand pulling the Christmas tree away from the door. A blur, the sounds of a struggle and then a figure is crashing down onto her with a scream and a flurry of flashing lights. It's Merry.

Merry is attacking her?

No, Merry was attacking her attacker.

The doors of the lift close. Fran pulls herself into a sitting position. Her shoulder feels strangely wet, her arm isn't as strong as it should be and that's what makes her look down.

Blood. Lots of it. She's been stabbed. But how come she doesn't feel any . . . *oh, there it is. There's the pain.*

And then the lift lurches, giving a low, metallic groan. The two women stare at each other.

Above them, something breaks, and the lift is in free-fall, plummeting.

Instinct makes her leap onto Merry, curl her body around the other woman, cradling the back of her neck with her hand as if to protect her from the impact. She hears Merry's squeak of protest from underneath as the lift crashes down.

She is going to die. She will never save the others, she will never be forgiven. The lift makes impact and pain explodes through her body.

The last thing she thinks before everything goes black: *Nobody ever knew.*

29

FRAN

FRAN IS NOT DEAD. THIS FACT SURPRISES HER AS SHE OPENS HER eyes. The lift has gone dark again, there are shattered remnants of broken glass scattered all around her. And she is being held down, pinned to the floor by an unknown assailant who is pushing brutally down on her shoulder wound. Fran screams, squirming.

'Hold still,' Merry says irritably. 'I'm applying pressure. Trying to slow the bleeding down – you're just making it worse.'

Fran groans. The tearing pain coming from her shoulder is all she can focus on right now.

'What were you thinking, getting into this lift?' Merry continues. 'It was so obviously a trap. I was hiding under Peg's piano when I saw someone creep after you. She – whoever it was – pushed you in and I tried to stop her, but she ended up shoving me in, too.'

The pain. The pain . . . Fran's mind pulses. But then she remembers something, the reason she is here.

'Phone,' she manages to croak.

'Oh, I've got that, but it doesn't work.'

Of course it doesn't. Merry was right – she has played right into the killer's hands.

'Are you OK?'

'My ankle hurts,' Merry says. 'But I think you kind of cushioned me from the worst. Er . . . thanks for that. Do you think you can move?'

Fran can barely even think let alone move, but she nods to be obliging. Slowly, agonisingly, she struggles to her feet, trying to regain that burst of adrenalin she'd had earlier, when she hadn't felt the wound at all.

Her legs ache and feel like jelly. There's a throbbing pain from where she banged her head and, of course, the pulsing agony in her shoulder, but there isn't that *wrong* feeling you get from a broken limb or a torn ligament. She can still just about move her arm. She tries to speak, but all that comes out is a sob. She nearly died, and her secret would have died with her.

Wasn't that what she wanted?

'I saw a glimpse of her face when we were fighting,' Merry says. 'Definitely a woman. She's white – like, pale white – and she was wearing a hoodie and a face mask; it all happened too fast for me to see any features. But she was wearing this too.' Merry holds up something tangled and matted in her hand.

'It's a wig,' Merry says. 'I pulled it off when I was fighting her. Ew, I think it might actually be real hair.'

269

Fran is near weeping with the effort of standing, of thinking, but still, her hands reach out, brush the hair. It's fine quality.

She's not repulsed by the idea of real hair, not after a lifetime of weaves. And she's seen the power that real-hair wigs can have. She has seen cancer patients, lost and afraid, slip one onto their head and immediately become themselves again.

All those people, all that suffering. Raising funds, denying herself all but the smallest pleasure – nothing she does will ever help them, ever undo her mistake. She could be the best person in the world, and still the secret would weigh her down forever.

A sickening certainty comes over her. There is only one way out of this.

The two of them force the lift door open and push out into the Hall of Wonders. Merry is limping slightly – just a twisted ankle, she says. Slowly and painfully, leaning on each other for support, they make their way up the main stairs. Back to Santa's grotto, to safety in numbers.

Josie sits on the floor, Benjamin's head in her lap. She is dabbing his brow with a rolled-up Christmas stocking from Santa's fire-place. *Why would Santa hang up stockings in his own grotto?* Fran wonders briefly, absurdly, but the thought flits away when she sees how bad things are.

'He's not waking up,' Josie's voice cracks. Merry produces an almost-empty Evian bottle from her bag and they try to dribble some of the liquid into his mouth in between his shallow breaths.

'He was poisoned,' Fran says blankly, explaining the vial she'd found, the sharp needles and dust she had discovered on Peg. Then she gives Merry a potted history of Benjamin's crimes.

A wave of helplessness crashes over her. What good does that knowledge do? She's not a doctor, she still has no idea how to save him. Even though she knows it won't work, she tries the phone she had found in the lift.

It's a real phone, a cheap Android model, reset to factory settings. There is no SIM card in it, and Wi-Fi has been disabled somehow. Those five bars of reception she had seen earlier were fakes – a screen shot taken of the phone when it was active, before the SIM card was removed. A cruel and simple trick.

'I was such an idiot to fall for it,' Fran curses herself.

'Look,' Merry says, 'this person knows you, even if you don't know her. She somehow knew you wouldn't be able to resist that trap.'

It takes a few moments for the idea to sink in. This person knows her guilt, knows that she would sacrifice herself for redemption. They see it as a weakness to be exploited. All the more reason to take control.

'I still don't get it, though,' Josie says. 'I'm sure it's Fire Kid. She's the one I hurt the most back in the day. But she loved this place, and now she's wrecking it.'

'Perhaps she's fallen out of love with it somehow,' Merry says, slumping back down on her blanket. 'Love turns to hate pretty quickly. She can burn this place to the ground for all I care, provided we're not in it.'

Fran feels weak, her eyes want to close and every time she lets them, she feels the lift plummet, that sickening certainty that she was going to die. And there is that thought again: *Nobody ever knew.* The thought hadn't comforted her as she expected, instead it had frightened her. At that moment Fran realises that, despite fighting to hide her secret from the world, she has to tell. It's the only way that she will ever find the punishment she is seeking, and the peace she needs.

'I need to do something,' Fran says, holding out the phone. 'I want you to film me and if I don't survive and you do, you have to promise to give it to the press.'

'Are you sure?' Merry says. 'You don't have to do this.'

Fran is taken aback, Merry has been trying to needle this secret out of her since the beginning of the night. Why hesitate now? Merry can see her surprise, looks slightly ashamed, twisting her sleeve.

'Look, all I'm saying is I trust you, whatever you did.'

Fran draws strength from these words as Merry fires up the phone camera and trains it on her. Her face instinctively rearranges itself into the expression she has always used when the camera is on her. Energised, smiling, ready to share – there's a twinkle in her eyes that in the early days used to send male reviewers into a state of agitation. She presses record.

'My name is Fran Silver,' she says. 'And I have something to confess.'

30

CHRISTMAS PAST – 2017

FRAN

THERE SHOULD HAVE BEEN DECORATIONS. THERE SHOULD HAVE been glitter on tinsel on foil decking every wall and surface, so much shininess that you couldn't see the shape of normality underneath it. There should have been a magnificent spread: chicken and curry goat, macaroni cheese and plantain, plus turkey, stuffing and roast potatoes to 'make it British'. There should have been dozens of friends and neighbours, the ones who were drawn to Mum's charisma not Fran's fame. There should have been Mum's big, broad laugh ringing out through the room, especially when the *Morning All!* Christmas TV special came on.

'There she is! That's my daughter on television! I'm so proud . . . but what do you think you're cooking there? That's not how you make roti!'

And Fran would cringe and smile and take the criticism (because Mum was right, that was not how you make roti – the producers insisted everything she cooked had a '*Morning All!* twist' that you couldn't find in recipe books). All the neighbours would pile in and attack her, but in a proud, happy way that made her feel part of her community, even if her working life had taken her away from it.

But this year there was none of that. Mum's house was gone – her cluttered, pungent kitchen and cramped dining room were currently being remodelled by a couple of lawyers who had snapped the place up and were in the process of turning it into their dream home. And across town, for the first time in her life, Fran kept her house decoration-free, with the exception of the felt Father Christmas figure her mother had had since she was a child, and which always sat on top of the mantelpiece clock.

Fran was watching the *Morning All!* Christmas special in her own home, with a bottle of wine for company, while on-screen Dahlia Whitty dipped her manicured finger into a mountain of whipped cream and licked it.

'Mmmm!' she said in her spoiled, posh drawl. 'Absolute heaven.'

Fran felt a rage rise in her belly, but she couldn't switch off, couldn't turn away. *Raising temperatures in kitchens across the country,* that's what the TV reviews were saying. *Dahlia Whitty's passion for food sizzles off the screen.*

Unlike Fran, Dahlia had never trained as a chef but she had three things that Fran did not: wavy screen-siren blonde hair, pouty lips and a phenomenal pair of tits. It also helped that she was married to one of the *Morning All!* producers.

'We're going to take the food content in a different direction,' said producer had told her. And they had certainly done that, Fran thought sourly. Pigs in blankets for Christmas dinner? Revolutionary.

She took another slug of Cava, felt the fizz settle on the back of her tongue, and tried to de-focus her mind enough to see her mother's ghost.

It had happened once, oh-so-briefly, about six months after Agnes died. Fran had been coming round from a wine-blackout and there she was, on the edge of her consciousness; a glimpse of a figure moving the way her mother always had, the flash of a smile.

So now she felt an extra hunger as she opened each bottle – a hope that she could find her mother at the bottom of one and tell her . . . She didn't know what. That she was lonely, that she was afraid, that she was forgetting who she was.

Cancer's a bitch. Branscombe's disease the worst, working its way through her mother's body, advancing sneakily day on day without any telltale lumps, any symptoms beyond tiredness that her mother had put down to old age. Fran wanted to travel back in time, beg her mum to get tested before it was too late, but even with the Sight that wasn't going to happen.

So instead, Fran kept her eyes fixed on the screen. Dahlia was on the sofa now, laughing and clinking Champagne glasses with Emma and Chris, the two main presenters. Fran ground her teeth. She had never been directed to join them on the sofa – the producers had said they wanted to keep the kitchen segment separate – but now here was Dahlia, simpering and serving them a little plate of mini mince pies like one of the family.

In the words of the tabloid press, Fran took to Twitter. She knew it was a terrible idea but she just had to look.

Dahlia Whitty is smoking hot #ChristmasMorningAll
That woman can stuff my turkey anytime

And from the @MorningAllOfficial account, a photo of the cast and crew gathered together. Fran noticed that every female presenter in the picture was blonde except for Rupa, the resident doctor.

Another great year for Morning All! What a team!

Fran drank and scrolled, and scrolled and drank. *Morning All!* faded from the feed after the broadcast ended, but there were other bruises she could press down on. So-called friends who had drifted away after she lost her job; ex-boyfriends posting photos with their new girlfriends; Dahlia's own feed, including a too-perfect Christmas dinner table with the producer-husband beaming dorkily and holding a glass aloft. Even a photo of Zelda, out celebrating with another, more successful client.

Fran drank again, then slumped forward over her kitchen table and let her eyes go blurry, searching for her mother in that liminal space. It wouldn't be Christmas alone if she could see her.

It was no good. She would have to keep drinking, keep trying.

The sound of the television woke her, the *Doctor Who* theme tune plus another weird buzzing noise she can't quite identify. The room was dark but for the flicker of the television. Flushed with shame, Fran glanced up at the windows and checked the curtains were closed – at least nobody had been able to peer in to see the absolute state of Fran Silver on Christmas Day. Not, she reminded herself, that anyone cared.

The buzzing sound happened again. Her phone. It took her a few moments to locate it, sandwiched between two sofa cushions. There had to be something wrong with it; it shouldn't be buzzing this much.

She ignored all the Twitter notifications – she was used to getting lots of mentions, even if they had tailed off recently. But she was not used to having this many text messages and missed calls. There were dozens and dozens of them. Including one from Marcus Raynsford, her mother's oncologist.

I've just heard. Please don't worry too much, if it's an early diagnosis there's lots that can be done. If you need any advice at all I am happy to offer it.

Bemused, Fran opens the next one, from Zelda.

Honey, why didn't you tell me? This is so shit on top of everything else. I'll be there for you, whatever you need.

Then another one, also Zelda: *Are you OK?*

Zelda again: *Fran, we need to get a statement out before this snowballs even further. I know you must be feeling like shit but if we handle it now, it'll be easier later.*

Fran stared at the messages, her booze-fogged brain failing to snag on anything that made sense. She coughed, tested her voice. No, she sounded too drunk to call Zelda. Instead, she went through the rest of her messages looking for clues. Nothing was making sense, and so with a due sense of dread, she looked at her Twitter notifications, which tell her she has received over ten thousand likes for one tweet.

What tweet?

Oh God, what tweet.

Fran navigated to her profile, and her heart dropped like a stone.

@realFranSilver: Cancer's a bitch.

Fran had no memory of tweeting it but after the initial post, people had immediately retweeted and replied, assuming she was the one with the diagnosis, and instead of putting them straight, drunk Fran had shared a stream of bitter, mournful tweets she could not remember sending. Until eventually, publicly and without ambiguity, she had told the world that she had Branscombe's disease. And the world had believed her.

Fuck.

Her phone buzzed again – a voice call from Zelda. Fran switched it to answerphone. She would need Zelda's help to get on top of this, but she wasn't ready to face that yet.

First she needed to throw up.

A heavy vomiting session followed by a shower should have helped Fran feel cleansed, but instead all she could think about was the deep, deep shit she was in. There was no weaselling out of this – she would have to draft a statement saying that she'd lied. Make a huge public apology, donate as much as she could to the Branscombe's Trust. She'd have to pay through the nose for a week at the Priory then go through a hideous round of interviews for weekly mags, saying how horrendously sorry she was. She would be apologising for this for the rest of her life.

Fran glanced over at her mother's Father Christmas decoration and was flooded with shame. For the first time she hoped Agnes' ghost was not here, that she would never know what her daughter had done.

Stay quiet and dignified, wait for Christmas to be over, then release a statement, that's what Zelda would say. But Fran could not stay offline, could not put her phone down and go to bed. Instead she spent the rest of Christmas night scrolling through all the wonderful, warm, supportive replies on Twitter, ignoring Zelda's calls. And through the shame, there was a flicker of hope, of wonder, because this showed she hadn't been forgotten. People cared about her, even though she wasn't on TV any more. How angry would those people be when they found out she'd lied . . .

Then a tweet jumps out at her:

@WhittyReparTea So sorry to hear about darling @realFranSilver's diagnosis. She's always been a great friend of mine and I'll be going over there with a freshly made jerk chicken as soon as I can!

'The fuck you will,' Fran growled. She'd met Dahlia once, maybe twice at the studios when she'd done a couple of guest slots. Somehow she managed to restrain herself from tweeting back, telling her exactly where she could stick her jerk chicken. If she could even make it, that was. Dahlia has probably just googled Caribbean food and named the first dish that came up.

Fran imagined what it would be like, meeting Dahlia and the rest of the *Morning All!* crew after the truth was revealed. The sting of humiliation, the shame.

But there was no other way out.

The next morning dawned bright and unseasonably mild, and Fran's headache was officially her worst ever. She did not return Zelda's calls. She did not go back on Twitter.

She spent Boxing Day watching *Miracle on 34th Street* on a loop, trying to draft her statement and imagining her future. She would never work in TV again, the money would run out, Zelda would drop her. She thought about opening her own restaurant. She googled *retrain as a midwife*. She checked how much money she had in her savings account then cried a bit.

On Twitter, in the absence of any word from her, the speculation grew. She had, it was generally agreed, been looking ill lately. Maybe that's why she'd left *Morning All!*. Or maybe *Morning All!* had fired her after finding out – there was a brief flare of anger against the programme over that. On the basis of no evidence whatsoever many people decided it was terminal and started speculating on how long Fran had to live.

Then of course there were the scum-suckers who fed on this sort of thing, people with pseudonyms, the word British in their bio and union flag profile photos. *Fran Silver's an attention seeker. She's just doing this to save her flagging career.*

Fran felt sick. Coming clean would make this guy's day. Him and all the other slimeballs, plus the better-paid media slimeballs who loved any story about a successful woman of colour fucking up. Oh, the sheer glee that would be felt in certain newspaper offices.

Just then her doorbell rang. She took another sip of wine and went to answer it, not thinking to check before she opened the door.

It was Zelda. Of course it was. She held out her arms wide, folding her into a hug.

'I'm so sorry, this is appalling, especially after what you went through with your mum,' she said.

Fran simply wept, clinging to her friend, her tears soaking Zelda's shoulder, guilt and shame pounding in her chest. And right in that moment she couldn't say it. She couldn't tell her what she'd done. And so instead she said:

'It does run in families, you know.'

Fran was fuelled by wine for the first fortnight of the year, agreeing a statement with Zelda confirming, not denying, her diagnosis, asking for privacy at this difficult time. Maybe she could do this, maybe if she played the privacy card, came off social media, distanced herself from her remaining friends, she could get away with it, pretend to have treatment and then bounce back a year later. But then the other messages began to creep in.

First, the Branscombe's Trust slid into her DMs with sympathies and suggestions for *ways we can work together to raise awareness of this terrible disease.* A group of *Morning All!* fans started a GoFundMe to raise money to help support her while she wasn't working. And then, worst of all, people with Branscombe's, and even relatives of those who had died, began contacting her offering solidarity, tips, recommending one consultant, warning her off another. Offering a shoulder to cry on when things got bad.

All these people suffering, dying. She was making a mockery of them all. The thought of it weighed Fran down day and night, driving her so deep into a lake of wine that she could no longer touch the bottom. She was the lowest of the low, the worst of the worst. Over and over, she'd open her Twitter app planning

281

to come clean but the thought of all that support turning to hate stopped her every time.

And then she picked up her phone and called Doctor Raynsford.

There was nothing remarkable about his consulting room. Despite his towering reputation as a physician it was NHS standard – impersonal with tatty furniture and uncomfortable chairs. She had sat in here with Agnes, holding her hand as he delivered the worst news in his soft, reassuring voice. It hadn't changed since.

Raynsford looked at her – her wretched face, her nervous, twitching hands, her skin which radiated the scent of booze.

'Tell me everything,' he said.

Back when he was treating her mother, she had appreciated his straight talking, his lack of judgement and now he listened patiently. As a doctor he'd seen everything, heard everything, and while he could never approve of what she'd done, he said he could understand how it had happened. The deal he offered was simple: he would help her, coach her in what to say about her treatment, how hospitals work and in return she would sort herself out, get clean and live a worthwhile life.

'But what if the press find out I'm not getting hospital treatment?'

'They'd never be able to prove it.' Raynsford shrugged. 'Hospitals aren't allowed to share your medical records without your permission. Search online and you'll find dozens of stories of people who faked cancer for years without being found out, or charged with any crime. As long as you don't gain anything personally from pretending to have cancer, provided you don't accept that GoFundMe or anything similar, I'm not even sure you're committing a crime. You've done something silly, Fran, but not anything illegal.'

At Raynsford's words, Fran felt calm for the first time in weeks. And maybe, she told herself, she could use this to make a difference, to make amends.

In this new life, there were no half-measures. She gave press interviews, posted about it on social media, always refusing direct payment for anything. She redirected the GoFundMe to the Branscombe's Trust and made sure there was a paper trail showing she had done it. And she began her new life, her sober life of raising money, striving to be good, of self-denial.

And of waiting, always waiting, to be discovered.

31

MERRY

AS FRAN STOPS SPEAKING, HER SHOULDERS SAG. SHE IS SITTING ON
the floor of Santa's grotto, her legs drawn up in front of her. She
is weeping.

Josie is the first to speak: 'But . . . I saw photos of you online,
having treatment.'

'You saw pictures of my hand with an IV drip in, empty
blister packs of pills. I didn't mention this on the video because
I don't want to implicate him but I had a doctor friend who
helped me, who supplied the props and the background information. It's not his fault, I was an absolute mess when I went
to him for help; he was worried about me, he was just trying to
get me out of it. I don't think either of us realised how much it
would snowball.'

Merry's head is a whirl of questions and all she can think of to
say is: 'You lost your hair . . .'

'I shaved my head.'

Josie makes a disgusted sound in her throat.

'I know.' Fran hangs her head. 'That was the worst thing of all, but I was in too deep by then. I felt like I was making a mockery of anyone who had ever had chemotherapy.'

'You were.' Josie speaks through gritted teeth.

Fran simply nods. 'If I ever get out of here I'm going to spend the rest of my life apologising – trying to make up for it – but it's still never going to be enough.'

Merry knows this is true. She has grown to like Fran, to respect her, even. And she can – sort of – understand how she got herself into this mess, but she is still appalled. She thinks of her grandfather, who died of cancer, of Kate from the office who tried to keep life as normal as possible and hated it when anyone called her 'brave'. And then there's . . .

Oh. Oh no.

A sickening feeling of realisation creeps over her. She holds her hand over her mouth as if to stop herself from screaming.

She knows who the killer is, and now, with brutal clarity, she understands exactly why she has been brought here.

Merry doesn't think she'd made any sound but she must have whimpered, because Fran looks up from her misery. 'What is it?'

But before Merry has a chance to reply, Josie cries out. She is kneeling next to Benjamin, holding her hand against the pulse point on his neck, the way Merry has seen people do in crime shows.

'Benjamin's not breathing.' Her voice comes out as a sob. 'I can't find his pulse. Does anyone know first aid? Oh shit, oh fuck, you funny, uptight little man, breathe. *Please.*'

He is still slumped next to Santa's throne. He looks like he is still sleeping – his features relaxed, no longer twisted in pain. His face is pale.

He is gone. Merry knows that, but she does not try to stop Josie as she leans over him, compressing his chest, breathing into his mouth with all the desperation of someone who saw this once on TV and will try anything to get someone back.

'Dammit, you stupid man,' Josie sobs. 'I'm sorry I called you a hypocrite. Don't die. Don't die, you rich wanker . . .'

Josie falls, sobbing onto Benjamin's chest. Fran goes forward to comfort her but draws back, afraid of Josie's disdain. So it is up to Merry.

She reaches out and lays her hand gently on Josie's shoulder, feeling the sobs trembling through her fingers. She waits for the storm to pass.

With a messy sniff, Josie pulls herself upright and wipes her eyes with the sleeve of her jumper. Merry can see her fighting to keep control.

Josie takes Benjamin's limp hand, looks at the tiny scratch on it. 'I can't believe one little scratch caused all this.'

'She planned this from the start.' Merry's voice is dull. 'She knew all our flaws, all our obsessions. She knew Benjamin wouldn't be able to resist the chance to touch that thing. She knew that Dean would lose it with Rudi and that he'd reject Evangeline. She probably knew Evangeline would goad him to climb down that ladder.'

Josie lets out a choking sob, gets to her feet. Her teeth are clenched tight together, and when she speaks, Merry can only just hear her. 'I am going to kill that fucking Fire Kid.'

'Don't,' Merry says. 'Please, just listen to me because this is all part of the plan. I don't know how or why yet, but I just know that's what she wants you to do. She's been controlling us from the start, and I know who she is. Her name's Rita. Rita Gliss. She's my friend Ross's mother.'

32

CHRISTMAS PAST – 2019

MERRY

IT WAS NOT A PART OF LONDON THAT MERRY WAS USED TO visiting. There was no litter here, no chewing gum stuck to the pavement and no tatty, quirky flats. Instead, there was a neat row of Georgian townhouses with uniform black railings and white columns on either side of the doors.

Merry became painfully conscious of the tattiness of her red winter coat, the hole in her gloves, the box of Belgian chocolates she was holding. They had looked upmarket when she picked them up in Waitrose, but they seemed paltry now. Ross was so normal, so unpretentious, that she had forgotten he came from proper wealth. His father was a member of the aristocratic Verity family (although at this point Merry was blissfully unaware of the existence of the Emporium) and his mother was the legendary Rita Gliss, dynamic perfume entrepreneur. Rita was famed for her educated palate, her exquisite sense of smell. It was said that Rita could tell what perfume you were wearing from across a crowded room. Merry had, of course, drenched herself in Glissful White for the occasion, which had made Ross laugh.

'Relax, she'll like you for who you are, because I do,' he'd said, but they had both known that he was lying. Rita was exacting, drove herself hard, and expected the best from Ross, too. She had chosen his university course, even introduced him to his girl-friend Emelle, one of her favourite employees and an eminently suitable future spouse. The very fact he'd gone to work at Stimp-son's had been a major form of rebellion, an attempt to break away from the future Rita had planned, following her footsteps into Glissful. And Merry, coming from Stimpson's, was already tainted with guilt by association.

Despite this, she had been desperately looking forward to this Christmas Eve get-together. Who wouldn't want to meet a genuine kick-ass feminist hero? Rita was an orphan who had escaped the poverty trap of a childhood in care, gone to Oxford, married an aristocrat and started a multi-million-pound business. You didn't meet people like that every day. When Emelle had pulled out of the gathering with another of her stress headaches, Merry had only been too happy to step in as Ross's plus one, hoping to bind herself more tightly to him, to become essential, to belong.

Truth be told, aside from the Stimpson's Christmas do, this was the highlight of her festive season. Everyone else she knew was going home to their families for Christmas but that wasn't an option for her. Her parents had opened an Instagram account a few months after she had moved out called @wanderingemptynesters and were living the brand to the max. It was Antigua this year; they had flown out the week before and already WhatsApped her a photo of the beach, the two of them wearing Santa hats and clinking cocktail glasses.

Don't worry if you can't get hold of us on the day, they had said. *Reception here is terrible. Merry Christmas and Happy Birthday, darling!*

Merry had tapped out a reply: *Please can you try?* But then deleted it. They'd just say no.

Maybe Boxing Day?

She had deleted that, too, it seemed too needy. Neediness always made them shut down and they had already sent her an M&S hamper and a pair of satin pyjamas, and considered their job done. So she had given up, and planned to spend the day alone in the flat wearing the pyjamas and eating Celebrations. She had told her friends, Jen and Farah, and even Ross that she would enjoy the peace and quiet.

Ross's family was pretty mixed-up – his dad was serially unfaithful, his mum controlling and quick to take offence – but at least they wanted him around. Maybe they'd want her too? They might even invite her to spend Christmas with them.

But now, as Ross stopped outside a glossy black door bearing an elegant, understated Christmas wreath, she wasn't quite so sure.

'This is the one.' He bounded up the concrete steps, but Merry hesitated, fixed to the spot on the pavement outside. Through the windows she could see the glinting of warm white Christmas lights, garlands of real pine fronds and ivy draped over a marble mantelpiece and trimmed with perfectly tied red and white silk bows. It looked Instagram-perfect, like a scene from a Christmas film.

'Perhaps this isn't such a good idea,' she said, gripping the chocolates so tight she felt the cardboard packaging give way.

Ross, unaware that she was serious, laughed and pressed the bell. 'Too late!'

They waited, but the door remained shut. Merry felt a crack of hope open up in her. Maybe they'd got the wrong day, and she didn't have to go through this after all. Ross pressed the bell again, holding it down. It made an ugly buzzing sound, nothing as middlebrow and suburban as a *ding-dong* for this household.

As they waited in silence, Merry realised she could hear shouting. A man and woman, screaming at each other, and finally a smashing sound. Ross later told her this was his beloved snow globe being dashed against a wall. The door opened abruptly, and Rita stood there. She looked exactly as she did in her perfume ads and press appearances – dressed all in white, with flame-red hair and scarlet lipstick. But in her publicity material she always looked serene, a knowing smile playing on her lips, her eyebrow arched as if posing a witty question.

Now, though, her eyes were blazing with rage, her cheeks scarlet under her beautifully applied make-up, her lips pressed tight together. She gave Ross a cursory hug.

'Darling, come in. Go to the kitchen and wait – your father and I are discussing something,'

'Discussing?' came an incredulous shout from inside. 'There's nothing left to discuss, Peg!'

Ross went through the door past his mother, and as Merry began to climb the steps after him, Rita noticed her for the first time. Merry froze on the second step, a butterfly trapped by a pin. Rita took in her shabby coat, her frizz-prone hair, the miasma of Glissful White hanging pathetically around her.

'Oh no, I don't think so,' Rita said, and shut the door.

Shocked, shaking, unsure of what to do, Merry crossed the road and leaned on the iron railings of the gardens opposite, texting Ross every few minutes.

WTF?!?

Erm . . .

Still here.

Merry was used to rejection – it had happened to her a lot, and when it did she turned her anger in on herself. What a fool she had been for thinking Rita would be impressed by her, for thinking that she would be welcomed, that there was a chance she could find a surrogate family with Ross. She had known from all Ross's stories how many red flags hung around Rita. She should never have let herself hope, or care. That's how people like Rita controlled you, by finding out what you cared about.

A sob pushed its way up inside her throat and she swallowed it down furiously. A few tears made it out, making her eyelashes sting with cold as she ripped open the wrapping paper on the chocolates, and shoved a praline into her mouth.

She was still shaking by the time the door opposite opened again, and Ross appeared, but the sugar hit had helped calm her down, get herself under control. Ross was clearly upset, his cheeks two spots of scarlet, his breathing rapid.

'Dad's leaving,' he said. 'He's met someone else and it's serious. It's someone he and Mum knew at uni, apparently, and Mum's going next-level batshit. I'm sorry, Mez, but I've got to go back in.'

So there was no warm family glow for Merry that year as she spent her Christmas/birthday alone with Netflix, reacting with happy emojis to the photos of Jen and Farah spending their first Christmas as a cohabiting couple and remotely coaching Ross on how to diffuse the situation over text.

This was the one and only time Merry met Rita Gliss – a split second of cold disdain on a doorstep that only served to confirm the conviction in Merry's mind that she should never put herself out there, let herself be seen wanting something. It only led to rejection and humiliation. It was why, when Ross and Emelle finally split, she decided that simply telling Ross how she felt about him would destroy the foundation of their friendship and expose her to heartbreak. In short, that was the day Merry stopped even trying to ask directly for what she wanted. Manipulation was her only option.

If she had looked beyond her own hurt, she would have seen that this was also the point at which Rita Gliss's carefully reconstructed life began to crumble. A year after Kit Verity left her, the board at Glissful called in a consultant to advise on a new direction for the company, and that new direction had not included Rita. The business she had built – the unique scents she had created, even her own name and flame-haired, red-lipped image – now belonged to someone else, someone who had pushed her out. Merry heard the news filtered through the pain of Ross's suffering.

'It's like she blames me for everything,' he said. 'She says if I'd gone into the business she'd have had more allies.'

Merry listened, comforted, told him that the collapse of his mother's career wasn't on him. And when Ross's father passed away, she held his hand through that, too.

'I sometimes think she was happy when Dad died. She keeps talking about how much he deserved it,' Ross said. 'Like, I know he was a complete dick, the way cheated on her, but he's *dead* and she's acting like he's lost some kind of game.'

Merry was desperate to tell him that Rita was toxic and he should go no-contact but she bided her time. Families were weird – this time next year they might be reunited and Merry would be accused of stirring up trouble.

'Talk to her,' she urged one night in the pub. 'Help her understand how you feel.'

Maybe that would make Ross see the light without Merry being the bad guy.

Ross leaned forward, running his slender fingers through his hair. 'She won't listen!'

'I know, but it's not really about her listening, it's about you getting to tell her what *you* feel. Sit her down and tell her that you need the space to grieve. Stand up for what you believe in. Own your life choices, even if you do feel guilty about them.' It was rare for Merry to speak so plainly, to tell someone straight that they need to do something, but she felt very sure this was the right thing to do. She had read it in countless Instagram posts, seen it in countless movies – *speak your truth and you will be free.*

And so he did, and the conversation went about as well as could be expected.

'She just told me to get out,' he said, face still blank with shock. 'She said I was either with her or against her.'

'She doesn't mean it.' Merry didn't really believe this, but was still hiding her true feelings in case Rita changed her mind.

'Oh, yes she does!' Ross just let out a short bark of a laugh. 'Mother's not built like most of us. You know she keeps a book in her bedside drawer listing all the people who have ever wronged her? I looked at it once – it had a bunch of names I never heard of, that woman Dad ran off with, and then Dad crossed off because he's dead. That's it, the only way off her shit-list is if you die.'

It seemed Ross hadn't quite made it onto the list, as contact between the mother and son rumbled on. There was always something that pulled on Ross's guilt strings. A setback with her new Phoenix perfume line, a drama with his dad's family. Each time, Ross would do his duty and support her, and Rita would pay him back with a toxic cocktail of compliments, gratitude, and, just as he started to relax, knife-twisting insults. Merry fed him ideas, watching *Sopranos* episodes featuring Tony's mother, showing him reels about people who have gone no-contact with their controlling parents. Ross still hesitated until, in a moment of frustration, she cried out.

'For God's sake, Ross, you have to cut her out of your life.'

Ross, taken aback by Merry's sudden outburst, nodded slowly.

'I can't do this anymore.'

294

It was almost as if Merry had written the line for him.

They drafted the letter together, laying it all out in black and white, reading it over and over, complimenting each other on how reasonable and rational it sounded. Ross posted it, then cried on Merry in the coffee shop afterwards. But it was the right thing to do.

The next week, Merry received a letter in the post at work. It was handwritten on quality stationery, a cream-coloured envelope with a thick sheet of paper inside.

I know you think you have got your claws into my son, pouring your poison into his ears, it said. *But you are wrong. You are nothing. He will always, <u>always</u> come back to me.*

It was official. Merry was on Rita's shit-list.

33

MERRY

'So, wait,' says Josie. 'There's a crazed perfume maker on the loose somewhere in the Emporium, picking us off one by one? Are you saying that *she* strangled Rudi?'

Merry's brain is virtually crackling with excitement. This is the most horrific, terrifying thing to ever happen to her and yet she feels alive as the pieces all start to come together.

'No, I don't think she did . . . at least not directly. Rita's a manipulator, it's what she does best. She gets people to do what she wants, whether by bullying or by getting them to believe her lies.' She glances up at the flickering lamp on the wall. 'Gaslighting, basically. So I think she somehow got Dean to murder Rudi. In his bag there was a note, supposedly from M.R. Verity, saying that he was open to the deal – I think Rita sent him that. Dean got something extra in his hot chocolate, too – the sprinkles Monty put on top – and maybe that made him more prone to lose his temper. He did kill Rudi, but he was driven to do it by Rita.'

'That's nuts,' Josie says. 'Surely if she wanted someone dead, she'd just do it herself.'

'She enjoys messing with people,' Merry explains, aware of the irony. 'She wants to see how far we'll go.'

'But she'd only be able to do this sort of thing if Monty-Nigel-whoever was in on it with her,' Fran says. 'Why would he agree to something that trashes the store and kills his employer? And let's face it, the publicity's not going to be great after all this.'

'This wasn't meant to happen,' a voice croaks. They look around to discover that Nigel Smallhouse has regained consciousness. His head still lolls to one side but his puffy eyes are open a crack, his dry lips moving. There are faint traces of a Birmingham accent now he's not being Monty. 'Sometimes I make money on the side renting the Emporium out as a kind of escape room. She paid me a fortune for Christmas Eve and even paid to have our windows properly preserved by some contact of hers . . . Looking at what he did to them, I don't think her guy really was from the National Trust after all.

'Her associate, a guy called Watton, came in with a team and set everything up. He told me she was going to give you all a scare, mess with your heads but in a fun way. I had no idea how far things were going to go until I saw Dean running out of here looking scared. But then she threatened me, tied me up in some secret room for hours, then brought me down here to "toast our success", she said. I didn't see what happened to poor Rudi until after I'd drunk *that* . . .' His eyes roll towards the mulled wine glasses. 'Turns out she's really good with drugs and stuff.'

'She's a chemist,' Merry says. 'I suppose perfume and poisons aren't that far apart. She must have wanted us to find you here, to realise we'd got everything wrong.'

'You're lucky she wasn't pissed off enough with you to kill you,' Josie observes.

'I don't feel lucky.' Nigel's voice is heavy with misery. The Christmas tape binding him creaks as he looks around, catches sight of poor Benjamin lying at his feet. Just beyond that, his former employer's decomposing body lies hidden under a blanket.

'You did lie to Rudi, though, trying to do a deal with Dean behind his back,' Merry says quietly. 'That's what you were arguing about when I saw you in the workshop, wasn't it?'

Nigel's head sags forwards. 'I was trying to save the Emporium – to save both of us. This place was in trouble from the start. There's no way it can survive in modern London selling hand-made toys for those prices. Watton suggested Dean as a business fixer, and I thought that he might talk him round. But it turns out Rudi had been sent a file on Dean, something about his early business practices which made him shut Dean down completely. I think that was the last straw for Dean.'

'So Dean did kill Rudi,' Fran says.

Nigel nods miserably. 'I didn't see it, but I think that's what happened. When we were hiding in that secret room Rita told me all about how she had planned it. She sent Dean false messages for weeks in advance, pretending to be Rudi, leading him on. Then she sent Rudi the file about Dean. She's been sitting on it for years, apparently.'

He fidgets in the chair, trying to move his bound ankles away from Benjamin's crumpled body. 'I don't suppose you feel like untying me?'

'Not really.'

Merry stops paying attention to Nigel. She will have questions for him later, but right now she's too busy trying to figure things out. 'So she messages Dean pretending to be Rudi, then she messages Evangeline pretending to be Dean and . . .'

'The ladder was a set-up,' Fran adds. 'She knew Evangeline would goad him until he climbed down.'

'That's complicated, though, unless she manipulated Barbara too,' Merry adds. 'Somehow she knew Barbara would be desperate to get to her son.'

Josie lets out a loud bark of cynical laughter.

'Come on,' she scoffs. 'Nobody thinks like this.'

'Rita does. I totally think she's capable of that. And . . .' Merry trails off because Fran is staring at her, her jaw open wide.

'Shit, I think she was trying to provoke me into killing Evangeline,' Fran says. 'She paid Evangeline to play along with her game, had her dropping hints about me all night. Maybe the plan was I'd kill her and she would come by afterwards and hoist her onto that horrible noose thing.'

Merry nods. 'I don't know how she found out, but I think you're right. Rita has a reason to be angry at you. She has Branscombe's.'

By the time he found out about the diagnosis, the relationship between Ross and Rita had deteriorated to the point that he had blocked his mother's phone number. To break the news, she had resorted to writing to him. Another letter, another creamy-white envelope which Ross considered tearing up on receiving, but reluctantly opened.

I have had every treatment possible, but the cancer is too far advanced, she had written. *Ross, your mother is dying.*

Any pity Merry might have felt had been cancelled out by the following line:

Did you know that stress is a contributing cause of cancer? It looks like I was right – the stress of losing a job, a husband, of betrayal by all my loved ones was enough to put me in an early grave after all. I suppose I am lucky to have survived this long.

Ross had sat with the paper on his lap for some time, just staring. Merry had stayed beside him, quietly, putting a cup of tea into his hand while he processed the information. And then finally, gently, she'd said, 'It looks like you have two options: go and see her, or don't.'

'What would you do?'

'Which scenario would make you feel worse? The guilt at not going, or the guilt she'd pile on you if you did see her?'

Ross crumpled up the paper, threw it across the room. 'I'm not going. I can't face it.'

He had thrown the letter away, and Merry hadn't stopped him.

Now, standing in the dim light of the grotto, Fran stares at Merry, her eyes wide. This was everything Fran had ever feared come true.

'There must have been some way she found out,' Merry says. 'Maybe it was something you shared online – the wrong brand of drug, hospital walls the wrong colour, something like that.'

'I guess she could have,' Fran agrees. 'I always thought carefully about what I shared but a couple of times people did pick me up on details online. Nobody pushed too hard, though – not when they thought I was ill – and I always managed to cook up some kind of explanation.' Fran is visibly cringing at her own words.

'Oh, Rita would see through all that,' Merry says. 'It takes a faker to know one. And that's why you're here. She's punishing you too.'

'I suppose that's what I'm supposed to do with this, then,' Josie says, reaching into her bag.

Fran flinches, her hand slides into Merry's as Josie pulls out a long, sharp carving knife. The end is wickedly pointed, the blade serrated steel.

Josie looks at the blade curiously, the expression on her face is strange, unreadable – a world away from the funny, warm, slightly sarcastic family-woman she met at the beginning of the night. This was the girl who had tormented Rita in a children's home, who had carried knives, threatened, stolen and set fires.

Merry finds herself gripping Fran's hand in return.

Fran takes a jagged breath, her eyes filled with fear as Josie holds the blade up, turns to and fro, letting its edge catch the light. Josie stares at it, as if transfixed.

'I don't know when this was slipped into my bag, but I'm supposed to kill you with it, aren't I?' An almost dreamlike smile touches her lips and she steps forward, closer to Fran.

'Josie, I . . .' Fran begins but Josie advances, pressing her against the wall of the log cabin, holding the knife in front of her face. Fran gives a frightened sob. Merry is rooted helplessly to the spot. Her mind whirls with the things she could say, and the million ways in which anything she says could go horribly wrong.

'I liked that they called me Knives at the children's home. It was good to know that people feared me – it made life easier, and more fun, too, watching people tiptoe around me. So yeah, I could do it, I could slide this knife between your ribs and make you bleed. But this . . .' The knife is an inch from Fran's face now, she gives a sob of fright. 'This would be over with way too quickly. Oh no, I want you to suffer. I want everyone to see what you've done.' She lowers the knife, and flashes a more natural grin. 'Besides, why would I want to do Fire Kid's dirty work for her? I'm not Knives anymore, I'm Auntie Josie now.'

Josie steps back, with an amused glance at Fran's face. 'Seriously, calm down,' she adds. 'I'm not going to stab you.'

Fran collapses back against the wall, her breathing hard and fast.

'Fucking hell,' a voice whispers. It's Nigel – Merry has almost forgotten about him.

Just then, without any warning, the electric lights flicker to life.

Suddenly, the grotto is filled with light and dazzling colour. All of them cry out as their eyes react to the brightness. Merry holds her hand up to her face, squinting. She has almost forgotten what colour looks like. As she looks down she sees Benjamin's face in light for the first time since they met in the Hall of Wonders. He is a wreckage of his former self – why hadn't they seen it sooner? Fran's face looks bloodless and tear-streaked, Josie's lines even deeper than they had been before. And Nigel, without Monty's self-assured strut, looks sad and alone, bound in the chair.

BING BONG

The store's PA system crackles to life, the speakers whine with feedback.

'Attention, shoppers, this is your murderer speaking.' The voice is smooth and honeyed, as if Rita is doing a voice-over for one of her ads. 'I have enjoyed your little talk. And yes, I have a listening device planted on you. Extra points if you can guess where it is.

'I am disappointed in you, Knives, but as Merry Clarke will confirm, the art of manipulation is not one for perfectionists,' Rita's voice continues. 'When human beings are your raw material you can never guarantee the quality of the final work of art, but that's what makes it so endlessly fascinating. Rest assured that whatever you do, by the time dawn breaks all of you will be dead. I don't care if I spend the rest of my life in prison – it won't be long for me anyway and I have nothing else to live for. Not since you stole my son, Merry.'

Moments after she speaks both the electric lights cut out. The gas lamps must have been switched off already, and once again they are plunged into darkness. But this time it's different, this time they're sure there's a killer out there.

As one, Merry and Fran press the buttons on their jumpers. The flashing lights are disorientating, but better than nothing. They enable Merry to see the snow globe on the table, the one she picked out for Ross and has carried with her like a talisman for the whole night. She dashes it down onto the floor. Glass shards and snowflakes scatter across the floor and the base cracks. Merry grinds her foot down and there it is, the microphone embedded inside.

'Oh yes,' says Nigel. 'I forgot we did that for her.'

Merry refrains from slapping him, taking out her frustration on the device under her foot. Glass crunches and something else, too – the happy couple that had stood in the foreground are crushed into powder. Merry thinks about surviving this, going home and spending Christmas with Ross and realises it will never

303

happen now. There will be no happy ending for them, not with this experience hanging over them both. Rita has succeeded in blowing her hopes apart.

But Merry will survive. She will get out of this. She cannot give Rita the satisfaction.

Josie, meanwhile, is pacing, still holding the knife. She has shifted her grip now, holding it outwards, like she means business. 'If she's messing with the tannoy that means she's downstairs in the Hall of Wonders, and I'm going to get her. Who's coming?'

Fran nods grimly, and Merry feels a surge of power. *Yes.* She wants to fight back, to hurt this woman.

But . . .

She knows Rita. She may have only met her that one time but a decade as Ross's friend has taught her something about the way she thinks.

'This is a trap,' she says. 'She wants us to go down there and confront her – there'll be something deadly waiting for us. Maybe she'll attack us, maybe the room will be full of gas and she'll strike a match. Maybe there's . . . I don't know, a pit of deadly fucking crocodiles. But if we go down there we're still doing what she wants us to do.'

Fran stops at the doorway, hesitates.

'I don't care,' Josie says grimly. 'I mean what I said before. I'm not stabbing anyone, but I'm going to find her and stop her.'

'Wait, Josie, I think she's right,' Fran says. 'I've been thinking about something. I've got a theory I want to check. Merry, what does Rita look like?'

'Don't you know? She's quite distinctive – bright red hair, red lips, always wears white, always has perfect make-up. Very

304

elegant. I used to think she was cool, if a bit overdone, until I knew what she was actually like.'

'And have you seen her recently, like, in the last year or so?'

'No, not since she stopped posting on social media. And Ross hasn't seen her for months.'

Fran shifts awkwardly. 'The chemotherapy that's most commonly used to treat Branscombe's has a significant chance of weight gain. Hair loss happens in ninety per cent of cases. It also results in a kind of puffiness around the face.' She turns to Nigel. 'When you met Rita tonight, what did she look like?'

'I'm not saying a word until you untie me!'

Fran sighs. 'Josie, would you do the honours?'

Merry approves: it's a clever idea to give Josie something to do with that knife. It doesn't take long – the tape is strong, but gives easily under the blade. Merry represses a shiver as she watches the other woman's expert work. Nigel stands up, staggering slightly, rubbing his wrists and muttering about the damage to his circulation. Now he is no longer performing – and without his signature hat and coat – he holds himself differently to Monty Verity; seems smaller somehow.

'So come on Nige, spill.'

Nigel huffs moodily, fusses with his cufflinks. 'I don't know why I need to – wasn't she here with you earlier on?'

A cold feeling prickles up Merry's spine at those words.

'Indulge me.' Fran's voice trembles.

'She's nothing like the way Merry just described. She's not slim, her clothes were drab and boring – she was wearing some kind of anorak with clouds on it and tacky Christmas tree earrings which definitely did not come from here.'

The three women stare at each other for a moment, taking in the news.

'Fuck me,' Josie says, 'Barbara.'

'I thought that voice on the tannoy sounded familiar,' Fran adds.

Merry's brain accepts the information as if she had always known it, because it makes so much sense. That's why Barbara had been staring at her in that odd way. That's why she thought she had seen Rita in the store when she was drugged-up and wandering around looking for the snow globe. Rita had pretended to escape via the candy cane ladder and retreated back into the store to hide – probably after sabotaging the ladder to ensure that whoever used it fell to their death.

She thinks of Barbara, chatting to her as they explored together, confiding her ladder plan, spinning some fake story about Australia to get sympathy and so they wouldn't be surprised when she disappeared. Nudging Dean into action, herding them towards her goal. Rita. Rita all along.

'Do you think she can still hear us?' Fran asks.

Merry looks at the smashed speaker on the floor and shakes her head.

'Right, then we'd better make a plan.'

Merry has noticed a slow shift in Fran's behaviour since she made her confession. She's still ashamed, but there's steel in her now too. She's willing to fight for her life.

There is no time to think too deeply about this. The clock is ticking – Rita has told them they'll be dead by dawn and already the light on the toy department floor is changing. The sun will be up in an hour and over in the more inhabited parts of London, young children are probably already scrambling out of their beds, dragging their sleepy parents to the tree to see what Santa has brought. Ross will be asleep in his flat, unaware of the destruction his mother has caused, excited to spend Christmas Day with his best friend.

'So, what have we got going for us?' Fran asks. It takes Merry a couple of moments to realise that this isn't a silly question, that they do have a few things in their favour.

'Right,' she says, counting off on her fingers. 'We've got Josie who knows every inch of the Emporium. We know roughly where Rita is – in the Hall of Wonders near where the tannoy system is so she can keep going back to taunt us. We know she's almost definitely expecting us, especially Josie, so there's a trap waiting somewhere. She's got things wrong about us, too, so she's not completely in control. And we've got Nigel who can tell us at least some of the delightful surprises she has in store, *can't you, Nigel?*'

Nigel looks undecided, as if this isn't his fight. Merry feels a wave of irritation and chooses her line of attack.

'You had a sweet gig going on here, didn't you? And now she's wrecked it.' Merry refrains from mentioning that Nigel did quite a bit of the wrecking himself. 'Surely you can't be on her side?'

Nigel nods slowly, rubs his wrists where Rita's bonds have chafed him.

'OK, I'll tell you everything I know.'

Josie snorts with derision. Fran stays quiet, possibly still feeling she can't judge anyone.

'First things first,' Fran says. 'Nigel, I don't suppose you know where our phones are?' *Good question, Fran. This double-act thing is starting to work out.*

Nigel looks down at his hands. 'She's got them locked in the safe in the office. The landline handsets are in there too. And my phone,' he says, wincing. 'But she's got the only key.'

'You gave her the only key to the safe? For a professional fraud you're pretty gullible,' Josie observes.

'She paid me a lot of money.' He shrugs. 'And locking phones away is a common escape room thing.'

'Yeah, but now we've got no sodding phones,' Josie says.

Merry suddenly feels a rush of excitement. She picks up the SIM-less handset Fran used to film her confession. 'She gave us a phone,' she says. 'She actually gave us a phone!'

'Yeah, a dead phone with no SIM.'

'OK, yes, but downstairs in the Hall of Wonders there's the phone Evangeline had. I think Rita probably smashed it when Evangeline was asleep to stop her calling for help, but I bet she didn't think to take the SIM out.'

Merry's heart is beating fast. This is Rita, the master manipulator, the woman who plans six steps ahead and imagines every outcome, and she has made a mistake. Merry is certain of it.

'There's no guarantee it'll work,' Fran says. 'It might not be compatible or whatever. But . . . it is worth a try.'

'She'll be waiting for us down there,' Josie says. She is still holding the knife, and Fran is still watching her closely but Merry is sure that she has no intention of hurting Fran now. Josie is holding the knife almost like a comfort blanket, a way to reassure herself that she's not powerless.

Merry shakes her head. 'No, Josie, not us. She's waiting for *you*. She knows you're going to go down there and confront her.'

'So we all march down together, a united front,' Fran suggests.

That is a lovely idea, very twee, very climax-of-a-movie, where they all work together to stand up to the bully. But Merry's cynical soul knows it won't work.

'I think Nigel might have a better plan,' Merry says.

Everyone looks at Nigel, who stares at Merry and utters a question along the lines of 'Whaaa?'

'What was it you said to me? It's all about misdirection. Getting her to look one way, to think she's still in charge, while we go for the phone.'

'I think there's something else you should know,' Nigel says. 'She's got a gun.'

34

CHRISTMAS PRESENT

RITA

RITA LIGHTS THE GAS LAMP THAT SITS ON THE WALL NEXT TO THE magical mirror in the Hall of Wonders, and looks at her reflection. It's not something she does often these days. She has grown to hate her body for its weaknesses, injuries, sickness and flaws. But tonight she feels powerful and strong. She is wearing her Barbara wig once more, having lost the vivid red one to Merry's grasping hands, and has placed Monty's hat on her head at a daring, rakish angle.

You did it, she tells herself. *You took back control. You showed them who's in charge.*

She can no longer hear what they are saying, huddled up there in Santa's grotto. Maybe that was a mistake, revealing her hand like that, but it was just too much fun to resist. Besides, they are all painfully predictable; she doesn't really need a listening device to know that things will not be going well.

Fran, that vile cancer-fraud, will be in a free-fall of self-depre-
cating guilt now her secret is out and will probably be useless. Josie
will storm down here any minute with a mouth full of swearwords
(Rita has always loathed cursing) and the knife in her hand, looking
for a confrontation. That charlatan Nigel will be completely useless
and none of them will trust a thing he says anyway. And Merry
will be herding all these cats, trying to manipulate them to her own
devious ends. Merry is the one she has to worry about.

Rita steps back from the mirror, taking a bite out of the
mince pie she is holding, as she surveys the chaos that remains of
the Hall of Wonders. Evangeline's corpse still lies where it fell,
surrounded by the shards of a hundred Christmas baubles. One
of the other inmates has laid a blanket over her face, but her legs
are still showing, one sticks out strangely displaying a common-
place-looking black sock and Evangeline's pale sun-starved leg. It
lacks the elegance Evangeline had when she was alive, and Rita
finds this very satisfying. The contents of Dean's and Evangeline's
bags are scattered all over the floor, evidence of the delightful
paper trail she's been laying for them over the past few months.

And . . . what's this next to the chair? An unopened Champagne
bottle?

'Don't mind if I do,' Rita says. She discards the mince pie and
fills the last remaining Champagne flute, glad that she thought to
provide one for herself when she was setting things up. It's not
perfectly chilled – Kit would never have drunk it at this temper-
ature – but it will do very nicely while she waits. She settles into
the chair and lays the gun across her lap, enjoys the crackling
from the fire. She tosses on another automaton elf-head which
begins to burn merrily. She feels almost Christmassy.

Once, Rita had loved the festive season. The chill in the air, the scent of cinnamon and ginger, her first bite of a mince pie and the wonder of visiting the Emporium. Even after her parents died in the fire, she had relished that build-up even more than the day itself. Then when she had gone on to have a family of her own, her nickname had been the Festive Fairy.

Every successful family Christmas has a control freak at its heart, creating a magazine-cover-worthy tree, timing the roast with military precision, wrapping each carefully thought-out gift with geometrically precise folds and adding a colour-coordinated satin bow. Magic is hard work for those who make it happen but her reward had come in the Fairy nickname; in the shining, excited eyes of little Ross on Christmas morning; in the approving nod of Kit's mother when she presented a faultless festive table, and in the feeling of Kit's arm around her, the way he'd call her a clever thing.

Then, her miracles performed, she would allow herself to relax. For a few hours she would rest the relentless drive inside her, feel satisfied for just one day. Other people might use the word happy.

But now that she had lost everything, that sense of anticipation had curdled into something twisted and wrong.

She glances up at the miniature version of the Emporium. She has laid the model Benjamin onto the Hall of Toys floor, next to the replica of Clockwork Peg. Dean lies shattered outside. Evangeline hangs from the ceiling. It was a shame the others had cut the real Evangeline down. Rita would have preferred to leave her there, twisting gently like a giant bauble.

Rita has called herself a feminist in countless press interviews. She is not one of those people who automatically blames the other woman when a man cheats. And when Kit had first started having his little affairs she had not blamed him, either. He had instinctively known that he would not make old bones, and had responded by living his life to the fullest, which included wine, women, song and rather too much fancy dress. He always came back to her in the end.

But *Evangeline Fall*, of all people. The woman who had seduced his best friend at university, then switched her attention to him, throwing herself at his feet with zero dignity. Back at Oxford he had chosen shy, self-effacing Peggy instead. But then Peggy had gained confidence – first as an adult, then as a mother, then as a businesswoman. Peggy became Margaret and then eventually – because the name Margaret doesn't sell perfume – Rita. Kit hadn't signed up for powerful, dynamic Rita. He wanted an audience for his exploits, an adoring partner, and at the right moment Evangeline had sidled up to him and given him exactly that. And the thought that Kit would leave her for keen, keen Evangeline – there was no coming back after that. Evangeline, of course, had lost interest as soon as he had blown up his life to be with her. She was always more about the chase than the happy-ever-after.

The love of the chase was how Rita had got to Evangeline, persuaded her to play along with the 'practical joke' she was planning. *Pretend I'm your assistant and, not only will I pay you, I will help you reunite with Dean Hallibutt, the one who got away.* Evangeline had sneered at Rita at first, calling her weird, but, persuaded by the messages from Dean's hacked PeelYu account, eventually agreed, unaware of the full extent of her plans. As they rehearsed their roles together, Rita had sensed a deep, desperate loneliness in her victim; a need for friendship which, of course, she had

313

leveraged to her advantage. Evangeline had done her job exceptionally well, for a hopeless attention-seeking flake.

After Kit left, the Veritys had closed ranks, pushing her out like the interloper she had always been. There were no more cosy Christmases, no more nods of approval from mama-in-law. But she had told herself it did not matter. She still had Ross, and she had the business. Glissful was her beautiful second child, something she had made by herself with sheer hard work, determination and talent. It could never be taken away from her.

Except, it was.

It was not her fault that there were a few off-years. That some fragrance lines were works of art, but did not perform at retail level. That some products were just too sophisticated for the mass market. But the board, which still contained a few members of Kit's family, brought in a business consultant to analyse the problem. And the problem, according to Business Fixer and out-and-out fraud Dean Hallibutt, had been Rita. She was too close to the product, too driven, too fanatical. The company needed to capitalise on the Glissful brand's reputation for quality with mass market products, not continue making bespoke, niche fragrances that sold for £150 a bottle. He recommended a change of leadership.

She wasn't sure he remembered her from that business course all those years ago, he had never given any indication that he did. But after she staggered out of that last meeting, shaking all over, feeling like the ground had been swept out from under her, Dean Hallibutt had suggested a five-minute coffee. She had been too bewildered to refuse, half expecting him to give her the kind of pep talk his videos were famous for. But he had smiled a slow, sharkish smile.

'Who's a fraud now?' he had said.

In the months which followed she had thought of some zinging comebacks, but at the time his words had summoned tears. Silent, traitorous floods flowed down her face, smearing her make-up as he gloated. But her tears came from rage, not help-lessness. He had waited for his revenge, she would wait too – and hers would be sweeter.

Rita was still not broken after this. She had received a generous payout from Glissful, she had her perfume-making talent, she had her adoring, supportive son who, admittedly, was a little busy these days building his own life. She would come back.

When Kit died, she felt strangely flat. Although she liked to tell herself that she was pleased that he was gone, there was so much unfinished business. Kit had died happily polyamorous, leaving two or three beautiful women in widow's weeds. His fancy dress funeral had been the social event of the year. He hadn't learned his lesson. He had never had to pay the price for how much he had hurt her.

And, in a way, when Kit died he took Ross with him. He was never the same after that, whining about the loss of his wastrel father. She needed a tower of strength but he had been distracted and moping. Often his phone went straight through to voicemail. Sometimes it didn't even ring before it did.

'Merry says I need space to mourn for Dad,' he would say. 'Merry's parents never ring her at all. Merry's helping me look for my own flat – it's time, isn't it?'

Merry, Merry, always Merry. That revoltingly cheesy name, that wide, eager-to-please face with its floppy curls staring up at her from the street like an over-zealous puppy at a time when

Rita had felt at her weakest. They weren't an item, Ross said, they were just friends, but she knew the conniving cow was playing a long game, working out how to control him. She was always pushing him to do this or that, telling him Rita was being 'weird' or getting him to question their close family set-up.

When he moved out, Rita had curled on his empty bed and wept. But when he began trying to cut her off, she had felt nothing but rage.

It was this anger which led her to plan to steal Clockwork Peg. Maybe if he had been around, he would have talked her out of committing theft, so it was his fault really. Why shouldn't she have something beautiful, and save the poor thing from rotting away in that store? It would also teach the Verity family a lesson in the process.

Kit had mentioned Benjamin and his odd obsession with Peg years ago. Now, she tracked him down and recruited him through a trusted third party but – control freak that she was – she could not resist going along to the pub where they were meeting, watching them both from a safe distance. She found Benjamin pathetic, obsessive, easily spooked and eminently controllable. Good.

Satisfied, she had left the pub, watched from the shadows as Benjamin scurried out moments later, then walked back through the darkness to her car. But halfway across the street, her world had abruptly dissolved into confusion and shattering pain. She felt the scraping of broken bone on bone, the bloody explosion of her nose.

And even worse, the accident had revealed the secret her body had been keeping from her. The vile cancer that had been growing there all along. She had lost her husband, her career, her son and now her health.

Benjamin Makepeace must have assumed she'd been unconscious, that she hadn't seen his panic-stricken, cowardly face
as he leaped back behind the wheel and screeched off. He had
repaired the dent in that ludicrous van and carried on driving
around in it as if nothing had happened. She could have reported
him to the police but she didn't – partly because Benjamin
would be bound to reveal the plot to steal Peg, but mainly
because prison was too good for him. Instead, she added him to
her special list.

His murder had been the first, the easiest. Benjamin is, or rather
was, so desperately predictable. Of course he wouldn't be able to
resist touching Peg, dusting off her cap. The poison she used was
an experimental drug, something which had formed part of her
treatment for Branscombe's in the US and which ultimately did
her no good. But, ingested in concentrated form, it had done no
good to poor weak-hearted Benjamin either.

She thinks of Clockwork Peg with a shadow of regret that she
was never able to take her home. Her love for the Emporium
is real and her joy on hearing of its reopening had been great.
She had assumed Rudi would welcome the chance to stock her
Phoenix perfume line, but he had refused, killing her hopes of
reviving her career and his own chances of surviving until the
New Year. The Emporium will pass to Ross now, and she is sure
he at least will respect its legacy. He always did love Christmas.

But for now, sitting by the fire, Verity's Emporium is all hers.
Nothing bad could happen here.

At least, not to her.

Josie should be here soon. Rita thinks. *It could be that the others are trying to talk her out of it, but they won't succeed. Knives hasn't changed that much, not when she's pissed off and someone's given her a weapon.*

Reaching into the pocket of Barbara's grey raincoat, Rita pulls out another carved figure, the one built to resemble Josie, complete with little wooden topknot. The wood is shiny, lacquered, crafted to perfection. He might have been a terrible judge of perfume, but Rudi Verity knew how to carve wood. Taking the tongs from the brass companion set by the fire, she pinches the model Josie in them, then lays them on the floor next to her, waiting for the flesh-and-blood version to arrive.

The gun is insurance but really there is only one way to destroy her first and darkest enemy, and that is with fire.

'This place has changed a bit.' Josie's voice rings out from the gloom.

She is standing near the entrance to the secret passage, casting a long shadow in the firelight. Rita fights to conceal her surprise. Josie is in her early sixties but has lost none of her soft-footedness.

'I mean, it's still a shoplifter's dream. No cameras, not even anyone on the door. But . . .' Josie's trainers crunch on the shattered baubles, 'the interior design's let itself go.'

'I heard they had squatters,' Rita says, then stands, indicating the easy chair opposite her. 'Come on, Knives, why don't you sit down?'

'So you can shoot me?'

'Oh, I'm not going to shoot you.'

Josie hesitates, looks around the room, and then seems to make a sudden decision to sit down, even plumping up the cushion to get comfy first. For a moment Rita wonders if Josie will be able to detect the lighter fluid, but decades of smoking has clearly taken its toll on her sense of smell.

Josie pours herself a glass of Champagne, sips it, wrinkles her nose. 'Too warm.' She puts her glass carefully down on the floor beside her and draws her bag up onto her lap.

Rita's hand goes to rest on the handle of the gun, preparing for Josie to draw the knife.

Josie laughs. 'Calm down, Fire Kid, I'm not going to stab you either.'

She falls silent for a moment, as if she's struggling to think of the right thing to say.

'I . . . back when I was living here I used to rehearse what I was going to say to you, if we ever met again,' Josie says finally. 'I'd run them by my mate Peg upstairs who can be quite critical when she wants to be. This wasn't exactly the situation I imagined, though. Nothing I had planned to say really works. But I'm going to give it a try anyway.

'Sorry isn't really good enough. It was a shit thing I did, burning your puppet. I have no excuse except that I was fucked up and trying to get some kind of control over my life. I think you might get that, at least.'

Rita presses her lips together to stop herself screaming. She will not allow herself to feel something in common with Josie.

Josie shrugs. 'Anyway, I made something when I was living here. It's been hidden under a floorboard in the old man's workshop ever since. This is the first chance I've had to get it back.'

She draws out a bundle – a grubby, perished old C&A carrier, and holds it out to Rita who recoils as flakes of degraded plastic fall onto her knees.

'Take it,' Josie urges. 'It's not a trap.'

The bag is so grimy, Rita's fingers are reluctant to touch it. This is the feeling she associates with Josie, always has. A feeling of being dirty, sullied somehow. Still, curiosity drives her to unwrap what is inside.

She sees limbs, she sees a tangle of hair, and string.

She pulls it out, a perfectly carved marionette puppet wearing a hand-stitched slip made from an old T-shirt. The face is hauntingly similar to her old puppet's. Her eyes are a different shade of brown, the hair looks a little odd, as if younger Josie couldn't find doll hair and snipped off some of her own, and the face is only partially painted, but she can see the craftsmanship that has gone into this and she is amazed.

'It's not perfect, I got arrested before I could finish,' said Josie. 'But that's it. That's what I made for you to say sorry.'

Since Rita was twelve years old, the memory of Knives has haunted her dreams. Vicious, unrelenting, endlessly confident. She had feared her, then she had tried to become her. And she had never imagined this. Her hands tremble as she holds the doll.

She feels . . .

She feels . . .?

She feels Josie's eyes watching her, hawk-like, sees Josie's hands reaching down to the carpet. Not to the Champagne glass but to something next to it, poking out from underneath the chair. It's the broken phone, the one she had specifically told Evangeline not to bring to the 'escape room evening'. The one she had smashed while her former room-mate was asleep. The phone is broken but the very fact Josie is reaching for it means it's something she has to stop. Rita grabs the tongs and plunges the wooden model into the fire. The paint should light up immediately, it's fresh, but it's not catching fast enough. Why isn't it more flammable? Her puppet had gone up like a rocket, but paints are probably safer now. *Health and safety gone mad.*

Josie is moving towards her, standing up, the phone in her hand. Rita shoves her back into the chair, throws the wooden figure, with one pathetic flame clinging to it, down onto the cushion next to her.

WOOMPH. the cushion catches fire, but Josie is too far out of the seat to be badly hurt. The fire licks at her leggings, melting the nylon and she cries out in pain, flaps at her leg with her sleeve. The flames do not spread. Josie stands up fully.

'Catch!' She throws the phone across the room into the darkness beyond and reaches back into her bag. She's holding the knife, now, face twisted into a snarl as the flames eat into the chair behind her. 'You absolute fucking bitch.'

Rita aims her gun and pulls the trigger.

35

FRAN

JOSIE'S BODY CRUMPLES TO THE FLOOR. FRAN OPENS HER MOUTH to scream, to roar with rage and denial but Nigel clamps his hand over her face, his palm sweaty and slick. Josie is not moving.

This wasn't supposed to happen, Josie wasn't supposed to get that close . . . But then what choice did she have when Rita was standing so near to the discarded phone?

The chair Josie had been sitting in is fully alight now, the flames licking at the discarded puppet on the floor – all Josie's hard work turning black and flaking away, just like its predecessor.

'Focus on the phone,' hisses Nigel. 'Where is it?'

There – lying two metres from them, right in the centre of the aisle close to Evangeline.

A beam of light cuts through the darkness, sweeping across the ruins of the Hall of Wonders. Rita has a torch.

322

'Come out, come out wherever you are,' she sing-songs, like the villain in a film. Fran knows that in the darkness on the other side of the aisle, Merry is crouched in her hiding place, cringing at the unoriginality of it. That knowledge is strangely comforting.

She can see Merry now, behind a display of stuffed reindeer, close but not close enough to grab the phone while staying safe. A heavy feeling lodges in her chest. Now is the time to make that big, sacrificial gesture.

'I'm coming out,' she says. 'I don't have a plan, I'm not trying anything, I just want to talk to you.'

She puts her hands in the air and steps out.

Fran has seen Rita Gliss as herself a couple of times before in her life – not to talk to, but they have overlapped at one or two awards ceremonies. And even though she spoke to 'Barbara' for some time at the beginning of the night, she is still shaken by the transformation. In her publicity material, Rita had been poised and perfectly presented. She'd had the kind of tight body that middle-aged women only maintain by getting up at 5 a.m. to run and row and lift weights. And the kind of bright, burnished hair that only comes with regular, extortionate appointments with one of London's top colourists. Now she is smaller, rounder and there is a clear bump in her nose where Benjamin's windscreen had broken it.

'Well?' Rita's voice is impatient. 'Are you going to offer to sacrifice yourself for the others or what?'

'Would it work if I did? Would you leave Merry and Josie alone?'

Fran takes another step forward, slowly, hands still raised. Behind her, she feels Nigel cringing more deeply into the shadows and wonders if she can trust him to grab the phone while she distracts Rita. If he doesn't do it, though, she knows Merry will. She can't tell if Merry has moved out of her hiding place, not while she's facing Rita. She will just have to trust her.

'I might,' Rita answers. 'You're pretty much the worst offender of the lot. You probably thought you were so convincing, all those photos you shared on social media, all that knowledge about treatment. But something about your story stank; little details were off. There's a few of us, an online community, who know you faked it, we just couldn't prove it. What you did wasn't just an insult to me, it was an insult to millions of people in this country. All to keep yourself in the public eye, to make yourself a national treasure.'

From the moment she confessed, Fran knew that she would spend the rest of her life explaining herself, apologising for what she did. But not here, not to this murderer. A decision clicks in her. She has to survive this. She has to get out of here, take her punishment and move on. She takes another step.

The flames from the chair are spreading across the floor now, worryingly close to Josie's feet. Is Josie dead, or just unconscious? It's impossible to tell from here, but Fran knows she has to get her away from those flames. She takes another step closer.

Rita watches her, tense as a mousetrap, the gun in her hand.

Another step.

And then Rita moves, grabbing Fran by the neck, cold metal presses to her temple.

Fran's breath comes rapidly, short, panicky. She can't think straight anymore. The world is reduced to a tight focus: Fran, the gun and the woman holding it, her body crushed uncomfortably close to Fran's, her breath smelling of mince pies and Champagne. All Fran can think is that she wants to live. Whether she deserves to or not, she desperately wants to live.

Just then, Fran catches sight of a movement over by the door, and Rita seems to see it too. Her body tenses. And then, to Fran's utter horror, Merry's reindeer jumper lights up.

Rita laughs to herself, loosens her grip on Fran for a moment and takes aim. Fran barges into her as she shoots, so the first shot goes wide, pinging into the Emporium ceiling, a strand of crystal filaments crashes to the ground.

Both of them have lost their balance and tumble forward. Fran is quick and flexible – years of training for charity events have seen to that. But Rita is powered by sheer bloody-mindedness and makes it to her feet first. A flicker of a smile appears on her face as she kicks the wound on Fran's shoulder. Pain explodes, Fran screams with the force of it.

Rita ignores her, turns and fires again. And again. And again. On the fourth shot, the reindeer jumper falls back, but instead of the slow thump of a body hitting the floor there's a clanging, crashing sound, exactly like an automaton elf toppling over.

Misdirection. That Merry is a genius.

She glances over to where the phone was lying – it's no longer there. Hope leaps inside Fran, but the agony in her shoulder won't let it last long. Rita seizes her, her fingers pinching into the wound. Pain blooms under her fingers, radiates outwards, blocking out all other thoughts as Rita orders Fran to stand up. The heat from the fire is burning the back of Fran's legs now.

'Merry Clarke, come out,' Rita orders, pointing the gun at Fran again. 'I have a bargain to make with you.'

Keeping the gun trained on Fran, Rita bends down and seizes the knife from Josie's limp hand. Fran thinks she can see Josie breathing, but it's too dark to know if that's the truth or wishful thinking. Rita transfers the knife to her right hand, gently lowers the gun to the floor and then presses the knife blade against Fran's neck.

'Come out, Merry,' she repeats. 'Or I will cut her throat.'

A figure emerges from the shadows. Merry is in her black office skirt with Nigel's waistcoat on top. She is holding the toy cricket bat, probably more for comfort than because she thinks it will help.

'What do you want?' Merry is trying to sound brave but the tremor in her voice is unmistakeable.

Rita nudges the gun with her foot and kicks, sliding it across the shiny boards in Merry's direction.

'I want you to kill me.'

36

MERRY

Merry looks down at the gun as if it's about to explode in her face. The cricket bat slithers from her hands; her palms are slick with sweat despite the chill on her skin now she's not wearing her jumper. *I want you to kill me.* She has not been expecting this.

'Come on.' Rita's tone is impatient, as if she's hurrying a child out of the door to school. 'Pick it up.'

Merry picks up the gun. She's never held one before and it's heavier than she was expecting. It's an old-fashioned gun, like something from World War Two, rather than the sort you see in American crime shows. It must have been in Ross's father's family for decades.

'You've already seen that it works. Just point it at me and shoot.'

'Why?' Merry says, and then because it sounds to weak she changes it. 'Why should I?'

'To save Fran's life. If you don't shoot me within the next minute, I will stab Fran in the neck and she'll bleed out right here on the shop floor next to Knives.' A slow smile spreads across Rita's red lips. 'Also because you want to. I'll be out of the way then, Ross will be free of my evil influence. Isn't that what you've always wanted?'

And now Merry understands what Rita is asking. Shooting her will free Fran, and it will free Ross, but it also means she and Ross will never be together. Whatever happens, Ross is going to be a mess after all this, and she'll want to be there for him, but she won't be able to. You can't seek support from the person who murdered your mother, even if it was in self-defence. Even if she told you to do it.

Fran whimpers. Rita is pressing the knife into the flesh of her neck and a bead of blood has appeared, trickling down the blade, dripping to the floor. Merry raises the gun, to play for time more than anything. No way is she going to do what Rita asks – *but . . . Fran.*

She glances back over her shoulder, wondering if Nigel has any bright ideas, but there is no sign of him.

'Oh, I wouldn't count on Monty,' Rita says. 'I think he's method acting a coward right now. I'm timing you – exactly one minute from now.' She checks the slim gold watch on her wrist.

'I'm scared I'll shoot Fran by accident,' Merry says.

Rita shrugs. 'Strangely enough that doesn't bother me. Fifty-four seconds.'

Merry and Fran gaze helplessly at each other, but then something shifts in Fran's body language. She is bracing herself. *Perhaps if they both rushed Rita together . . .*

But Merry needs to be closer.

'The thing is,' Merry says, taking a step towards Rita and keeping the gun raised, 'I'm not you. I don't have my claws into Ross in the way you think. I just love him, a lot. I want him to be happy, which is why I decided tonight that I wasn't going to push him into a relationship. The poor guy's been so messed up by you, the last thing he needs right now is anyone else pressuring him.'

Merry takes another step closer. She's close enough now to hear Fran's rapid, uneven breathing. She can see the way she's holding her shoulder differently, compensating for the injury. She's going to need all the help she can get.

'Nigel!' Merry calls. 'Please tell me you've got that phone working!'

There is silence.

'Nigel?'

Rita smiles a savage smile, her red lipstick like a smear of blood. *She's right, Nigel's gone*, Merry thinks. *What a dick.*

'Twenty seconds, and don't come a step closer . . . AARGH!' Rita screams in pain, crumpling downwards.

There's something pulling at her leg. Josie has grabbed Rita's ankle and sunk her teeth into her flesh. Rita's face twists into a snarl. She bends down and plunges the knife into Josie's back. One. Two. Three. Josie lets out a cry and slumps down again, her hands limp.

Merry drops the gun, she doesn't trust herself to fire it anyway. As one, she and Fran throw themselves towards Rita, pushing her back from Josie. The heat from the fire is getting more intense now, scorching their legs as they try to push Rita down. The woman's strength is incredible, though, despite her illness. She flails out with the knife, scratching Fran's face just above the eyebrow. Fran screams.

'Nearly got your eye there! Come on, do it, Merry Clarke, kill me,' Rita pants, her eyes wide and crazed as she strikes out again. 'I swear, I will make your life hell until the day I die. I will never give up.'

Merry is still frozen by indecision when Fran grabs Rita's knife hand, wrenches the weapon from her grasp and holds it up against her chin. Fran's hand is trembling, her jaw tight. Rita's eyes sparkle with excitement, her lips part in an ecstatic smile.

'At least someone here's got the guts. I knew you were a killer, Fran Silver . . .'

Moments later, she is gone.

Fran and Merry stare at each other for a moment in shock, and then the realisation crashes in that the danger has passed. Rita can't hurt them anymore.

Merry can see things more clearly now. She can feel the wreckage of broken toys and baubles under her knees, see the rise and fall of Josie's chest, hear her laboured breathing . . . *She's alive – just.* And see Rita's blank eyes, staring in glassy triumph.

Nigel's voice calls out in the darkness. 'I've done it.' His voice is trembling with pride. 'It was fiddly in the dark and I had to go right up to the window to get reception but I did it. They're on their way.'

Fran and Merry are still holding hands when the police and ambulance pull up, fingers clasped together, sticky with blood.

Nigel was the one who pulled Rita's and Josie's slumped forms away from the fire, as it spread slowly up the side of the oak panels. The flames took the model of the Emporium, spitting and fizzing as they consumed the miniature figures inside. They licked around the cogs of the Great Clock, creeping up towards the ceiling.

So much seasoned, lacquered wood. And so few fire extinguishers. Benjamin would not have approved.

It takes the police some time to get Fran and Merry to let go of each other's hands, to lead them away from the paramedics who are crowding round Josie's and Rita's bodies. To lead them gently outside.

Outside. There is an outside. Merry has almost forgotten.

Police cars are there, fire crews working to quell the growing blaze, even though Quockerwodger Court is too narrow to fit a full-sized fire engine. Merry is given a blanket to cover her bare shoulders and taken out of the court to the main street beyond, where an ambulance is parked. Real London, empty and silent on Christmas morning, awaits. It feels less real than the Emporium.

37

JANUARY

MERRY

MERRY AND ROSS ARE SITTING ON JEN AND FARAH'S SOFA, watching *Love, Actually*. It's not the first time they have watched it together and it's something which usually unites them in loathing. Merry would rant about the saccharine schlock of the boy running through the airport to confess his love. Ross would bemoan the disgusting treatment of Emma Thompson's character by her husband. Then they would both agree that nobody on earth would ever consider Martine McCutcheon fat.

But today they are both just staring at the screen, each lost in their own world. In the kitchen, their hosts are taking a long, leisurely time pretending they're washing up, when in truth they're hiding to give the two of them space. This was their idea – inviting them round for a meal, creating a safe, neutral place for Merry and Ross to talk. Somehow she had always assumed that Jen and Farah only tolerated her for Ross's sake, so she was touched by Farah's hug when she first saw her, by their promises of support. She really does have friends after all.

Merry looks down at her hands. It keeps happening, this instinct to check that the blood has finally been washed off. It had been there for what felt like hours afterwards – the police swabbing and scraping under her fingernails. She knows that when tests eventually came back they will find a mixture of Fran's, Rita's and Josie's blood, hopelessly mingled together. A forensic nightmare, like the charred but still-standing Emporium itself. Technically, as Rudi died childless, this prime piece of real estate belongs to Ross now. Maybe that's what Rita wanted – a bloodstained legacy for her only son. But she hadn't known about the sheaf of papers that Fran found hidden in Clockwork Peg. Ross plans to hand it over to Peggy Goodchild's descendants as soon as they are traced.

Right now, the police are more focused on the main facts of the case. Rita brought about the deaths of four people, and now she, too, is dead. Fran had confessed to stabbing her and Merry had made a statement backing her up, saying Fran acted entirely in self-defence. In films, this part of events is usually glossed over. The victim-turned-killer is released almost immediately and the charges go away. But in reality, Fran's dark secret gave her a strong motive and the fact Rita died lying flat on her back made the stabbing look like an act of aggression. Only Merry's testimony and the fact Fran had already confessed to the cancer lie on video convinced the police that she was telling the truth.

In the eyes of the general public, though – based on her own confession and the limited information the authorities had released so far – Fran is a con-artist who murdered a terminal cancer patient. She might not have any charges looming over her, but she'll certainly never work in TV again.

I've made my peace with that, Fran told her by text. They had agreed not to meet up in the aftermath, to avoid upsetting Ross. *Quite happy not being famous. Am working with Gary Shrike on producing Peggy documentary.*

'Holy fuck,' Ross says, breaking Merry's train of thought. It's a phrase he has repeated over and over in the past three weeks. He had never been one for swearing, his mother's distaste for it had ingrained in him a long time ago, but he is making up for lost time now.

Merry stops herself from looking down at her hands again.

'I mean, I don't think I'll ever get over what she did.' His face is still fixed on the screen, where Hugh Grant is shaking his hips in 10 Downing Street. 'I mean, she's my *mum*. She taught me how to ride a bike, she made the most epic birthday cakes, and now . . . I don't know. She killed people, and she was murdered too. By that annoying TV presenter. I mean, holy fuck.'

Merry can't answer. She doesn't consider Rita's death to be murder, more a desperate act of self-preservation. And she owes the TV presenter everything.

They fall silent again. Merry gazes at him, wishing she could read his mind, but it's only at the end – at the worst, most schmaltzy point of the film – that Ross speaks again.

'I think I'm in love with you.'

Merry's heart is hammering. She fights to control herself, to react in the right way, still afraid that she will frighten him away.

'I can't believe you did this,' she says eventually. 'You created a romantic moment at the end of *Love, Actually*. I'm feeling feelings, and people are going to think it's because of the film.'

Ross kisses her. And it's every bit as amazing as she thought it would be.

She keeps kissing him, partly because it feels so wonderful but partly to resist the urge to question, to ask if he is sure. She lets the sensation overcome her. Ross is a grown man and they will figure it out together. His complicated grief and mummy issues, Merry's traumatic night at the Emporium, her ongoing fight to be more merry and less Rita and that lingering, nagging feeling of guilt . . . They'll work it out. Love will find a way.

Ugh.

Well, actually, not ugh.

Jen and Farah are delighted, smiling, talking about how they always knew this was going to happen and saying that they should all go on holiday somewhere next Christmas. Somewhere far away, where they won't have to wear festive jumpers. And at last Merry can see a way forward, a future, and friendships.

She hasn't looked at her hands for at least a couple of hours.

It's midnight by the time she looks at them again. Alone in bed in her cramped little flatshare she stares, and lets the flashback break over her head like a tidal wave.

Fran dropping the knife, sobbing that she isn't a killer, that she just doesn't have it in her, talking about Evangeline, and goodness and badness. Rita's cruel, mocking laughter. Merry overwhelmed with frustration, grabbing the knife and plunging it into Rita's stomach, feeling it slide in easily, her hand warm and slippery. Rita's laugh becoming a gurgle and then just . . . stopping. She had done it. She had killed Ross's mother. And at the time she felt nothing but relief.

A strange calm settled over her as she made a series of decisions. She decided to let the knife slither to the floor. She decided to sob hysterically until she could barely breathe, to lean in to Fran's hug, to confess to Fran precisely how Rita had won. That she was losing the love of her life over this.

'Shhhh, don't worry,' Fran soothed. 'I'll say it was me. Nigel didn't see. Josie's unconscious, I'll say it was me. That's how to clear my slate. That's my punishment.'

Just like Merry had hoped.

They had both got something out of the deal. Merry got her freedom, Fran got the punishment she had craved for years. Win–win. Rita might have lost her complicated game of vengeance, but she had been right about one thing: Merry is a master manipulator.

The tsunami of memories over, Merry takes deep breaths to calm herself. She is OK. Fran is OK. She has the rest of her life to process what she has done and she will make sense of it someday. And, thanks to Fran's selflessness, she will have Ross at her side. She turns over to sleep – leaving the light on as she always does these days. Just as her head hits the pillow, Merry's phone beeps. She picks it up, eyes blurring as she opens a message from an unknown number.

I'm awake now, thanks for asking. Getting better every day. Police want to interview me about what happened again, fill in the gaps so to speak. I was awake, see, when you stabbed Rita. She was on the floor, unarmed, with you sitting on top of her. I saw your whole little performance after, too, and what you talked Fran into doing. My niece needs money for her cancer treatment and I'll do whatever it takes to get her there. So what's it worth to keep me quiet?
Happy New Year,
Knives.

ACKNOWLEDGEMENTS

First of all, thanks to you for making it to the end of this book. I really hope you enjoyed it, and if you didn't I'll try hard to do better next time. My stories never feel real to me until someone else has read them, so just by reading it you have made this book exist. Cheers for that!

The Emporium, with all its festive magic and weirdness, wouldn't exist without the fearsome imagination of my editor at Zaffre, Kelly Smith. Thank you Kelly for leading me into ever darker and more devious territory and also to Isabella Boyne for your insight and encouragement. Thanks, as always, to my agent Lina Langlee for your wisdom, your calm and the fact you always come up with a plan. If I was trapped in a shop with a killer on the loose, I'd want you there at my side. Sort of. You know what I mean.

Grateful season's greetings also to Will Speed, the creator of my beautiful shiny cover, Sophie Raoufi for the brilliant marketing,

Clare Kelly for giving me a platform to shout about my book and Mireille Harper for her sensitivity read.

Huge thanks also to Aran Osman, aka Instagram's @london_lamplighters, for explaining how gaslight works as it really is difficult to search it online without getting the wrong kind of result. If you're intrigued by the automata in this book then I thoroughly recommend you check out @thehouseofautomata on Instagram, and thanks to Tiffany Sherlock for sharing the original automaton link that set the cogs in my mind whirring.

My incredible UKYA group has kept me sane throughout, particularly Kat Ellis for the brainstorming; Dawn Kurtagitch, Gina Blaxill and Kathryn Foxfield for the critical read. Also, Amy McCaw for the YouTube chats. Cheers also to the Witches, and to Emma and family from whom I nicked the name Duncan Biscuits. And to all my parents for being wonderful and supportive.

Heartfelt apologies to my children Rufus and Elena for the fact that I wrote 'another murder book' instead of focusing on our bedtime epic *Dinosaur vs Unicorn* just because my silly publisher asked me to. Most of all thanks to Richard for his loving support, his helpful 'the butler did it' advice and of course, the delicious lunches.

Merry Christmas one and all!

**Enjoyed *Murder at the Christmas Emporium*?
Don't miss Andreina Cordani's first
Christmas murder mystery**

Twelve years ago, eight friends ran an exclusive group at
university: The Murder Masquerade Society. The mysteries
they solved may have been grisly, but they were always
fictional – until their final Christmas puzzle, when one of
the group disappeared, never to be seen again.

Now, the remaining members receive an invitation to a
reunion masquerade, to be held in a beautiful and remote
country house in Scotland. The game begins, and it
feels just like old times.

Until the next morning, when Lady Partridge is found
hanging from a pear tree . . .

Available now

1

You Are Invited to a Murder.

Charley has been holding the heavy, cream-coloured invitation card for four hours now, running her fingers over the glossy, embossed calligraphy. The details: time and place of killing, dress code, RSVP. The black edges of the invitation are becoming worn away by the constant stroking of her fingertips.

The coach trip from London to Inverness lasts twelve hours when the traffic goes well, but this is Christmas Eve and it is as if everyone in the British Isles is trying to get home to their loved ones on the same section of road between Peterborough and Perth.

After three hours, Charley's book began to blur in front of her eyes, and after five hours her phone battery died in the middle of her favourite true-crime podcast. Now it's been nearly ten hours. The atmosphere on the coach has passed through restless to flat out, please-Lord-let-this-end exhaustion. Children wail a long, grumbling litany of misery and boredom, adults shift in their seats, huffing and sighing. The sharp-elbowed manspreader sitting next to Charley tuts every time she fidgets from one numb buttock to the other. Charley stares out into the dingy light, watching the acres of traffic ahead and reminding herself yet again that this was the cheapest option. She needs to save every penny if she's going to move out of Matt's in the New Year, even if Ali does come through with the money.

When Charley had first shown the invitation to Matt, the idea of walking out on him hadn't been clear in her mind – it had just been a wisp of future intention, a thing that she might do at some point, if things got really bad. She was still telling herself that love wasn't about hearts and flowers and mutual support, it was about knowing someone's soul. They knew each other so well that Charley could always guess what he was going to say next, especially when it wasn't something she wanted to hear.

'What a load of pretentious bullshit,' he'd said, peering at the embossed heading. 'Who would give up their Christmas to play some silly game?'

'Well, I . . .' Charley had started to explain, but how could you put it into words? The marvellous creativity of it, Karl's brilliant inventiveness, the fun of shuffling off your old insecure-student identity for a few hours, or even a few days, and becoming someone different, someone glamorous or sneaky or downright murderous. When it was good, it had been so good. *Karl* had been so good. And then it had all gone wrong.

Matt just rolled his eyes. 'You'd have to be mad to spend time with those people. All you've ever done is moan about how they made you feel like crap,' he'd said.

And he was right, of course, on one level. He always was. But while Charley couldn't help but agree, another tiny voice inside added, 'But *you* make me feel like crap, and I spend time with you.'

Still, the sensible part of her knows she should have ignored Ali's invitation – torn it up, thrown it in the recycling as Matt had suggested. She has worked hard to wean herself off the sense of longing she had felt during her time in the Murder Masquerade Society, that baked-in belief that if she was that little bit funnier, that bit cleverer or quirkier, they would forget that she wasn't like them – that her father was a hard-working cook, her house only had five rooms and that nobody had heard of the school she went to – and pull her into the fold.

But it's not the sort of feeling you can just shrug off. It had clung to her like static electricity to nylon, shadowing her to every audition. It was a kind of hunger, but the sort that makes people pity you, rather than give you the job. That whiff of desperation was probably what had attracted Matt in the first place. He likes his girlfriends pliant and eager to please.

At first she had decided it was easier to ghost Ali. After all, it's what most of the other Masqueraders had done to her since the group broke up. But Ali isn't the ghostable type. A few weeks later an email had arrived, a persuasive, sweet-talking message.

I know they're not your favourite people but it's been a long time and they're all dying to see you again. And if you're still hesitating, just treat it like any other acting job!

Ali had followed that up with the offer of a tidy sum of money in advance, with another even larger sum to come to her in the New Year. The kind of money that could help her get a fresh start. By that time her vague intention of leaving Matt had hardened into something real. She had told him it was over, but was trapped, sleeping on his sofa as she tried to scrape together a deposit for her own place.

'This is what I mean, Charley,' he'd said during one of his nicer moments. 'You need me; you'll never cope on your own.' Well, maybe with a kick-start from Ali, she could.

Ali had spelled it out in her email: *don't forget, I've hooked you up with roles in the past and I've got a couple more opportunities in the pipeline already . . .*

That had been enough to convince her to set her worries aside and say yes.

All the remaining members of the Masquerade Society – well, everyone except Charley – had done amazingly well in the past dozen years. Ali was currently blazing a trail at one of the most successful advertising and PR agencies in the country. This year she is being lauded as the brains behind the tear-jerking Christmas advert that has had the whole country talking about #theboyandthetortoise. Even Charley has seen it and cried.

So the idea of having someone like Ali in her corner is hard to resist. If she does this right, there could be more lucrative advertising gigs in the future, which could lead to more connections, then more gigs . . .

What was it Matt had said? 'I don't know how to introduce you to people these days. Are you a failed actress or a successful receptionist?'

This could be the opportunity to change all that.